Adironda

MW00738042

A STORY IN THREE PARTS

"Someone should write an ode to the arm of an Adirondack chair," said Mrs. Ferguson. "You can put your morning coffee on it, you can put your glass of wine on it, you can put your plate of dinner on it. You can put a book on it, you can write a poem on it. You can keep your binoculars on it, or your camera with a telephoto lens, ready for a loon to swim by. There is no other chair in all the world so well suited to a person's soul, as an Adirondack chair."

Looking up at the nearly completed wind turbine, Tony remembered the question which Mr. Jacobsen had asked, "What are the cathedrals of our age?" He knew that he was watching the construction of something more than a machine which would provide clean energy. It would uplift humanity as well, by beckoning the human spirit to awaken more fully, to rise to new heights, to reach more generously around the curve of the planet.

"Every American should visit Walter Reed Army Medical Center. Every American television should take us on a tour, for two hours every evening during prime time, night after night after night, until the war has ended. Because until you see and fully comprehend what has happened to those children, you cannot claim to be able to cast an educated vote."

Adirondack Green

Volume I

Copyright 2006
John Slade

ISBN 1-893617-15-7
ISBN 978 189 361 7155

Library of Congress Control Number
2005910036

WOODGATE INTERNATIONAL
P.O. Box 190
Woodgate, New York
13494

www.woodgateintl.com

Distributed by
BookMasters, Inc.
1-800-247-6553
www.atlasbooks.com
and major distributors

Cover photography by the author
Cover design by Clarissa Vogel

Adirondack Green

Volume I

John Slade

Maps by Carolyn Aldridge

WOODGATE INTERNATIONAL

All characters in this novel are fictional.

Balsam Corners is a fictional town.

DanishWind is a fictional company.

But the wind that blows across the top of Bobcat Mountain is very real.

Other books by John Slade

A DREAM SEEDED IN THE EARTH

CHILDREN OF THE SUN

DANCING WITH SAMUEL

A JOURNEY OUT OF DARKNESS

HERBERT'S MOUNTAIN

THE NEW ST. PETERSBURG

ACID RAIN, ACID SNOW

COVENANT

GOOD MORNING, DADDY!

BOOTMAKER TO THE NATION
The Story of the American Revolution

OSLO IN APRIL

WOODGATE INTERNATIONAL
www.woodgateintl.com

distributed by
BookMasters, Inc.
1-800-247-6553
order@bookmasters.com
or
Ingram, Baker & Taylor

v

NEW YORK STATE

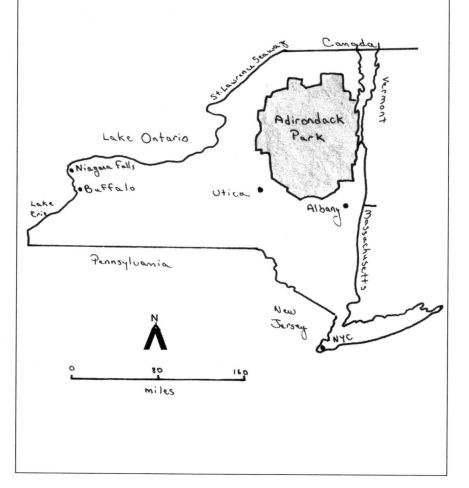

ADIRONDACK PARK

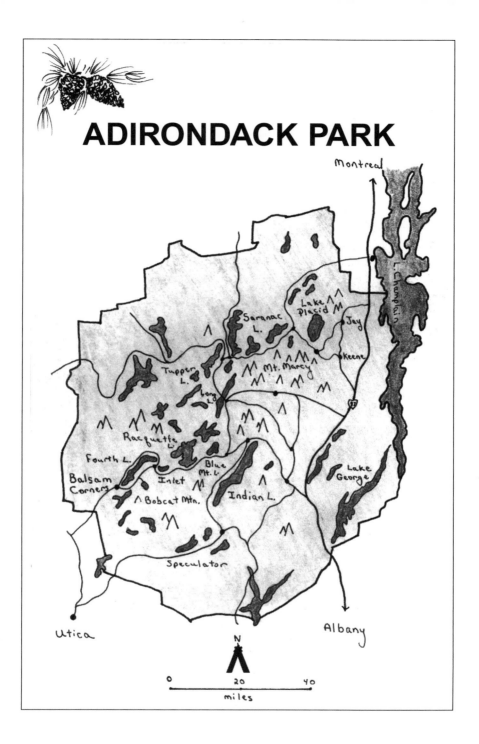

Acknowledgements

From deep in my heart
Thank you.

Ursula Baekkegaard
and Vestas Wind Systems A/S of Denmark

Mike Merrick

Jenny Briot

Bill Moore

Natalia Bulava

Julia Zhigulina

Joe Antinarella

Sarah Fisher

Bert Theiss
Pat Casler

Mary Wiik
Thrond Stenberg

Ann and Bill Guiffré

Major Edward L. Jones

Susan Marie Chappelle

Carol Chrabas

Carolyn and Ken Aldridge

Dedication

This novel is dedicated to

Svetlana Mikhailovna Zhigulina

Thank you for the bedrock foundation
of your encouragement.

The world was made for love
And if ye love it not,
So much the less ye liveth.

Prologue

The people of Balsam Corners, a small American town nestled deep in the rolling Adirondack forest of northern New York, made a decision. For over thirty years, they had watched their glittering blue lakes slowly succumb to the poison of acid rain. The fish were down to ten percent of what they had once been. The frogs were almost silent. You hardly ever saw the nose of a turtle poking up anymore. The sun sparkled on a multitude of blue lakes that were virtually dead. The mercury level in the Fulton Chain had risen so high that local fishermen could no longer eat their own Adirondack fish. In the forest, increasing numbers of red spruce were turning brown. The old folks would tell you that winters were becoming warmer, the snow slushier, the January rains more frequent.

For over thirty years, experts had conducted studies on acid rain, and politicians had given speeches about acid rain, but the people of the Adirondacks saw very little real action against acid rain. The coal-burning power plants, both in New York and further west, continued to burn their coal. The automobile industry continued to build cars of every sort, containing every sort of gadget, all powered by gasoline. Every winter, the people of Balsam Corners listened to the roar of more and more two-cycle snowmobiles: snowmobiles that filled the forest and the town with fumes, snowmobiles that kept their fragile economy going.

A growing number of folks in Balsam Corners understood that their beloved Adirondacks were dying, by poison, by starvation. Other folks in town vehemently disputed that fact, while many simply ignored it.

During the year 2002, while America fought its war in Afghanistan, some of the people of Balsam Corners turned their eyes to Denmark. During the 1970's, the Danish people had the vision to launch a long-term program in the development of wind turbines. Thirty years later, the Danes were selling their wind turbines to the world. Their slender white windmills were shipped by the hundreds to a growing number of countries, where the turbines provided abundant energy, new jobs, and a growing global network of shared research.

In Denmark, thousands of new jobs were created, long-term jobs, not likely to disappear when a bubble burst, for the peoples of the world needed clean energy.

The people in Balsam Corners knew they had a prime spot for a wind turbine: on the peak of their local ski mountain. Bobcat Mountain was really a large foothill, with a forest of hemlock and maple wrapped around it, reaching almost to the top. The peak was a flattened dome of glacier-polished granite, about two hundred feet in diameter: a perfect sturdy platform for a wind turbine.

But of course, not everybody in town liked the idea of putting a wind turbine on top of their beloved mountain. The Adirondack peaks were sacred.

In January of 2003, a group of worried but determined people, roughly a dozen pioneers, invited the villagers of Balsam Corners, population 1,932, to a town meeting in the school gymnasium, so that the Friends of the Wind Turbine could introduce the concept and benefits of installing a wind turbine atop Bobcat Mountain.

The result was nearly an earthquake. The contention at that meeting was severe. People were out-and-out angry, and they stood up and said so. Several stated vehemently that they would refuse to allow the natural peak of an Adirondack mountain to be "uglified" by some technological contrivance. Others were certain that the migrating geese would be slaughtered by the blades. Turbines made a horrible noise that could be heard for miles. The blades emitted dangerous vibrations. And of course, everyone's electricity bill would skyrocket, whereas coal and oil kept the town warm all winter at a modest cost.

And Denmark? Well, that was somewhere far away, where they had cradle-to-grave socialism and other strange ideas. The hams in the local supermarket came from Denmark; no need for any further imports.

Following that town meeting, people wrote letters to the *Adirondack Express*, for and against. Their letters appeared on the same page as letters for and against the war in Afghanistan.

The "wind turbine fanatics," as neighbor now called neighbor, decided that someone from Balsam Corners should visit Denmark, so that he could see for himself what these big machines were all about. He could hear for himself what Danish farmers and teachers and business people had to say about them. He could find a small Danish town powered by its own turbine, and talk with the folks there.

By unanimous vote, the Friends of the Wind Turbine, a group of now forty-two, selected Gerald Jacobsen, former president of Balsam Corners Community Bank, to visit Denmark during one week in March. He would then report back to the people of Balsam Corners at another town meeting.

Gerald Jacobsen had spent his entire career making sure that local businesses had the loans they needed at a fair cost; that family farms stayed in the family, even during lean times; and that bright high school graduates had the scholarships they needed to study through all four years of college. His goal had never been to become a wealthy banker. His goal had been to enable the town, which he loved, to prosper. Thus when he visited Denmark during one fascinating week in March, 2003, he kept the needs of his community clearly in mind.

When Gerald returned to Balsam Corners, he addressed the second town meeting. He stood on the stage at one end of the school gymnasium and spoke into a microphone, a situation very different from the quiet privacy of his office above the bank. Speaking slowly and clearly, as was his nature, he explained—to an audience that packed the gym—what he had learned during an hour-and-a-half meeting with the CEO of the DanishWind company at corporate headquarters. Gerald described his visits to three strikingly modern wind turbine factories, two of them right on the Atlantic coastline of Denmark. In one enormous plant, he watched people carefully making the blades, forty-four meters long. He stood at the tip of one slender blade and gazed along the curving length of a giant white feather.

Then Gerald explained to his audience what he had learned from talking with dozens of Danes, many of them from small towns like Balsam Corners. Most of those folks had nothing but good to say about their turbines.

Gerald told his Adirondack neighbors that one day he was standing near the Danish coast, within sight of dozens of turbines, both on land and offshore, when suddenly he heard the familiar sound of a flock of Canada geese. He looked up and saw his old pals, flapping overhead in a large but ragged V, the way geese do when they're about to land. Thousands of geese wintered along the Danish coast, as did flocks of wild white swans. They did not seem to be bothered by the blades of the wind turbines.

The angry debate of the first town meeting was replaced at the second meeting by a long session of questions and answers. Gerald took a swing at each ball pitched at him: his answers were clear and concise, and convincing.

He reminded his fellow citizens that during the Depression, President Roosevelt had led the nation toward a whole new way of doing things. "The time has come again," he said, holding up one finger, "with the damage from acid rain still very much with us," holding up two fingers, "with the damage from global warming already started in many places around the world," now holding up three fingers, "and with Washington quite determined to prolong the Dark Ages of Coal and Oil." He lowered his hand, gripped the podium, then slowly scanned his audience as he said, "Yes, the time has come for the good people of Balsam Corners to announce to all the other towns in the Adirondack Park, that we shall be the first town to put up a wind turbine."

He paused to let that thought settle in.

"I recommend that we finally stop waiting for somebody else to do something for us. I recommend that we do it ourselves."

He heard a healthy murmur.

"I recommend that we power our ski mountain with clean energy. That we power our school, K through 12, with clean energy. That we power our medical clinic and our nursing home with clean energy. We can power all of the town's streetlights, including the Christmas lights in December. We can power all of the shops along Main Street, as well as over five hundred homes. Yes, one wind turbine can power the entire town of Balsam Corners, without a smidgeon of pollution."

He heard a fervent buzz.

"And what's more," said Gerald, "we are going to teach our children to respect Mother Nature. We are going to teach our children that we have to clean up our mess. We are going to teach our children that if we explore, we can find bright new ideas that work."

After the second meeting, the town mulled over the issues for another few weeks. Then they set a date for a third town meeting, at which they would vote on a proposal to install one DanishWind V-90 wind turbine, able to produce 3.0 megawatts of electricity per hour, on the peak of Bobcat Mountain. The wind turbine would last for at least twenty years; after it paid for itself in three to five years—with no hike in anyone's electricity bill—the turbine would provide the town with a steady profit.

78% of the people of Balsam Corners voted Yes. Those who voted against the turbine did so, as they later explained, as a cautionary voice: they were airing their skepticism rather than blind resistance. More than a few who hated to put any sort of tower atop an Adirondack mountain, nevertheless voted for the wind turbine because it would be less unsightly than a future forest of dead trees. Folks didn't want to wait until the last peeper was gone.

The town board of Balsam Corners thereupon notified DanishWind in Denmark that the town would like to purchase a wind turbine. DanishWind sent over a vibrant young woman who addressed a fourth town meeting. She answered every question with examples from several countries. She clarified every detail in the contract. She explained that the "infrastructure," consisting of a concrete foundation embedded in the granite, and electric cables leading down the mountain to the grid, would be installed during the course of the summer. The turbine itself would be installed during ten days in September. She welcomed the people of Balsam Corners to ride their chair lift up the mountain through the summer and fall, so that they could get off at the top of Bobcat Mountain and watch every step of the process.

"When the blades begin to spin in September," she told them, "it will be the wind turbine, not some coal-burning power plant, that will power your chair lift. The wind will carry you people up the mountain."

No one in Balsam Corners anticipated the changes which one wind turbine would make in their lives. They discovered that once they had chosen to leave behind the Dark Ages of Oil and Coal, they quickly entered the first stirrings of a global Renaissance. Whereas before they had felt themselves to be citizens of Balsam Corners, of the Adirondack Park, of Herkimer County, of New York State, of the United States of America, they now reached out to the entire world. The kids, especially, seemed to wake up.

This is the story of the people of Balsam Corners, during September of 2003 to August of 2004: their first year with a wind turbine atop their mountain. This is the story of people who called upon their Yankee ingenuity. Who called upon their love for their Adirondack home, and their hopes for their children.

This is the story of people who called upon their growing awareness of a shared destiny with the peoples of the world.

Part I

THE FIRST DAY OF CLASS

CHAPTER 1

Dale and Cynthia Shepherd, principal and nurse at Balsam Corners Central School, attended an educational conference in Ohio at the end of June, 2003. The war in Iraq had begun in March. Delegations from around the United States discussed the present state of American schools, and the bleak outlook for the future. After three days of mostly bad news, Dale and Cindy drove home deeply saddened. While America fought her wars around the world, American schools were increasingly neglected.

It wasn't good for the kids; it wasn't good for the country.

Dale and Cindy spent July and August at their home on Blueberry Lake. They settled, with relief after the long school year, into the peaceful balm of summer vacation. They sat in Adirondack chairs on their dock and baked in the hot sun. They paddled their kayaks to the wild southern end of the lake. They swam in the chilly water at dawn, swam in the refreshing water at noon, and swam in the warm, star-sprinkled water at midnight.

But they never stopped thinking, as principal and nurse, about the mess that America had made of her schools. And further: they were the parents of three grown children who would soon—the sooner the better—present them with a brood of grandchildren. The future was already very much a part of the present.

Their school, they promised themselves, was not going to slowly unravel. They were going to make some changes, changes that would be announced to the students on the first day of class in September.

Dale and Cindy had July and August to think about those changes.

Andy Charboneau was always pleased when the other kids addressed him as "V K," Video King. Andy was the video trivia wizard. He knew every video made in the last nine years, since he had begun at the age of eight, without even trying, to remember titles and names of actors and actresses. He especially remembered all the big computerized special effects. He knew the best car chases, and exploding helicopters, and severed heads. He knew exactly in which film a hand was cut off in slow motion by a chain saw, then stuffed, fingers first, into the victim's screaming mouth.

Andy was the King. And now he was surfing the new DVD wave, the next generation. Sometimes the kids addressed him as "V K," sometimes as "DVD K." He was equally pleased with both.

Home alone every afternoon, he began a five-hour stretch of videos and/or DVDs in the sanctuary of his bedroom. He wore headphones so he could really hear the sudden blast and deep rumbling growl of the explosions. He liked the sirens loud. The gunfire got him pumped. He kept a book on his desk, so he could grab it if his father, or occasionally his mother, knocked on his bedroom door.

Andy was the King. After graduation from high school, he was outta this dump of a town and on his way to L.A. He'd hitchhike if he had to. Andy was going to drive those cars in wild chases on the freeway. He was going to roar on a Harley along California Route One. Andy and the computer special effects man were going to do some incredible things together.

Then the gang back home could rent a DVD at the gas station and see what the Real Andy was doing.

Kate Sommerfelt wanted to be a beautician. She thought that two kids would be nice, and a husband who had been born, if not in Balsam Corners, then at least in the Adirondacks. They could alternate Sunday dinners with the two sets of parents. They would need a big enough house, right in town, so that once the kids were in school, she could walk to her beauty parlor.

She was seventeen now in September, would be eighteen next February, and hoped to be a high school graduate in June. A year in Beauty

School in Utica or Syracuse, then she'd be back home. It would be nice if she could spend that year of schooling engaged, so when she came home, they could have the wedding.

The problem was, the best looking boy in her senior class was Tony, and Tony never stopped talking about joining the idiot Peace Corps. She knew that Tony was going to break her heart; she had already accepted that.

Beyond Tony, who always spoke kindly to her at school whenever she said hello in the hall, there wasn't much male talent in the senior class. The senior class was only thirty-two kids, and most of them had known each other since kindergarten. Other than Tony, whose dark handsome face she could stare at for hours, her Prince Charming was definitely not one of the boys at Balsam High.

Maybe during her year at Beauty School, she could find someone whom she could bring home to Balsam Corners over Thanksgiving, so that he could see the town. If they got engaged at Christmas, that'd be perfect.

Raphael Baxter had worn through three living room sofas by the time he was seventeen. He liked to watch the NASCAR races on cable TV. Football and baseball and hockey were all right, but what he really liked to watch was NASCAR.

He had his driver's license, and was studying for his heavy truck license. Next spring, a month or two before graduation, he would apply to the county highway department for a job laying asphalt in the summer, plowing snow in the winter. His uncle worked at the highway department. Raphael had worked with the guys for three summers already. Next June, he would almost for sure have a full-time job.

Now, during the school year, he'd work on Saturdays as a mechanic at Brill's Garage. Give him a Chevy and he could fix it. The part-time job would pay for his gas until graduation, when a real job would take over.

Raphael could have gone out for football, could have gone out for wrestling. He was a big kid, strong. But he was lazy too. If he wasn't behind the wheel of his old battered blue Chevy pickup, cruising Route 28, he was on the sofa, keeping track of several NASCAR drivers. He followed three drivers closely, and a couple more he kept his eye on, in case they burst up through the ranks. He had a secret dream, of being a pit man, changing those wheels in seconds flat.

But he had sense enough to know that if the county highway department gave him a job, he'd grab it and hang onto it. He could watch the team in the pit on cable, unless he was out plowing.

Tony Delmontico was by far the best looking boy in Balsam Corners Central School. He was the only child of parents who had moved from the city of Utica to the village of Balsam Corners when Tony was a year old. His mother and father had worked, until recently, at the Nathaniel Greene Furniture Factory, a few miles north of town.

By the time Tony was five years old, he was riding his bicycle up and down the sandy road that wound along the shore of Blueberry Lake. By the time he was ten, he was riding twenty miles a day on hilly back roads through the forest. By the time he entered high school, he was training on mountain roads all over the Adirondack Park. In school, he was mastering French. Next August, after graduation and a summer of intense training, he hoped to ride for the first time in the Tour de France. He wanted to be able to give interviews on French television, with all his verb endings correct.

His other goal was the Peace Corps. He had it good. He knew that he had it good. Time for him to help some other kids to have it good too.

He would ride in the Tour de France next August (if he qualified), then (if Georgetown accepted him), he would spend four years at a top university, right in Washington, D.C. He would major in international affairs, while he minored in global economics. Then two more years at the University of California at Berkeley (if he was accepted), working on a masters in global ecology. If it felt right, he'd extend that masters into a doctorate.

With his degrees in his pocket, he'd spend two years in the Peace Corps, maybe in French-speaking Africa. Then he'd put on the blue beret and serve as a United Nations peacekeeper for two or three years, perhaps in the Middle East.

And then, with all of that experience in his portfolio, he would set his sights on the Big One. If there was still some lightweight in the White House, Tony was going to boot him out and do the job right.

He had it good. But it wasn't going to last long. Though most people didn't yet notice any change in their own backyard, the world was already warming. Icecaps and glaciers were melting: the early warning lights were flashing red. The sea was warming, and reefs were dying. Here in the Adirondacks, few people noticed. The majestic white pines looked as healthy as ever. The sun still glittered on the lakes. The robins came back every spring.

Tony devoured books at the Balsam Corners Library. Whatever he studied, he studied deep, and what he studied now was an unprecedented threat to human existence. Around the world, the increasingly abnormal weather would cause crop failures. Crop failures would drive tidal waves of refugees from country to country, desperate for food. Wars of a sort that had never before existed would become commonplace.

He had been thinking about all of that while he was riding his bike.

It was time for something new.

Katya Cherkasova, a silent, dark-eyed girl who had immigrated with her parents from Russia to the United States two years ago, was without a doubt the shyest girl in the school. Her written English improved steadily (it had been remarkably good when she first arrived, a waif of fifteen), and she scored well on all exams, but she never spoke a word of English unless it was absolutely necessary.

Katya loved to ski. She was from Saint Petersburg, a city in northern Russia, and thus she had grown up on skis, crossing greater and greater distances through spruce forests every winter with her mother and father. During her first winter in Balsam Corners, she joined the school's cross-country ski team, and soon was coaching the other kids along the trails around the base of Bobcat Mountain. But back in the classroom, she was her old silent self.

Now, at the age of seventeen, she would begin her third year of school in America, as a high school senior. Katya had tutored her father and mother in English, three evenings a week for the past two years, and thus both could speak their adopted language well enough to find a job. Her father worked as a car mechanic at a garage, and her mother worked as a cook at a diner.

Yuri Cherkasov, like most Russian men, could fix any car from the Sixties, the Seventies, and the Eighties, as long as Jackson Brill could get the parts for him. He was not only capable but extremely diligent, and soon proved to be one of the best mechanics Jackson had ever hired.

Svetlana Cherkasova started as a dishwasher at the Maple Diner, but when the cook phoned in sick and Sveta made Russian *blini* instead of pancakes, she was promoted. Regulars at the diner loved Sveta's blinis: thin pancakes, golden brown, rolled around a dozen different fillings, including Sveta's own homemade blueberry jam.

Their daughter had one more year in high school, then she must begin to study at some university. Which university, in this giant country called America? And how to pay for four years of university education? And then how to pay, as they hoped, for medical school or law school? Their Ekaterina had many years of schooling ahead of her. Yuri and Svetlana worked long hours at the garage and diner, and saved every American dollar that they could.

CHAPTER 2

Tony sat at the kitchen table eating a bowl of corn flakes. Staring out the window, he watched the yellow sun rising above the forest across the lake, while he listened to his parents argue in their bedroom upstairs. He glanced up at the grated vent in the ceiling over the wood burning stove; in the winter, warm air could rise to the second floor. He could hear his mother's exasperated voice quite clearly, and his father's voice too, exhausted, defeated, too tired to meet anger with anger.

Ever since his mother and father had lost their jobs at the furniture factory, they had become almost strangers to him. They worried, they bickered, they went looking for work—driving further and further from home—then they came back even more laden with despair. Nearly everyone who had been laid off was looking for work; some families were moving to Atlanta, Phoenix, Seattle. If his parents could not find work anywhere near Balsam Corners, then the family would have to move to some strange place. Already, they were four months without health insurance.

Today was the Tuesday after Labor Day, the first day of school. Tony would be a senior at Balsam High this year. He would apply to universities. He would take the SAT's. He would train for the Tour de France. If he were uprooted now, if he had to do his senior year in Atlanta or Phoenix or Seattle, he'd probably never make it to Georgetown. Or to Paris. He'd end up at some state college, working twenty hours a week on top of classes.

All he asked for was to be able to live here in this house with his mother and father for another nine months, until he could graduate in June. If the family could somehow hang on . . . even if his mother and father had to commute to Burger King in Utica . . . then he would have a good shot at a top university, and a scholarship.

"Antonio," cried his mother, as if she could not believe how far they had fallen, "we didn't even go to church on Sunday!"

"I can't, Larisa. I just can't." His father had been in bed for three days, going on four.

"But why?" asked his mother. "Why can't you get up?"

"Larisa, I have tried to explain as much as I possibly can. There is nothing more that I can say. I cannot possibly look at another want ad. I cannot possibly make another phone call. Please, please understand, I just can't."

Tony heard his mother sigh. He heard her feet shuffle across the ceiling, heard her feet coming down the stairs. He stared down at his half-eaten bowl of corn flakes.

"Oh Tony, I'm sorry." His mother stood beside him in her bathrobe. "I forgot to make you oatmeal." Ever since first grade, his mother had made a bowl of oatmeal for him before the first day of school, with Adirondack maple syrup on it. That was a family tradition.

"It's all right, Mom." He looked up at her as she put her hand on his shoulder. Staring at her worn face, her exhausted eyes, he could see what she was going to look like ten years from now. "I'll ride the bike tonight until dark. Don't wait dinner. I'll make a couple of grilled cheeses when I get home."

He could see that she was hurt: hurt that more and more often he made his own dinner. Didn't want to eat with his parents. The bike was his escape, his peace.

"Home before dark?" she asked, her eyes proud of him.

The September evenings would become shorter and shorter as winter's darkness carved into them. Nevertheless, he promised, "Home before dark."

He finished his bowl of corn flakes while she made herself a pot of coffee.

Then he swung on his backpack, strapped on his helmet, and gave his mother a kiss on the cheek, another family tradition.

She kissed both his cheeks. "Have a great first day."

"Thanks. I will."

He opened the inner door, stepped through the little room for coats and boots, then opened the outer door and stepped outside. As if freed from prison, he took a deep breath of the cool morning air.

Maybe tonight, if his father was still in bed, he'd try to have a talk with him.

Tony walked his mountain bike out of the garage and along the driveway—a sandy driveway with a strip of grass up the middle—to the smooth black asphalt road that followed the western shore of Blueberry Lake. He faced the bike north, swung onto the pedals and began to pump for speed. On lazy days, he'd warm up in a mid-range gear. But to counterbalance the dreary wallowing inside his house, he wanted to push himself this morning as hard as he could. He pumped the pedals until he was cruising at a good clip along the smooth black road, cabins and the lake to his right, the forest to his left.

He had spent the summer working full-time in Sunny's Bike-n-Ski Shop, nine to five back in the repair room. After work, the long summer evenings had enabled him to cruise the Adirondack back roads, some of them paved, many of them hard-packed glacial sand. He regretted, as every boy regrets, the end of summer and the beginning of school. All he wanted was to ride and ride and ride his bike, through the rolling green Adirondack Mountains.

Most of the cabins along Blueberry Lake were summer camps, but a few, like his own, had been converted into all-year homes. Tony waved to the Schaeffers, already out working in their yard. They had retired a few years ago; now Philip fished while Margaret painted landscapes. "Hello Tony!" they called, their voices in tandem.

He rang the bell on his bike, "Jing jing!"

A little further down the lake, he passed a modern log cabin, a handsome two-story home with a balcony wrapped around the second floor. Dale and Cindy Shepherd, principal and nurse, had built their dream home five years ago on the site where an ancient hunting camp had stood, its foundation rotten. They each had a kayak; Dale's was green, Cindy's red. They had taught Tony, who had paddled a canoe on Blueberry Lake since he was three, that he could cruise in a kayak in much the same way as he cruised on his bike.

The smooth black road dipped and rose over gently rolling contours, contours carved by a glacier eleven thousand years ago. Breathing hard as he pumped, Tony inhaled the scent of balsam.

Now he could see the chapel just up the road: a small white clapboard church, with a square-topped bell tower that caught the morning sun. The chapel stood on a point of land at the northern end of the lake. It had been built, with planks fresh from the sawmill, by lumberjacks over a century ago. It still had no electricity, only kerosene lamps. On cold summer mornings, Philip Schaeffer got the wood-burning stove going an hour before the service; then the chapel smelled of wood smoke and warm pews and old hymnals. As he pedaled past, Tony could see, in the grove of giant hemlock trees flanking the chapel, a whitewashed outhouse, distinctly leaning. He had used that old outhouse more than once, and not only on Sundays.

His family had missed the church service last Sunday, because his father had been unable to get out of bed. That had been the final Sunday of the summer season; Mr. Schaeffer would board up the chapel's windows before the snow fell in October. Through the winter, Tony and his parents would attend services at the Methodist Church in town, but it wasn't the same. The little Woodgate Chapel, with its windows open on a sunny Sunday morning, and a breeze off the lake drifting over the pews, was Tony's idea of something sacred.

Now the road, leaving the lake, snaked downhill through the forest for a couple of miles. Tony pumped the pedals and leaned through the curves at an exhilarating speed. A parade of turkeys started to cross the road ahead of him; rather than brake, he whooped with joy, scattering the big birds to both sides as he whooshed between them.

All he wanted was his family back. He felt so alone, as if he had lost both his mother and father, though they still lived in the same house. What sort of company was it that just dumped three hundred people on their asses? And what a joke, that now everybody would find a job sitting at a computer. As he grew older, he was increasingly stunned by the stupidness of the adult world.

Blueberry Lake Road came out on South Shore Road, a two-lane road that skirted the southern shore of Fourth Lake, one of the Fulton Chain of Lakes. Tony squeezed the brakes as he approached the junction; he glanced in both directions at the light traffic of people driving to work. Without having to stop, he crossed the highway and now pedaled along its right edge. He didn't mind the few cars on this stretch of road. Most of the traffic followed Route 28 along the northern shore of Fourth Lake. South Shore Road, eleven miles long between Balsam Corners and Inlet, was one of his favorite routes for cruising on a golden summer evening.

He rode for three miles—past the marina to his right, past the motel on the lake, past the medical clinic and nursing home tucked into the forest to his left—then, entering the town itself, he hooked left onto Park Avenue, which ran parallel to Main Street. He pedaled with houses and a church to his right and the forest to his left, then hooked right onto Gilbert Street and approached the two-story red brick school from the rear.

He rode slowly now, wary of the heavy traffic—parents bringing their children to school, and high school students looking for a place to park—then he hopped his bike over the curb, crossed a narrow lawn to the side of the building, and came to a halt at a half-filled bike rack. With great reluctance, he dismounted from his mountain bike, set the front wheel between two bars, took off his backpack, reached inside for a cable with a lock, then ran the cable through his spokes and around the bars, and fastened the lock. His prison term had begun.

He walked around the corner of the building—the morning sun shone warmly on the red bricks—to the school's front lawn, where a towering white pine and a towering Norway spruce flanked the broad concrete sidewalk that ran from Main Street to the school's big white door. The sidewalk bustled with students; Tony waved to Raphael, a fellow senior. Then he climbed the granite steps, passed through the open door and smelled freshly waxed linoleum.

Mr. Shepherd stood in the lobby, as he always did before the first bell, greeting students and parents, giving directions, and clapping his hands at anyone who dawdled on the way to homeroom. Tony caught his eye and gave him a smile.

Mr. Shepherd raised a hand with a brief greeting, then he set his hand on the shoulder of a boy who was trying to sneak in with a Walkman.

Tony headed down the crowded corridor toward his homeroom with Miss Applegate.

CHAPTER 3

DVD K sat at his desk in Miss Applegate's homeroom, his nose twitching with an incipient sneeze because of Miss Applegate's geraniums. He always sat in the back row, with her geraniums on the window ledge behind him. When he sneezed, he liked to do so with a lot of noise.

"Andrew!" squawked Miss Applegate with a voice as shrill as the shriek of a swooping hawk. "All seniors are to report to the auditorium."

Comfortably slumped in his chair, DVD K, who could handle "Andy," but cringed when anyone called him "Andrew," shuffled his feet a bit. "Auditorium?" He would have been glad if he could just remain slumped where he was for the next nine months.

"Toute suite!" piped Miss Applegate, who taught English but liked to use a bit of French.

DVD K thought that Miss Applegate was already so ancient, that surely during the course of his senior year, she would be removed from the classroom and placed in the mummy collection of some museum.

He shuffled his feet with another bit of inefficient protest, then he slowly stood up from his desk and shambled, with a well-chewed pencil in one hand and last year's ratty notebook in the other, up the aisle and out the classroom door, without even a nod to Miss Applegate.

While walking along the crowded corridor toward the gym, alias "auditorium," he waited for someone to call out, "Hey DVD K!" Or even better, "Hey, there's the King!" But no one seemed to notice him. They were all too busy hurrying to homeroom or the gym or the john.

He shuffled into the gym; the frayed and rumpled cuffs of his jeans dragged across the freshly polished wooden floor of the basketball court. He sat in the second row of two rows of sixteen folding chairs: thirty-two seniors, unless somebody new showed up, or somebody had bagged it already.

He glanced up and down the rows of chairs at the same old girls. Nothing like the talent he'd find in L.A.

He slumped in his chair and waited for the show to begin.

Mr. Shepherd stood in front of the seniors, clapping his hands for attention. DVD K glanced up and down the rows of chairs: every seat was filled, exactly thirty-two.

"Welcome, seniors," said Mr. Shepherd with his hearty voice.

DVD K slumped deeper in his chair and quickly zoned out. He recalled, vividly, an especially well done scene in a DVD last night, in which a helicopter had fired missiles into the (computer simulated) Empire State Building. Inside the skyscraper, aliens had linked their brains to the building's computer system and were downloading the New York Stock Exchange into their heads. When the missiles crashed through the windows, the Empire State Building was filled not with an explosion, but with a greenish glowing poison gas. The aliens, trying to escape, came writhing like long silvery-purple snakes out through the shattered windows. The aliens dropped into the canyon of Fifth Avenue. Some of the aliens were still alive enough to start writhing up the block.

Mr. Shepherd was climbing the steps up to the gymnasium stage. "Now I would like each of you," he was saying, "to cross this stage today as you will cross it nine months from now, on graduation day. I will hand you your community service assignment." He held up a handful of white envelopes.

Community service assignment? Aw, gimme a break.

CHAPTER 4

Dale Shepherd stood in the lobby of Balsam Corners Central School, welcoming the tanned faces of summer, the sour faces, the giggles, the proud mothers, the frightened first graders. He stood as if in the middle of a river of people coming into his school, and he felt, as he felt every year on this first day, that he had the best job in the world. He loved every child, even the brats, even the bullies, and yes, even the sullen teenagers looking for trouble. He loved to encourage them, he loved to guide them, and, when necessary, he was willing to discipline them. Most often, he saw problems before they became serious, and caught the boy before the police did. In his twenty-seven years as principal, he had rarely had a senior drop out before graduation, and he had never lost a single boy or girl to prison.

When the first bell rang, he clapped his hands to send loiterers in the lobby to their homerooms. Then he peered out the open door and clapped his hands at the stragglers dawdling on the lawn. "Let's go! Let's go! Don't be late on your first day of school!" He put two fingers into his mouth and whistled to Raphael Baxter, another twenty pounds heavier since last June, leaning against the sturdy trunk of the school's white pine.

Raphael came shuffling across the lawn. As he lumbered up the steps, he gave his principal a grin. "Hi, Mr. Shepherd."

"Seniors to the auditorium, Raphael."

"Yes sir." Raphael paused for a moment to accept Mr. Shepherd's handshake, then he shuffled without the slightest urgency down the long corridor.

Dale stepped out the door to the top granite step. He looked up at the blue morning sky. Acknowledging his gratitude for this annual miracle, he said aloud, "Thank you." Then he stepped back into his school, a building filled with the most beautiful people in the world, and closed the door behind him.

When he walked into the gym, he saw that all thirty-two chairs were filled, although several had been turned around to accommodate a conversation between the first and second rows. He liked this senior class. It was one of the best bunch of seniors that the school had ever produced. Several of the students were real standouts, and even the laziest ones were at least fairly polite about it. No knives, no guns, limited drugs, and no teenage mothers yet. He would get most of them off to college. A few would choose the military. Raphael would probably work at Brill's Garage, unless he got lucky and landed a highway job. But he was a good kid, with a big heart beneath all that baby fat.

Dale stood behind a portable wooden podium; most of the seniors became quiet, a few kept whispering. He clapped his hands for attention. With a principal's stern but compassionate dignity, he looked briefly at each of the thirty-two faces.

Then he addressed his seniors. "It is my great pleasure and honor, to welcome the Class of 2004 to the first day of your senior year."

A few of them smiled, one nodded, several continued to slouch. They were seventeen years old, able to drive, soon able to vote.

"My job is to prepare you for life after graduation." He turned and pointed at the stage behind him. "In June, you will cross that stage and receive from my hand to your hand a diploma. A diploma which says that you are now ready to enter the adult world."

They were listening to him. Even Andy Charboneau with his orange Mohawk, who could look at you with the blankest eyes, seemed to be watching him.

"I want you to know that calculus and world history and senior English and physics and French and gym are not, even if you pass them all with an A, enough to prepare you for the world that is waiting for you."

Katya stared at him with her dark Russian eyes. Yes, she knew something of the difficult world out there.

"So I have made a decision. On top of all of your classes and activities, on top of the part-time jobs that many of you have, I am going to ask something more of you."

They waited, a few of them already looking sullen, angry, belligerent.

"After a great deal of thought this summer, I have decided to ask the Class of 2004 to begin what I hope will become a school tradition. I think that you are tough enough and big enough to do it, so I'm asking your class to be the first."

Tony Delmontico, with a heavy load already on his shoulders, would be the kid who would carry this project through. He was the class leader, and though Dale had said nothing to the boy during the summer about this new requirement for graduation, he knew that Tony, watching him intently with his hands folded on top of a green backpack in his lap, would quietly take the lead.

"In order to graduate from Balsam Corners Central School in June of 2004, I am asking that you serve one hundred hours of volunteer service in our community. I have already prepared," he held up thirty-two white envelopes, "your assignments."

He had worked the entire month of August on those assignments, phoning dozens of people in town, visiting businesses, visiting old friends in the nursing home. He and Cindy, out in their kayaks on Blueberry Lake in the August sunshine, had talked about this possibility and that, what might work and what certainly would not. She had helped him with the phone calls, helped him with the interviews, until they had paired all thirty-two seniors with just the right person in Balsam Corners. Now the question was, Would it work?

Dale climbed up the steps at one end of the stage, then walked to the center of the stage and stood exactly where he would stand next June. He looked down at his audience; they were looking up at him. "As I call your names, I would like each of you to climb the steps at that side of the stage," he pointed to his left, "then to cross the stage as you will cross it at graduation in June. I will hand each of you your community service assignment."

He paused. They looked pretty grim. So he asked them with a hefty measure of enthusiasm, "Big Thirty-Two of Oh-Four, are you ready?"

Kate raised her hand and said that she already worked long hours at the beauty shop. Raphael raised his hand and said, "Ditto. I'm working Saturdays at Brill's Garage." Several others voiced their objections, complaints and protests.

Dale nodded. "I know. I understand. And what is more, nearly three hundred people from Balsam Corners and the surrounding area lost their jobs at the furniture plant last April. This town got socked right in the jaw. A lot of you kids are working after school so that you can take home pay to help put food on the table."

They stared at him, their faces worried, serious.

"So maybe I'm wrong. Maybe I should not ask this of you." And maybe he *was* wrong. Maybe the project was right, but the timing was wrong. Tony's parents: both of them were out of work. Worried sick. That's a lousy load for a kid.

"I believe, however, that you seniors can show this town what you've got in you. I believe that by June, you can show the *world* what you've got in you." He searched their faces. "Yes, I know each of you fairly well. And I believe, without any doubt, that each one of you can rise to the occasion and do it."

Kate raised her hand again and asked, "When do the hundred hours have to be? Can I do them instead of homework?"

"No, you cannot do them instead of homework. They must be something separate. You can fit them in on a Sunday afternoon. Or on a Saturday morning. You may find time during Christmas vacation. During Easter vacation. But you must contribute one hundred hours of your time to the good people of this community in order to graduate in June."

Andy raised a limp hand and asked, "Who's keeping score?"

"What do you mean, Andy?"

"I mean, like, who's counting the hours?"

"You count your own hours, keep a tally on a sheet of paper, with dates and the sort of work that you did. You add up your hours until you reach one hundred."

Andy asked, "Cn'I do a hunnert hours at the video shop?" He grinned. "Volunteer work for the good of the community."

"No, Andy, I've got your assignment right here," Dale held up the envelopes, "and the video shop is not it."

Andy let out a sigh of long-suffering exasperation, closed his eyes and continued his indolent slump.

Dale had considered taking a vote on this project. He would have liked to begin with the seniors' unanimous consent. But he sensed that democracy on such shaky ground might lead to disaster. Best just to proceed.

He held up the first envelope and called out the name he had written on it, "Raphael Baxter."

"Always first, always first," complained Raphael as he stood up from his chair and shuffled toward the steps. "Why aren't there any Aardvarks in our class?"

Dale watched the boy slowly climb the steps, shuffle across the stage and take the white business envelope with fingers stained black by engine grease. "Raphael," he held out his hand, offering to shake on the deal, "good luck."

Raphael's grip was firm, his young smile genuine. "Thanks, Mr. Shepherd. I'll give it my best."

In what everyone understood to be a dress rehearsal for graduation, the seniors ascended the steps, then crossed the stage and took their assignments. Some of the seniors seemed intrigued with the idea, while others let their principal know with look of bland indifference that this was really too much.

When Tony hopped up the steps two at a time, then strode across the stage, Dale saw a boy who one day would stride toward a podium of his own, his speech prepared. The assignment, which Dale now offered, would lift the boy to a new level of responsibility, but with the finest of guidance. He had paired Tony with Gerald Jacobsen, the retired director of Balsam Corners Community Bank. Gerald was already in the process of moving a mountain, and Tony would help him to move it.

"Good luck, Tony."

Tony gave him a firm handshake. "Thank you, Mr. Shepherd. We'll give it our best shot."

The students were now whispering among themselves as those who returned to their seats opened their envelopes and read the names of the people whom they were supposed to meet, as well as a brief job description. Andy Charboneau was audibly complaining with disbelief.

After Brenda Zekendorf had crossed the stage, Dale said to his seniors, "Please phone your contact person this afternoon after school, or this evening at the latest. Your contact person is expecting to hear from you today, following the final bell at three o'clock."

He paused, then he explained an important point. "Should you have any expenses which arise from your community service, please keep track of them in a notebook. Put all of your receipts into an envelope. You will be reimbursed every week at the front office, during homeroom on Tuesday mornings. Any questions?"

No questions. The seniors were busy whispering, telling each other what they knew about old So-and-So.

Dale walked to the front edge of the stage. "The Big Thirty-Two of Oh-Four, I want you to know that I am deeply proud of you. You have the makings to be one of the finest classes that ever graduated from Balsam Corners Central School. I am sure that each one of you will surprise yourself in the stature and generosity of your contribution to our community."

He could tell by the murmur that interest outweighed defiance. The project was already gaining momentum.

"If you have any questions about your community work, and certainly if you run into any problem, please come to see me at my office." He looked at his watch. "All right then. We have ten minutes more of first period. Please return to your homerooms. And be sure to pick up your class schedule from your homeroom teachers."

The seniors stood up, rattling their chairs. Cindy appeared at the door at the back of the gym. He gave her a subtle thumbs-up. She beamed her gorgeous smile and gave him an equally subtle thumbs-up. She was his bedrock, her belief in these kids as solid as Adirondack granite.

When he descended the steps from the stage, he was met by a cluster of students with questions. Kate wanted to know if she would have to change her hours at the beauty shop. Raphael wanted to know if he was going to lose hours at the garage on Saturdays, his only full day of work. Katya wanted to know where the Towering Timbers Nursing Home was located.

* * *

Dale had sat down in his office for only a few moments, during which he leafed through a stack of fresh memos from his secretary, when he heard a knock on his door.

He called, "Come in."

The door swung open: there stood Andy Charboneau with his orange Mohawk, a white envelope in his hand. "Mr. Shepherd, there's gotta be some mistake."

Dale stood up from his desk. "Come in, Andy. Close the door behind you." He walked around his desk to meet the boy. "There's no mistake, Andy. I think that birdfeeders might be your specialty."

"But I've never built a birdfeeder in my life."

"Then it's an art you surely need to acquire."

"Mr. Shepherd, *twenty-five birdfeeders*?" Andy spoke with injured exasperation. He was suffering from an unfair punishment.

"Andy, I am sure that your technique will develop in both style and quality. Birdfeeder number twenty-five will probably have gothic steeples."

"And I'm supposed to put 'em up at the nursing home?" He spoke as if this was beyond all credulity.

"Yes, you are to build twenty-five birdfeeders in the school shop, where Mr. Wilkens will help you. And then you are to install these twenty-five birdfeeders outside of twenty-five windows at the Towering Timbers Nursing Home, so that the good folks inside can look out their windows and watch the finches and chickadees."

"Mr. Shepherd, I wouldn't know a finch from a chickadee."

"Time you learned, Andy, time you learned. Now I recommend that when you order the wood for these birdfeeders, you order cedar. Cedar holds up well in the Adirondack weather."

Andy stared at his principal as if he had just been assigned to clean a dozen chicken coops. He shook his head at the injustice of it all.

"Give it a try, Andy. Please give it a try. Your contact person is Mr. Bennet, the groundskeeper at the nursing home. He'll show you around the building. You should stand outside twenty-five windows and calculate where and how you'll install your birdfeeders."

"Sir, I will promise to do better in my classes this year. And as we agreed last spring, no cell phone from eight to three. But this thing about birdfeeders, it just doesn't make sense."

"Andy, there's a whole new world awaiting you." Dale held out his hand. "Will you give it your best?"

"Uh." The dull eyes quickened, as the lost boy deep inside enjoyed for a moment the attention of an important adult who believed in him. Andy offered a fairly committal handshake. "It's a deal, Mr. Shepherd. I'll give them birdfeeders my best shot."

"Atta boy. Tell you what, stop by my office in about two weeks and tell me how it's going."

"All right."

Andy turned and headed out the door, a walking ragbag with a weird haircut. A lost boy with a hidden heart.

CHAPTER 5

Ekaterina Yurievna Cher*ka*sova, known to her fellow students as Katya, was born in Leningrad in 1986 at the beginning of the Gorbachev era. Now at the age of seventeen, she was beginning her third year at an American high school. After her first day of classes, she did not walk to the Balsam Corners Library, where she usually studied until dinnertime. Instead, following the principal's directions, she walked along the edge of South Shore Road toward the Towering Timbers Nursing Home, "about a quarter-mile out of town."

Why do they still think in miles, she wondered, when the whole rest of the world uses kilometers?

After a five-minute walk along the broken edge of the road, she could see two red brick buildings set back in a grove of hemlock and maple. The trees seemed to have stepped out from the forest so they could gather protectively around the buildings. She recognized the further building as the Balsam Corners Medical Center, where she and her parents had had their immigration exams, including an X-ray for possible tuberculosis.

The nearer one-story building was set back a bit further into the trees. It was three times as long as the medical clinic. She spotted a sign on the front lawn: TOWERING TIMBERS NURSING HOME. A home not in town, but at the edge of the forest. That, she thought, was good.

Her community service assignment was a man named Walter Bower. He was eighty-five, about the same age as her mother's father, who had fought in the trenches around Leningrad during all three winters of the

Blockade. She missed her grandfather, her *Dyeh*dushka. She phoned him in Saint Petersburg every first Sunday of the month. She and her parents allowed themselves a five-minute phone call. They were about to enter their third winter in America, and those calls home helped them to keep their spirits up.

As she walked up a broad asphalt driveway, she spotted four of her classmates getting out of a car in the parking lot. She waved to them. They waited for her on the sidewalk to the nursing home, so that everybody could walk together.

"Katya, who ya got?" asked Bobby, her partner last spring in biology dissection lab.

She held up her envelope. "Walter Bower."

"Don't know him. I've got Mildred Somebody." He rolled his eyes.

She was glad for the company as the five of them walked through the glass doors that opened ahead of them. The seniors approached the front desk. The receptionist greeted them as if she had been expecting them, then she looked into her computer screen for room numbers, as each of the five seniors said the name of the person to be visited.

When Katya said, "Walter Bower," she was told, "Room 126. West wing." The receptionist pointed toward the long corridor to Katya's left.

"Thank you," said Katya, remembering one two six, one two six.

She walked down the brightly lit corridor, not only sniffing but breathing the smells of medicine and old people. Along the yellow walls were a dozen watercolors, each one a scene from the Adirondacks. Katya marveled at the care that Americans gave to their grandmothers and grandfathers. In Russia, the elderly barely survived on their tiny pensions; few could afford such a luxury as a modern, well-equipped nursing home. The Soviet system, which had promised to take care of them in their old age, had vanished.

Room 126 was at the end of the corridor, to the right. The door was partially open, though not enough that she could look inside the room. Yes, there was his name on the door: WALTER BOWER. She raised her hand and lightly knocked.

"Come in, come in." It was the voice of an elderly man, but a firm voice nevertheless.

She pushed the door fully open and stepped into the room. Walter Bower sat in a rocking chair in the space between his narrow bed and a large window. Wearing a coat and blue silk tie, he was properly dressed for company. He looked at her expectantly, then he gestured toward the empty rocking chair facing him. "Please, it's a bit hard for me to get up. Won't you have a seat?"

"Thank you."

As she walked around the end of the bed, she glanced at a print of Leonardo da Vinci's *Last Supper* over the headboard of the bed. Above the dresser was a picture of the Virgin Mary. On the dresser was a small wooden cross. Walter was clearly a religious man.

She sat in an elegant rocking chair, then glanced out the big window at scattered hemlocks and maples, and even—her heart gladdened—a few white birches. Further back, about thirty meters from the window, the lawn ended at the edge of the forest.

Then, looking at Walter Bower, she leaned forward—the chair rocked forward with her—and reached out her hand. With a smile, she said, "My name is Katya Cher*ka*sova. You may call me Cathy."

Most Americans, she knew, had a hard time with Katya. They liked Cathy.

"Katya," he said, taking her hand in both of his thin cold hands. "You may call me Walter. I am told by your principal that you are from Russia."

"Yes. Saint Petersburg. I came to America two years ago, during the summer of 2001. My family arrived a month before September Eleven."

"Ah. Then you know about our tragedy."

"Yes," she said, and wondered, as she often wondered, why so few Americans knew about Russia's tragedy.

"Well," he said, relinquishing her hand and sitting back in his chair. He wrapped his white hands over the curved ends of the armrests, then gave himself a push with his foot, so that he rocked back and forth with a gentle rhythm. "Tell me about yourself."

"I was born in Leningrad," she told him, "which is now Saint Petersburg. I was born in the Soviet Union, part of which is now Russia. The old country is gone, but the new country is not yet sure what it is going to be. In August of 2001, I immigrated with my parents to America, where people are so confident that they are exactly what they ought to be. I can only say that one day, I want to go home."

"May I ask why you emigrated to this country?" He raised his eyebrows and looked at her with wry sympathy.

"Because my mother and father lost their jobs in 1991, when I was five. They both had university degrees in electrical engineering, and like 70% of the work force in Leningrad at that time, they worked on military contracts. Nuclear submarines, nuclear missiles. Then suddenly, when the Soviet Union collapsed, everyone was out of a job. My mother was forced to sell potatoes in the street, while my father drove an old battered taxi."

Her earliest memories, the memories of a five-year-old, were of long worried talks between her parents at the kitchen table.

"We would still be there, struggling like everyone else in Saint Petersburg, had my parents not won green cards in the American lottery. It was as if God said, 'You may leave. But you must never, never forget your country.' "

"Certainly not," said Walter with immediate understanding.

She explained further, "Peter the Great himself—as my grandfather taught me even before I learned it in school—traveled abroad for his education, to the Netherlands, to England, so that he could return home to build a new Russia. That is what I want to do. I will study in America, but I will one day return to my people."

Walter gave himself a slightly stronger push with his foot, then rocked with a bit more energy. "Yes, that is how we felt. Way back then, we felt that we were building a better world."

"When?" she asked. "When was that?"

"During World War Two. When Hitler was besieging your Leningrad. We were in England, flying missions over occupied France, then over Germany itself. We were bombing the hell out of them, and they were shooting the hell out of us."

She rocked forward and stopped her chair. Unable to believe her good fortune, she asked him, "You are vete*ran*?"

He stared at her, then set down his foot and slowed his chair to a stop. "Veh-teh-*rahn*," he said with a smile. "Is that how you say it in Russian?"

She wrapped both her hands over his hands on the armrests and squeezed them. "You are veteran!" Her mother and father would be thrilled. Here was a man who knew about Leningrad. "Wait until I tell Mama and Papa. You must come to dinner. Mama will prepare a banquet!"

He looked at her with surprise. "Is it so much, to be a veteran? Here, they wheel me out once or twice a year to watch a parade. Then they wheel me back in and give me my pills."

She shook her head with disbelief. "You are veteran! In my country, on Victory Day, it is *veterans*, not school bands, who march in the parade. Of course!"

"Well, I suppose I could march, fifty yards at least."

Letting go of his hands, she sat back in her chair and rocked with the deep satisfaction that she had almost certainly found a new friend. Here was a man who knew about Leningrad.

"You were a pilot?" she asked.

"Bombardier. In an B-17, Eighth Air Force, 92nd Bomb Group, 407th Squadron. We were a crew of ten, tight as brothers: pilot, co-pilot, navigator, and flight engineer. Top ball turret gunner, lower ball turret gunner, waist gunner, and tail gunner. Radio operator. And me, bombardier." He began rocking again. "We went through training together on a dozen bases Stateside, then we flew our buggy to Bangor, Maine. Up to St. Johns, Newfoundland. Then across the pond to Prestwick, Scotland.

"We landed in Europe on the third of July, 1943. While the Germans were pounding the hell out of Leningrad, we were getting ready to pound the hell out of the Germans."

He paused, delighted to meet someone who actually listened to him as he talked about the war. "At Prestwick, we were socked in for nearly a week by lousy weather. Then we finally hopped down to England. We were based at Alconbury, with the 407th Squadron. They called our bombing runs over Europe suicide runs, and they surely were."

Katya encouraged Walter with questions and questions, until he seemed to be growing tired. Standing up from her chair, she promised to return tomorrow, Wednesday afternoon, at four o'clock. She almost leaned down to kiss Walter on the cheek, but offered a handshake instead.

Walter wrapped both of his hands around her hand. "Tomorrow," he said, not a question but a statement. "You promise."

"I promise. My mother is done working at the diner at three. May I invite her to come with me? She would love to meet you, I am sure."

"What is her name?"

"Svetlana. My father is Yuri. He works at Brill's Garage. Perhaps he might visit you on a Sunday?"

"Oh, with great pleasure, with great pleasure," said Walter, gripping her hand.

He stared at her with his warm blue eyes, then he let go of her hand. "Thank you, my dear."

"You are welcome."

She paused in the doorway to wave goodbye to him. He raised a thin white hand and waved back.

Walking home with the late afternoon sunshine warm on her face, she decided that she would stop tomorrow at Mr. Shepherd's office, to thank him.

CHAPTER 6

DVD K, well into a state of Video Withdrawal, walked in a sort of daze around the rectangular red-brick building of the Towering Timbers Nursing Home, listening to the groundskeeper's nonstop lecture about where and where not could a birdfeeder be, with regard to mowing the lawn in the summer and clearing ice off the roof in winter.

The groundskeeper, whose name DVD K had forgotten, was explaining that a birdfeeder with a piping disk six inches in diameter attached to its bottom, could be screwed onto the top of a five-foot piece of two-inch pipe. The pipe would already have been driven into the ground, "twenty-six inches out from the wall. Then just swivel the feeder so the folks inside can see the birds from their windows, and you've got it."

DVD K considered terminating his senior year on its first day. He could just head out to L.A. and start getting his career started. He had saved money enough for a bus ticket, and about five hundred in cash in his pocket when he got there. That oughta do it.

"Howerya gonna load yer seed?" the groundskeeper was asking him.

"Huh?"

"Tilt yer roof is the style I like. Coupla hinges, brass, with good-quality cedar, and you've got a feeder that'll last you a good ten years."

Near a window on the rear side of the building, the groundskeeper knelt and picked up a soupspoon from the lawn. He glanced into the room. "She tosses 'em out her window. I check here 'bout once a week."

DVD K could see, inside the window, a woman with white hair looking out at him, watching him. She wore a pink dress, and was sitting in a wheelchair.

"That's Emily," said the groundskeeper. "She's a corker."

DVD K saw that if he put a birdfeeder on a pipe right where he now stood, about two feet out from the window, then Emily would be able to see the birds clearly. The feeder shouldn't be too high. Maybe four feet up from the ground, so she could see the birds standing on the platform.

She was waving to him now. Her sleeve was pink. Her hand was clearly beckoning him to come in.

"She's in room two thirty-six. You oughta visit her. She's a corker. But I'll warn you. She's got Alzheimer's. When you come back to visit her again, she may not remember you."

At the end of the tour around the building, DVD K thanked the groundskeeper. He said he'd give him a call when the first of the bird-feeders was ready.

"All right, Bub," said the groundskeeper, who clearly hadn't remembered Andy's name. "I'll help ya put 'em up. Just give me a ring the day before."

Then DVD K had a choice. He was standing in the front yard of the nursing home, gazing down at pine cones that had fallen from the spruce trees. He could walk home, put on the headphones and crank up *Cosmic Chicks*. Or he could go into the nursing home and ask the receptionist where he could find room two thirty-six.

He reached into his pocket for his cell phone so he could check the time: five-fifteen. He had done his first hour and a half of community service, counting time talking with Mr. Wilkens in the school shop. There was no rush to get home. Dinner would be whatever he popped into the microwave.

Probably a good idea to check out the placement of the birdfeeder from the viewpoint of a person looking out the window at the birds. He'd say hi to Old Lady Pink, check the view from her window, then boogey home having covered all the bases.

The glass doors opened ahead of him as he entered the building. Right away, he wanted to hold his breath. Something smelled really weird, like some poisonous toxic gas.

There was still time to bolt. Nothing in his crazy birdfeeder assignment said that he actually had to meet someone.

He proceeded, however, to the front desk, where he asked a woman his mother's age, "May I visit Emily in room two thirty-six?"

"East wing," said the woman, pointing to his right. "Last room on the left."

"Thanks."

The further down the corridor he walked, their weirder the smells got. But the place looked nice. Paintings on the walls, birds twittering in a big birdcage, and a cat that darted ahead of him into a room. Passing one room, he heard someone half moaning, half calling for help. Should he go in? Maybe someone had fallen out of bed.

He almost bolted. He wanted to hurry back along the corridor and get outside as soon as he could. He wanted a big breath of fresh air. He wanted to look up through the trees at the sun shining in the blue sky.

But he kept going until he came to room 236. On the door was a sign with her name: EMILY VAN DER HOOVEN. Dutch. The Dutch, he knew, were among the first to settle in New York. Maybe she was from some old Dutch family.

He knocked gently on her door. "Hello? Emily?"

"Yes! Yes! Yes!" she called, as if she had been anxiously expecting him.

He swung the door open and stepped into a rather messy room in which Emily, sitting in her pink dress in a wheelchair, stared at him, her lavender eyes filled with delight. He cringed for a moment when he thought how disappointed she would have been had he not come to visit her.

"Hello," he said. "My name is Andy." It felt all right to say Andy.

"Hello!" she said, sitting up tall in her chair. "My name is Emily." She had a white lace collar around the top of her pink dress, and white lace at the cuffs of her sleeves.

"I'm supposed to put up a birdfeeder outside your window." He looked at the big window behind her: double-paned Anderson windows that could be cranked open. That's how her spoon got out.

He glanced around the lawn where he had walked with the groundskeeper.

"Do you see any deer?" she asked him. She swiveled her chair around so that she could see out the window too.

Standing behind her, looking over her shoulder, he peered out at the lawn near the edge of the forest. "Deer?"

"Sit," she said, reaching out her left hand and patting the bright flowered quilt that covered her bed. "If we keep an eye out, I'll bet we see a deer within half an hour. A doe and a fawn is what we'll see, coming out of the woods right over there." She pointed a shaky finger toward the far corner of the yard. "The little one still has its spots."

Andy stepped through the narrow space between Emily's wheelchair and the wall, then stepped in front of her to the bed beside her. He brushed aside a few wadded Kleenexes—wondering if he shouldn't be wearing rubber gloves—and sat on the rumpled quilt. Then he slowly scanned his eyes along the edge of the forest from one end of the yard to the other. "Do you ever see raccoons?"

"They come out at night. Sometimes the staff will leave a spotlight on, so I can watch them snuffling around the yard. But there's certainly no garbage out there for them, or we'd have bears too."

"Bears?" He peered deeper into the trees, hoping he might spot a bear.

"What kind of birds are we going to have?" She wheeled herself closer to the window, then peered out at the spot where he had been standing.

He shrugged, "I don't know. Don't know a darn thing about birds."

She turned to him with a grin, "Well, then we'd better get started!" She searched around her room, twisting to the left and then to the right in her wheelchair. "Do we have a bird book?"

"Uh." What was he supposed to do now, buy a bird book? He'd have to keep the receipt, put it in an envelope. "Yeah, I could get you a bird book."

"Us!" she corrected him. "Us!" Then she asked him, "Do you think our birdfeeder will attract flamingoes?"

He wasn't sure whether she was kidding him, or whether she was some cracked old lady. "I don't know. Don't know much about flamingoes."

Behind them a voice said, "Emily, time to get ready for dinner."

He looked over his shoulder at a nurse standing in the doorway, then he stood up from the bed. "Nice to meet you, Emily. I'll set up a birdfeeder outside your window as soon as I can. You'll be Number One."

He walked around her chair, then he paused as she swiveled deftly around to face him. She held up her thin shaking hand. "Thank you, young man. We'll use sunflower seeds. The chickadees love sunflower seeds."

Gently, gently, he shook her hand. "Then sunflower seeds it shall be."

He bowed slightly to her while he held her hand. She bowed back to him in her pink dress.

Then she let go of his hand. He stepped past the nurse and out the door. Before he headed down the corridor, he glanced back into the room: she was staring at him, her hand raised, ready to wave good-bye to him. He cringed when he thought how disappointed she would have been, if he hadn't stopped to wave good-bye.

"Good-bye, Emily," he called, waving. "I'll be back in a couple of days."

"Don't make me wait until Friday."

"I won't."

As he walked down the long corridor, he decided that he would stop at the bookstore on the way home.

The bookstore was tucked in a back corner of the sprawling Balsam Corners Hardware Store. He found a multitude of books about birds. He finally selected a book about Adirondack birds, with good clear pictures.

Then he spotted a poster on the wall, with life-size pictures of Adirondack birds, including an amazingly large pileated woodpecker. Searching from bird to bird, he found a chickadee, about the size of a sparrow, with a black cap and white cheeks, and a black throat. He vaguely recalled that chickadees said their name, "Chick-a-deeeee."

The poster was numbered 17. Looking down at an upright barrel, he rummaged until he found a cardboard tube numbered 17, with a rolled-up poster inside it.

At the front checkout, he bought both the book and the poster. He'd visit Emily tomorrow, put the poster up on her wall. Then she'd just have to be patient while he figured out with Mr. Wilkens how to build a darn birdfeeder.

CHAPTER 7

Larisa Kharkova Delmontico, born of Ukrainian parents in Utica, New York, married to Antonio Demontico, born of Italian parents in Utica, New York, was searching, searching, and searching her computer screen for some way to salvage her American Dream. She had been at the computer all day, as she had been at the computer for so many days all spring and summer. But today, she had crossed the border into Canada.

If she could find good jobs for herself and Antonio in Canada, then she would strongly consider leaving the United States, even her beautiful home on Blueberry Lake. She was deeply frightened by the war in Iraq. The government promised not to start the draft, but she knew what such promises were worth. The moment her boy Tony was threatened, their family of three was over the border into Canada within forty-eight hours.

So she searched the websites of furniture makers in Montreal, Ottawa, and Toronto, then points north. She sent nicely written letters via email to each company, touting Antonio's skills as a master cabinetmaker, and her own skills in the business office. She stated very honestly that Nathaniel Greene Furniture had closed, putting them out of work.

It took a lot of hope to write those letters, and she had little hope left. She was as exhausted as her husband, who lay in their bed upstairs in the dark bedroom. But she kept going, searching every day, every day, every day for a job. What kept her last tattered remnant of hope alive was her beautiful son, this startling creature with so much talent and ambition, who didn't get his bowl of oatmeal this morning. His dreams—he had so many of them—extended far beyond himself. Somehow he was going to reach up and gather handfuls of stars, so that he could share them with his friends and neighbors.

She turned her eyes from the tiring computer screen, closed them to rest them for a long moment, then looked out the window at the lovely blue lake. How odd to be inside on such a beautiful day. But there had been no spring for Antonio and her, there had been no summer, and now there would be no autumn. No bright, blazing, jubilant Adirondack autumn, because she would be ruining her eyes at this damn computer.

She stood up from her desk, then hesitated, torn between going out on the porch, and maybe even down to the dock, or lying down beside Antonio in the dark room.

She walked to the stairs and climbed wearily up to the second floor. She opened their bedroom door quietly, stepped into the pleasantly dark room, took a breath of the cool air that stirred the curtain over the lakeside window, then quietly closed the door behind her.

When she lay down beside Antonio, he turned his head toward her and whispered, "Hi, Angel. I love you."

"I love you too, Antonio." She snuggled against him.

Within half a minute, she was sound asleep.

CHAPTER 8

Kate learned from talking with her friends that Raphael's community service was with a retired couple living on Blueberry Lake. Her own contact person was Dorothy Ferguson, who also lived on Blueberry Lake. Kate knew that Raphael would probably drive out to the lake in his Chevy pickup, so she asked him, while they were standing in the cafeteria lunch line, if she could hitch a ride.

"Sure," said Raphael. "I'm gonna phone the Schaeffers just after three o'clock. If they want me to come out to the lake this afternoon, then you might as well ride with me. Phone your person and ask her if you can show up at four, for about an hour. We'll roll at five."

"Okay."

Right after the three o'clock bell, Kate went outside and stood on the lawn in front of the school, where the reception was good, so she could call Dorothy Ferguson with her cell phone.

"Hello, Mrs. Ferguson?"

"Yes. . . . To whom am I speaking?" The voice was soft, though not especially old.

"Hi, I'm Kate Sommerfelt, a senior at the high school. We're supposed to . . . We're supposed to do some sort of community service together."

"Yes, dear. We're going to start fighting back."

The soft voice said "fighting back." Kate wondered if she was getting into somebody's family quarrel. She'd had enough of them, that was for sure.

"Um, Mrs. Ferguson, would it be all right if I stopped by your house at about four o'clock this afternoon? Like, in about an hour? I could stay for an hour. Then my ride is picking me up at five."

"That would be just lovely. I shall see you at four o'clock."

"Um, thank you. Bye."

"Good-bye, Kate. See you soon."

Not so bad, thought Kate, a bit proud of herself for managing a phone call with a complete stranger. Well, if Mr. Shepherd had picked out Mrs. Ferguson, then she must be all right.

Kate met Raphael in the parking lot behind the school. "Hop in," he said.

She climbed into his old battered blue Chevy pickup, a hand-me-down, she had heard Raphael complain a dozen times, from his older brother.

"So earn the money and buy your own truck," she had told him a dozen times.

"I'm workin' on it."

He had worked all summer with the highway department, filling potholes, but he was especially excited about his new job on Saturdays at Brill's Garage. He liked working on Chevies best. He said he could "hear them," could tune the engine just perfectly, "the way that Russian guy at Brill's can hear and tune a Volvo."

Kate and Raphael rattle-banged out of town on the South Shore Road. Kate looked out the dusty windshield at Fourth Lake, so pretty in the afternoon sunshine.

Further up the road, she spotted several friends in the parking lot by the nursing home. Waving, she called from her open window, "Hey guys!"

Now she sat back and enjoyed the ride through the forest. The maples were just getting their color. Her eyes danced from one sunlit red tree to the next. No orange yet; the orange came later in September.

Raphael turned off South Shore Road onto Blueberry Lake Road, a thinner strip of asphalt. The road wound uphill through spruce and maple for a few miles, then approached a small white chapel. Kate had never been in that chapel. She had always attended the Methodist Church in town, where she sang in the choir.

They drove with the long narrow lake to their left. She looked out between the camps at the water, but she didn't see any boats. She had water-skied all last summer on Fourth Lake, and wondered if anybody water-skied on Blueberry Lake.

"That's the principal's house," said Raphael, pointing at a two-story log home as they passed it.

"Mr. Shepherd's?"

"Yup."

"How do you know? You were there on detention?"

"Ha." Then he pretended to ignore her.

Further up the road, Raphael slowed his truck, read an address number on a post, rolled slowly forward to the next driveway and spotted the name SCHAEFFER on a sign. Kate and Raphael both looked out his open side window at a dark brown cabin, set—almost hidden—in a grove of hemlocks. "That's the place," said Raphael as they rolled by. "I'll drop you off, then come back."

"Okay."

A short distance up the road, Raphael pointed out his window and said, "That's where Tony lives."

"Tony Delmontico?" Her heart jumped.

"Yup, Utica Italian Tony."

"C'mon Raphael, Tony came to Balsam Corners when he was a little kid. For heaven's sake, the three of us went through kindergarten together."

"Born in Utica. Born Utica Italian."

"Well, just because you're a Mayflower family in Balsam Corners."

"Yup."

She leaned forward and stared out Raphael's window at Tony's two-story house, brown with red trim, and felt in her heart the worst pang of sadness. She had never been in that house. She had never been invited. Tony was always friendly whenever she said hello, but that's as far as it went, and would ever go.

They drove to the very end of the road—an asphalt circle where the snowplow could turn around—and spotted, beside the last driveway, a green sign with red letters:

FERGUSON
TRAIL'S END

Peering up the driveway, she saw a dark red cottage with white trim.

"Wish me luck," she said, hoping Raphael would give her a smile. "See you in an hour."

"Good luck." He gave her a brief encouraging smile.

"Thanks."

She stepped down from the truck, shut the door—she had to slam it—then waved through the window to Raphael. He lifted one hand from the wheel, then roared back down the road. One day the police were going to stop him and make him buy a new muffler.

As she walked along the driveway, enjoying the softness of sand beneath her feet instead of hard concrete, she heard the twitter of chickadees. She was a town girl, and though she loved the snugness of her little village, it was nice too to be out in the forest. She watched the small flock of chickadees flap from branch to branch, as if they were following her.

The door of the red cottage swung open and a woman stepped out. She wore a blue denim shirt and blue slacks, as if her outfit had been cut from the blue of the sky. "Welcome," she called.

"Hello," Kate called back. She walked now along a path of pine needles edged with thick frilly ferns. Mrs. Ferguson, who looked to be about her grandmother's age, stood in a dappled patch of sunshine. A blue ribbon held her long silver hair in a sort of ponytail.

Remembering Mr. Shepherd's instructions to be both outgoing and polite, Kate held out her hand. "Mrs. Ferguson, I'm Kate Sommerfelt."

As she shook hands with her community service contact, she was surprised at how comfortable she felt. It was as if she was on some adventure, visiting a stranger's house, and then Raphael would pick her up at five.

"Kate, I'm so glad to meet you. I'm Dorothy Ferguson. Dale Shepherd has told me wonderful things about you."

Mrs. Ferguson looked very fit for her age. In her blue shirt, blue slacks, blue sneakers, she might have been out paddling a canoe.

"I've made a fruit salad," she said. "Shall we have it down on the dock?"

Kate said, "A fruit salad down on the dock would be wonderful."

"Please come in." Mrs. Ferguson gestured for Kate to precede her through the open door into the cottage. Kate stepped into what was clearly an old Adirondack camp, built when the lumberjacks and their families had first settled along the lake. The walls were made of rough-cut boards, although the bookshelves, rising from floor to ceiling, were clearly more modern. The old wooden floor had a slight spring to it. Kate recognized the rocking chairs facing the stove: all four were from Nathaniel Greene, before it had folded.

The kitchen with its old hand pump was in one corner of the camp. "If you'll carry the salad," said Mrs. Ferguson, handing her a glass bowl filled with melon balls and blueberries, "I'll bring our bowls and spoons. Do you like apple cider? I bought the first jug of the season."

"Apple cider would be fine."

Kate followed Mrs. Ferguson out a screen door to an elevated deck, then down a set of steps to a path that led through ferns and blueberry bushes to the lake. Glancing ahead, Kate saw the dock, almost as broad as it was long. A red kayak was tied to one side, a green canoe to the other. Perched on the end of the dock were four green Adirondack chairs, facing the lake.

When Kate stepped out of the woods onto the dock, she stepped into sunshine. Glancing over her right shoulder, she saw the sun still fairly high over the forest along the western shore. September afternoons could be almost like summer afternoons, and this was one of them.

The floating dock moved beneath her feet as she followed Mrs. Ferguson to the end. They each sat in a green chair; Kate set the salad bowl on one of the broad flat arms of her chair. The sun had been warming the chair, for now the chair warmed her bottom. She slid back into it, a princess on a throne, then she looked out at sunshine glittering on the lake. A cool breeze brushed her cheek. If this was community service, she could handle it. She could do a hundred hours on a peaceful little Adirondack lake, with a woman who seemed to be very much at home here.

"So," said Mrs. Ferguson as she spooned fruit balls into two brown bowls, "I hear that you sing in the church choir."

Kate was very shy about her singing. Her choir director was always telling her, "Sing with a *big* voice." Then he would complain, "You sing like an exquisitely talented soprano mouse."

But she never could make herself do it. She loved to sing, but quietly, just for herself. "Yes, I sing in the church choir. In the high school choir too."

"Well, you are so fortunate to have a voice." Mrs. Ferguson filled two glasses with apple cider, one on Kate's flat armrest, one on her own; the cider shone with a deep golden glow in the sunshine.

Then she settled back in her chair, lifted her glass and suggested, "Shall we have a toast?"

Kate picked up her glass of cider. She looked at the weathered face with lively green eyes, and felt: at last, at last, at last, something was about to begin.

"To our friendship," said Mrs. Ferguson, her eyes warm and welcoming. "And to our victory." She raised her glass toward the glittering blue lake. "Our victory on behalf of this poor dead lake."

"What do you mean?" asked Kate, surprised. The lake certainly did not look dead, but beautiful. And a victory of what sort? She remembered Mrs. Ferguson's words on the phone, about "fighting back."

Mrs. Ferguson clinked her tall glass against Kate's glass. "Our community service shall include a community of fish and frogs and snails. Fellow creatures in God's great kingdom. Don't you think?" Mrs. Ferguson sipped her cider and watched Kate, waiting for an answer.

"Um." Kate loved to sing the old hymns in church, loved the "Faith of our Fathers," loved "The Old Rugged Cross." God's great kingdom was snug and safe inside her Methodist Church.

Mrs. Ferguson reassured her, "You don't have to answer now. Let's just enjoy our picnic." She scooped her spoon beneath a red ball of watermelon, then moaned with delight as she savored the fruit.

Kate watched with surprise as Mrs. Ferguson, like a little girl, spat the seeds into the lake, "Ptoo! Ptoo!"

Half way through her fruit salad, Kate felt that she could easily fall asleep right here in the warm sunshine. She closed her eyes, leaned her head against the back of the chair, and listened to the lapping of water against the dock.

"Could we start on Sunday afternoon?" asked Mrs. Ferguson. "Say around one o'clock? Does that give you enough time to have lunch after church?"

Kate couldn't think of anything she was supposed to be doing on Sunday afternoon, except maybe homework. She opened her eyes and looked at Mrs. Ferguson. "Sunday at one would be fine."

"Until five?"

"One to five. Four hours. I'll have to ask my ride if he can bring me and pick me up."

Mrs. Ferguson patted her hand on her flat green armrest. "I'd like to paint these Adirondack chairs. The old paint is beginning to chip."

Kate looked more closely at her chair: in several places, the green paint had chipped away and she could see a layer of red beneath, and a spot of yellow.

Mrs. Ferguson pointed at the yellow spot. "My husband liked yellow." She pointed at a red spot. "Our son liked red. I let them have their way. But I've always said that the only color for Adirondack chairs is Adirondack green."

"Forest green," said Kate.

"Yes, the deep dark green of a healthy forest."

That sounded easy enough, thought Kate. Paint four old chairs, and probably listen to a sermon about God's fish and frogs and snails. She could handle that.

Then Mrs. Ferguson gave her a determined look. "Ask your chemistry teacher, please, to order a good professional pH meter for us. The same quality meter that a professional lab would use."

"A pH meter?" Kate hated chemistry. Hated, hated, hated chemistry.

"Yes, and then we're going to go to work. You and I are going to test the pH of every rain and every snow that falls through the autumn and winter and spring. *Most* important," she raised her finger for emphasis, "we are going to test the pH of the snow that melts in the spring, when the blanket of deep snow is a bank of acid from the entire winter." Her eyes narrowed as she told Kate, "Each time we test the precipitation, you will phone our results to the radio station in Canton. We want them to include the pH of last night's rain or snow in today's weather report."

"I will phone the radio station?" asked Kate with a pang of panic. She hated phoning strangers.

"Yes. We shall ask them, when the snow is especially acidic, to record your voice over the phone. Then our friends and neighbors will hear a local girl telling them that the snow in their forest and the snow on their farms is a blanket of nitric acid, a blanket of sulfuric acid, waiting to melt into our Adirondack soil. Waiting to leach aluminum into the lake, waiting to carry mercury into the lake. Waiting to leach the calcium out of the soil, year after year, while the trees slowly starve. I think that if people hear your voice, two or three times a month through the winter, they might begin to pay attention."

Kate would never be able to speak on the radio. She barely dared to raise her hand in class. This acid stuff didn't seem like a good idea.

"Um, maybe I could help you do the testing. But I think it should be you who phones the radio station."

"No, no, no, that would never work. I'm the old crank tree-hugger. Old Gloom-and-Doom. They'll just dismiss me. They have to hear it from one of the youngsters at school. It's your voice they want to hear."

Kate stared out at the lake. She wondered what sort of deal Raphael was getting roped into.

Then she looked at her watch. Ten minutes to five. "My ride is picking me up at five."

"Yes," said Mrs. Ferguson. "We've had a good first meeting. Now I shall walk with you out to the end of the driveway. Please tell your ride that his old noisy truck is a nitric acid machine."

Kate stood up from her chair, picked up the empty salad bowl with one hand and her own empty bowl with the other. She took a final look at the lake, so pretty, so peaceful. No matter what this community service was going to entail, coming back to Blueberry Lake would be nice.

They walked up the path, Mrs. Ferguson leading, to the dark red cottage. In the kitchen, as she set the bowls on the counter, Kate recognized a maple cutting board from Nathaniel Greene. Her mother had one just like it.

She followed Mrs. Ferguson out the door toward the road, then along the path through the ferns, ferns beginning to turn brown in September. They walked side by side up the sandy driveway. Mrs. Ferguson showed Kate the scarlet berries of a jack-in-the-pulpit, hidden a few feet back in the woods. Chickadees twittered overhead.

Raphael was right on time. Kate introduced Mrs. Ferguson to Raphael, while his embarrassing muffler rumbled. He reached out his window and shook her hand. "Nice to meet you, Mrs. Ferguson."

Mrs. Ferguson didn't say a word about nitric acid. She did, however, invite Raphael to come in next time for a glass of apple cider.

Kate asked Raphael if he could bring her out to Blueberry Lake next Sunday at one, and pick her up at five. If the three of them figured out the schedule now, she could avoid phone calls later.

"One to five is perfect," said Raphael. "I'm doing just the same hours at the Schaeffers." He asked Mrs. Ferguson, "You know the Schaeffers," he pointed, "about halfway up the lake?"

"Of course. I learned to swim with Margaret."

Kate climbed into the truck. They all said good-bye, then Raphael roared and rumbled down the road.

He looked at her and said with a grin of disbelief, "Wait till I tell you what happened! Wait till I tell you!"

CHAPTER 9

After dropping off Kate, Raphael drove his truck, "Tyrannosaurus Rex," back to the Schaeffer driveway. He parked by the side of the road, climbed out and shut the door with a "Bang!" Then he glanced across the road at a long brown shed back in the woods. It had a steeply pitched roof, and a red brick chimney standing tall above the middle of the peak.

As he walked around the front of his truck, he gave its faded blue fender a pat. Then he headed down the sandy driveway, toward a camp so dark brown that it almost disappeared into the forest.

He heard a "thunk, thunk" to the right of the camp, then spotted a big pile of split firewood, a huge heap of it, as if dumped out the back of a good-sized truck. A man wearing a green shirt was picking up pieces of firewood, a split log in each hand, then carrying them into a long empty woodshed. He set each log on a growing wall of wood, "thunk, thunk."

Uh-oh, thought Raphael. Here was his community service: stacking a truckload of firewood. Aw, shit.

"Good afternoon," called the man as he stepped out of the woodshed. He wasn't all that old, no older anyway than Uncle Bill, Raphael's oldest uncle. "I hope you're ready to work up an appetite."

"Good afternoon, sir." Raphael walked around the waist-high pile of wood and offered his hand. He liked meeting new people, liked his job at the garage because he met all kinds of people in town. "I'm Raphael Baxter. Senior at Balsam High. I'm," he made himself say it, "looking forward to doing some sort of community service with you."

"Philip Schaeffer here," said the man who looked as if once he could have split that whole load of wood himself, but now he needed a little help in stacking it. He took off his glove and gave Raphael the handshake of a man who had handled an axe for fifty years. "Glad to meet you."

Then Mr. Schaeffer nodded toward the heap of wood. "That's the first load. Two more coming."

Raphael silently groaned. He was going to lose a lot of Nascar while he was stacking that wood.

"After we fill up the wood shed," said Mr. Schaeffer, "we'll fill the bin in the shed across the road, and the bin at the chapel. You saw that pretty little white chapel when you drove in?"

"Yes sir." A team of six men could work around the clock for a week to stack that much wood.

"The chapel's closed now for the winter, but I like to have the bin filled with good dry wood, ready for spring."

Philip picked up two more split logs from the woodpile, each a little over a foot long, and walked with them into the long woodshed. He laid them neatly atop a stack of wood no more than two feet high, a stack that extended about half the length of the shed's back wall. The shed looked wide enough to hold three or four such stacks of wood.

Ol' Philip was just getting started, when lucky Raphael showed up.

Stepping back out from the shed, Philip pointed a gloved finger at an orange plastic wheelbarrow standing beneath a nearby hemlock. "The most efficient way to carry logs to the far end of the shed is with the wheelbarrow. Load 'er up, wheel 'er to the far end of the shed, and start building a stack back toward me. You ever stack wood before?"

"No sir."

"Well, you'll find a new pair of gloves in the wheelbarrow. Don't wear your fingers out."

Philip picked up another two logs from the pile and continued his slow but steady work.

Raphael walked over to the orange wheelbarrow, saw the pair of new work gloves with a cardboard tag stapled to them, and considered for a moment that right now, had things gone otherwise, he would be home on the sofa, eating salsa-flavored Crunchoos, while he watched motorcycles roaring through the black muck of a Louisiana swamp in the World Cup Mud Derby.

But Mr. Shepherd had told the seniors that he believed in them. And so did Raphael. Though he knew some of the seniors better than others, they were a damn fine bunch of kids. Most were from Balsam Corners. The town grew fine people. Best town in the Adirondacks, and certainly a world apart from the flatlands outside the Park. Balsam Corners, that was home, and Mr. Shepherd was right: the seniors were going to show the town what they could do.

He put on his gloves, then rolled the wheelbarrow toward the monster pile of wood.

Half an hour later, having made a barely visible dent in the mountain of wood, Raphael set down the loaded wheelbarrow at the far end of the shed and groaned while he arched his back and rolled his shoulders. Even his fingers ached. Five o'clock couldn't come soon enough.

"That's what I say," said Mr. Schaeffer as he stepped out of his end of the shed. He arched his back and rolled his shoulders, while he vented an exuberant, "Aaaaaahh!"

Then he walked to Raphael's end, stepped into the shed, set his gloved hand on Raphael's foot-high wall of wood and shook it. "Try to wedge the pieces into each other. Look for a triangular log to fit into a triangular space. Set square logs on either side of a round log. Pack 'em tight, and you can build a wall eight feet high."

"All right." Raphael inspected the gaps along the top of his wall, then peered at the wood in the wheelbarrow for a triangular piece. He saw two, took one in each hand, and began to move the load from wheelbarrow to woodshed. He got so he liked the way a piece of wood could be made to fit firmly between two others.

Ten minutes later, when he set down the empty wheelbarrow beside the woodpile, he could feel an ache in his legs, he could feel an ache in his shoulders, and he certainly could feel an ache in his back. He was going to be hurting tomorrow, as he had always hurt after the first day of wrestling practice. Maybe if he took a good long hot bath tonight, and went to bed early, he wouldn't be all that sore in the morning.

"Tell you what," said Philip, stepping out of his end of the shed, "let's take a look at the wood bin in the shed across the road. I think there's maybe half a cord still in it. And I want to check how much kindling's in the kindling box."

"All right," said Raphael with great relief. He wanted to glance at his watch, but he didn't want to appear impolite.

"Sorry you haven't met the Missus," said Mr. Schaeffer as they walked side by side up the driveway with a strip of grass between them. "She's writing a letter to our nephew, her brother's boy, over in Iraq. You'll meet her next time, I think."

Raphael thought for a moment. "You mean Bobby Dyson? He's your nephew?"

"Yeah, Bobby. You know him?"

"He graduated two years ahead of me. My older brother was his best buddy, always neck and neck with him on the ski team. Well, *almost* neck and neck. Nobody could ever beat Bobby Dyson, King of Bobcat Mountain. He holds almost every downhill record in the Adirondacks. Got to Iraq about a month ago, didn't he?"

"Five weeks and two days. First letter his parents got from him, he wrote he was going out on patrol, without body armor. Seems the Army came up short."

"Hmm." Raphael hadn't thought much about the war in Iraq. It was so far away, and though a local kid was over there, Bobby could certainly take care of himself. Just a matter of time before he was outta the Army and back home in Balsam Corners.

Everyone expected Bobby to coach the high school ski team. He had a job waiting for him.

After glancing up and down the empty stretch of road, the two wood stackers crossed the asphalt, then followed a grassy driveway into the forest, to a long brown windowless shed, with a pair of big barn doors. Raphael guessed that Mr. Schaeffer had an old horse carriage inside, or maybe a sleigh.

Mr. Schaeffer turned a key in the padlock on the door's latch, pulled the latch free, then swung one door open and stepped inside the dark shed. A moment later he switched on a light. "C'mon in."

Raphael stepped through the big door and saw Philip at the left end of the shed, peering into what looked like a kindling bin. Raphael looked at an old black potbellied stove standing in the middle of the shed, its pipe connected to the brick chimney standing behind it.

Then something to the right caught his eye.

He stared at a red Chevrolet Corvette convertible, with white scoops in the sides, almost certainly 1957, covered with dust, its ragtop spattered with bird droppings. Here was the Princess of all Chevies, with just about enough power in her V8 to take off and fly.

He heard Mr. Schaeffer ask, "Know anything about Chevies?"

Raphael took a deep breath. "A bit." The tires looked to be the originals, almost half a century old. He could order new tires from Coker, down in Chattanooga. Two sets, winter and summer. Maybe even winter studs. "When was the last time you drove it?"

Philip patted his hand on a red front fender, leaving a print in the dust. "She was our courting car. I was back from Korea, Margaret was waiting for me, so I bought this red-hot little Corvette and life began. The summer of 1957, we drove all over the Adirondacks on our honeymoon. We had a tent and a couple of zip-together sleeping bags, and we were the happiest kids in the world."

"I guess." Raphael inspected the spokes on the wheels: they needed a good polishing. "How's it run?"

"Well, that's where I thought you might be of some help. Your principal tells me you work at Brill's. Got a good hand with a wrench. I thought that maybe on Sunday afternoon, we'd stack some wood for a couple of hours, then we'll roll this beauty out into the sunshine and you can turn the key." Mr. Schaeffer tapped his knuckles on the red hood. "I start her once or twice a year, but after twenty years, she'll probably need a new set of plugs."

Twenty years! How could such a car sit for twenty years?

"Whatdya say? You got time on Sunday afternoon? One to five, four hours, first the firewood, then a little fun. Margaret'll be thrilled if you can get her old Chevy running."

Raphael peered through a dusty window at the old dashboard. The seats were low and snug. He nodded, "Sunday, one to five, you've got it. I'll bring my tools. Points and condenser. Cap and rotor. I'll dig right into it."

"Thanks."

Mr. Schaeffer switched off the light, gestured for Raphael to precede him out the door into the dappled sunshine, then swung the big brown door shut, latched it and locked it. "Good."

As they walked together along the overgrown driveway, Mr. Schaeffer said, "We don't have to look at the chapel today. But I want to get firewood in the bin, and the windows covered with plywood, before October."

"All right." Still thinking about the red Chevy, Raphael barely heard whatever it was about the chapel.

When they reached the road, he was a bit embarrassed by his faded blue truck with one gray rear fender. The thing about community service was, he wasn't earning one damn dollar toward buying a new truck.

"Sunday at one?" asked Philip, confirming the day and time.

"One o'clock sharp," said Raphael.

As he drove down the winding road to pick up Kate, he imagined taking her out for a spin in that red Chevy. Not courting her, certainly. But still, cruising with Kate up Route 28 to Blue Mountain Lake on a sunny autumn day with the top down wouldn't be half bad.

CHAPTER 10

Gerald Jacobsen, seventy-two years old, born in 1931 and thus between ten and fourteen years old during the Second World War, peered out his office window on the second floor of the Balsam Corners Community Bank. He watched a boy peddling his bicycle up Main Street. Gerald was a tall man, tall and slender, with striking blue eyes; his sense of quiet leadership—his hand on the tiller, his eyes on the sails and the sea ahead—indicated his descent from a Norwegian sea captain about ten generations back. He knew quite a lot about the boy peddling toward their meeting at four o'clock, for Gerald had a summer camp on Blueberry Lake. He and Tony talked two or three times every summer, whenever they met each other out on the lake in their canoes. Gerald knew not only who Tony was, but more importantly, who he could become.

Yes, the captain was about to take the lad on a voyage, in order to teach him how to handle the tiller, how to read the wind.

Gerald glanced up and down Main Street at the sunlit storefronts. He knew every store, every shop: they were the businesses which he had nurtured—even kept alive—during the past half century. He sometimes counted, when he peered down from the window, a dozen people on the sidewalk whom he knew. Though he shunned microphones and the spotlight, he had quietly spoken on one occasion or another with at least half the population of Balsam Corners. If a child opened a bank account, Gerald always went downstairs to sign the papers, and to congratulate the child with a handshake. Twenty years later, he would meet the same child, now a young man, with a young woman, in order to give them a loan for their first home.

Peering almost straight down, Gerald watched as Tony, wearing a red helmet and green backpack, locked his bike to a lamppost. Then Gerald walked around his big desk, stepped past an empty chair facing his desk, walked through the conference room and down a short hallway, opened the door at the top of the stairs, and waited for Lucille, working late this afternoon, to escort Tony to the bottom of the stairs. Gerald stood on the wooden landing, looking down. He felt the excitement that comes with every launching.

When Mrs. Brady swung open the oaken gate in the oaken railing that divided the bank's lobby from the offices behind it, Tony stepped from the world of customer to the world of banker. He followed Mrs. Brady along a corridor with a squeaky wooden floor, office doors on both sides, to a back corner of the bank. Mrs. Brady turned the brass knob on a door, which led to, as the sign on the door indicated, the CONFERENCE ROOM. But when she opened the door, Tony saw that it did not lead to a room, but to a set of stairs rising up the back wall of the bank to the second floor. At the top of the stairs stood Mr. Jacobsen, smiling down at him.

"Hi, Mr. Jacobsen," said Tony.

"Hi, Tony," said Mr. Jacobsen. "Come on up."

Tony thanked Mrs. Brady, then mounted the stairs two steps at a time.

When he reached the top landing, Mr. Jacobsen shook his hand. "How's that bike of yours?"

"Getting ready for the Tour." Tony had talked with Mr. Jacobsen about his training for the Tour de France. Tony did not tell everyone about his dream, but he had known Mr. Jacobsen since he was a little kid, and trusted him to understand such a dream.

"The Tour is what I want to talk about," said Mr. Jacobsen.

Tony's heart jumped. Mr. Jacobsen wanted to talk about the Tour de France! Perhaps he would help with the airplane ticket.

He followed Mr. Jacobsen down a hallway, then through the conference room; the long oval table, made of cherry, with a spindle chair at each end and four spindle chairs along each side, was a showpiece from

Nathaniel Greene. The table was covered with neat stacks of papers and brochures and photographs, and a calendar. The walls along both sides of the conference room were filled with bookshelves, holding easily over a thousand books.

Tony followed Mr. Jacobsen into his office. Mr. Jacobsen gestured to an oaken spindle chair facing his desk. "Please have a seat." Then Mr. Jacobsen walked around the biggest oaken desk that Tony had ever seen, and sat down in a Nathaniel Greene oaken swivel chair that Tony's father might have made.

Tony slipped the straps of his backpack off his shoulders, set the backpack on the floor beside a bookcase, then sat in the spindle chair.

Mr. Jacobsen held up a thermos from his desk. "How about a cup of hot cocoa? And I've got some good Danish rolls," he held up a brown bag, "still warm from the bakery."

"Sounds great," said Tony. He never ate anything after school if he was going to train on the bike, but today he was meeting Mr. Jacobsen.

While Mr. Jacobsen poured steaming cocoa into two green mugs, Tony looked around the office. Three of the four walls were lined with bookshelves; the fourth was almost all window, looking out at the town and the green hills beyond it. Tony wondered what sort of books Mr. Jacobsen had in his library.

Reaching his arms across the desk, Mr. Jacobsen handed Tony a mug of cocoa, and a plate with three Danish rolls on it. Tony stood up from his chair, reached over the big desk and took the mug and plate. "Thank you, sir." He set the plate on a side table to the left of his chair.

"You're welcome." Mr. Jacobsen sat back in the swivel chair and savored his cocoa. "Aaaahhhh."

Tony looked at his own chair. The elegant spindle back, and strong curving arms, were certainly his father's style.

Now the factory was shut down. His father was lying in bed in a dark room. If the family had to move, they'd probably have to sell their home on Blueberry Lake. His senior year, and Georgetown University, would be right out the window.

So what was he doing in this office? What sort of community service was he going to do in a bank?

He was surprised at how comfortable he felt here, a guest in the inner sanctum of one of the most important people in Balsam Corners. He felt as if something were about to begin, something at a higher level than bike training and homework assignments.

"Tony," said Mr. Jacobsen, setting down his mug, "there's been a run on the bank. Deposits are being withdrawn at an increasing rate, and soon the vaults will be empty."

He stared across his desk at Tony with angry indignation. "It takes a long time for assets to accumulate. They are not to be squandered."

Tony held the warm mug in his hands while he waited for some further explanation.

"Water," said Mr. Jacobsen, "has gathered as ice on mountain tops around the world for millennium after millennium. The glaciers are water banks. During the winter, snow adds to the bank. During the summer, some of the ice melts and flows down the mountainside as water. The forests and plains and people below depend on that water. When all the ice melts and the bank runs dry, everything that depends on that water will wither and die." He paused, then he thumped his fist lightly on his desk. "I'm talking about global warming."

"Yes sir, I understand. The glaciers of Switzerland are a water bank."

"As are the snow caps in the Andes, the snow caps in the Himalayas, the snow caps in the Adirondack Mountains. The snow that falls on Algonquin Mountain in December is the water that pours out of a faucet in Manhattan in August. Take away that snow, and they'll have water until June. After that, the bank is empty."

Tony heard a twinge of anger in Mr. Jacobsen's voice. Whenever he thought about his own dead lake, he felt more than a twinge.

"And I don't think," continued Mr. Jacobsen, "that the fools who live on this planet have yet found a way, once the bank has run dry, to put ice and snow back on the mountaintop."

Tony was only seventeen, but he had already noticed that adults were often not quite as bright as he had supposed them to be. They seemed to squabble, and grab, much the same as children in a sandbox squabbled and grabbed.

"Son, we have watched our own lake die from acid rain, while the politicians dithered and the power plants thumbed their noses at us. Do we now watch the whole world die in much the same way? Do we dither and bicker and plunder and ignore while the glaciers quietly trickle?"

Mr. Jacobsen swung around in his chair and peered out the window. He pointed his finger at the street below. "Those good people decided to make a decision. They decided that if Washington wasn't going to do anything, anything *real*, and if the State of New York wasn't going to launch a major program, then they would do it themselves. They applied for all the permits. And they wrangled: neighbor was angry at neighbor, neighbor finally listened to neighbor, neighbor slowly came to understand neighbor. Until working together, the good people of Balsam Corners found the vision and the courage to purchase the first wind turbine in the Adirondack Park. A wind turbine big enough to power the entire town. Soon they will be able to say to the other towns in the Park, 'Look at us. Look at what we have done. We're not melting any glaciers anymore.'"

Mr. Jacobsen swiveled toward Tony. "Except, all the motors are still running. Our cars. Our snowmobiles, our power boats, our jet-skis." He paused. "But at least our lights are clean. Or will be, as soon as our turbine is up and running. The commissioning is scheduled for the third week in September. That's this month, Tony. Balsam Corners, during the next two weeks, is about to do something extraordinary."

Tony knew all about the clamorous deliberations over the proposed wind turbine. He had attended meetings, he had read countless articles in the *Adirondack Express*. His parents had supported the proposal every step of the way, and had voted for the turbine at a town meeting last winter. But then Nathaniel Greene had closed, and they had other things to worry about than megawatts and blade diameter and the threat to migrating geese.

Tony also knew that Mr. Jacobsen had ultimately tipped the balance toward approval. Everyone respected the town's retired banker, for nearly everyone had been helped by him in one way or another. The man who had provided college scholarships for dozens of kids over the span of two generations was a man whom people trusted. When he came back from Denmark, he spoke at a town meeting about his talks with farmers and shopkeepers. He spoke about his talks with investment bankers in Copenhagen. People in Balsam Corners believed him when he said, "The Danes have been doing the right thing for thirty years with their wind turbines. More and more people have jobs, the local economy is growing, the national economy is growing, and a real future is unfolding, because they are selling their big clean machines to the world."

Whereas in Balsam Corners . . . Whereas in Utica . . .

Mr. Jacobsen held up the thermos. "More cocoa?"

Tony nodded. "Sure. Thanks." He stood up from his chair, but Mr. Jacobsen gestured for him to sit.

Then the banker, holding the thermos and his own cup, stood up from his chair, walked around his desk, filled Tony's mug, filled his own mug, set the thermos on the desk, then pulled up a second chair and sat. "Don't forget your rolls," he said, taking one from the plate on the table between them.

"All right. Thanks." Tony picked up a roll, took a bite, took a sip from his mug. He liked listening to someone who had talked with investment bankers in Copenhagen.

"So," said Mr. Jacobsen, holding up his own green mug with the Bank's logo on it, "I propose a toast. A toast to the slender beauty with three white wings that will soon stand atop our Bobcat Mountain."

Tony raised his mug and the two gentlemen clinked. "To doing things right," he said.

"Ah, that's just the key," said Mr. Jacobsen with fervent agreement. "To explore, to think, to bushwhack about a bit in the woods, until we learn the difference between what is right for today, and what is right for the next hundred years. Because, Tony, we've reached a juncture in our human history. We have fueled the industrial revolution with coal and oil, fueled the big engines and furnaces for a century and a half, and brought unprecedented prosperity to the peoples of the world. But now it's time to change the fuel. Either that, or we wallow and wither in our own poison. Time to harness the wind, time to harness the sun." He stared at Tony with absolute conviction. "And do you know what? We will find that the wind and the sun will transport us to a new and unprecedented revolution. Never before have the peoples of the world worked together to produce clean energy. Aside from the economic and ecological benefits, that global cooperation alone can launch us into the next Renaissance."

Mr. Jacobsen paused to take a long drink of his cocoa.

Then he looked at his watch. "They're running the chair lift today up Bobcat Mountain until six o'clock. What do you say we take a ride to the top, so we can look at the site where our turbine is going to stand?"

Tony liked the idea of riding with Mr. Jacobsen on the chair lift up the mountain. "Sounds good to me."

"Then drink up and let's go."

CHAPTER 11

Gerald drove his sun-faded maroon Volvo, vintage 1971, down the driveway behind the Bank to Crosby Boulevard. He did not turn left, however, toward Main Street and Bobcat Mountain. He turned right, toward his neighborhood.

"I like driving through the neighborhoods," he said to Tony, who sat in the passenger seat, silent, staring ahead. "I always want to know: How fares the nation?"

Tony nodded, indicating that he had heard.

The *Boulevard*, of course, was just another quiet street in town. Gerald's house was number 221, across the street from the library. He was the only one in the house now. He looked ahead to the left at the blue two-story house, with a wrap-around verandah . . . the verandah where the kids had camped out on a cot when they were eight, and where they had courted on the wicker swing when they were eighteen. Now they were gone, all three, to banks in New York, San Francisco, and Vienna. They were flourishing.

He swept his eye along the empty veranda, wondering how many more years he would be able to live in that big old house, before he had to move into the nursing home. What would he do with the dozens of photographs on the walls of his bedroom, the living room, and the kitchen, when he moved into some tiny room?

He passed the library on the right, a handsome, two-story, brick-and-beam edifice with an Elizabethan window, then he turned left onto

Garmon Avenue. He headed west past modest but sturdy homes, several with maples just turning red in the front yard.

"It's a question of economics," he said, glancing at Tony. Both of them had rolled down their windows; the warm air of a September afternoon flowed through the car. Ahead, the late afternoon sun flickered through the trees, casting its dappled light through the windshield onto Tony's blue denim shirt, and Gerald's grey suit and blue silk tie.

"The wind turbine which the town of Balsam Corners is going to erect on the peak of Bobcat Mountain will produce three megawatts of electricity per hour. That's three thousand kilowatts an hour. Now the average home, with four people in it, uses roughly seven hundred kilowatts a month. You can check your family's electricity bills to see exactly what you've used each month. So. Multiply three megawatts per hour by twenty-four hours, and you have the megawatts produced by a wind turbine in one day. Multiply by thirty, and you have the power produced in a month."

He paused, then repeated, "the power produced in a month."

Tony looked at him and nodded that he was listening.

Gerald continued, "The DanishWind V 90, operating under normal wind conditions in this area, will produce 2,160,000 kilowatts per month. At 7,000 kilowatts per home, our turbine will be able to power over three thousand homes."

Tony asked with surprise, "One turbine can power over three thousand homes?"

"Absolutely. And in a town of roughly five hundred homes, sheltering a population of about two thousand, we shall have a lot of extra power." As he drove, he looked to the left, to the right, at homes along both sides of the street, many of which had been bought, repaired, or painted with a low-interest loan from his Bank.

"Of course, the turbine will power all the businesses in town too. Every shop on Main Street will be powered by the wind. The wind will power all the municipal lighting: street lamps, stop lights, the Christmas lights in December."

Then he shook his head sadly. "We had hoped that the turbine would power Nathaniel Greene, so that we could have advertised that every stick of furniture was whittled by the wind. An excellent selling point. But Nathaniel Greene's headquarters is in Rhode Island, and they got bought by a conglomerate out of New Jersey." He thumped his fist on the steering wheel. "There wasn't a damn thing I could do."

He turned left onto Riverside Street and drove parallel to the Moose River, which he could glimpse through the trees. He slowed as he drove past the Canoe and Kayak Outfitter, with its wharf on the river. Canoes of every bright color were stacked upside down on racks for the winter.

"When the people of Balsam Corners made their decision to erect a wind turbine, the town floated bonds and the citizens invested. Thus the good people of Balsam Corners are the owners of that turbine. Our DanishWind V 90, generating over two million kilowatts per month, will pay back the original investment in three to five years." He tapped his hand on the sun-cracked leather dashboard for emphasis. "Our turbine will pay back the original investment in three to five years. A DanishWind turbine is designed to run for at least twenty years. Thus, after the first five years, the town begins to turn a profit. A portion of that profit shall be dividends to shareholders, and a portion of that profit can be invested into a number of community projects. We'd like to upgrade some of the equipment in the nursing home. We'd like to give a boost to the school's library budget. That sort of thing."

He turned left onto Spring Street, waited for a break in the traffic on Main, then continued on Spring for a couple of blocks. A jog to the left, to the town's Highway Department, home to a fleet of red snow plows, now parked at one end of the gravel yard, and home to a fleet of yellow school buses, now out on the road taking the hooligans home.

Hooking right, he drove up the gentle slope of Brown's Tract Road, out of town and into the forest that wrapped around Bobcat Mountain.

"The wind turbine is going to power the Ski Center. Ski lifts, snow machines, and the chalet. You'll meet Steve Barkauskas, the mountain manager. He'll tell you that the annual electricity bill for Bobcat Mountain Ski Center is between sixty-four and sixty-eight thousand dollars. The peak month is mid-December to mid-January, when they're making snow. The average electricity bill for that month is twenty-five thousand dollars. That's one huge bite out of their budget. So, imagine what the Ski Center could do with an extra sixty-eight thousand dollars a year."

He glanced at Tony. The kid stared straight ahead, silent.

"First off, they could string lights along the twenty kilometers of cross-country ski trails, something that even the Olympic trails in Lake

Placid don't have. The good folks of Balsam Corners could come home tired from work, have dinner, put their feet up and read the paper, and then decide, at about eight or nine o'clock in the evening, that they're going to go skiing for an hour or two. And they *could*, because the ski trails would be lit until eleven. Beautiful white trails winding through the dark forest, with stars glittering overhead. By golly, that's civilization!" He accelerated a bit as the road grew steeper.

"Of course, we'll light the downhill slopes as well, so that alpine skiing could run until nine or ten at night. What a difference that would make, for both the Ski Center and the motels in town: Friday evening skiing, all day Saturday and Saturday evening, all day Sunday, and Sunday evening too if they want it. Three evenings a weekend, that's a selling point. Even Lake Placid can't offer that."

He glanced at Tony, a serious boy if ever there was one.

"And then you know what?"

Tony looked at him, listening.

"We can begin to innovate. Stretch out a bit. Do things new. For example, with the town's extra revenue from our turbine, the cross-country ski trails could be extended deep into the forest along several old logging trails, left by the lumberjacks back in the 1880's. Most of those trails are still fairly open, or at least not so overgrown that they couldn't be cleared again. Mind you, we shall not touch one foot of snowmobile trail. Let those guys roar around all they want. We shall clear logging trails that go deep into the forest, while the yahoos go racing from bar to bar."

"Deep into the forest," said Tony.

"That's right. We can build some lean-to's, way back in, for winter camping. Think what a draw that would be: a hundred kilometers of wilderness ski trails, about a third of them lighted, with scattered lean-to's that could accommodate fifty, maybe a hundred campers every winter weekend. Then we'd start to draw not just the usual skiers, but the wilderness people too. I'll bet they'll come all the way from Cleveland to camp in gorgeous Adirondack wilderness, snow on the spruce and a black pot of coffee on a campfire. Tony, we could bring in a Boy Scout troop every weekend. Those kids would have the time of their life."

He drove past Old Indian Trail, angling off to the left. His wife Marion had grown up in her daddy's rough-hewn timber house on the Trail. She was a wild creature of the woods, she was.

"Something else I been thinking about. With the Dyson boy over in Iraq, and casualties piling up in Walter Reed Hospital down in Washington, I think the town of Balsam Corners might consider developing a winter sports center for people with physical limitations. The guys are coming home now with their legs blown off. With an arm missing. With their eyes burnt to the sockets. How about we develop a sports center with special skis, special lifts, so that we can welcome home a few soldiers who deserve more than a parade."

Tony was looking at him now, staring at him with those dark Italian eyes.

"So, in summary, our turbine shall power the lights, power the lifts, and make its steady investment into the town budget." He paused, then asked, "But how do we handle this extra revenue? We must be sure to use it wisely."

He angled left onto Bisby Road, downshifted into third gear, then patted the dry leather dashboard. "Atta girl, ol' Bess."

The sun was behind them now, dappling the maples ahead. He savored the brighter blush of red in the woods up at this elevation. The Volvo climbed from early September to mid-September as it ascended the mountain.

"Last night, the town board decided to hire two consultants, who will investigate a number of projects. The board spent well over three hours going through a stack of job applications. Many of the folks had been laid off from Nathaniel Greene last April. They filled out the applications in early June. Most of them knew next to nothing about doing a 'feasibility study.' They had worked on a lathe, they had done payroll. But the board narrowed the field down to a couple of people who we felt would apply themselves with all the motivation necessary, and who, equally important, understood both the history of the town and the town's future needs. They didn't have to be old timers, a family with roots going back for generations. The board felt that such a limitation would be unfair. What the folks hired had to have, was an understanding of the *soul* of the town. If you see what I mean."

Tony nodded.

Teenagers were like that. Sometimes they made noise and noise and noise, and sometimes they were the very definition of silence. Deep moody silence. What was the kid thinking about?

"So now it's my duty," he continued, "as corresponding secretary for the board, to tender a letter offering employment to two members of the Balsam Corners community. But I would like to check with you first."

"With me?" asked Tony, surprised.

"Yes. Because the two people whom the town would like to hire are your parents. We'd call them in for a final interview, certainly. But I thought, just between you and me, that I should ask you whether you minded if they took the job."

"Whether I minded?"

"Yes. We'd like them to conduct a long-term study of possible innovations at the Ski Center, based on projected income from the turbine quietly spinning on top of the mountain for twenty years. We'd like them to survey the needs of the nursing home, the medical center, the school. We'll set them up with an office, downstairs here at the Bank. Your mother seems to have the requisite computer skills."

"She's a whiz."

"Good. Myself, I hate the damn thing. But what I want to know is, do you mind if your parents become involved in such a complex and demanding undertaking? A lot of evenings, they'll be out at meetings. And as you know from the Turbine Wars of 2002, folks in town have strong opinions, aye and nay. Your phone's going to be ringing day and night, out there at your quiet home on Blueberry Lake. Are you ready for the revolution?"

"Am I ready for the revolution?"

Now the forest opened and Gerald drove into a big grassy parking lot at the foot of a ski slope. He could see, beyond the roof of the brown chalet, the green chairs of the chair lift slowly rising through the air up the slope, about half of them filled with folks who wanted to watch what was happening on the peak of Bobcat Mountain. He pointed, "We'll ride together up the chair lift, take a look at the autumn foliage, say hello to the deer, and talk about your bicycle race. All right?"

"Mr. Jacobsen, do you really mean that the town is going to hire my parents? The town is going to give them jobs? Do you really mean that?"

"Yes, Tony, that is what the board decided yesterday evening. By a unanimous vote, I might add. Your mother and father will both be on the payroll for one year, with the option to extend for five."

"And you're asking me if I approve?"

"Yes. Before I disrupt your senior year, which, as I understand from our talks, is a crucial year for you, I think it only right that I ask you for your advice and consent. You would, of course, have a much better crack at Georgetown if you can just stay put right here in Balsam Corners."

The dark Italian eyes burned with conviction. "Mr. Jacobsen, I will tell you for certain: my parents can handle the job. Ski trails, nursing home: they'll dig right into it. They've been in Balsam Corners for sixteen years, worked steady at Nathaniel Greene, and haven't missed a PTA meeting since I was five. They will do a super job, I assure you."

Tony paused, then he asked, puzzled, "But why are you worried about me?"

Gerald swung his door open. "C'mon. I'll tell you on the chair lift. I've got an idea for that bike of yours."

CHAPTER 12

Tony and Mr. Jacobsen did what a surprisingly large number of people were doing: they got in line, shuffled forward for two or three minutes, then stood on the proper spot, and sat down as the green chair gliding toward them swooped them off the ground. Tony pulled down the green safety bar in front of them. The chair carried them to a height of ten, twenty, thirty feet, level with the red crowns of the maples. He had ridden the chair lift countless times in the winter, but he had never ridden through the treetops at the beginning of autumn. And he had certainly never ridden the chair while seated beside a former director of the Community Bank, who seemed to have something in mind about the Tour de France.

Mr. Jacobsen, peering down, pointed with a grin. Tony spotted three deer, a doe and two fawns, standing in the middle of the slalom run where Bobby Dyson had won the Adirondack gold. Tony could see, faintly, spots on the fawns.

"Tony, I don't want to disappoint you, but I'm not sure that the Tour de France is the right thing for you to be training for."

Tony looked at the man beside him with disbelief. Hadn't they talked a dozen times about the Tour de France? Tony had been training since he was ten years old.

"I don't understand, sir."

Mr. Jacobsen nodded. Wearing a grey suit and blue tie as he glided through the air up the mountain, his white hair gently tousled by the breeze, he swept his arm toward the distant rolling hills of the

Adirondacks. "Tony, next July, I want you to ride in the first annual Tour d'Adirondack." He pronounced the word "Ah-di-ron-DAHK," as if it were French. "I would like you to organize, and then compete in, a seven-day race, in seven stages, on a course that loops through the entire Adirondack Park. We'll close off traffic, bring in the press. If we can get fifty riders, with some contenders from Canada, we can turn the eyes of the nation, of the world, to our fragile Adirondack sanctuary."

Mr. Jacobsen glanced at Tony with a look of confidence. "Your gang will ride exactly when the other gang is riding in France, and I'll bet we can get the bigger draw. No cars, no motorcycles anywhere near the riders: nobody's going to ride in gasoline fumes. Every vehicle associated with the race must be either hybrid or electric. That's a selling point. That'll stir up interest. We can plug electric cars into the wind. We can plug electric motorbikes into the wind. Then you ride, ride, ride, in seven stages through these beautiful mountains."

"A big loop through the entire Adirondack Park."

"That's right. One of the rules is: all bikers camp out. No biker goes inside any sort of building for seven days. Your road crew brings along tents, campfire wood, healthy food, sleeping bags. Do you see, it's an *Adirondack* race. Beautiful, healthy, and clean."

"You want me to organize a Tour d'Adirondack?   And then ride in it?"

"You don't have to win. I expect we'll have some professional riders. But if you can at least finish in the middle of the pack, then Balsam Corners would be extremely proud."

"Sir, is this my community service?"

"Yes, if you'll accept it. I propose such a bike race, but I ask for your advice and consent."

Tony swept his eyes across the red and green forest rolling to the horizon. Looking over his shoulder to the left, he could see the slate blue water of Fourth Lake. He couldn't see Blueberry Lake; it was hidden behind Little Moose Mountain. But he would be riding home to Blueberry Lake tonight. Riding as a contender in a race that would plug people into the wind.

He reached over the safety bar to shake hands with Mr. Jacobsen. "Sir, Balsam Corners shall host the first annual Tour d'Adirondack. And I shall train on mountain roads from one corner of this Park to the other, so that I might bring some distinction and honor to my native town."

Gliding ever higher into the blue sky, the ski slopes sweeping down beneath them, Tony and Mr. Jacobsen shook hands with something more than mere agreement; they gave to each other their pledge, that though the race was but a dream and nothing more, they would each work diligently through the next eleven months to make that dream a vibrant reality.

"Thank you, Tony."

"Mr. Jacobsen, it is I who thank you, and the good people of Balsam Corners."

The two gentlemen rode the rest of the way up the mountain in silence. The sun was low enough now that the reddish light it cast kindled an even deeper red in the wind-ruffled crowns of the maples.

The chair lift took them to just short of the peak of Bobcat Mountain. The operator at the top slowed the lift, as he always did when he saw Gerald coming, then he stopped it completely, allowing Gerald to step off.

"Thank you, Roy."

"You're welcome, Mr. Jacobsen. We hadn't seen you, sir. Thought you weren't coming today."

"Not a chance."

Gerald led Tony up the last bit of grassy slope, through a few stunted pines that clung to the mountaintop. Then they reached the clearing that capped the peak: a flattened dome of glacier-polished granite, roughly two hundred feet in diameter. As Gerald walked carefully across the cracked and uneven granite, he said to Tony, "You probably know about the old logging road leading up the back of the mountain. An old skidder trail used by horses, way back when. Trucks managed to come up it when the chair lift was installed in 1973. Trucks will try to use it tomorrow when they bring the crane up in sections. I hope they make it." He shook his head with a laugh. "I certainly wouldn't attempt that road with my old Volvo."

Now, standing near the center of the granite dome, he pointed at a disk of gray concrete, thirty-four feet in diameter. "There it is."

About fifty people, folks from town who had ridden up the chair lift, stood alone or in clusters around the concrete disk, inspecting it, muttering for or against it, walking around it on the Adirondack granite. Some took pictures of Step One.

Gerald explained to Tony, "That's a plug of concrete twelve feet deep. That plug caused one of the biggest battles: some folks were absolutely dead against blasting a hole in the top of a mountain. They said that such an injury was sacrilege, and I agree. But finally they decided that a small hole blasted in a granite peak was less of a sacrilege than a starving forest and poisoned lakes and a dead Park. So the hole was blasted, and the concrete trucks rumbled up here last August. Now the base is ready for the turbine's tower."

He pointed at a ring of bolts in the middle of the concrete disk, a ring about twelve feet in diameter. The shiny bolts stood almost a foot tall. "See that ring of bolts? You can bet they're high quality steel. The bottom section of the tower will be bolted to the concrete base. In the circular seam between them will be a thin layer of rubberized concrete, so that the tower has some flex. It's amazing what those Danes have figured out."

He pointed at a rectangular field of gravel covering part of the peak. "The crew built a pad for the crane: a bed of crushed gravel. The base of the crane comes up the mountain tomorrow on a flatbed truck. The sections of the derrick come up on other trucks. Then the crane assembles itself. That's the theory anyway. Usually the crew operates in somebody's cattle pasture. They won't have as much room up here on Bobcat. But DanishWind has put up turbines on mountain peaks in Austria, so I guess they'll manage here."

Gerald's eyes traveled once again around the ring of upright bolts. "I must admit," he said to Tony, "that despite blowing a hole in the top of a mountain, and despite running a parade of trucks up and down, it still makes more sense than sending Bobby Dyson to Iraq. That kid was king of this mountain, and he ought to be here now, watching what his town can do."

"Maybe I could take some pictures and send them to him," said Tony. "Step by step."

"Do you think G. Washtub would allow it?"

Tony smiled. "I don't think G. Washtub is paying much attention to what's happening in Balsam Corners."

"Good," said Gerald. "It's always best to start a revolution quietly."

CHAPTER 13

They rode down the chair lift together, then drove in the maroon Volvo to the grassy parking lot behind the bank. Tony and Mr. Jacobsen got out of the car and stood at the bottom of three granite steps leading up to the back door of the bank.

Mr. Jacobsen held out his hand. "Thanks, pardner."

"You're welcome, sir."

"I'll be phoning your parents from my office. Quicker than a letter. So they'll have a little good news for you when you get home."

"Thank you, sir. They've both been so worried. My father especially. He is a very strong man, but when he lost his job," Tony envisioned his father's worried stare, "he lost his confidence."

Mr. Jacobsen nodded with understanding. "That's why the board knew that your parents would understand the soul of this little town. Because fear is a part of that soul now. Fear that all the good and beautiful things which this town has built, will suddenly be snatched away."

"Right. Do we have an appointment for tomorrow, sir?"

"Tony, I'll be up on the mountain all day. I'll be up there for the next two weeks, until they flip the switch and our wings are feeding the grid. Ride up on the chair lift when you can. Bring your parents. This is their show too."

"Thank you, sir. I certainly will."

Mr. Jacobsen climbed the steps to the steel door at the back of the bank. He reached into his pocket and pulled out a bundle of keys.

Tony walked beneath the silver-blue sky of twilight along the alley between the backs of several stores to his left, and a hardware store warehouse to his right. When he emerged onto the sidewalk of Crosby Boulevard, he glanced back toward the rear door of the bank. He was surprised to see Mr. Jacobsen still standing on the top step. The tall white-haired man was looking at him with a smile and a wave.

Tony waved back.

He was beginning to understand this thing called community service.

CHAPTER 14

When Walter Bower awoke from his nap, he lay in bed with a very unfamiliar feeling: he was not lonely. He was always most lonely when he first woke up, from a nap or from his labored sleep at night. Because when he first woke up was when he missed Anna the most.

But now he felt so peaceful, not lonely at all. That girl's visit had filled him with the most wonderful sense of ease. He had a friend. She would be back.

He liked her, with her serious dark eyes and her lovely Russian accent. She was full of questions, wanted to know, wanted to know. He hadn't talked that much about the war for years.

He wondered if he would be able to sleep tonight. He had tormented poor Anna with his nightmares for forty-seven years.

They were badly hit, three engines gone. The pilot struggled to control the plane long enough for the crew to bail out. His chute on, Walter stood at the edge of the open nose door. There below were French farms and German snipers. The plane shook like a freight train jumping the tracks.

A short distance beneath them, about three hundred yards at ten o'clock, a crippled Fortress, struggling to stay aloft, exploded into a fireball. Trailing black smoke, the blazing B-17 nose-dived like a comet toward the earth.

Then Walter jumped into the blast of wind, and the war waiting below. God help the pilot to make it out too.

Katya talked about her Leningrad with such love. Her eyes lit up when she told him about Tchaikovsky at the theater.

I think she's in love with him. Poor girl, I doubt she'll find anyone quite like herself in this little town. Not many folks in Balsam Corners have seen Swan Lake seventeen times.

Pretty girl, when she lets herself laugh. She's the bud of a Russian flower, waiting in April, waiting, waiting. Well, if she doesn't mind keeping an old bombardier company, I'm very grateful.

It'll be nice to meet her folks. Katya promised a Sunday dinner. Imagine!

"Mr. Bower, are you ready for supper?"

He lifted his head from the pillow and saw Nancy, his afternoon nurse, standing in the doorway. She would walk beside him, while he thumped his cane to the dining room.

"Yes, Nancy. Thank you." He sat up, swung his feet over the side of the bed, then reached for his cane, hooked over the footboard. He tapped its rubber tip on the linoleum floor. Then he smiled at Nancy and asked, "What sort of goulash are they serving tonight?"

CHAPTER 15

Larisa was dead asleep when the phone rang. Groping in the dark, she understood that it must be Tony, calling to say he would soon be home on his bike. And she had nothing for dinner, the same as she had forgotten to make the poor boy his oatmeal this morning.

Her hand found the phone. She picked it up and pressed it to her ear. "Hello?" She wondered whether she had any spaghetti noodles in the cupboard.

"Good afternoon. This is Gerald Jacobsen calling from the Balsam Corners Community Bank."

My God! she thought with utter panic. The bank's going to repossess the house!

"Do I have the pleasure of speaking to Larisa Delmontico?"

"Yes." She sat up in bed, swung her feet over the edge. She did not reach for the light, but sat in darkness and listened with a thumping heart.

"Mrs. Delmontico, the Balsam Corners town board came to a decision at our meeting yesterday evening, with regard to feasibility hiring. I am very glad to tell you that the board has recommended that you and your husband Antonio be hired for one year, at a comfortable compensation, to investigate and report on potential opportunities for development in Balsam Corners. I wonder if we might meet tomorrow morning at ten o'clock in my office at the Bank. Then you and Antonio and I could go over the details together, and hopefully sign a contract."

She was shaking Antonio now—she gripped his arm and then his shoulder and shook him so hard that finally he rolled over—because she was hoping that maybe Gerald Jacobsen at the bank would repeat all of what he had just said, to Antonio.

But she heard herself say, "Yes, that would be fine. Tomorrow morning at ten."

"Thank you. And may I add, that I have just spent a most wonderful couple of hours with your son Tony. We are going to work on a project together. He's quite a boy. You must be very proud."

"Yes," she said, "we are very proud."

"Then, until tomorrow at ten. Good-bye, Larisa."

"Yes, good-bye, Mr. Jacobsen."

Still in a state of disbelief, she set the phone in its cradle, pulled the chain on the light beside the bed, then looked at Antonio, who was sitting up now, looking like a cadaver that had been raised from the dead.

"Antonio, we have a job."

"A job? Both of us?"

"I think so. That was Mr. Jacobsen at the bank. He helped us with our mortgage when we first moved here. Do you remember? Tony was a year old."

"What kind of job?"

She tried to remember what Mr. Jacobsen had said. "Something about the development of Balsam Corners. We're supposed to investigate and report."

"Did we apply for this job?"

"I vaguely remember filling out some applications at the town hall last June. For town jobs. One of them was life guarding at the beach." She smiled. "I guess we didn't get that one."

Antonio scooted across the rumpled bed and sat beside her on the edge of the mattress. "Tomorrow morning at ten, at the bank, we have a meeting?"

"Yes." Her heart welled with joy when she saw the life in Antonio's eyes.

He stood up from the bed, still wearing the clothes he had been wearing to a job interview in Syracuse—a job as an all-night grocery store security guard. He said to her, "Then I propose we go jump in the lake."

She laughed, "Jump in the lake?"

"C'mon." He reached his hand as if asking her to dance. "We hardly went swimming all summer. Let's wash away half a year of sludge and start living again."

Taking his hand, she stood up. "Let me get my bathing suit."

They hurried like two children down the stairs, undressed in the bathroom and threw their clothes—their grave shrouds—into a laundry basket. Then they grabbed their bathing suits, hanging on pegs on the bathroom door.

They hurried out of the house and down the path to the floating dock that bobbed beneath their feet. The sun was down; the air was cool; the sky was silver-blue.

Larisa and her Antonio paused at the end of the dock. Standing beside each other, holding hands, they looked out at the silver-gray lake. With its bays and islands, and patches of water lilies, the lake had been here all summer, waiting for them. As steady as a church, it had been waiting to embrace them, to comfort them, to buoy them up.

"Thank you," she whispered, as she had whispered a thousand times to her lake.

"Thank you," he whispered, his voice strong, filled with life again. He squeezed her hand.

Then with a whoop, they dove into the chilly water of September. Frolicking like a pair of otters, they swam and dove and splashed toward the middle of the lake.

When they floated on their backs, puffing for breath, Larisa wondered what Tony had been doing with Mr. Jacobsen. Did Tony know about their new jobs? Well, at least the poor boy could finish his senior year in Balsam Corners.

CHAPTER 16

Tony stopped at the Chinese restaurant, up the street from the bank, to get a couple of quarts for dinner: one fried rice with shrimp, and one chicken lo mein. He and his parents could have a picnic down on the dock. There was half a jug of cider in the fridge.

Then, wearing his helmet and backpack, he rode out of town on South Shore Road, ready to do some climbing. He maintained a good speed along South Shore, but began to really pump on Blueberry Lake Road. This wasn't serious climbing, certainly nothing like the slopes in the High Peaks further north, but it was enough that he could feel the mountain.

The mountain wanted him to be strong. Those long gorgeous glides downhill were fine, but the real biking was uphill, when the mountain trained his legs, his lungs, his heart. The mountain had been waiting for eleven thousand years, since the mile-thick glacier had melted, for Tony to come pumping up its flank. Something ancient was making him strong.

The race was not in France now, it was in the Adirondacks. Imagine that. The first annual Tour d'Adirondack, and all he had to do was organize it, then ride in it. That was his community service.

A race in seven stages, over seven days, Monday to Sunday. In July. This fall and next spring, he'd have to ride dozens of routes around the entire Adirondack Park, to pick out the best sequential seven. Perhaps north from Balsam Corners, east across the Newcomb plateau, north through the High Peaks, west into the lakes, then south on the last day through Saranac and Tupper Lake, past Blue Mountain and the Museum, past Sagamore, the tight turn to the left in Inlet, then the final stretch along South Shore Road all the way to . . . He'd have to figure out an exact finish line. Did he want curves at the end? Or a long straight final sprint?

A bird flew across the dark turquoise sky ahead of him; he could tell by its size and the bobbing way it flew that it was a flicker. It disappeared into the forest, and must have known what tree it was looking for, because Tony could hear it hammering already when he rode past.

So how was he going to organize this bike race? Yeah, what if he held the Tour d'Adirondack and nobody came? He might get a couple of local riders, but the big guys on the circuit could easily thumb their noses. And of course the top pros would be in France.

Well, he could try to get all the bike shops in the Park to promote it. And he could contact high schools around the Adirondacks, asking for a team from each school. So what if the race turned out to be a bunch of local kids, and no big names at all. So much the better.

He pumped up the road home, pumped with a heavy load of books in his backpack. He could train through September, October, and hopefully some part of November, but then the snow would come. He would ski and pump iron through the winter, until he could get back on his wheels in April. Although in some years, May. In any case, May, June, and half of July: roughly three months of flat-out training, before the big last week in July.

Ride the race, then head off in August to Georgetown. Yes, he could handle that.

He spotted the pale white chapel now, just up the road, its bell tower rising into the first stars. He loved the summer services in the chapel, though he couldn't say that he had yet found any firm religious foundation. He liked the breeze off the lake when it blew through the open windows. He liked the morning sun when it shone through the stained glass window behind the altar. He liked the smell of the old pews, the musty scent of old hymnals, and on cold mornings, the smell of the wood-burning stove.

He liked to see his summer neighbors, liked to chat before and after church.

As he rode past, he looked at the tall dark windows, pointed at their tops, along the pale white length of the chapel.

But he had not yet reconciled the fact that such a living church stood on the shore of such a dead lake.

When he arrived home to an empty house, he looked out the window and saw silvery ripples on the black water: his parents were swimming a little ways out from the dock. He knew immediately that the family, which had stumbled and crumbled all summer, was back together again.

He took off his helmet and backpack, took off his sweaty clothes, put on his bathing suit, then walked barefoot down the path of pine needles to the dock. As he used to do when he was a crazy little kid, he ran the length of the dock as hard as he could and then belly flopped into the lake. He swam beneath the surface, frog-kicking through the cool black water, until he had to pop up to breathe. As he puffed, he could taste the damp tannic air over the lake.

He swam out to meet his parents. He could see that his father was his old self again, breast-stroking beside his mother and squirting fountains of water at her from his grinning mouth.

"Sweetheart!" called his mother. "We have the best news! Do you know? Your father and I have jobs!"

"Yes," boomed his father's voice. "Your old man is gainfully employed."

"Did you meet today with Mr. Jacobsen?" asked his mother, treading water now in front of him. "Do you know what these jobs actually are?"

Tony took in a mouthful and squirted his father. Then he said, "You are to calculate how to best use the projected earnings from a three megawatt wind turbine. It will pay for itself within three to five years, and it will run for at least twenty. The town of Balsam Corners wants you to develop a community plan."

His father squirted him back, then he asked, "And what is your part in all this business?"

"Me?" laughed Tony. "I ride my bike!"

He disappeared underwater and frog-kicked toward the dock.

Part II

WHITE FEATHERS
ON THE MOUNTAIN

CHAPTER 17

On Wednesday morning, September 3, 2003, during second period, Andy Charboneau sat in chemistry class, listening to Mr. Schwartz's lecture on "The Origin of the Elements."

"The elements that we find on planet Earth," said Mr. Schwartz, "were created inside a star. Eons ago, in the core of that star, intense heat, plus great gravitational pressure, formed a furnace in which new elements were forged. Through the process of fusion, four hydrogen atoms combined to form one helium atom. Three helium atoms formed one carbon atom. Four heliums formed one oxygen. Five made neon."

Neon! thought Andy. The orange neon sign, ADIRONDACK SOUVENIRS, in the window of his parents' store, came from the hot core of an old star.

"Tremendous heat and pressure continued this transformation," said Mr. Schwartz, "so that the light elements became heavier elements. At 1.4 billion degrees Fahrenheit, neon atoms combined to form magnesium. At 2.7 billion degrees, aluminum, silicon, sulfur, and phosphorus were formed. At 4 billion degrees, titanium, chromium, . . ."

Chromium on an old Chevy bumper!

". . . manganese, iron, cobalt, nickel, copper, and zinc."

Smoley hokes! thought Andy. Do I have to remember all this?

Mr. Schwartz kept chugging along. "That ancient star, growing old, began to shrink. The core of the star became even hotter, and the gravitation more intense. Now the furnace was really hot, and the hammer was clanging on the anvil in that forge, creating all of our elements."

Mr. Schwartz clapped his hands with a *bang!* "Finally the star exploded, throwing vast clouds of star dust into space. We could say *launching* clouds of star dust, for this dust wandered great distances across the universe."

Andy imagined a cloud of hydrogen and carbon and oxygen, mixed up with all the other stuff, whirling through space.

"Eventually, this dust was caught in gravity's web. Gravity likes to collect things, and to spin things, forming circular balances. Round balls of star dust began to form, while they traveled in orbits around larger round balls of star dust."

Andy imagined an early Earth, round but rough, with clouds of dust and dirt swirling around it.

"Our star, the sun, today still a young star, was made from the dust of that older star. Our Earth was made from star dust. The carbon in our muscles, the iron in our blood, are star dust."

The class murmured at this discovery: they were all made of star dust.

"The chemical Tinker Toys of which we are made," said Mr. Schwartz, "were assembled in the furnace of a star that evolved through a life of its own. The birth and life and death of that star made possible your birth seventeen years ago, and your life today."

Andy thought of something. He began to rummage through the ratty pages of last year's notebook, looking for a fresh page.

"Of course," continued Mr. Schwartz, as he always continued and continued and continued, "we can ask the question, 'How did that old star come to be born?' We can also ask, 'How, in this vast universe, where trillions of furnaces are burning, did life begin? How did the earliest forms of life manage to evolve to more complex forms of life? How did we reach such a complex level that today we are able to think?'" He swept his hand, encompassing in one gesture all the students in the classroom. "Because here we are, pondering our origin. Pondering how it could be possible . . . that elements hammered together by heat and gravity inside a star . . . could become, inside each one of you, a beating heart, a thinking brain."

Andy found a blank page near the end of his notebook.

Raphael raised his hand, which he rarely did in chemistry class.

Mr. Schwartz nodded. "Yes, Raphael."

"Mr. Schwartz, where did the original hydrogen come from? I mean, the hydrogen before it started to make everything else."

"Ahhhhh," said Mr. Schwartz with satisfaction. "Good question, Raphael. Where, in the very beginning, did that hydrogen come from? Where, in the very beginning, did *we* come from? I believe that some of you may spend the rest of your lives trying to answer those questions."

Mr. Schwartz looked at his watch. "Golly, three minutes." He picked up a clipboard from his desk. "Your homework for tomorrow will be to answer, in essay form, questions two and five on page twelve in LIVING CHEMISTRY. You will find that these two questions require you to ponder a bit."

Andy wrote at the top of the blank page: Q 2 and 5, Pg. 12.

Then he zoned out, his mind on its own tangent. He wrote on the blank page,

> Emily is made of stardust.
> Chickadees are made of stardust.
> Pink flamingoes are made of stardust.

He liked that Emily was a part of the universe.
He wrote,

> A pink rose is made of star dust.
> Emily is like a pink rose.

He saw that what he had written was a sort of poem. He had never written a poem before.

The graphite in his pencil was made of carbon. The graphite lettering of his poem was made from star dust.

He wondered if Emily would understand him if he tried to talk with her about all this.

CHAPTER 18

Larisa and Antonio Delmontico sat in Mr. Jacobsen's office—she wearing her most businesslike blue dress, he in his handsome charcoal suit with a maroon tie—listening to Mr. Jacobsen describe the job which they had been hired to do. Larisa watched Antonio, watched Mr. Jacobsen, her eyes flicking back and forth between the two men. Once Antonio was convinced that they really did have real jobs, with adequate and equal salaries, as well as a solid health care program, he began to relax. He glanced at her with a smile in his eyes, then he looked back at Mr. Jacobsen and kept listening,

The retired director of the bank sat behind his huge oaken desk and spoke to them with increasing excitement, as the financier became a visionary. "To our best calculation, 86% of the power generated by our wind turbine will be used by the town. By 'town' I mean homes, businesses, municipal lighting, the school, medical center, nursing home, and the Ski Center. That leaves 14%, which we shall sell to the grid. The profits from that 14% shall be earmarked: to the general benefit of our community." He nodded toward the two of them. "Your job is to make the rounds, talking with folks, asking what they need. Books for the school library, books for the town library. A new X-ray machine at the medical center. Computers for patients who can use them in the nursing home. These are the practical sorts of things we need to investigate."

Mr. Jacobsen lifted his green mug, discovered that it was empty, then looked at Larisa with a surprised smile. "More cocoa?"

Her cup was empty too. "Yes, thank you."

Mr. Jacobsen stood up behind his big desk, picked up his steel thermos, then walked around the desk, unscrewed the cap on the thermos and poured steaming cocoa into Larisa's cup, then into Antonio's, without the least embarrassment that he was doing a job usually done by a waitress.

He filled his own cup, set the thermos on his desk, then drew a spindle chair toward them. She and Antonio shifted their chairs a bit, so that the three now faced each other in a circle. Mr. Jacobsen was no longer the boss behind the desk, but one of a threesome.

"I think that you can take it a bit further," he said, then he paused to savor a long sip of cocoa. Larisa and Antonio drank from their mugs as well. She wondered whether Mr. Jacobsen made the cocoa himself, or whether he perhaps stopped at the diner to have his thermos filled. It was certainly good cocoa.

"For example, when I visited the DanishWind company in Denmark, I discovered that the Danes have done something very special with the beaches along their Atlantic coast. The Danes have built wooden walkways for people in wheelchairs, so that folks who have been hurt in one way or another can wheel themselves from the parking lot to the beach. There are special picnic areas built on wooden platforms, with tables that have only one bench, so that a wheelchair can pull up to the other side. The resorts up and down the coast have made such an effort to be wheelchair accessible, that people in wheelchairs now come from all over Europe to the Danish seacoast." Mr. Jacobsen thumped his fist on his armrest. "Now *that's* the sort of tourist destination a place could be proud to be."

He looked toward the window; his blue eyes caught the morning light. "You see, we could help people out of their wheelchairs and onto the chair lift, then we could carry them on a long quiet glide through the sky to the top of the mountain. On the peak, they would find a wooden walkway that would take them to a platform with picnic tables, where they could look out at miles and miles of rolling Adirondack forest. While they have their picnics, they will be able to hear a faint whoosh, whoosh, whoosh above them. You see, if I were in a wheelchair, stuck in some little room, I would be very glad to perch up there where the angels perch."

Larisa watched Antonio: she could see his mind working on a new sort of furniture. Furniture that he could build on a mountain top, for people in wheelchairs.

"Or let's take another example," said Mr. Jacobsen. "We have twenty kilometers of cross-country ski trails around the base of Bobcat Mountain. Twenty kilometers, without lights. We have a dozen beautiful downhill ski runs, without lights. Our wind turbine is offering to light the mountain. A boon for the tourist business. And a boon for everybody who lives in Balsam Corners. With night skiing, winter would no longer be one more bout of cabin fever."

Yes, she hated the long months of winter when she went to work in the dark and came home in the dark. Every evening, television and tiredness, or a book and tiredness, or a ho-hum walk along a dark road and tiredness. How nice it would be to go skiing with her boys, two or three evenings a week.

"But let's take it a bit further. In the forest around the mountain are old logging trails. They're a bit overgrown, but they could be cleared. I'd like to run our cross-country ski trails deep into the forest, until we have a network of about a hundred kilometers, with lean-tos along the trails. Folks could ski with a backpack along a lighted trail on Friday evening, to a lean-to where they set up camp for the weekend. Who else in the American northeast offers winter skiing, winter camping, with lit trails? And I mean *wilderness* camping. At eleven o'clock, the lights go out, and the coyotes begin to howl."

Mr. Jacobsen pointed toward the conference room. "I've got topographical maps there on the table. A few of the old logging trails are marked on them. The other trails we'd have to find ourselves. I'll bet some of the old timers in town could help us."

Larisa asked, "You want to string a hundred kilometers of lights through the forest?"

"Oh, we don't have to light every trail. Just a few of the major boulevards, so that people can get where they're going at night. If folks want to ski with just the moonlight, just the starlight, they could follow the unlit trails."

"And in the summer," she said, "these would be hiking trails."

"Of course. Some of them with wheelchair walkways, wheelchair lean-tos. I'm tired of selling beer and gasoline to the snowmobilers. I'm tired of the stink of exhaust in town. Is that the best that Balsam Corners can do?"

Mr. Jacobsen paused for a moment; his face became deeply serious. "The town's got a boy now over in Iraq. What if Bobby comes home with his legs blown off? We say to him, 'Sorry Bobby, you can't go up your mountain anymore? You can't go into your forest anymore?' And what about all those other kids, men and women both, down in Walter Reed Hospital, arms and legs gone? How about we *really* support our troops, with a corner of the Adirondacks that welcomes them."

Yes, she thought, here was something that the town could do, which WalMart could never take away from them.

Mr. Jacobsen's voice was vibrant with conviction as the told them, "We could develop an entire program, winter and summer, for people with physical limitations. Out in Minnesota, they guide blind people on skis down the slopes. Isn't that the American dream? Equal opportunity for all? Maybe we need to wake up that old dream again."

"Sir," said Antonio, "I have a question."

"Yes?"

"Why is all this suddenly possible now? Where is the money coming from? Why didn't we do this years ago?"

Mr. Jacobsen shrugged. "Well of course, it's always a matter of economics. If oil and coal power your economy, you never have any extra power, because you have to pay for every bit of oil and coal. But if the *wind* powers your economy, there's usually plenty of wind, more than we could ever use. Plenty of sunshine, plenty of ocean currents, plenty of geothermal heat. So it's not so hard to have a bit of extra power, power that we can sell to the grid. Yes, occasionally the wind fades, and we have to buy from the grid. But more often than not, the wind is blowing. The wind is very generous, don't you see?"

"Then why haven't we done this sooner?"

"The Danes have. The Spaniards have, the Italians have, the Germans have, the Irish have. The whole world is putting up wind turbines, the whole world is creating new jobs, while Americans worry about their oil supply." Mr. Jacobsen grimaced with contempt. "Address your question to the oil boys. Address your question to G. Washtub. Ask *him* why he insists that America stay stuck in the Dark Ages of Oil."

"You truly believe that the wind will be so bountiful?"

"Ask a Minnesota farmer, who has a dozen turbines out in his pasture. The profit that he earns from wind turbines enables him to keep the family farm. The wind pays his mortgage at the bank much better than the cows ever could."

"And that's the job you want us to do," said Antonio. "Something beyond just clean energy."

"Exactly. I want you two to come up with concrete and beneficial dreams. For the town, for the Adirondack Park, for this poor struggling country, for the world. I want to take the road not yet taken."

Antonio thought for a long moment, then he asked, "And how long would be our term of employment?"

"Well, DanishWind builds their wind turbines to run for twenty years, at least. How would you like to dream and build during the span of one generation? Where do you think this little town could be in twenty years? I'd like to be the town that lit the first candle in the dark."

"Twenty years." Antonio looked at Larisa. "What do you think?"

Larisa had been watching the transformation in Antonio. His confidence had come back, and with it, that special ability of his to see a full range of possibilities, all of them positive. He had designed such beautiful furniture because he was always exploring toward something more beautiful. He had done the same with their son: always guiding, always encouraging, as he helped Tony to build a positive foundation.

Today in Mr. Jacobsen's office, she saw once again the man she had fallen in love with years ago.

She held up her mug. "I propose a toast. Here's to the troops in Walter Reed Hospital. May we truly welcome them home."

Mr. Jacobsen raised his mug and toasted, "May we welcome them to a new blossoming of democracy in America."

Antonio held up his mug, "To concrete and beneficial dreams."

The three clinked their green mugs together, then savored their cocoa.

CHAPTER 19

At the end of chemistry class, Kate Sommnerfelt stayed after the bell to talk with Mr. Schwartz.

"Mr. Schwartz?"

"Yes, Kate."

"Um, I need like, a, um, pH tester. One of those things for testing pH in snow and stuff. But a good one, a professional one. It's for my community service."

"What are you going to test, Kate?"

"Um, rain. And snow. The snow in the spring when it melts."

"Acid precipitation, Kate. Good for you."

"My, um, community service person wants me to phone the results to a radio station. She says that if the rain is acidic, the farmers ought to know. But I don't think I could ever, ever, ever talk on a radio."

"Kate, you might surprise yourself. This is your senior year. This is the year when you kids are supposed to blossom."

"Um, like, do you know what sort of pH tester to order?"

"Certainly. I'll contact Cole-Porter in Illinois. They carry the best in scientific equipment. We'll make a pro out of you, Kate. A tester, two buffers, a thermometer and a notebook is what you need. You can post your findings on the classroom bulletin board. And you can practice explaining your information to your classmates. They're a tough crowd. If you can handle the seniors, you can handle a little ol' radio station."

"Thanks, Mr. Schwartz."

"You're welcome, Kate."

When she went out the classroom door, she felt like skipping.

CHAPTER 20

When he rode his bike to school on Wednesday morning, Tony Delmontico carried his camera in his backpack. After school, he would ride the old logging road up the back of Bobcat Mountain, so that he could take a picture of Step One: the wind turbine's concrete base. He planned to take step-by-step pictures over the next two weeks, as the wind turbine was erected, so that he could send an album of four-by-six-inch prints to Bobby Dyson in Iraq. He wanted Bobby to see what was happening back home, as a counterbalance to the violence of the war.

Within minutes of Wednesday's three o'clock bell, Tony was pumping his bike along Park Avenue toward the mountain. He pumped up Brown's Tract Road, in forest now, then he hooked left and climbed Bisby Road. At the fork with Bobcat Mountain Road to the left, leading to the Ski Center, he took the right fork: the old logging road.

Winding up the southwest flank of the mountain toward the peak, the road was sometimes a stretch of grassy earth, sometimes a patch of polished granite, sometimes a bed of new gravel. The road was steep, but not too steep: a century ago, horses had managed to bring down a sledge of logs on a good bed of snow.

He noticed freshly cut trees and bulldozed stumps: the road had been widened in places during the summer. The trucks that would bring up the sections of the wind turbine would have to be big. The blades were forty-four meters long, almost half the length of a football field.

He liked pumping so hard that his legs ached. He liked the red maple leaves scattered on the earthen roadbed. He was training, training for the Tour d'Adirondack. He might not reach the top of the mountain in one push today, but in two weeks, he'd be cruising up.

He downshifted, but had to stop twice. He walked the bike about a hundred feet each time to rest his legs. Then he was pumping again. He could hear the wind in the maples. Sometimes the breeze reached down and cooled his sweaty face.

He emerged from the forest of spruce and maple onto the flattened granite dome of Bobcat Mountain. He squeezed his brakes, then puffing for breath, he stared with astonishment at the most enormous red bulldozer he had ever seen. Its treads were at least twenty feet long. Around it stood a dozen men wearing bright orange overalls. As he walked his bike over gravel and granite, he realized that the giant red machine was not a bulldozer, for it had no blade. It must be the base of the crane.

He spotted Mr. Jacobsen on the opposite side of the dome, standing near the top of the chair lift. He was talking with someone. Tony walked his bike toward the man who had called him "pardner."

As he approached the two men, Mr. Jacobsen spotted him and called, "Good afternoon, Tony."

"Good afternoon, Mr. Jacobsen." Tony swung down his kickstand, parked his bike on a fairly level bit of granite, then shook hands. Mr. Jacobsen stared him square in the eye, as if to reaffirm all they had said to each other the day before.

Then he turned to the man beside him. "Tony, I'd like you to meet Yuri Cherkasov. Yuri, this is Tony Delmontico."

As Tony shook Yuri's hand, he realized that Yuri must be Katya's father. "I'm very pleased to meet you, sir."

"It is my great pleasure," said Yuri, with a much stronger accent than Katya's.

"Yuri is our engineer," explained Mr. Jacobsen. "Down at Brill's, he's the best Volvo mechanic I've ever found. He'll keep ol' Bess running for another twenty years. But Yuri can do a whole lot more than tune a Volvo. Yuri and his wife are both electrical engineers, with university degrees. They both had top jobs in the Soviet defense industry, until

1991, when the Soviet Union collapsed. Seventy percent of the workforce in Leningrad had been doing military work: designing and building and preparing for launch the missiles that were aimed at New York and Washington."

Mr. Jacobsen paused to look at Yuri for confirmation.

"Yes," said Yuri, "both Sveta and I graduated with highest marks. She worked on a satellite navigation system for naval destroyers, while I built the guidance system for submarine-launched missiles. We were defending our country, and proud of such work. We did not know that one day we would be living in the land of the enemy," he glanced with a smile at Mr. Jacobsen, "able to work with such bright and generous people."

"So," continued Mr. Jacobsen, "as part of the contract, DanishWind trains a qualified local person to maintain the V90 wind turbine. DanishWind told us that they prefer someone with an electrical background, who is also handy with tools. Fifty-seven people applied for the job last June, but the only person nearly as qualified as Yuri was Svetlana. But she's not as handy with tools as she is with Russian cooking. So Yuri got the job."

Yuri nodded. "I trained for five weeks last summer at the DanishWind office in America, far to the west in your state of Oregon. *Excellent* training. As they showed me the turbine, the gears, the generator, I felt that I was myself again. I learned more English during those five weeks than I had learned during the two years before. Now, in September, I will help the DanishWind crew with the assembly and commission. When they leave, I will listen to the turbine as I listen to a Volvo, and your light bulbs will never flicker."

"So," said Tony with satisfaction, "we'll have a Russian engineer taking care of a Danish wind turbine, on top of an American mountain, where the wind blows around the world."

"That's right," said Mr. Jacobsen. "Where the wind blows around the world."

Tony took off his backpack, opened the top flap and took out his camera. He zoomed in on the red crane base, focused on the name MARINO in white letters, and took a picture of Step Two.

Step One was the concrete base with its ring of steel bolts. He asked, "Can we walk closer? I'd like to get a shot of the concrete plug."

"Certainly," said Mr. Jacobsen. "If the crew wants us out of the way, they'll wave an orange arm at us."

The three walked across the cracked and glacier-polished granite toward the ring of bolts. Twenty feet from the ring, Tony took a look through his lens. He focused on the nearest bolt, gave himself as high an f-stop as possible for good depth of field, drew back the zoom so as to show the plug of manmade rock lodged in Adirondack granite—the ring of steel bolts was gleaming in the afternoon sun—then pressed the shutter, CLICK.

The mountain had endured a bit of blasting, had suffered a tiny pockmark, so it could become the pedestal for an unprecedented set of wings.

He wanted Bobby, who had raced so bravely down this mountain, to see that now the mountain was reaching up.

"I remember way back when," said Mr. Jacobsen. "I was a young fellow at Colgate, majoring in economics. We had an excellent professor, Dr. Winthrop, who asked us to consider the question, 'What are the cathedrals of our age?' What will stand the test of time over the next millennium? What will lift us out of our day-to-day drudgery? What will instruct our spirits, that we might evolve beyond ourselves?"

A cathedral, thought Tony. He had long dreamed of visiting the cathedrals in France.

Mr. Jacobsen pointed at the giant red base of the crane. "That's what they call a 'crawler crane,' Tony. It's on treads, not wheels. During the next three days, they'll be trucking up a smaller crane, then pieces of the crawler crane's boom. The smaller crane will help to build the big one. By Saturday afternoon, they'll have a boom three hundred and ten feet tall, ready to snatch down the moon."

Tony would ride his bike up the mountain tomorrow after school, and Friday after school, and on Saturday after work at the bike shop, so that he could take pictures of whatever sort of crane it would be. He regretted that two days of school and one day of work would take him away from the mountain. He would have liked to simply camp up here, with a sleeping bag and tent, food and cooking gear, and his camera. Yes, he would like to camp right here on the mountaintop for the next two weeks.

But for now, he needed a picture of Step One. "How about a photograph of you two?" he asked. "I think you should be a part of the story. Why don't you stand in front of that ring of bolts?"

Mr. Jacobsen and Yuri gladly obliged. They stood side by side in front of the gleaming ring. Mr. Jacobsen wrapped his arm around Yuri's shoulder; Yuri did likewise. Wearing a grey suit, and blue mechanic's overalls, they were a team. Tony focused on their faces, then drew back his zoom lens toward a wider angle: now he had the ring of bolts, then the red crawler crane in the background, and in the further background, the rolling red-tinged hills of the Adirondacks in early autumn. CLICK.

As he rode his bike down the old logging road, his tires jounced on the roots and ruts. A grouse burst into the air ahead of him, startled from a hobblebush. The late afternoon sun blinked through the trees.

He heard the labored rumble of a truck approaching. He braked to a stop, then walked his bike off the road into the ferns. Standing at the edge of the woods, he stared in awe at the size of a blue flatbed truck transporting a section of the crawler crane's boom. Tony waved to the driver when he rumbled past in low gear. As the long red derrick on the flatbed now passed him—part of some architectural skeleton—he remembered the question, "What are the cathedrals of our age?"

Though he had to breathe a cloud of oil fumes when he walked his bike back onto the road, he felt extremely fortunate.

He was here at the very beginning.

CHAPTER 21

Just about everyone in Balsam Corners visited Bobcat Mountain on Thursday. They drove to the grassy parking lot at the bottom of the ski slopes, then they joined the crowd staring at three long white cylinders, like sections of a rocket, strapped to the flatbeds of three enormous blue trucks. The white cylinders looked to be about ten feet in diameter, big enough that a man could walk inside with a child riding on his shoulders.

The three trucks would carry the three sections of the tubular tower one by one up the old logging road on Monday, when the crane on top was ready for them.

After staring at the cylinders, people walked across the bottom of the ski slopes, past the brown chalet, to the line of people waiting at the bottom of the chair lift. While folks waited their turn, they watched the lift's green chairs carrying pairs of people up the mountain, until the chairs disappeared out of sight. People riding the chairs down the mountain stepped off at the bottom, then mingled with people waiting in line to go up. Friends chatted with friends, telling them what they had learned up on the peak.

People from Balsam Corners who had never ridden the chair lift except in winter, and people who had never ridden it at all, stepped quickly from the front of the line to the spot where they should stand. They peered over their shoulders at the approaching green chairs, then set their bottoms down firmly on the seats and gripped the safety rail which the operator lowered in front of them. They felt the chair sweep them gently up into the air. They glided smoothly between the red crowns of maples as they rose higher and higher up the mountain.

They peered down at the grassy slopes between groves of trees, searching for the famous Bobcat Mountain deer. They peered up at the blue sky that reached further and further over the distant Adirondack horizon.

And now they saw, as they neared the top of Bobcat Mountain, a slender vertical finger of red latticework, pointing nearly straight up into the sky: the lower section of the crane's growing boom.

At the top of the lift, people stepped quickly off the gliding chair, then they walked a short distance further uphill, first on grass, then on granite, until they came to a yellow DO NOT ENTER ribbon strung between orange traffic cones around the work area. From a safe distance, they watched a yellow hydraulic crane on wheels as it lifted section after section of red lattice from the ground, then hoisted the section into position atop the lengthening boom. With each section installed, the red boom reached higher and higher into the blue sky.

On Friday, just about everyone in Balsam Corners visited Bobcat Mountain, this time bringing their cameras. In the parking lot, they stared at the "na*celle*," as it was called: a white housing about the size of a school bus. The nacelle was transported on a long blue truck with more wheels than anyone had ever seen on one vehicle. The nacelle and its specially designed truck looked like something from the Cape Kennedy space program. People felt proud that such a thing had come to their little mountain.

Inside the nacelle—as an article in the *Adirondack Express* had explained when the paper came out last Tuesday—was the three megawatt turbine. Its coils of copper wire, spinning inside a strong magnetic field, would turn wind power into electrical power. Many people brought the newspaper with them to Bobcat Mountain, for a half-page diagram showed the interior of the nacelle. While folks stood outside the big white housing, they studied the diagram: gears, turbine, transformer, a hatch to the roof.

That turbine was going to power every light bulb in town. Without burning one barrel of oil, without burning one lump of coal.

People asked their friends to take their picture in front of the nacelle. One by one, two by two, in clusters of friends, or gathered as a family, the folks of Balsam Corners stood in front of the big white housing, with the name DanishWind printed in blue letters above them. Then they gave the photographer a thumbs-up.

People walked with their cameras to the chair lift. They rode once again up the mountain to see how high the crane had been built by Friday afternoon.

On Saturday, the people of Balsam Corners, as well as people from a dozen other cities, towns, villages, and hamlets, from Blue Mountain Lake to the north, to Utica and Rome to the south, gathered in the Ski Center parking lot. They marveled at the size and the elegance of three long white blades, strapped atop three specially built blue trucks. People could run their eyes along a curve as graceful as the curve in an eagle feather. Each long narrow blade had the dimensions of a wing's pinion stretched to about twice its natural length. The blades were forty-four meters long, nearly half a football field. How, people asked, would they ever get these giant white feathers to the top of Bobcat Mountain?

Folks told folks that if the trucks could not climb the old timber road, then a helicopter would lift the blades one by one to the top. Danish-Wind had already erected turbines high in the mountains of Austria. Well, then they would probably manage Bobcat Mountain.

People carried their cameras and small picnic baskets to the chair lift. The picnic baskets sat on their laps, just inside the safety gate, while folks rode up the mountain. At the top, they found three dozen picnic tables, which had been trucked up the old logging road to the granite dome by the Highway Department. The spectators enjoyed their macaroni salad and fried chicken while they watched the final sections of the towering red boom hoisted into place.

The crane was completed on Saturday afternoon, September 6, 2003. The slender red boom reached like a needle three hundred and ten feet high, braced by a shorter boom and a stack of enormous weights.

When a worker wearing orange overalls stood atop the giant red crawler and called out to the watching crowd that the crane was now functional, a great cheer went up. The crane was something magnificent. Imagine that next week, after a quiet Sunday, the crane would build something even more magnificent.

CHAPTER 22

On Wednesday afternoon, the second day of senior year, Andy Charboneau transferred out of French IV and into Wood Shop. He had to get signatures from his French teacher and the shop teacher, as well as from his homeroom teacher, Miss Applegate. His French teacher told him, "Andy, I would be *delighted* to sign your transfer."

So during sixth period, Andy stood in the school's wood shop with a dozen other students—mostly boys, though with a couple of girls—listening to Mr. Wilkens explain the operation of the jigsaw.

"Now you've got your choice of blades," said Mr. Wilkens, holding up five sample blades, "broader for the heavy cutting, and more slender for the frills. You'll practice with all of them, so that while you're working on a project, you can choose exactly which blade you want to use."

Andy didn't think a birdfeeder would have much in the way of frills. Just the major cuts, and a hinge for the roof.

In study hall during seventh period, Andy studied the book which Mr. Wilkens had loaned him, a book with carpentry plans for birdhouses and birdfeeders. Andy found a basic birdfeeder that looked pretty good.

During class, Mr. Wilkens had asked Andy if he had time to work in the shop after school. Mr. Wilkens said he worked with students on special projects during the afternoons. He thought that maybe Andy would want to get started on his birdfeeder. The only thing Andy had going this afternoon was maybe a visit to Emily, but he could visit her at five or six, so he said Yes, he would like to get started.

As it turned out, he was the only student working in the shop that afternoon, so he had Mr. Wilkens' full attention. They worked with white pine, rather than cedar. "You'll work with cedar when you start building birdfeeders for real. Right now, you're working on a model, a prototype. You want to get the wrinkles out before you use a good wood like cedar."

Following a diagram in the carpentry book, Andy cut a board of pine into a ten-by-fourteen-inch rectangle, for the birdfeeder's base. Then he cut the side supports, pointed at the top to support the roof. He cut the twin boards of the angled roof. Then he learned from Mr. Wilkens how to cut the upper edges of the two roof boards at an angle so that they fit together at the peak.

He liked wearing the shop apron, liked the way the rough blue denim gathered the fine sawdust. And he didn't mind wearing the goggles. He thought they would fog up, but they didn't.

He was amazed that by five-thirty that afternoon, he had cut out all the pieces, had hammered them together with small nails, and had attached the V-shaped roof with two hinges so that it lifted perfectly, enabling a person to put bird seed onto the eight-by-twelve-inch tray. He had even sanded the rough edges, so that there on the carpentry bench stood a completed birdfeeder.

"Good job!" said Mr. Wilkens, though Andy could see that some of his cuts were not very straight.

"Thank you, sir. Thank you for your help. I thought it would take us about three days."

"Three days! You show up at nine o'clock on Saturday morning, and I'll have enough cedar for you to build ten birdfeeders. And brass hinges too, not this tin stuff."

Andy carried his birdfeeder, or really, a prototype birdfeeder, in his arms as he walked along South Shore Road to the nursing home. He wanted to show Emily what her birdfeeder was going to look like. He could build the real thing on Saturday morning, though he wasn't sure exactly how he would install the birdfeeder atop a pipe outside her window.

When he got to Emily's room, his arms were about to fall off. She was sitting in her wheelchair, wearing a dress as bright yellow as a daffodil. He stood in her doorway, smiled at her and said, "Knock, knock."

She stared at him as if she had never seen him before. "Did you bring my apple? I've been waiting for my apple."

"No, I . . . Emily, may I come in?" He was going to drop the darn birdfeeder right there on her floor if he couldn't put it down. "May I put this on your bed?" He stepped quickly across her room and set the one-ton birdfeeder on her flowery quilt. "There you go, Emily. That's what it's going to look like."

"I want to share my apple."

"What?"

"I want to share my apple with my brother. Did you bring my apple? We have to cut it in half, part for me and part for my brother."

She did not recognize him, nor did she remember talking about a birdfeeder.

He shook the aching out of his arms, then he took off his canvas Boy Scout rucksack; he'd been a Scout for exactly two weeks, another flop in his long career of baseball, football, and Boy Scout flops. He unfastened the flap, then took out the bird book, and the poster wrapped in its tube. "Emily," he said, turning to page seventy-eight, "do you remember *chickadees*? Chickadees. Chickadees."

She stared at the picture of the little grey bird with a black cap and white cheeks. Then she puckered her lips and whistled three high tones with clear precision, so that she sounded almost like the bird itself, saying its name.

Andy tried to whistle the chickadee's name, but made a blurry botch of it.

Emily whistled "chickadee" a half-dozen times. Then she smiled at him. "They stay all winter. The other birds abandoned me, but the chickadees kept me company all winter."

"That's right, Emily. That's right." He put the book into her pale thin hands, then he pulled the poster out of the tube, unrolled it and showed Emily the life-size chickadee, right next to a life-size blue jay. "Here's your friend, Emily. May I put this poster up on your wall?"

Her eyes widened. "Certainly!"

He glanced around her room, then pointed at the bare wall beyond the foot of her bed, close to the window. While she was lying in bed, if she looked beyond her feet, the poster would look like a window with a lot of birds outside. "How about right there?"

"Do you have tape?"

"Yup." He held up his thumb, with a roll of adhesive tape around it. The woman at the front desk had given it to him. "I think this tape'll stick to the plaster. Let's give it a try."

Emily swung her wheelchair around so she could watch him. The tape stuck well: the poster hung flat against the wall. Andy thought briefly that he might one day build a window frame around it.

He pointed at the chickadee, its little feet gripping a twig. "There's your friend, ready to stay with you through the whole winter."

"Is it winter yet?"

"No. Look out the window. Do you see any snow? It's fall. Autumn. The leaves are turning red. Look into the forest. Do you see those red trees?"

She pivoted her chair and stared out the window. "Ayah. That's why I'm waiting for my apple. It's autumn."

"All right. Just a sec."

He went out to the corridor, looked for a nurse—they were all busy—so he followed the long hallway to the front desk. He asked the receptionist, "Excuse me, do you know where I could get an apple for Emily? Is there a kitchen?"

The woman pointed, "Down the west corridor, the first big door on your left goes into the cafeteria, the second big door goes into the kitchen."

"Thanks."

He found the kitchen door, talked with one of the cooks, and returned to Emily's room with a ring of thin apple slices on a blue plate. With red peels, the circle of apple slices was distinctly red, white, and blue.

He put a small table between his spindle chair and Emily's wheelchair, then set the plate on the table. She looked at the apple slices with delight, though she did not reach for one. He picked up the plate and extended it to her. "Go ahead, Emily. There's your apple."

"May I?"

"Yes, you may. The chef wants you to know that it's a Cortland."

"A Cortland! My favorite!"

She carefully picked up a white wedge with red skin, raised it to her mouth and took a bite. She closed her eyes, savored the apple, then opened her eyes and proclaimed; "Now it is autumn."

She insisted that they split the apple slices equally, five and five. The two of them ate in silence, too absorbed for conversation.

When she had finished her five slices, Emily sat back in her chair and stared at him. "Thank you, young man."

"I'm Andy," he said. "Andy."

"Oh."

Then she was quiet, still watching him. Though she could easily see the birdfeeder sitting on her bed, she hadn't paid the slightest attention to it.

She asked him, "Do you have a brother?"

"No," he said. He saw the disappointment in her eyes, as if she felt sorry for him.

He had once had a baby sister, for two weeks. He had been only three then, and could not remember her. He couldn't remember his mother and father either from that time. By the time he was five, and could begin to remember things, his baby sister had been dead for two years.

"My brother went away in the war," said Emily. "He went to France. When the war is over, he'll be coming home." She smiled at the thought.

He heard himself say, "That's right, Emily. That's right."

"Then we're going to have a party," she said, clapping her hands three times. "And everyone will be there."

A voice behind them said, "Emily, it's time to get ready for dinner, dear."

He looked over his shoulder and saw a nurse in the doorway, then he stood up and moved his chair back to its corner.

"I'll see you soon, Emily."

"All right, young man. Thank you for the apple."

"You're welcome."

He swung on his rucksack, picked up the bird feeder and stepped out the door. Then he glanced back at Emily: she held her hand up, ready to wave. He waved the fingers of one hand as best he could while holding the birdfeeder. "G'bye, Emily."

"Good bye, Mr. Chickadee."

As he walked down the long corridor, he decided that it didn't matter whether or not she recognized him. He would put up a cedar birdfeeder outside her window, and then she could watch her chickadees all winter.

CHAPTER 23

When he got home, Andy glanced into the living room: his parents were as usual going over the books from the souvenir store. The card table between them was covered with bills, catalogues, the account books. They both looked up when they heard him, but he hurried down the hallway to his bedroom. He set the birdfeeder on his unmade bed, then shut the bedroom door.

He looked at the television on his desk, at the video player, the DVD player, and at the computer screen and keyboard. He looked at the stacks and stacks of videos on his desk, and at the ragged heaps of videos on the bookshelves flanking his bed. The bedroom walls were covered with posters of space aliens wielding futuristic weaponry. The room smelled of electrical circuitry and old socks. The window behind the cluttered desk hadn't been opened for years.

He could either put on his headphones, crank up *Ballistic Chicks*, then venture out to the kitchen so he could put a frozen dinner into the microwave, which he would eat in his room while he watched a DVD, or he could do something else. He looked at the birdfeeder on his rumpled bed.

Charles Charboneau was not sure which one was the greater failure, himself or his son. Himself for having failed to raise a child able to join and contribute to the world around him. Or his son, for being some strange, self-absorbed creature, who once had been part of the family, but now lived a separate existence.

Had he been too severe with the occasional discipline when the boy was younger, or too lax? Andy had been such a nice kid, though always a bit of a loner. And then suddenly, he seemed to vanish. He had the headphones on, he was gone. Perhaps Charles should have scolded him more at that point, should have demanded that Andy at least speak once in a while with his mother and father.

The transition, when Andy was about thirteen, tore up Annette. She had already lost one child, and now she felt she was losing her son. Andy simply rebuffed her attempts to say hello. Charles told her that it was just a teenage phase, but it went on and on and on.

They had hoped that when Andy reached the age of fourteen, he would be able to help part-time at the store. But even if he had been willing, they couldn't have such a distant ghost waiting on customers. So they gave him twenty-five dollars a week, as an allowance. He was home and out of trouble, and the money enabled him to buy his videos. As long as he was in his bedroom, evening after evening, all day Saturday, all day Sunday, then at least he wasn't out dealing drugs.

It was as if the television had snatched their child away. Then came the video. And now DVD. The non-stop music, the non-stop noise. What happened to the kid who used to help his mother when she was packing a picnic? What happened to the kid who had his own little shovel, so he could help his father shovel snow?

None of the teachers at school had been able to reach him. The principal had tried to counsel him. Well, Dale Shepherd had had some success, for at least Andy was still in school.

But it broke Annette's heart. She had one child, one beautiful son, and he was quickly growing up as a stranger to her. He was losing his childhood by spending the time somewhere else, and she was losing it too. What does a mother do with all that love? What does a father do?

When Andy appeared in the living room doorway, holding something made of wood in his hands, both Charles and Annette looked up. They were surprised to see him, but they were utterly stunned when he said, "I want to apologize."

Neither said a word. It would have sounded stupid to ask, "Whatever for?"

Andy stepped into the room, holding what appeared to be a newly built birdfeeder. He must have made it at school.

"What do you have there?" asked Charles.

"No, wait," said Andy. "Let me say this." He was clearly struggling, and wanted to get something out.

Charles set down his calculator. Annette set down her pencil. They looked at a boy whose troubled green eyes were looking openly at them.

"I think I've been . . ." He shrugged, baffled himself. ". . . on a long trip. Like I had to get away for awhile. I had to listen to something that seemed to make sense." He paused. "But while my ears were listening, my eyes were closed."

"Sweetheart," said Annette.

Andy set the birdfeeder on the floor, then stood near his mother. She stood up from her chair, clearly aching to hug him, but hesitating, afraid she might chase him away.

"Mom, I'm sorry. I can't begin to think of how rude I've been."

"Sweetheart, we all go through difficult times."

"Yeah. But now something new has started, and I don't want to muck it up with all that old stuff."

"What's that, son?" asked Charles, standing up as well from his chair. "What's something new?" Somebody had gotten through to Andy. One of the teachers had finally gotten through.

"Her name is Emily. She's at the nursing home. She's my community service. She doesn't remember things very well, but that's okay. The thing is, I have to build all these birdfeeders," he glanced at the birdfeeder on the floor, "twenty-five of them. The first one will be outside Emily's window. I don't want to mess up Emily and her chickadees." He shook his head against ever letting that happen. "I can't say much more than that. I just met her, you see. But I know that I don't want to be the same jerk that I've been, with Emily."

"Sweetheart," said Annette for the third time.

"Wait, Mom." He waved his hand, stopping her. "You've got an apology coming, an apology about as big as this house. I'm sorry, deeply sorry, for being . . . whatever it was that I've been."

Andy looked at his father. "Dad, I think it was four years ago that you gave me a fly rod for my birthday. I just shrugged my shoulders and turned away. It's September now, not exactly trout season, but I want to say, finally, 'Thanks for the fly rod.'"

"You're welcome, son. You're welcome." Charles marveled at this miracle, wrought by a woman in a nursing home. Somebody named Emily. How did she do it?

"So," said Andy, reaching down to pick up his birdfeeder, "this is what I made in shop today."

"Wait a minute, young man," said Annette, reaching down and grabbing her son's hand before he had taken hold of the birdfeeder. "Your mother wants a hug."

"Mom, don't be crying," said Andy, his voice shaking.

Charles watched his wife wrap her arms around her son. "My boy, my boy, my boy," she said, as if a dam had burst and all her pent-up love could finally pour out.

Charles picked up the birdfeeder and set it on top of the account books on the card table. Then he stood ready to shake his son's hand.

CHAPTER 24

On Saturday, Kate worked at the beauty shop while Raphael worked at the garage. She washed and curled people's hair while he changed oil and adjusted carburetors. They both got out of work at five.

Everybody in town had been talking all day about their trip to Bobcat Mountain. In the Ski Center parking lot, people stared at the three huge white cylinders that would form the wind turbine's tower. They studied the na*celle*—people pronounced the word with stress on the second syllable—with the three-megawatt turbine inside it. And they looked from several angles at the three blades, each blade atop a separate truck. It was the blades that people marveled at the most. The other parts were big, but the blades were something that "stirred your heart," as one woman said while Kate tinted her hair.

So Kate and Raphael decided, when she climbed into his rumbling truck at the curb in front of the beauty shop, to take a look for themselves. Tyrannosaurus Rex rattle-banged up the mountain, to the parking lot at the bottom of the ski runs. Kate and Raphael stared out her open window at the white cylinders, the white nacelle, the white blades, each on a separate truck surrounded by a crowd of people.

Raphael had to park on the far side of the lot, then they hurried together toward one of the blades, perched atop an amazingly long truck. The blade was even longer than the truck: the tip of the feather extended over the roof of the blue cab.

"Kate," said Raphael, "think of the torque on that blade."

Kate did not think about the torque. She understood that the people in the beauty shop had been right: something very special was happening in their little town. She was glad to be here watching it happen with Raphael. She liked the wonder in his eyes, the excitement in his voice, while he imagined the size of the gears inside the nacelle.

They walked together past the chalet to the bottom of the chair lift. She would have liked it if he had held her hand while they were walking, but he didn't.

They waited in line together, said "Hi" to friends in front of them, then they stepped quickly to the take-off spot. They looked back over their shoulders, set their bottoms down on the gliding green seats and took off smoothly into the sky. They looked down at the grassy slopes, looked ahead up the mountain, and glanced higher up at the gathering clouds, clouds that might bring rain tomorrow.

Rain was no good, thought Kate. She was supposed to help Mrs. Ferguson to paint her Adirondack chairs.

When friends passed them on a chair gliding down the mountain, Raphael laughed and called, "Any snow on top?"

They glided so quietly, so peacefully, that Kate would have liked to ride that way forever.

"Do you know what?" she asked Raphael.

"What?"

"This is our first date."

"This is our first date?" He sounded a little worried.

"Yup. You picked me up, we decided to do something together, and here we are."

"Well, then." He let go of the safety bar in front of them and wrapped his arm around her, squeezing her closer to him. "If it's going to be a date, then it had better be a *hot* date."

"That's right," she said, snuggling against him.

It didn't matter if he didn't kiss her yet. Gliding through the sky with Raphael was just great.

CHAPTER 25

After Katya's first meeting with Walter Bower on Tuesday afternoon, she visited him again on Wednesday afternoon, and Thursday afternoon, and Friday afternoon. They did not talk about the war, either in Russia or in Western Europe. Katya knew that some veterans preferred to go back to that time only rarely, if at all. Instead, Katya read to Mr. Bower from the book which Miss Applegate had assigned to the senior class, *The Grapes of Wrath*, by John Steinbeck. Mr. Bower said that he had read the book once, a long time ago, but in any case he knew about the Dust Bowl during the Depression: he had been a boy of twelve in 1933, here in Balsam Corners.

Katya liked to read the smooth clear sentences (marking any word she did not know). She tried to enunciate clearly, pausing now and then to ask Mr. Bower to pronounce a difficult word. He would say, "Okla*ho*ma," slowly and clearly, then she would try to repeat his pronunciation, "Okla*ho*ma." He would nod and say quietly, "Just right, just right." Then she would go on reading and he would go on listening.

They sat in their rocking chairs, sometimes facing each other, sometimes side by side, rocking gently while Steinbeck unfolded his tale.

During breakfast on Saturday morning, Katya and her parents agreed that they would invite Mr. Bower for dinner on Sunday afternoon. The three of them would work this evening, Saturday evening, in the kitchen, preparing borsch, preparing at least three Russian salads, maybe four, preparing *pelmayni* with beef wrapped inside the dough. Katya would make an apple cake with absolutely fresh apples. Her father would have the fireplace ready, and of course some Russian cranberry liqueur. They wanted Mr. Bower to feel completely at home.

Her mother and father did not work that Saturday at the diner and garage; they were taking two weeks off from their regular jobs to work with the DanishWind people up on the mountain. Her father would maintain the turbine—a part-time job—after the set-up crew left. Her mother, also working part-time for DanishWind, would be his assistant engineer. Both would spend all day Saturday inside the nacelle, still on its truck in the parking lot, inspecting the components inside.

After Katya had finished washing the breakfast dishes, she walked to the nursing home. She stood at Mr. Bower's door at five minutes before ten o'clock on Saturday morning.

"I have a question for you," she said as she shook his hand, a formality which he enjoyed each time they met.

"What's that?" he asked with interest.

"Will you come for Sunday dinner tomorrow afternoon? The entire meal will be Russian. My parents would be delighted if you would come."

He stared at her. "A real Russian dinner in a real Russian home?"

"Well," she laughed, "cooked on an American stove in an American house. But otherwise, yes, the beet soup and the potato salad and the apple cake with be absolutely homemade."

Letting go of her hand, he sat back in his chair and rocked. "Do you know, I have not been in a real home for seven years. Since I came here. The kids are all scattered and," he shrugged, "nobody wanted the house. So they sold it."

"May we pick you up with our car at one o'clock?"

"Oh," he nodded, his blue eyes filled with anticipation, "with great pleasure! With great pleasure!"

Deeply pleased, Katya settled into her chair and read to Mr. Bower about the Joad family and the tragedy of losing their farm. She liked to read about this American family; she imagined their farm in the vast wheat country of the Russian steppes.

At a little before twelve o'clock, she walked with Mr. Bower out of his room and down the corridor toward the dining room, for lunch. (She had brought a plastic container of her mother's cabbage salad for herself.) Katya was surprised at how well Mr. Bower could walk. He tapped his cane but did not lean on it, and progressed at a steady pace.

She had a special place where she wanted to take Mr. Bower on Sunday afternoon, after the dinner, but he would have to walk a bit to get there.

After lunch, Mr. Bower lay down on his bed and took a nap. Katya shifted her chair so that she could read her chemistry with light from the window. She would stay with Mr. Bower until three, and then she would go shopping for tomorrow's big dinner.

CHAPTER 26

Tony Delmontico worked at Sunny's Bike-n-Ski Shop on Saturday from eight to five, back in the repair shop. He repaired bikes, he tuned bikes, he inflated tires to the proper pressure. But today he did something more. He wore Sunny's telephone headset, with headphones wrapped over his ears and a microphone clipped to his shirt, so that he could talk with the owners of the other bike shops in the Adirondacks while he worked.

He opened the *Yellow Pages* to BICYCLES, laid the phone book on the bench where he tightened spokes, then phoned the bike shop in Saranac Lake, the two shops in Lake Placid, the shop in Keene. Once he had the right person on the line—not a clerk, but the owner, or at least the manager—he pitched the Tour d'Adirondack with as professional a tone as he could.

A seven-day race, in seven stages, next July. The roads would be closed to traffic in whatever region the bikers were riding. He made clear that he was "open, completely open, with regard to the route of the race." He preferred input from the other bike shops, so that together they could design a race that suited the Adirondack Mountains. Perhaps they could all meet, a month from now in October, at some central spot, so that together they could design the race, and agree on the rules.

Most of the owners sounded interested. They took his name and number, and welcomed him to phone back. They would think about an Adirondack bike race—none of them took up the name "Tour d'Adirondack"—and get back to him with some good routes.

Once the bike shops in the Adirondacks had designed the race and agreed on the rules, Tony would start phoning bike shops in Utica, in Rome, in Syracuse, in Albany. He would phone the high schools, the colleges, in central New York. He needed to get at least a hundred riders for the First Annual Tour d'Adirondack, if there was ever going to be a Second.

At five-fifteen, he locked up the shop—Sunny had gone home at four—then he rode his bike through town and up the mountain to the Ski Center parking lot. He had his camera in his backpack; he wanted to get pictures of the crane. People in town had told him that the crane was now fully assembled and as tall as the Eiffel Tower.

But it was the blades, the white, forty-four-meter carbonfiber blades, and the crowds of people staring at them, that he first took pictures of. The blades looked like three giant white feathers that had floated down to earth, and then had been loaded onto trucks. The trucks would carry the feathers up the mountain next week, so they could catch the earthly wind, rather than a celestial wind.

With his long black lens, Tony zoomed in on the faces of people from Balsam Corners as they gazed, admired, and marveled at the long elegant blades. In half an hour, he had shot two and a half rolls of slides, about ninety pictures, out of which at least a dozen ought to be excellent portraits. Along with pictures of the crane and wind turbine, Tony wanted to send pictures to Bobby of the people in his hometown, watching the whole process. Tony imagined himself as Bobby, somewhere in a hot gritty desert, laden with military gear, looking at an album of pictures when he was off duty. Whenever Tony spotted one of Bobby's old classmates in the crowd, Class of Oh-Two, he'd snap a shot.

Tony especially liked taking pictures of the older folks in town. He shot them with a high f-stop, to fully catch the lines in their faces.

With daylight soon fading, he hurried over to the chair lift. He was about to get in line when he saw the opportunity for a unique shot. He knelt on the grass about fifty feet in front of the loading platform, where he could shoot portraits of people in that first delighted moment when they were swept up into the air.

He could not focus on their faces where they stood, waiting for the chair, but somehow had to focus on them as the chair carried them the first few feet. So he focused on two, three, four faces in that first moment as they launched toward him, until he was certain that the faces would be sharp. Then he drew back his zoom so that the frame included both faces, and the full chair with four hands that gripped the safety bar.

He shot another two rolls of slides. Among the pictures was one superb portrait of Raphael and Kate, she with a smile of blissful happiness, he with a big grin.

He was just about to stand up and hop on the chair lift himself, when he saw the Picture of Pictures about to happen. His mother and father stepped out from the line and took their places on the loading platform. Both of them looked back over a shoulder, then they sat together as the chair swept them up. His mother laughed, as she always laughed when she set forth on a bicycle or canoe or skis. She loved the first moment of some adventure.

And his father, holding onto his hat as if in a high wind, rose to the occasion with exuberance. "Here we gooooo!" CLICK.

Tony had his family back. He'd give them that portrait at Christmas.

CHAPTER 27

Andy had the best Saturday he'd had in years. He worked in the shop all day with Mr. Wilkens. Mr. Wilkens' old collie, Daisy, was there too. Daisy came every day to school with Mr. Wilkens, but she usually stayed in his office, sleeping the way an old dog sleeps, because she didn't like, as Mr. Wilkens said, "so many kids making so much noise." But on Saturday, when Andy and Mr. Wilkens were the only two working, Daisy came out and slept on the floor near Andy's jigsaw, her fur increasingly covered with sawdust.

Andy and Mr. Wilkens talked about the requirements of this bird-feeder community service project. Did Andy have to cut every board of all twenty-five birdfeeders? Did he have to nail all the pieces together? Did he have to screw in all eight brass screws on each of the two hinges? Did he have to screw each steel disk to the bottom of all twenty-five feeders? Did he have to screw the end of a six-foot pipe into each disk, to be sure they fit together?

Or could Mr. Wilkens help him with some of the job? Because they had to get all twenty-five birdfeeders mounted on pipes outside of twenty-five windows before the snow came. And because they didn't want some people at the nursing home to have a feeder outside the window, busy with birds, while someone right next door did not.

So they decided that Andy would cut every piece to exact dimensions, thus developing his skill on the jigsaw. He would nail together about a third of the feeders, enough to practice with a light hammer; Mr. Wilkens could do the rest of the nailing. Andy would screw on a few

137

disks; Mr. Wilkens could screw on most of them. That way they could cut and hammer at the same time, and make twenty-five people happy as soon as possible.

Andy's mother had packed him a lunch of fried chicken and macaroni salad, a lunch big enough for Andy and Mr. Wilkens both. Mr. Wilkens was delighted to have something for lunch other than his "same old liverwurst." Andy sat with Mr. Wilkens on a green wooden bench in the shop, the big window behind them casting its light on the quiet shop in front of them. Andy shared his thermos of cold apple cider with Mr. Wilkens, who had his own cup.

After cutting pieces for the first half-dozen feeders, Andy was able to cut accurately and efficiently at a smooth and steady pace. He began to kid Mr. Wilkens that the hammering had better hurry up, because another set of pieces was on its way.

Though Andy was reluctant to stop working during the afternoon, they took a couple of breaks. Mr. Wilkens called, "Daisy!" and the old dog woke up. She stood up slowly, then shook herself, sending up a fragrant cloud of cedar sawdust. Daisy followed them out the shop door to the grassy yard behind the school. She sniffed around the trees while Andy and Mr. Wilkens brushed the sawdust off their sleeves and looked at the progress of the sun across the cloudy southern sky.

"Ya know," said Mr. Wilkens during the second break, "I'll bet we have twelve, maybe fourteen birdfeeders done by six o'clock."

"Awesome," said Andy. "We're way ahead of schedule."

"Now I don't like working on Sunday. That's the good Lord's day of rest. But I do think He would not mind if we set up the first fourteen birdfeeders outside of fourteen windows on Sunday afternoon. Whatya say?"

Sunday afternoon. Andy could put up Emily's birdfeeder tomorrow. And a dozen others. He and Mr. Wilkens could work again next Saturday, and put up the rest of the birdfeeders next Sunday. Job done, which he could say to Mr. Shepherd on Monday morning.

"Mr. Wilkens, what do the rules say about digging the holes for the pipes? My father has a posthole digger. He said he'd show me how to use it."

"Fine," nodded Mr. Wilkens with approval. "Hell of a good thing to learn, how to use a post hole digger."

"So, would it be all right if both my parents helped us tomorrow? I sort of wanted them to meet Emily, and tomorrow might be the right day. You could bring Daisy, so she could sniff around the yard while we're working."

"Good. Very good. How about one o'clock to five o'clock, Sunday afternoon. We ought to be able to dig fourteen holes and stand the pipes in them and screw on fourteen feeders in four hours. Maybe the folks inside would like to come out and watch."

Andy looked up at the sky and wrinkled his nose. "Clouds today, maybe rain tomorrow."

"Naw," said Mr. Wilkens. "Them ain't rain clouds. Not too hot tomorrow, not too cool, just right for folks to come out and say hello to Daisy."

The two carpenters worked in the shop until six. They managed to cut and assemble fourteen birdfeeders, each of them, as Mr. Wilkens said, "a handsome piece of handiwork." The fourteen feeders stood in three orderly rows on a workbench, waiting for tomorrow.

Andy did not visit Emily on Saturday evening. He knew there would be no point in telling her that he would be back tomorrow to set up her birdfeeder, because she would never remember. Besides, he had something else he wanted to do.

After dinner with his parents, during which he pleased his mother by telling her how much Mr. Wilkens liked her macaroni salad, he cleared the junk out of his room. His father kept empty cardboard boxes in the loft over the garage; Andy filled them with videos and DVD's. Everything, out. He carried the boxes down to the basement. He'd put an ad on eBay, get what he could for the whole collection. The one rule was: the buyer had to take everything. He wasn't going to sell piecemeal.

Some video shop would grab the stuff, then sort through it and keep what they could use. Andy had some real classics.

He put the video player, the DVD player, and the television back into their boxes, which he had kept down in the basement. He'd get what he could for the stuff. Some dumb kid who thought the world was on a DVD would snatch it up.

With a wet sponge, he wiped the dust off his desk. He moved the computer, keyboard and screen, dusted where they had stood, then set them back in place.

He cleaned the window behind the desk with Windex and paper towels, then wiped up spiders and assorted bugs on the window ledge. The spiders looked to have been dead for centuries. He swung the latch, pushed open the sticky window, and took a breath of cool evening air.

He took the sheets off his bed, pulled the pillow case from the pillow, then asked his mother to show him how the washing machine worked.

Then he peeled poster after poster from the walls, wadding each one and tossing it toward the bedroom door. When he had them all down, and had peeled off the last bits of tape from the pale blue walls, he carried the posters out to the back yard and burned them in his father's cinderblock grill.

While the smoke rose into the overcast night sky, he decided that he would repaint the walls, one afternoon next week, with a deeper blue.

CHAPTER 28

On Sunday morning, Kate sang in the church choir. Raphael admired her from a pew near the rear of the church.

On Sunday morning, Katya rode with her parents in their old silver Volvo down to Utica, where they attended a service in the tiny Russian Orthodox Church. She loved to be able to speak Russian with the small congregation after the service.

Andy slept late on Sunday morning, as did his parents. They didn't go to church very often, though of course on Christmas and Easter. They had a long, lazy breakfast: his mother's perfect golden pancakes, with maple syrup that his father had bought at the barbershop. Andy had a question that he wanted to ask his mother and father, but it wasn't the right time yet.

On Sunday morning, Tony rolled his bike out of the garage in the first pale light of dawn. He was going on a big one today. He had been cooped up in classrooms all week, had met with Mr. Jacobsen, had taken pictures for Bobby, and now he was going to cruise.

He rode down Blueberry Lake Road to South Shore Road, turned right toward Inlet, and began to pump on one of his favorite routes: along Fourth Lake to Inlet, then on Route 28 to Raquette Lake, Blue Mountain Lake, and finally Long Lake. That route might be—in the opposite direction—the final stage of the Tour d'Adirondack. Lots of long

141

rolling hills along 28, the sharp left turn in Inlet, then a sprint through the forest along South Shore, to a finish line at . . . the Blueberry Lake Road? A spot closer to Balsam Corners? He wasn't sure.

The sun was up now, blinking through the red maples ahead of him. Pumping hard, at the edge of what his aching legs would tolerate, he focused his attention on his heart: letting go of the handlebars with one gloved hand, he touched his ungloved fingertips to his throat and felt a steady quick beat, a beat that was certainly not racing.

The heart was good; the legs needed work.

CHAPTER 29

On Sunday afternoon, Raphael stacked wood with Mr. Schaeffer for two solid hours. Mr. Schaeffer carried light pieces of maple one by one in his hands from the dwindling heap of wood to the woodshed, while Raphael loaded the orange plastic wheelbarrow with logs, then wheeled his heavy load to different spots along the length of the woodshed, where he stacked the wood with increasing skill. Raphael liked the soreness in his muscles while he worked. That soreness meant that his muscles were coming back.

He told Mr. Schaeffer that he had ordered tires for the Corvette from Cooker down in Tennessee, and that the tires would be shipped to him at Brill's Garage. "They oughta be here sometime next week."

"Good," said Mr. Schaeffer in an absent way. "Very good." He didn't even look at Raphael, but just kept stacking his wood.

Raphael wondered if he was going to have a chance to work on the Corvette's engine today. He had all his tools in the truck.

Mr. Schaeffer just kept carrying and stacking light pieces of wood, so Raphael continued with his job without any further conversation.

Mr. Schaeffer paused to look at his watch. "Whatdya say we load a cord into the back of your truck, then drive it up to the chapel? I'd like to fill the wood rack."

So Raphael backed Tyrannosaurus Rex down the driveway to the heap of wood, dropped the tailgate, then tossed pieces of wood into the back. Mr. Schaeffer disappeared into his house.

Raphael was working today from one to five, four hours. He'd already spent two hours stacking wood. Now they were going to the chapel. Another two hours there, and he'd never get to the Corvette.

Mr. Schaeffer came out the door with Mrs. Schaeffer, a woman nearly as tall and thin as he was. They both wore a plaid flannel shirt, his red and hers green. They might have been a perfectly matched couple on an Adirondack outing. Except that they both looked so serious, so sad, as if they were on their way to a funeral.

"Raphael," said Mr. Schaeffer as he crossed the chip yard toward the truck, "I'd like you to meet my wife Margaret."

"Hello, Mrs. Schaeffer," said Raphael. He took off his glove and shook her slender hand.

"Hello, Raphael. Philip tells me nothing but good things about you."

"Yeah?" Raphael looked at Mr. Schaeffer, who gave him a brief smile, then looked into the back of the truck.

"Toss in a few more pieces, if you would. That looks to be about enough."

"All right."

While Mrs. Schaeffer climbed into the passenger side of T. Rex, and then Mr. Schaeffer climbed in beside her, Raphael tossed another dozen pieces into the back. He was going to be a taxi driver today. He certainly would have cleaned up the cab a bit if he had known that grown-ups would be riding with him.

They didn't seem to mind the crumpled Burger King containers on the floor. They didn't seem to mind, when he started the engine, that thunder rumbled under the hood. They didn't comment about the loose fender banging on the frame when he drove over a rough patch of asphalt. Not a word about the muffler. The Schaeffers sat in absolute silence beside him, staring straight ahead through the bug-smeared windshield.

He pulled into the grassy semicircular driveway in front of the chapel, then, careful of a hemlock trunk that was a bit in the way, he backed the truck's rear end toward the chapel's front door. He glanced at the Schaeffers, who looked ashen, then he opened his door and climbed out.

The Schaeffers stepped slowly out of the truck, then, holding hands, they climbed a set of granite steps to the chapel's big white doors. Mr.

Schaeffer turned a key in a lock, then pulled open one of the doors and swung it to one side; the door's inside color was dark red.

Raphael followed the Schaeffers into the chapel, a church so small that it did not have two sets of pews with an aisle between them, but one set, with aisles down both sides. The cool air inside the chapel smelled of old candle smoke, old books. Though the sky was cloudy, a bit of light shone through the tall stained glass window behind the altar.

Mr. Schaeffer went directly to a wood-burning stove at the back of the chapel; he swung open its black iron door and peered in. "We gotta take out the ashes." Then he looked at the nearly empty wood rack standing nearby. "Raphael, can you bring in the wood while I take out the ashes?"

No "please," no "thank you." Mr. Schaeffer didn't even look at him when he asked the question.

"Sure."

When Raphael stepped from the cool dimness of the chapel into the warm brightness outside, he wished he were on Fourth Lake fishing. This community service stuff was going to be one hundred hours, period, and not an hour more.

As he carried an armload of wood into the chapel, he noticed that Mrs. Schaeffer was sitting in the middle of the front pew. She did not seem to be praying, for she stared straight ahead, toward the pulpit.

Mr. Schaeffer was shoveling ashes from the stove into a metal bucket. Raphael stepped around him, then took pieces of wood one by one from his armload and set them into a wood rack made of black pipes. He wished for a moment that Kate were here with him. Maybe she could figure out what was going on.

After Mr. Schaeffer had cleaned the ashes out of the stove, he sat beside Mrs. Schaeffer in the middle of the front pew. They looked like two people who were either very early for church, or who were still sitting in church after everyone else had left. Raphael kept loading wood into the wood rack.

When the truck was empty and the rack was full, he stood in the quiet at the back of the chapel and waited for the Schaeffers to be done with whatever they were doing.

He looked at the three elegant kerosene lamps hanging from the beams; the chapel clearly had no electricity. There were four stained glass windows along each side. He wondered how old the place was, and who had built it. Occasionally the sun shone a bit brighter through the window behind the altar, bringing its colors to life. A tall red cross, framed with yellow, stood in a blue sky above green mountains.

Mr. Schaeffer looked back over his shoulder. "Raphael, would you mind joining us?"

This was beginning to feel a little spooky. Raphael walked up the side aisle, past the dimly lit colored windows, then sat on the pew a short distance from Mrs. Schaeffer, who looked at him as if her heart were broken.

"Raphael," said Mr. Schaeffer, "Margaret and I are trying to do something that is very difficult. Sometimes it seems just plain selfish, and sometimes it seems to be the right thing to do."

"All right," said Raphael, leaning forward on the pew and looking past Mrs. Schaeffer so he could see Mr. Schaeffer, who stared right at him.

"Margaret and I would like your help."

"Yes, sir."

"You see," he nodded toward the pulpit, "Amanda drove that little red Corvette."

Raphael looked at the pulpit, an elegantly crafted podium made of cherry. Then he noted a brass plaque on it, glowing dimly against the dark wood. He read the words etched on the plaque,

In Memory of
AMANDA LOUISE SCHAEFFER
1953-1978
Rest, Child, in the Peace of God

"Margaret taught Amanda to drive in our old honeymoon Corvette. Amanda drove the Corvette to school during her senior year, then she drove it off to college. She was a graduate student at the Eastman School of Music in Rochester, only twenty-five years old, her life blossoming, when she discovered that she had advanced breast cancer. The poor kid lasted eight months." His shaking voice gave way to silence, a silence that filled the chapel.

Raphael understood now why the red Corvette had not been driven for so long. They couldn't drive it, neither could they sell it. They left it parked in the shed, gathering dust. But now they wanted him to tune the engine, put on new tires. Were they finally going to sell it?

"That was a quarter of a century ago. Antonio Delmontico, a neighbor up the lake, made that pulpit to honor Amanda. The congregation put the memorial plaque on it. The whole town wrapped its arms around us."

Raphael recalled comments he had heard about a girl, a girl who could sing, who had died before he was born. This must be the girl.

"So now, a quarter of a century later, Margaret and I have decided that with what little time we have left, we should try to live again. We ought to give each other a little happiness. We ought to leave the grief behind."

Raphael nodded with understanding. "You want me to fix up your old courting car, is that it?"

Their eyes shone at him with gratitude.

"Well," he said, "I can soon have that little red beauty humming like a kitten. I think your Amanda Louise would be very glad that you are out cruising the roads of the big green Adirondacks again. I think she'd be a little upset with you, to know that you have been grieving for so long."

"Ayah," said Mrs. Schaeffer, patting his arm as if to thank him for saying the right thing. "She'd be darn mad at us, I'm sure, if she knew that we spent the remainder of our lives so miserable."

"So we're very grateful to you," said Mr. Schaeffer, "because we didn't want some tow truck to take the Corvette down to a garage. It's so much nicer to have a mechanic," he smiled, "who makes house calls."

"I've got all my tools in the truck."

"We thought, once you get the engine running and the new tires put on, we'd like to wash and wax her, outside in the sunshine. Then we'd like to take a couple of short spins. Just to be sure everything's in order." He put his hands on Mrs. Schaeffer's shoulders. "And then we'd like to go on a second honeymoon, all through the Adirondacks. Right around the end of September, when the color in the maples is at its peak."

"Well, get your bags packed," said Raphael, "because that little red beauty is soon going to be on the road."

The three of them sat together in the chapel, in silence, for another ten or fifteen minutes. Then Mrs. Schaeffer stood up. Mr. Schaeffer and Raphael stood up. With a final glance at the brass plaque that shone against the dark wood, they walked up the aisle toward the open chapel door. They could see, beyond the grassy driveway, the grey scaly trunks of the hemlocks, ancient giants which the lumberjacks had spared.

Mr. Schaeffer glanced over at the full wood rack. "Good job, Raphael. Thank you very much."

"You're welcome, sir."

Raphael walked down the steps beside Mrs. Schaeffer, then stood on the grass beside her while Mr. Schaeffer closed and locked the door. Then everyone got into his truck.

As he drove back toward the Schaeffer's house, he glanced at the clock taped to the dashboard: 4:05. He had less than an hour to work on the Corvette. He could hardly get started.

With the red hood lifted, he leaned over the engine and turned his wrench on each of the eight old spark plugs, taking them out.

Even though this was something new, something very different from anything he'd ever done before, he liked what he was doing. He was a mechanic, yes, but he was also a high school senior, as their daughter had once been a high school senior. As if they needed the energy of somebody young to get them going again.

Yes, he liked doing that. It was as if, through him, Amanda Louise was giving her folks a little nudge.

CHAPTER 30

Kate didn't really want to be with anybody right now. She had been so happy while she was riding in the truck with Raphael from town to Blueberry Lake, and she didn't want to lose that feeling. When he dropped her off at the Ferguson driveway, then drove away to spend the afternoon with the Schaeffers, she wanted to walk into the forest and find a nice log to sit on, just to feel happy for a while.

She didn't want a sermon from Mrs. Ferguson. She didn't want to fight some battle about dead fish in the lake. Grown-ups had made such a mess of the world. Why did they think that kids were supposed to clean it up?

Her eyes followed the empty road to where it curved into the forest. She cheered herself with the thought that Raphael would be coming back for her in four hours. Then she looked down the sandy driveway at the red cottage with white trim, wrapped with a frilly skirt of ferns. Maybe one day she and Raphael could live in a little cottage tucked away in the woods.

She had hardly started down the driveway when Mrs. Ferguson came out the door, smiling. "Hello, Kate!" she called, clearly ready for a long afternoon together.

"Hello, Mrs. Ferguson."

When they met at the bottom of the driveway, Mrs. Ferguson laughed, "Well, aren't we a couple of rag bags!"

It was true. Kate had worn her old work clothes, spattered with paint from helping her father around the house. Mrs. Ferguson's outfit was spattered with white and red.

"Yeah," said Kate with the best smile she could muster, "I'm ready to paint your green chairs."

"Thank you, Sweetheart. Now how about hot apple cider and fresh brownies for a picnic? I thought we might take the canoe out on the lake before we get to work."

She called me Sweetheart, thought Kate. I hardly know her, and she calls me Sweetheart. Maybe she's one of those people who calls everyone Sweetheart, or Darling.

"Um. Hot cider would be fine."

"Good. C'mon in."

Mrs. Ferguson led Kate into the cottage, which smelled of wood smoke and hot cider and freshly baked brownies. Mrs. Ferguson handed her a thermos. "Our life jackets and paddles are down on the dock."

"All right."

Kate followed Mrs. Ferguson out the lakeside door and down the path to the dock, where Mrs. Ferguson had everything ready: the four green chairs stood on a paint-spattered tarp that covered most of the dock, so that paint couldn't drip into the lake. Two quart cans of green paint, with their lids still on, stood on the tarp beside the chairs. Atop each can was a brush.

Across the flat arms of the Adirondack chairs lay two canoe paddles of about equal length. Over the backs of two chairs hung life jackets, sun-faded orange.

"Are you a pretty good paddler?" asked Mrs. Ferguson. She set down a container of brownies on an arm of a chair, then reached for a life jacket.

"Um. I've paddled some." Her father had tried once to take her canoeing on the Moose River. It didn't work.

"Good. You'll be in the bow," Mrs. Ferguson pointed at one end of the green canoe tied to the side of the dock, "and I'll take the stern. Have you ever been walking on a bog?"

Kate wrinkled her nose. "You mean those spongy things that float on the lake?"

"Yes, they're floating islands of sphagnum moss, rooted to the bottom. They have their own species of orchid, but we'll have to visit in June if we want to see them."

I thought this was going to be about painting chairs, thought Kate. I didn't sign up to walk on swamp stuff.

Kate set the thermos on the dock by the bow of the canoe. She put on her life jacket, took a paddle, laid the paddle on the dock beside the thermos, then climbed into the bow of the canoe. She knew enough to sit facing the canoe's pointed end, rather than its middle.

She set the thermos on top of a towel behind her seat. Then she held the paddle with one hand while she tried to grip the edge of the dock with the other.

Mrs. Ferguson untied a rope at each end of the canoe, then Kate felt the canoe jiggle as Mrs. Ferguson stepped into it. Kate tensed.

"Let go of the dock, Sweetheart, so we can push off."

Kate released her grip on the edge of the dock. If the canoe tipped over, it had better not be in shallow water where the bottom was black muck.

Mrs. Ferguson pushed with her hand against the dock, sending the canoe backwards. Then she paddled: the canoe glided in a backwards curve, until the bow pointed directly into the early afternoon sun, faintly visible behind a gauze of clouds.

Kate squinted as she looked down the silver-gray lake: she saw a distant island, and a bay, and some camps along one shore.

"Kate, did you bring sunglasses?"

Kate looked over her shoulder and shook her head. Mrs. Ferguson was wearing sunglasses, and a blue ball cap. "I didn't think of 'em."

"Here, try these." Mrs. Ferguson reached into a small wicker basket at her feet and took out a pair of sunglasses. She set them on the blade of her paddle, then carefully reached the blade up the length of the canoe toward Kate, who took the sunglasses off the blade and said, "Thanks." They were good Polaroids, with no smudges on them. She laid her paddle sideways across the canoe, then put on the sunglasses, wrapping their arms behind her ears. They were dark, and snug, and would never fall off into the lake.

She twisted on her seat and looked back at Mrs. Ferguson. "Thank you. They're great."

"You're welcome. Now let's head south toward a channel that runs between bogs and beaver houses. We're probably too early in the day, but you might see a beaver out on patrol."

A beaver! Kate felt like a Girl Scout again, setting off on some great expedition. She curled one hand over the top of her paddle, wrapped her other hand around the neck, then began to sweep with long smooth strokes; she tried not to bang her paddle against the canoe.

The sunglasses were perfect: they cut the glare from the gray sky and the gray lake. The clouds were more distinct: dark fluffy puffs against a pale grey background.

She looked around, but didn't see any other boats on the lake. She and Mrs. Ferguson were the only ones out, on a peaceful Sunday afternoon.

They paddled for about half an hour toward the southern belly of Blueberry Lake, then they entered a narrowing channel with shallows along both sides. Kate watched the lily pads—round pies with a slice cut out—as the canoe glided past them. Few of the pads were still green; most were turning brown, or autumn red. They had been chewed on by bugs all summer and were pretty ragged.

Mrs. Ferguson steered the canoe up a long winding stripe of open water between patches of lily pads. Kate saw few white water lilies; the flowers were done for the summer. Looking ahead, she could see the first of several bogs, reddish-brown islands along the edges of the channel. She looked down at her paint-splattered sneakers. The question was, did she dare to walk barefoot on a bog, or was she going to wear wet sneakers for the rest of the afternoon?

They paddled between several small bogs, then, a little further along the channel, Mrs. Ferguson tillered so that the bow pointed toward the edge of a large bog. Kate tensed as the bow rode up on an arm of moss—moss that bubbled as it sank.

"Here we are!" said Mrs. Ferguson with a lilt of celebration. "Take off your shoes and roll up your cuffs. I'll hold the canoe steady while you step out."

Kate cringed: it was barefoot on the bog. With great reluctance, she laid her paddle across the sides of the canoe, then bent down and untied her laces. She took off her sneakers, took off her socks. She hated gishy things. She hated especially to step on gishy things. The worst was walking barefoot at night in the rain on the lawn and stepping on an earthworm.

She rolled up the frayed cuffs of her jeans, then she held her breath as she lifted one foot over the side of the canoe and set it down on . . . soft warm moss, not so bad.

"Wait," said Mrs. Ferguson. "Bring your foot back into the canoe."

Kate brought her foot back into the canoe, with some reluctance, for she had mustered the courage to do this horrible thing, and now there was some interruption.

"First, lay your paddle along the bottom of the canoe behind you, with the handle toward you. Then it can't fall out of the canoe, and it's ready when you need it."

Kate carefully laid her paddle along the bottom of the canoe behind her seat, with the handle toward her.

"Good," said Mrs.Ferguson. "Now lean forward, grip the gunnels, lift your bottom from the seat and *then* step out. You steady yourself by holding both sides of the canoe."

Kate leaned forward and gripped the two sides of the canoe, then she lifted her bottom from the seat and shifted her weight forward. Yes, it was easy now to lift one foot over the side of the canoe and to step down on the bog. But the moss immediately began to sink. She quickly lifted her foot from the bog. She could smell the weird muck gasses bubbling up.

"You're all right," said Mrs. Ferguson. "Just step out of the canoe and then walk further onto the bog. It's only the edge that sinks."

Only the edge, only the edge. She would sink on that edge right down between the canoe and the bog into black muck, and roots and giant snapping turtles. Her last scream would bubble up with the bubbles of muck gas.

"Um."

"Go ahead, Kate. You can do it."

Mustering her courage once again, she set her foot down on the bog, shifted her weight so that she was *really* sinking now, quickly lifted her other foot out of the canoe and then ran about ten feet toward the middle of the bog. Now she stood on soft wet moss, sinking a little but not much. The bog was like a firm sponge, not at all gishy.

She looked at Mrs. Ferguson in the stern of the canoe and declared with triumph, "I did it!"

"You certainly did."

Holding a rope tied to the stern of the canoe, Mrs. Ferguson stepped out onto the bog, and didn't mind sinking up to her calf as she swung the bow of the canoe out into the channel, then pulled the stern about three feet onto the bog.

"There!" she said with a smile to Kate. "We have landed."

Kate wished for a moment that Raphael could see her now. Could see how brave she was.

"Now watch for frogs," said Mrs. Ferguson. "Green frogs, bull frogs, leopard frogs, and peepers. Watch for garter snakes too. They swim out to the bogs to hunt. And we might see a great blue heron. They feed on the frogs too."

The frogs had better darn well hop out of the way, thought Kate. If she stepped on a snake, she was going to scream. She stared with sharp eyes at the moss ahead of her with every step she took.

They walked together across the gently bobbing bog, looking at pitcher plants, at cranberries, and at a baby tamarack tree, its needles turning autumn yellow. They walked, about six feet in from the edge, along the entire perimeter of the bog. The bog was not round, but had the shape of a giant protoplasm, with mossy peninsulas like pseudopods reaching into the lake.

Mrs. Ferguson pointed a warning finger at various black muck holes in the bog: spots where the carpet of moss was not solid. "Step in a muck hole and down you go!" She made the most awful sucking sound.

Kate felt the skin prickle up her back. "Do they ever come up again?"

"The people who disappear down a muck hole?"

"Yeah."

"Never. They get tangled in the roots, and try to claw their way up through the moss, but the moss is too thick, and the muck is absolutely black, and even though the whole bog shakes while they struggle, they eventually drown. Then hundreds of leeches attack the corpse and suck the blood out. After a few years, the tannic acid in the bog turns the corpse into a nearly indestructible mummy."

"You're kidding me, right?"

"Kidding you? We are right now as we speak walking above five mummified children, all of whom at one time or another disobeyed their mother."

Kate smiled. "Is that what you told your kids?"

"Ayuh. And as a result, the Muck Monster never got a single one of them."

"You had five children?"

"Five beautiful children. They went to sleep, every spring and every summer, listening to the frogs."

When they had walked around the entire bog and had returned to the canoe, Mrs. Ferguson asked Kate, "How many frogs did you see?"

"Frogs? I didn't see any."

"How many snakes?"

"No snakes, thank heavens."

"Any great blue herons, on this bog or any of the other bogs?"

Kate looked at the bogs up and down the channel. "No, I haven't seen any birds."

"Well then," said Mrs. Ferguson, looking at her intently. "What you have seen today, or *not* seen today, is the end result of thirty years of incremental death. Acid rain, acid snow. Nitric acid from oil, sulfuric acid from coal. The snow especially is an acid bank, for it stores all the acid that falls through the winter. When the snow melts in the spring, the streams in April carry acid from the first blizzard in November. And spring, of course, is just when creatures are waking up and laying their eggs. The frogs lay their eggs in pools of snowmelt, snowmelt that is not natural water, but acidic water. The eggs have a tough time developing. The tadpoles have a tough time surviving. The number of frogs diminishes each summer, until," she swept her hand over the bog, "they are completely gone."

The bog had become a wet sponge that Kate could trust. But now it also became something very strange: a place where everything had died.

"That is why," continued Mrs. Ferguson, "our little town, the first town in the Adirondack Park, voted to put up a wind turbine. So that maybe the other towns might follow our example. More wind, less coal. People say they don't want to see these turbines. All right. We could build hundreds of wind turbines along the coast of the Great Lakes, the way the Danes are doing, the way the Irish are doing. Wind farms five miles offshore, steadily pumping power. Our little mountain is just the first candle."

Kate remembered the elegant white blades of the wind turbine, still on trucks in the Ski Center parking lot. She and Raphael had stared at them with amazement. They were so different from anything else in Balsam Corners, and yet so real.

"I guess I feel a little proud," said Kate, "that our town is the first."

"Very proud," said Mrs. Ferguson. "We finally stopped whining at the power plants. We finally stopped whining at the government. Neither one ever cared two toots on a tin whistle about us anyway. We finally got angry enough, and smart enough, to do something ourselves. At least it's a first step. At least we have done that. So that sometime in the future, within the next century or so, we might begin to have a few frogs again."

Kate remembered now to tell Mrs. Ferguson what she should have told her when she first met her on the driveway, "I ordered the pH tester. I talked with my chemistry teacher, and he said he knew exactly what to order. It ought to come sometime next week."

"Good. Then we'll wait for a downpour of lemon juice, and get you on the radio, telling folks about it."

"I'm not sure about the radio part. I'm not much of a public speaker."

"Neither are the frogs, Kate. They need you to be their voice."

Well, thought Kate, maybe for the frogs I could do it. Maybe for the tadpoles that never had a chance.

Standing together near the canoe, they had a picnic of fresh brownies and hot cider. Neither of them spoke. They savored the brownies, savored the cider, while their eyes roamed over other bogs, or followed a dragonfly among the lily pads.

Kate looked beyond the lily pads at the edge of the forest. The trees were a deeper red now than even a few days ago. But still no orange yet, except for one jubilant tuft that ruffled in the breeze against a background of dark green balsam.

Then they got back into the canoe—Kate embarked much more gracefully than she had disembarked—and paddled back up the channel toward the open water of the lake. At the lake's far end, hardly more than a tiny white spot, stood the chapel.

They were back at the dock with still two hours to paint the four chairs. How nice it would be just to sit in one of them, close her eyes and listen to the waves wash against the dock while she fell asleep.

But Mrs. Ferguson was all business. She tied up the canoe, then leaned her paddle against a tree on shore, and hung her life jacket on the sawed-off stub of a branch. Kate did the same with her paddle and life jacket, then she joined Mrs. Ferguson on the dock.

Working a screwdriver around the lids, Mrs. Ferguson opened the two new cans of dark green paint. "Brian shook the cans on his machine at the hardware store a couple of days ago," she said, "so they won't need more than a little stirring." She handed Kate a brush about three inches wide, still in its plastic cover.

"Thanks," said Kate.

"You're welcome."

Mrs. Ferguson then handed Kate a whiskbroom, brand new. She picked up one of her own, well worn. "Before we can paint, we have to sweep away the needles and cobwebs." She showed Kate all the little nooks and angles in an Adirondack chair that needed to be swept clean before the chair could be painted. That included turning the chairs upside down on the tarp and sweeping underneath as well.

While the chairs were still upside down, Kate and Mrs. Ferguson dipped their brushes into the lush green paint, then began by putting a good coat on the bottoms of the uplifted feet. "That's where they first begin to rot," said Mrs. Ferguson, "if you don't keep them properly painted and properly stored."

The undersides of the two chairs changed from a faded, mildewed green to a rich dark green, the green of a healthy forest. Kate watched Mrs. Ferguson, then spread her paint not too thick, not too thin. She kept up with Mrs. Ferguson, board by board, working her brush up and down in the spaces between the boards. She liked the dribbles of green paint on her jeans, on her bare feet. She was beginning to look like a frog.

When the undersides were done, they turned the chairs over . . . and got their fingertips green in the process. Kate wiped her fingertips on the stomach of her blue work shirt.

She painted the boards of the chair's slatted back, then she painted the boards of the chair's slatted seat. She worked her brush into all the little nooks and gaps, especially along the seam where the seat and back were joined. She made sure that the paint on the top of the chair met the paint on the underside all the way around: a uniform coat of green with no old paint showing.

"Now," said Mrs. Ferguson, pointing her brush toward the broad flat arms, "the *pièce de résistance.*"

Kate looked at the chips in the old paint on the arms of her chair, where layers of red, and yellow, and blue showed through the green.

"Someone should write an ode to the arm of an Adirondack chair," said Mrs. Ferguson. "You can put your morning coffee on it, you can put your glass of wine on it, you can put your plate of dinner on it. You can put a book on it, you can write a poem on it. You can keep your binoculars on it, or your camera with a telephoto lens, ready for a loon to swim by. There is no other chair in all the world so well suited to a person's soul, as an Adirondack chair."

Kate painted a coat of shiny green on the flat arm of her chair, sweeping her brush back and forth to smooth the paint, occasionally daubing to fill a chip, to fill a crack. There were four chairs on the dock. Maybe Raphael might sit here with them sometime.

"You know, Kate, you should talk with Tony Delmontico about all the years that he's been snorkeling in this lake. Do you know Tony? I think you're in the senior class together, aren't you?"

Kate could feel herself blushing. "Yes."

"Well, you ask him sometime about snorkeling in this lake. He's done it since he was a kid. My husband Ed taught him. Ed had been snorkeling in this lake since *he* was a kid. The two of them used to set up a thirty-gallon aquarium every summer. They'd fill it with water from the lake, then they'd put in green plants from the lake, and tadpoles, baby bluegills, crayfish, and snails. It was so pretty at night: we'd turn out all the lights in the living room," Mrs. Ferguson nodded toward her cottage, "with just the aquarium light on. Then the three of us would sit in chairs, watching tadpoles wriggling about, and crayfish scuttling along the bottom. The little bluegills would gobble up pieces of a worm. Tony always had a magnifying glass, so he could look for tiny hydras with their long white tentacles. He'd watch the clouds of microscopic daphnia that gathered beneath the light. Snails laid their eggs on the glass: day by day, we could watch the eggs develop. Water beetles holding a silvery bubble in their folded legs would dart around the tank. You never knew what you might discover in that aquarium."

She paused, though her hand kept sweeping the paintbrush up and down the arm of her chair. "You ask Tony. He'll tell you that summer after summer while he was growing up, there were fewer fish. The bullheads disappeared, the minnows disappeared, the perch all but disappeared. The snails vanished, the crayfish vanished. All the beautiful green salamanders with their bright red spots: gone. When Tony and Ed went snorkeling along the shoreline, around the bogs, they would find only a few surviving bass and bluegills, big ones, ready to eat anything that moved."

She gave Kate a look of angry devastation. "Four years ago was the last year they bothered to set up the aquarium. Now it sits empty in my house, like a thirty-gallon coffin of a dead lake."

Kate was glad to have something to talk about with Tony, something serious, something real. Even with Raphael as her . . . new best friend, it would still be nice to talk a bit with Tony.

She finished painting both arms, then lifted her sunglasses and admired the true green: not quite so dark, but definitely more lustrous.

A bug had gotten stuck in the wet paint on the seat; she swept it up with her fingertip, wiped her finger on her jeans, then smoothed the paint with her brush.

"Good job!" said Mrs. Ferguson as she stepped back to admire the two freshly painted chairs.

While Kate looked at the two chairs, equally green, she wondered what had happened to Mr. Ferguson. Maybe he had died just recently. She wondered how many cups of morning coffee there had been, while the two of them sat side by side in their chairs and looked out at the lake. How many glasses of wine at sunset? She wondered if Mr. Ferguson had written poems, or if maybe Mrs. Ferguson did.

She wondered if painting the chairs today wasn't, somehow, a fresh start. She looked at the two outer chairs, still unpainted, in the row of four. Maybe Mrs. Ferguson needed some friends.

The two painters paused for another round of cider and brownies. Then they turned over the two outer chairs, brushed off the needles and cobwebs, and painted the bottoms of the feet with a fresh coat of Adirondack green.

The chairs were done, the brushes were washed, and the half-empty cans of paint were put away in the garage, by ten minutes to five.

Mrs. Ferguson ran the water at the kitchen sink until it was "the cold water right from the well," then she filled a glass and handed it to Kate.

"Thanks," said Kate, happy that the afternoon had been so nice, but a little anxious because Raphael was coming soon. She wanted to be up at the end of the driveway, ready for him.

She drank the entire glass. The water was wonderful, cold from deep in the earth, much better than town water.

Mrs. Ferguson washed her face at the sink by cupping her hands in the running water, then splashing her face again and again. "Ohhh," she cried with delight. "Ohhh!"

"Try it, Kate," she said as she dried her face with a dishtowel. "You'll feel as clean as clean can be. Then we'll walk up the driveway to meet your gorgeous hunk."

Gorgeous hunk? Kate felt herself blushing again.

She washed her face in the cold water, and yes, it felt heavenly. She splashed her face until her fingers began to ache, then she turned off the water and accepted a dishtowel from Mrs. Ferguson. "Thanks."

As they walked together up the sandy driveway, Mrs. Ferguson laughed again. "Aren't we a couple of rag bags?"

Kate giggled, "More green than before." They both were sprinkled with green spots.

"Thanks for your help."

"You're welcome."

They had just reached the road when Kate could hear, before she could see it, the rattle-banging truck with only half a muffler. When it lurched into sight, rusty blue, she wondered if once, just once in her life, her Prince Charming might arrive on a white horse.

Raphael braked to an abrupt halt where Kate stood with Mrs. Ferguson, then he showed that he could be a gentleman. He didn't just idle the truck while he waited for Kate to get in. He turned off the noisy engine, got out of the truck and walked over to Mrs. Ferguson with a smile of greeting. "Hello, Mrs. Ferguson. Was Kate of any help to you today?" He grinned at Kate with a teasing smile.

"You'd have to work darn hard," said Mrs. Ferguson, "if you want to keep up with Kate."

Then she said something that took Kate by utter surprise.

"If you two want to take the canoe out, you go right ahead. The paddles and jackets are down by the dock. But of course, Raphael, I should give you Ed's paddle. He was about as tall as you."

To go out in the canoe with Raphael! Kate looked at him, wondering if he would go with her.

Raphael looked at her. "You got anybody waiting dinner for you?"

She laughed with scorn. "Dinner is when I make it."

"Well, my folks had Sunday dinner at two o'clock, so I'll get leftovers whenever I get home." Then he laughed. "You know how to paddle a canoe?"

"She certainly does," said Mrs. Ferguson, already heading back down the driveway. "I'll pack a picnic for you, then off you go."

Kate, in the bow, looked over her shoulder at Raphael in the stern, as they paddled south across the lake toward the channel. She was going to take him walking on a bog.

"You know what?" she asked.

"What?"

"You don't steer as well as Mrs. Ferguson."

"I'll bet I steer better than you."

She wondered if she looked really good in the sporty sunglasses that wrapped around her ears. Raphael looked very handsome in a pair of Mr. Ferguson's Polaroids.

Then she asked, "You know what else?"

"What?"

She smiled at him, her gorgeous hunk. "This is our second date."

He grinned. "You're right, it is. And we still even like each other."

She turned around, immensely pleased, and began to sweep her paddle.

CHAPTER 31

Annette Charboneau watched Sunday afternoon's proceedings with astonishment. Her son Andy was completely in charge, handling both the installation of the fourteen bird feeders, and the welfare of his elderly audience, with cordial efficiency. She had never seen anything like it.

Charles drove the family to the Towering Timbers Nursing Home, where Annette's aunt had once stayed. Andy asked his father to park beside a yellow school bus, then he led his parents along the sidewalk to the front door as if he were their guide. Inside at the front desk, he actually introduced his mother and father to the receptionist. "Estelle, I'd like you to meet my parents, Annette and Charles Charboneau. Mom, Dad, this is Estelle Richards."

Then he led the way down a corridor to a room at the end. "Knock, knock," he said, peeking into the room. "Emily, today's the big day."

He introduced his parents to Emily, a small, weathered woman who sat in a wheelchair. She wore a lilac dress with white lace at the collar and cuffs, and had a lilac ribbon in her white hair. She looked surprised, but delighted, that company had arrived.

"Emily," said Andy, speaking with a slow, clear voice, "I'm going to put up your birdfeeder today. Listen, it's warm outside. Do you want to come out and watch?" When she looked at him blankly, he added, "There's a dog outside, Emily. Her name is Daisy. She's a nice, old collie, very gentle. Wouldn't you like to come outside to meet Daisy?"

"A dog?" asked Emily, her soft voice filled with excitement.

163

"Yup." He pointed out the window. "She's sniffing around the yard, waiting to meet you."

"A collie?"

"Yup. Do you want me to wheel you, or should we get a nurse?"

"You can. We don't need a nurse."

"All right." Andy lifted a quilt that covered the foot of Emily's bed, folded it neatly, then set it in her lap. "Emily, you tell me if you start to get cold."

"I *always* tell people when I start to get cold."

"Good."

Annette and Charles followed their son—a perfect gentleman—as he wheeled Emily down the long corridor and out the front door. He angled her to the left, then followed the sidewalk that formed a rectangle around the nursing home.

"You certainly ordered a perfect fall day," said Charles to his son.

"Yup, not too hot, not too cold," said Andy over his shoulder. "I'm going to try to get as many as I can outside, so they can watch us put up their birdfeeders."

As Andy pivoted Emily's chair around the back corner, he leaned over her shoulder and said, "Keep an eye out for your deer. You might see them at the edge of the forest."

"Yes! Are we going into the forest with them?"

"No, were going to be in the backyard outside your window."

"Oh."

Andy stopped outside the first window along the back facade. "Here we are. That's your room inside, Emily. We're going to put up your bird-feeder right here."

Annette marveled at her son's gentleness, his thoughtfulness, his enthusiasm.

They were joined by a man who came walking toward them from the edge of the forest, a man wearing an olive green shirt and olive green trousers: the uniform of an old Adirondack native. He wore a fisherman's hat, festooned with a dozen bright flies.

Andy introduced him, "Mr. Wilkens, these are my parents, Annette and Charles Charboneau. Mom, Dad, this is Mr. Wilkens, my shop teacher."

Annette smiled with gratitude at the man who had helped to produce the miracle.

"Emily," said Andy, leaning down to her, "this is Mr. Wilkens, who helped me to build your birdfeeder."

"Call me Arthur," said the man with jovial eyes as he leaned down and shook hands with Emily. "I didn't do a darn thing but tap in a few nails."

Puzzled, Emily looked at Andy. "Who are these people?"

"They're going to help us put up your birdfeeder."

"Oh."

Andy turned to Mr. Wilkens. "Where's Daisy?"

Mr. Wilkens nodded toward the forest. "She's in there sniffing for rabbits."

"I promised Emily that she could meet Daisy."

"All right." Mr. Wilkens put two fingers into his mouth and whistled. A moment later, a collie came bounding out from the trees.

"Daisy!" called Andy. "There's someone here who wants to meet you."

Emily stared at Daisy with delight as the dog came prancing toward her.

"Emily, this is Daisy." The collie sat beside the wheelchair. "Daisy, this is Emily." Emily patted Daisy's head. Daisy moved a bit closer and reached her long nose toward Emily for a proper scratch behind the ears. Emily obliged with both hands, knowing just what to do.

With Emily comfortably occupied, Andy and Mr. Wilkens led Annette and Charles across the wooded yard to the parking lot. Charles took the posthole digger out of his trunk. Mr. Wilkens opened the door to the school bus. Inside he had fourteen wooden stakes, which would mark where the holes would be dug, as well as fourteen iron pipes, each pipe six and a half feet long. The fourteen birdfeeders, fragrant with cedar, each sat separately on a seat of the bus.

Andy carried a birdfeeder in his arms down the school bus steps. Annette carried a bundle of stakes. Mr. Wilkens carried two pipes, one in each hand. Charles, with his posthole digger, completed the parade that walked among the hemlocks toward Emily's window.

Andy set the birdfeeder down beside Emily's wheelchair. Emily paid no attention to it. She was talking with Daisy.

"Now Mom," said Andy, "would you please go into Emily's room, sit in a chair where she would sit, and give me directions while I hold the birdfeeder outside. Then we'll know where to dig the hole for the pipe."

"All right."

Annette walked back around the nursing home to the front door, nodded to Estelle, followed the corridor, found Emily's room, then drew a spindle chair from a corner and sat where Emily would sit in her wheelchair. Andy stood outside the window, holding the birdfeeder at about shoulder height. Annette cranked the window open so she could talk to him.

"That looks perfect, right where you are."

"Can you see the tray where the sunflower seeds will be?" he asked. "Or is it too high?"

"Maybe down an inch or two." She slumped in the chair until she was about Emily's height. Andy lowered the birdfeeder to chest height. "That's it," she told him. "That's perfect. She'll see every finch."

"It's chickadees she wants to see."

"Oh."

Andy put down the birdfeeder, then knelt and hammered in a stake beside his foot.

"Dad," she heard him say, "could you dig your post hole right where I've put the stake? Mom and I will continue around the building, putting in stakes at every other window, so you'll know exactly where to dig the holes. Please dig a foot and a half deep. That gives us five feet of pipe above ground."

"All right."

Emily watched with great interest as a woman appeared in the window, talking to a young man who hammered a stick into the ground.

She liked the dog. The dog had soft fur and alert ears. The ears kept listening toward the forest.

Andy called in through the window, "Mom, since we have only fourteen feeders and not all twenty-five, we'll install them outside every other window. That way we'll get around the whole building, and folks can watch what we're doing. I want to be sure that everyone gets in on the action."

So Annette worked her way down the corridor, entering every other room. She spoke with people in wheelchairs, people in regular chairs, people in bed. She tried to explain her mission, but most of the people just stared at her, then noticed Andy standing outside the window with a birdfeeder at chest height.

"How's this?" he would ask.

She would kneel beside an old man in his chair, or lean down over an ancient woman in bed, then wave her hand, "A little closer. And a bit to the left."

Andy shifted his feet. "All right, how's this?"

"Good. She'll be able to see the feeder from her pillow."

"Thanks."

After he had hammered in the stake, Andy wheeled Emily from window to window, so that she could watch. Daisy followed along, sniffing in the grass nearby.

As her son had done with Emily, Annette invited the people whom she met to go outside. "Do you see the dog?" She would point out the window at the collie rolling on her back in the needles beneath a hemlock tree. "Her name is Daisy." When Daisy stopped rolling and stood up, needles and twigs and bits of green moss clung to her fur. "She's waiting for you to come out and meet her."

When Annette had finished the first wing and was crossing through the lobby to the second wing, she said to Estelle at the desk, "Some of your guests want to come outside. Could a nurse check on them, to see who needs help?"

Estelle nodded, "Andy already explained the drill to me. A half dozen nurses will be bringing out the residents. We're going to set up some chairs and a picnic table."

"Oh," said Annette, her astonishment unabated. Then she started along the second wing.

By the time Andy and his mother had put the fourteen stakes into exactly the right spot, people were leaving their rooms and shuffling down the corridors and blinking at the pearlescent sky as they stepped out the front door. Wearing a sweater for September, a shawl for September, they shuffled slowly or rolled in their chairs along the sidewalk around the building. They smiled and pointed at a collie the color of taffy as it bounded happily around the back yard. The dog was making sure that every chattering squirrel stayed high in a tree, and never dared set foot on the ground.

Nurses in white uniforms unfolded metal chairs around the site of the first birdfeeder installation, now nothing more than a hole in the ground, the first of several holes along the back of the building. People sat in the folding chairs and looked at the birdfeeder and a length of pipe on the grass outside somebody's window. Daisy came to visit, moving from chair to chair as different hands reached out to scratch her.

The nurses set up a card table with plastic cups of cider and paper plates with oatmeal cookies. Andy offered a cookie to Emily; she asked for two, then looked around for Daisy.

Charles walked from the seventh hole back to the first, pointed at the first hole and said to his son, "See if that's deep enough."

Andy stood a pipe in the hole. He had already marked a foot and a half with a piece of red tape on the pipe: the tape lined up with the roots of the grass. "Perfect."

Then he said to his mother, "Mom, you hold the pipe as straight as you can, while I push the dirt back into the hole and pack it down."

"All right." Annette held the pipe as straight as she could, while her son knelt in the grass and pushed the black earth back into the hole with his hands. He tamped down the earth with a piece of two-by-four. Then he stood up and tried to wiggle the pipe: it was very sturdy.

"Good job," he said to his mother. "Now while I put the birdfeeder on top of the pipe, will you go in Emily's room, and check to be sure that her birdfeeder really is at the right height?"

"All right."

Andy brushed the dirt off his hands, then he said to Emily, seated with about twenty of her friends in a horseshoe around the first Bird-feeder Installation, "Now Emily, this is *your* birdfeeder that we are about to put up." He pointed at the cedar birdfeeder on the grass.

She watched him now, paying attention. "All right."

He picked up the birdfeeder, raised it to shoulder level, set the threaded ring screwed to the bottom of the feeder atop the threaded pipe, then carefully spun the feeder around and around, until the top inch of the pipe had threaded into the ring, and the feeder came to a snug halt. Gently, he turned the feeder a bit more, so that its tray faced Emily's window.

He stepped back to admire his work, then he called in through the open window to his mother sitting in a chair where Emily would sit, "What do you think?"

"Sweetheart," said his mother, her voice trembling, "It's perfect. It's beautiful. She'll be able to see every chickadee that comes to visit."

Despite the emotion in his mother's voice, Andy laughed and clapped his hands. Then he turned to Emily, knelt on the sidewalk and asked, "Emily, what do you think?"

"Is this where the chickadees will come?"

"Yes, this is where the chickadees will come. You can watch them from your window, all winter."

"And shall there be flamingoes?" She looked at him with high expectation.

"Yes, you shall have a whole pink flock of flamingoes. But not yet. They come in the winter, when the snow is deep."

"Good!" Looking now with keen eyes at her new birdfeeder, Emily raised her thin hands and began to clap.

Andy clapped as well. His mother clapped inside Emily's window. His father clapped with his work gloves on. Mr. Wilkens clapped, as did most of Emily's friends. The Installation of the First Birdfeeder was a grand success.

Andy and his mother and father and Mr. Wilkens now worked at a steady pace. While his father went back to digging holes, his mother held the pipes straight, and Andy pushed the dirt back into the holes, tamping down the earth so that each pipe was sturdy. Mr. Wilkens brought all the birdfeeders from the bus and set them on the grass around the building.

After Andy had screwed on each birdfeeder, and had led the applause, he wheeled Emily to the next spot. Many of her friends were able to follow. The cortege of residents enjoyed a moveable feast as they followed the activity along the back of the building. They not only clapped but now cheered with each new birdfeeder fastened to its pipe.

At one point, the sun became a bit brighter as it shone through the clouds. Emily's eyes, looking up at Andy, caught the sunlight; he saw that her eyes were a deep lavender, darker than her lilac dress.

By a quarter to five, all fourteen birdfeeders had been installed. They stood like sentries in a rectangle around the building. Emily and a dozen of her friends had made the entire loop, and were now gathered back at the first birdfeeder, Emily's. Mr. Wilkens had brought a twenty-five-pound bag of sunflower seeds. The time had come for the Filling of the Feeders.

Mr. Wilkens took out his pocketknife and cut open the top of the bag. With an empty cottage cheese container, Andy scooped up the black seeds, then he lifted the hinged roof of the birdfeeder and spread the seeds evenly across the birdfeeder's tray.

He lowered the lid, then turned to Emily and said, "Emily, the chickadees are going to need a day or two before they find your sunflower seeds. Don't get impatient. They'll be coming."

"I can wait. I don't mind. They always found me in the fall."

"That's right."

Carrying the bag that became less and less heavy, Andy walked around the building, filling all fourteen feeders. Emily and a few of her friends accompanied him, making a second loop.

He filled the last feeder at ten after five. The residents were heading inside now. They had to get ready for dinner. His mother and father followed as he wheeled Emily back to her room.

Annette stood beside Charles, just inside Emily's door, ready to say good-bye. She watched as Andy knelt and looked out the window, his face beside Emily's face, so that he could see the birdfeeder as Emily would see it. Her son was an absolute gentleman with Emily, a gentleman and something more. It was as if he had suddenly started to speak Chinese.

Andy stood up and nodded to his parents: he was ready to go.

"Well, good-bye, Emily," said Charles.

Emily slowly swiveled her chair around. She pointed at Charles. "Are you the father?"

"Yes, I am Andy's father."

She pointed at Annette. "Are you the mother?"

"Yes, I am Andy's mother."

Emily paused for a moment, staring at Andy. She asked him, "Then who am I?"

Andy touched Emily's cheek with his fingertips, very gently, as he had not touched his mother's cheek for years and years. "You are my best friend, Emily. You are my best friend."

"Oh," she said, very pleased.

Andy joined his parents as they walked out the door. Looking back, he gave Emily, her hand raised and waiting, a jubilant wave.

She waved back. "Good-bye, Mr. Chickadee."

"Good-bye, Emily. I'll be back soon."

CHAPTER 32

Walter Bower had hoped and hoped and hoped, as the decades went by, that the nightmares would end. But they never did. Anna knew about them, of course, for she had been awakened by them nearly every night of their marriage. But he had hid them from the children. Even today, his nine beautiful offspring, scattered around the country as they pursued their careers, knew little about his war years.

He had remained silent about the war for many reasons. Child after child kept him busy, and filled him with joy; why go back and dwell on those years of struggle and anguish? He wanted his children to have a happy childhood, unscarred by tales of some hideous war before their time. And besides, how could they ever understand what it was like to be in a B-17 Flying Fortress on a bombing run over Germany? No one could understand what a soldier, or a sailor, or an airman goes through, except other soldiers who had gone through the war too. Certainly, those who had never been shot at could never comprehend the cost, in shattered lives, in brutally ended lives, paid by the troops in every war. So why tell a son, a daughter, about Ethridge Lamm, a turret gunner on their B-17, a nineteen-year-old kid killed on their very first mission over Germany?

Now it was worse, without Anna beside him in bed when the terror gripped him in his slumber . . . *as he stood with his parachute on in the jolting plane with three dead engines. The wind was screaming past the open hatch, the French countryside was whirling far below, and . . .*

Anna would grip his shoulders and call to him, "Walter! Walter! It's all right, Walter. I'm with you. I'm with you. I'm right here with you."

And then what could he do? Apologize that he woke her up again? Have a drink of warm milk? He would let her hold him, as he gradually calmed, until he said quietly, "Thank you, Anna. I think it's all right now. You can go back to sleep."

And she would, because he left her in peace. He would get up out of bed, put on his bathrobe, step out of the bedroom and close the door behind him. Then he would go down the hallway, peering into the four other bedrooms: younger sons in one room, older sons in the next, and across the hall, younger daughters in a room, and the two oldest daughters in a room large enough that they could each have a closet. He opened the four doors quietly, stood so silently that the children never awoke, as he stared at their faces while they slept. Nine healthy children, each one vibrant and distinct, all because he had been allowed to come home, while thousands of other men did not make it out of the plane before it exploded.

Eventually he would return to the bedroom, where Anna was asleep. He would lie down beside her, and hope that before dawn he might fall asleep too.

This girl named Katya, Katherine, with her serious dark eyes, and yet such beauty in her face when she laughed, was coming at one o'-clock on Sunday afternoon to take him to dinner at her home. A real Russian dinner in a real Russian home. Both her mother and father were coming with her to fetch him, rather than just one or the other to drive the car. "They want to see," Katya had told him, "where Mr. Bower lives, so that they might stop by to visit you from time to time."

The anticipation that he felt as he lay in bed on Saturday evening, the excitement that tomorrow was Sunday and he was going to have dinner with new friends, in their home, kept the nightmares at bay all night. He did not awaken until the light of dawn was shining through his window. He felt like a kid at dawn on Christmas day.

Katya hurried along the corridor ahead of her parents, then stood in Mr. Bower's open door. He was sitting in his rocking chair, wearing a gray suit that was a little too big for him, and a red silk tie. He of course had to shake hands with her, and then with her mother, and with her father, who each leaned down to take his firm hand in theirs. He was dressed in his best, as if to go to church on Easter, or to someone's home for Sunday dinner.

Katya liked this Mr. Bower so much, and felt that somehow they were already old friends.

She braced the back of his rocking chair while he stood up. He reached for his cane, lying across his bed. Then he led her family out the door and down the corridor, tapping his cane lightly, hardly needing it at all.

She hoped that later in the afternoon, he would be able to walk across the grass to the chair lift up Bobcat Mountain.

As soon as Walter stepped out the nursing home's front door, he took a deep breath of the cool fresh outdoor air. He tasted immediately that good Adirondack tinge of hemlock.

Katya walked beside him along the sidewalk to the parking lot. He glanced up at the sky: it was cloudy. Never mind. He was out!

She insisted that he sit in the front passenger seat of her father's old silver Volvo, because he was "the guest of honor." She and her mother, Svetlana, sat in the back seat, while her father, Yuri, drove slowly out of the parking lot, then slowly along South Shore Road, as if he had a fragile and extremely valuable antique on the seat beside him.

Walter enjoyed driving through Balsam Corners. His eyes darted from building to building to see what had changed, what was still the same. They drove past the old baroque movie theater on the right, the little green triangular park on the left. They passed the granite facade of the bank on the right, then turned the corner onto Crosby Boulevard. He feasted his eyes on the most elegant building in town, the beam-and-yellow-brick library, with its Shakespearean window.

Now they turned left onto Fern Avenue, passed Harvey Street, then pulled into the driveway of a small red house nearly hidden by a grove of cedars. It was the sort of house, Walter saw, that hard-working immigrants could afford to rent.

He got out of the car without Katya's help, then tapped his cane up a short sidewalk to the front door. Yuri unlocked the door, then he and Svetlana stepped inside and turned on lights. Now they stood in the doorway, beaming smiles at him as they invited him, "Come in! Come in!"

He entered a small living room, with one picture on the wall. Even with his untrained eye, he recognized the picture as a Russian icon of the Virgin Mary. He remembered his own picture of the Virgin Mary, in the Catholic style, on the wall over his dresser.

A bookcase, made of simple pine boards, unstained, was more than half-filled with books. A green sofa, a little worn, clearly second-hand, faced a stone fireplace. Split logs nestled on a bed of kindling and wadded newspaper: the fire was ready to light.

"Welcome!" said Yuri.

"Thank you," said Walter. He could smell a fresh apple pie in the kitchen.

Yuri and Walter sat for a few minutes in front of the blazing fire, talking about firewood—Yuri burned maple here in Balsam Corners, but in Russia people burned birch—while Katya and her mother readied the table. Then Katya stood behind the sofa, put her hands on her father's shoulders, leaned over him playfully and said, "Dinner is served."

The four of them sat around a small dining room table, each with a bowl of steaming red borsch as the first course. Katya leaned across a corner of the table and said quietly to Walter, "Would you like to say a blessing?"

He looked at her with surprise. Usually the host would say a blessing.

"Yes, please," said Yuri. They clearly did not want to say a Russian blessing, and thus exclude him.

"All right," said Walter. As he folded his hands on the edge of the table and bowed his head, Katya and her parents, Russian Orthodox with a Roman Catholic guest in their home, folded their hands and bowed their heads.

Speaking the words he had said a thousand times to his own family, he prayed, "Bless us, O Lord, for these gifts which we are about to receive from Thy bounty, through Christ our Lord. Amen." He remained silent, his head bowed, for another few moments, letting them have time for their own prayer in Russian. Then he looked up at Katya and said, "Thank you."

"You are welcome. Now try Mama's borsch." She looked at her mother with a teasing smile. "She's very nervous until you try it."

Walter took his soupspoon, dipped it into the steaming red broth and took a first sip. "Oooooohhh," he moaned with delight, looking at both Katya and her mother. "I taste the beets from my grandmother's garden."

"Well, almost," said Katya. "Mama works at the Red Maple Diner. The cook special-ordered the beets for her. They are very good beets, I think," she took a sip from her spoon, "but not quite straight from the earth."

"Exactly right," said her mother. "My mother's borsch, when we harvest the beets at the dacha, ah!"

"Well," said Walter, dipping his spoon again, "I am honored, I am honored."

While Katya put a spoonful of sour cream into Walter's soup, he heard Yuri say to his wife, in Russian, "Kara*shoh*, Sve*toch*ka. *Oh*cheen kara*shoh*." Her name was Svetlana, but he called her Svetochka. One of those Russian nicknames.

Sensing that his host and hostess were still a bit shy, Walter gave them a topic for conversation which he thought they might enjoy. Addressing Svetlana, he asked, "What did Katya like to do in Russia when she was a little girl?"

"Katya? In Russia?"

"Yes." He looked at the lovely young woman who had come from somewhere on the other side of the world, and who had paid more attention to him in one week than anyone in his own hometown had for years. "What did this wonderful person like to do before she left her beloved Saint Petersburg?"

Svetlana looked proudly at her daughter. "She loved to ski. But she loves to ski here too."

"Da!" said Yuri. "Every weekend, we took the train from Saint Petersburg north to the forest. Even when Katya was only five, she could ski twelve, fifteen kilometers a day with us. By the time she was ten years old, she was skiing so far ahead," he laughed, "that she had to ski back to see what was taking her old mother and father so long. She would call to us with such impatience, and then off she would race on a trail through the forest, like a rabbit, like a deer!"

Walter said to Katya, "I too was once a skier." He had to be, for he had nine kids skiing on Bobcat Mountain as they grew up. If he wanted to see them on the weekends in the winter, he had to be up on the mountain too.

"Now she skis with the high school ski team, yes, Katya?" said Svetlana.

"Yes," said Katya shyly. "When the snow comes, we will be skiing again."

"And when Katya was a little girl," said Yuri, "she liked to sing. In School Number Eleven, she sang in the choir. When she was a little girl, she had the sweetest voice."

"She has a sweet voice now," protested Svetlana. "She sings in the school choir here," she looked at her daughter, "and you like your choir director, don't you?"

"Yes," said Katya. "Mrs. Fisher is very good."

Katya, pensive, ate another spoonful of borsch. Then she looked at Walter, her dark eyes filled with regret. "Do you know what I really wanted to be?" she asked. "My secret dream . . ." She glanced at her father. "My secret dream was to be a ballerina."

"Da!" agreed Yuri. "She could ski and she could dance. So many things this girl could do."

"But I had no talent for dancing," said Katya, admitting the sad truth.

"Yes, you had talent!" protested her mother. "But if you want to ski, you must go to a special school for sports. If you want to dance, then of course you must go to a special school for children who train to become professional dancers. But you, Katya, you were always the student. Books and books and books. Especially English. You loved School Number Eleven because your English teachers were so good."

"That is true," said Katya. "I had no real talent for ballet, but I so much wanted to speak this language that maybe, maybe, *maybe* would let me travel. I wanted to see the rest of the world."

"And here you are," laughed her father. "In Balsam Corners. America!"

"Why," asked Walter, looking at all three of them, "did you come to America?" He had been wondering, ever since he had met this extraordinary girl, how on earth she ended up in Balsam Corners.

They were quiet for a long moment. Then Yuri said, "This is a very complex question." He looked at Svetlana, as if to let her answer.

She shook her head. "Yuri, you say."

He took a deep breath, and then began his saga. "You see, Walter, in the year 1991, when the Soviet Union vanished, and Leningrad became Saint Petersburg again, our government stopped building submarines and missiles. Sveta and I, we worked in the military industry. And then, in 1991," he shrugged, "finished. The Cold War is over. Russia has no money. Do you know, Walter, how many people were out of work? In Leningrad, seventy percent of the people had worked in military industry. Now seventy percent of the workers were suddenly without a job. The same all over Russia. This is nightmare!"

"Da," agreed Svetlana. "You cannot imagine such a frightening time. The Soviet dream vanished. Our country vanished. Our rubles vanished. We had a child five years old, and had planned on a second child, but now that was impossible. We had to keep *one* from starving."

Yuri continued, "Some said that the West would help us. Some said that Europe, and America, would reach out a helping hand." He shrugged again. "I do not blame them for what little help they gave. From America, it was mostly the wrong sort of help. Too much money, from American banks to banks in Moscow, and then, of course, it disappeared."

Svetlana stated firmly, "We have only ourselves to blame. Our oligarchs, our own Russian oligarchs, stole the nation's wealth from their own people. A handful of thieves, they plundered their own people."

"Da," agreed Yuri. "The richest man in England today is a Russian oligarch. He owns a football club. He stole from his mother country, so he could drive around London in a black Mercedes." Yuri puckered his lips, then made as if to spit.

"Before the collapse," said Svetlana, getting back to the story, "Yuri designed navigation systems for nuclear submarines. I designed guidance systems for nuclear missiles. But *after* the collapse," she almost wailed, "he repaired old cars, while I sold potatoes in the street. Just like that," she snapped her fingers angrily, "we were at the bottom. Selling our books, selling shoes we no longer wore, selling for cheap, for kopeks, because everybody else was selling old boots for kopeks."

Walter had been only distantly aware of the collapse of the Soviet Union. He had lost his Anna in May of 1991, seven months after their fiftieth wedding anniversary. The rest of the year was a black tunnel of grief.

"After three years of this . . . this exhausting struggle with no end in sight," continued Yuri, "I did something which even today hurts my heart. For it was like going against my own people. It was like becoming a traitor, hoping to abandon them."

"Yuri Mikhailovitch, you did right," insisted Svetlana. "Look where we are now. Look at our Katya. On her way to an American university."

"Da, da," agreed Yuri. "But still." He looked at Walter as if he were making a confession. "I took the train to Moscow. I went to a special office of the American Embassy. I applied to what they called a lottery for green cards. For work cards, for permission to work in America. I told no one, only Sveta of course. Then we waited. I reapplied each year, and we waited another year, and another year. Now I did not just fix old cars, I drove one as a taxi. Sveta no longer stood out in the snow selling potatoes. She had a job in a shop, selling potatoes. And our Katya was now in school. Skiing, singing, dancing. I told myself that Peter the Great had studied in Holland, in England, learning to be a shipbuilder. Then he returned home to Russia to build ships. It was therefore no sin to dream that maybe, maybe one day our Katya could study in another country too. Then, it would be her decision whether to return to Russia to build ships."

"Which I surely will," said Katya. "I just don't know yet what sort of ships they will be."

"Then suddenly," continued Yuri, "in the fall of 2000, the American Embassy notified us that we had green cards. Like a gift from heaven, Sveta and I had green cards! Katya was fourteen now, flourishing in school. Do we take her out of school? Do we really go to this America on the other side of the world? Do we leave my old father, who had just lost one son, Maxim, frozen to death on New Year's Eve? Do we leave Sveta's mother, out in the village? We had already lost one country, our Soviet Union. Were we now to lose our Russia too?"

Yuri paused; he stared at Walter with deep worry in his eyes, as if he were still back in that time, struggling to make an almost impossible decision. Whatever blessings he had found for his family in America, they clearly did not fully compensate for what the Cherkasov family had lost by leaving home.

"For Katya," said Svetlana firmly, "for Katya, always at the head of her classes in English, six and six and six—like your A-plus here—on every English exam. We took our green cards and we told ourselves, 'We shall go to America.'"

"So," said Yuri, "I stopped driving the taxi. I managed to get a visa to Finland, then I took what little money we had and spent three days in Finland, looking for an old car that I could buy and drive home. I bought a Volvo that was little more than junk, but I kept it going from Helsinki to Saint Petersburg. I repaired it fully, with parts that I could find at this market, that market, and then I sold the Volvo for dollars. For dollars, which were then flowing freely in the Russian black market. Right away, I went back to Finland and bought another Volvo, a better one, and drove it home. All through the winter and spring of 2001, I bought old cars and repaired them and sold them for dollars to the people in Saint Petersburg who had such money. I did not ask where they got it. I took what they paid me and saved the hundred dollar bills, your Ben Franklin, so that we could buy three plane tickets to New York. Every trip to Helsinki was really part of the journey to New York."

"He was never home," said Svetlana. "He was sleeping on buses, he was driving through blizzards. He was bringing home money that was not Russian money, but it was money that kept its value. Money that could buy plane tickets. Money that we could take in our pockets to New York."

"Finally, finally, finally," Yuri shook his head, "though I was almost a dead man by now, we had enough. In May of 2001, we bought our tickets for a flight on Aeroflot to New York in July. Katya was fifteen now, saying good-bye to her friends. Saying good-bye to her Grandfather Mikhail, alone in his apartment. Saying good-bye to her grandmother Elena, Sveta's mother, a woman not so old, but with knees that ache with such pain, she can hardly stand."

"Everyone at school," said Katya, "was so excited that I was going to America. But I cried. I wanted to go, but I cried."

Walter thought of his own daughter, Mary, who lived on Long Island and worked in New York. Years ago, he and Anna had worried terribly about Mary, when she first moved to the big city at the age of twenty-two, to attend medical school at Columbia. The leap from Balsam Corners to New York City had seemed enormous. But at least Mary could speak fluent English, and knew that Columbia would take care of her for the next four years. And she could always hop on the train from Penn Station to Utica for Thanksgiving and Christmas and Easter.

He looked at Katya with growing admiration. Imagine a fifteen-year-old kid, the only one in the family who could speak English, translating for her parents as they went through customs at Kennedy Airport. He told her, "You were a very brave girl."

"Brave?" she asked. "You are a veteran. You know what bravery is. You have your job and you do it. My job is to become something, and then to go back home so that I can help to build a new Russia."

"Did you know that when you were fifteen? That someday you would return to Russia to build ships?"

"Yes, I knew even then. Otherwise, I could never have left."

"And are you becoming something here? Have you found something to become?"

"Perhaps," she said. "Maybe after dinner, the four of us can ride in Papa's Volvo to Bobcat Mountain, to see the sort of ship that I would like to build in Russia."

CHAPTER 33

After everyone had finished the borsch, Svetlana and Katya took away the empty bowls, and then they brought out four fresh plates from the kitchen, followed by four serving bowls containing four different salads, and a tureen filled with what Svetlana called, "Pel*may*ny. Pieces of beef wrapped in dough, like a pillow in a pillowcase. And then boiled. I hope you will like it."

"Thank you, thank you," said Walter as she ladled pelmayny onto his plate. He leaned forward and took a breath of fragrant steam.

After Katya and her mother had sat down again, Walter asked, looking at the three of them, "And New York? How was New York? And how did you manage to get from New York to Balsam Corners?"

"Oy!" said Yuri. "We arrive on the twelve of July, and the city is hot. Hot!" He puffed his cheeks, remembering how he had sweltered. "We go from Kennedy Airport by this bus and this train to Brooklyn, where we find the friend of a friend of a friend, who lets us stay, for one month, in a corner of his apartment. He had an air conditioner in his bedroom window. But the rest of us in the living room: hot!"

"I never know so hot," agreed Svetlana. "In Saint Petersburg, we can go out to the forest in the summer. We can swim in the lakes. But in New York, we don't know where to find some forest. We walk on streets so hot, our feet stick to the black pavement."

"So," said Yuri, continuing his saga, "I find work in a truck garage, owned by a Russian in Brighton Beach. I tell him I can fix any car, any truck, and he puts me to work. So we have money after one month to

183

leave our friend of a friend of a friend, who was less and less friendly toward the end, and we move into our own apartment, about the size of a corner of a corner. But now we have job, and home."

"But where will Katya go to school?" asked Svetlana, holding her head with her hands. "In this big, big city. We are afraid to let her walk down the street out of our sight. We know no parents, no children. How should we find the right school?"

"And then," Yuri stared at Walter with those dark eyes that spoke from soul to soul, "after one month in this new apartment, after one month of buying new plates, new chairs, I am getting ready to go to work when the radio tells us that a plane just crashed into some building in New York City. We have no television, only radio. We cannot see what is happening. We look out our windows, see only traffic in the street in Brooklyn. Then we hear that a second plane crashed into a second building. This is not accident, this is attack. And I think, we have come to America, and now America is at war. This is the beginning, like the German attack on Leningrad."

Walter had been on the phone all day with Mary, calling her again and again. She was safe on Long Island. Arthur was safe, the children were safe.

"We have no telephone," said Yuri. "I go down the stairs four flights to the street, then stand in all the noise around a phone booth while I try to call my boss at the truck garage. He tells me to stay home. No work today. Something horrible is happening, but he does not know what. So I go back upstairs, and all morning the three of us sit on the edge of Katya's bed and listen to her radio. Like three prisoners in a jail cell, while the world outside is blowing up."

Yuri was silent now; Svetlana reached across the corner of the table and laid her hand over his.

"First one building collapses," said Yuri, "then the second building collapsed. After the second building collapsed, Svetlana says to me, 'We must go to Utica.' We had heard there were Russians in a little city called Utica, somewhere in another part of New York State.

"'Utica?' I asked. Then I said, 'Maybe we buy three more airplane tickets and we go home to Russia.'

"But Katya said, 'No.'" Yuri looked at his daughter with pride. "She said, 'Mama is right. We get out of Brooklyn, we get out of New York

City. If they have a war, it is not our war. We take a train to Utica. No one has ever heard of Utica. There will be no war in Utica.'"

"That is right," said Katya. "New York City was a target. During the Blockade, people evacuated Leningrad because it was a target."

"So I worked for one more week at the truck garage. My boss phoned a Russian friend in Utica, a friend of a friend of a friend, who said he would meet us at the Utica train station on Sunday afternoon.

"So, we wait in Brighton Beach until Sunday. No more planes crashed into any more buildings in New York City. Maybe it wasn't a war after all. On Saturday night, we pack our suitcases. On Sunday morning, we carry our suitcases down four flights of stairs, then along the street to the subway. We ride the subway to the railroad station in New York City. We hope that no one will bomb the station while we are there."

"Pennsylvania Station," said Katya.

"Da, Pennsylvania Station. My boss had already phoned the station. He gave me the train schedule. We bought our tickets, three train tickets to somewhere in America. Then we rode for six hours to this place called Utica."

"Where we probably would have stayed," said Svetlana, "for Utica was nice. A small city, and people welcomed us."

"Da," agreed Yuri. "For the first time, we felt that we might be able to survive in America."

"But this friend of a friend of a friend," continued Svetlana, taking over the story, "really became a good friend. He welcomed us into his home, and gave us *two* rooms. Can you imagine, two! Boris Ivanovitch knew all of the companies in Utica where immigrants could look for work. He phoned and phoned, found nothing, but kept phoning. He told us not to worry, not to worry, he would find something."

"Yes," agreed Katya, "Boris Ivanovitch is a very good man."

"No job, no job," continued Svetlana, "but then, one day in the middle of the week, a Wednesday or a Thursday, the sun was shining outside the kitchen window. My family, we were having breakfast—I had made *kasha*, oatmeal, for the four of us—when Boris Ivanovitch called us all outside to his back yard. We go out, wondering, 'What is it? What is it?' And he told us, pointing his finger, 'Look up at that blue sky.' Boris and Yuri were still in their bathrobes. 'Today is a *perfect* September day,' said Boris. 'Today we must drive north to the Adirondacks to see the maple trees.'"

Svetlana slapped her hand lightly on the table. "And that was it. On this sunny day in September, we would not look for jobs. We would drive to somewhere to see some sort of tree."

"Of course," said Walter, delighted that the story was now tending toward his neck of the woods. "I have lived here for eighty-five years, and every September is still a miracle."

Svetlana shrugged. "What do we know? We have seen nothing but city, city, city in America."

"Da," said Yuri. "I think, is there no forest in America?"

"So we get into Boris Ivanovitch's silver Volvo—the car we rode in today, it was his, he sold it to us, nearly gave it to us—with a picnic, a big Russian picnic, and Boris Ivanovitch drives us north, with the sun behind us. We drive on a big highway, so smooth, so nice, then we turn off on a smaller road that very soon is winding through a forest. Green pine, not big, but at least green. And spots of red and orange. But Boris Ivanovitch says, 'That's nothing. Wait till we get further north. Whole mountainsides of red!'"

"That's right," said Walter, kindling with anticipation. "And that miracle is coming again, in about two weeks."

"So," continued Svetlana, "we drive through little villages, not even villages, just cottages along the shore of a lake, American *dachas*. We cross a river with many rocky islands."

"The Moose River," said Katya.

"Yes, the Moose River, with red trees along the banks. And then the road begins to climb. No one is talking, we are just looking, looking at more and more bright orange trees. And yellow too. How you call it? Tamarack, green needles turning yellow, the same as we have in Russia. Some white birch, not many, but some."

"The white birch are further north," said Walter, "up around Lake Placid. We're a little too far south here, although the birch *will* grow fairly well here if somebody plants them."

"And then," Svetlana's voice brightened with excitement, "after we have been driving for about an hour, we cross a small river and drive into a little town. Not a city, not a cluster of American dachas, but a little American town. We see nice houses along the street, with big trees in the front yard, big trees in the back yard. We see a post office, not a giant city building, but a little red brick building where we could walk in and mail a letter to Yuri's father, and a letter to my mother. We see— Boris Ivanovitch stopped at the curb so we could really look— a beautiful school, two stories, red brick, just the right size, with grass and big trees in the front yard. We try to see through the windows, because today, in the middle of the week in September, children are learning their lessons in the school. And I think, 'Here is a school for our Katya.'"

"Yes," said Katya, "I knew that we had finally found America. We could live here, we could breathe here. And whatever war was happening in America, it would never find us here."

"We have our picnic basket in the trunk of Boris's car," continued Svetlana, "but Boris Ivanovitch drives us through the heart of the little town, with shops on both sides of the street, then he parks in front of the Maple Diner. 'Let's go in and have a cup of tea,' he says to us. So we go into a little restaurant and we sit in a booth, just like in an American movie. Boris Ivanovitch does not order just tea. He orders a full dinner for each of us. Yuri tries to protest, but Boris Ivanovitch waves his hand at him. Later in the car, Boris explained, 'If you want information, you must buy a dinner. A cup of tea will get you nothing.'"

"Da," laughed Yuri, "and we had dessert too! But look at the information we got. Here we are today."

"Yes," said Svetlana, "we had dessert. And then Boris Ivanovitch asked the waitress if she knew about any jobs in town. She said, 'Just a second, Hon,' and then she disappeared into the kitchen. When she came out, the cook came with her. He was wearing a wet and greasy white tunic, with the sleeves rolled up. He said hello to us, very politely, then he asked, 'Can anybody wash dishes? I'm fed up with turning burgers and washing pots at the same time.'

"Now of course I didn't know that's what he said, because he said it in English. But Katya looks at me and asks in Russian, 'Mama, can you wash dishes?' She knows of course that I can, but she wants to know if I am *willing* to wash dishes. I am, you know, an engineer in electronics. I once worked on a guidance system that would direct a Soviet missile toward New York City. And now, would I wash dishes? 'Kan*yesh*na!' I say. Of course! Katya tells the cook in her best English that her mother is an excellent dish washer, and that she is learning English very quickly, and that as soon as we find a place to live, she can go to work."

"Exactly right," said Katya. "How long does it take to learn 'plate' and 'pot' and 'spoon' and 'cup'?"

"Boris Ivanovitch talks with the cook and the waitress a bit more, and learns about the town's one industry, a furniture factory that employs about three hundred workers. It is just north of town, on the left. Nathaniel Greene Furniture. 'Thank you,' we say. 'Thank you, thank you.' Boris Ivanovitch paid the bill, and left a ten-dollar tip."

"You know," said Walter, "I would like to meet this friend of yours, Boris Ivanovitch."

"He lives in Utica," said Katya. "We saw him this morning in church. We must invite him up for Sunday dinner, and then you can meet him."

Walter liked that. Already he was invited for another Sunday dinner. And with another new friend to meet.

"So," continued Svetlana, "we drive in the silver Volvo out of the little town, on a road that is winding, winding, winding through the red forest, and then we see a big wooden sign on the left, NATHANIEL GREENE FURNITURE. We are so nervous that no one talks. Boris Ivanovitch turns in, then parks in a spot with a little sign, VISITORS. I think, How nice, a place for visitors. These Americans can be very polite.

"We go inside, where Boris Ivanovitch talks with a woman at the front desk. She calls someone on the telephone. Two minutes later, a man appears in the lobby, wearing a blue shirt with light sawdust on it, and holding a clipboard. Boris Ivanovitch talks with the man, and the man at first looks skeptical, for of course Yuri can speak only Russian. Katya later told us that Boris Ivanovitch told the floor manager that Yuri would work the first week without pay, to show that he could do the job. Finally the man nods and says, 'C'mon back into the shop and I'll show you what the job entails.'

"We follow him down a short hallway, with offices on both sides, then we pass through a swinging door and enter the factory. Many men are working on lathes and saws, so there is much noise. A few men look briefly at us as we walk among them, then focus again on their work. I see a rocking chair, still without arms, but with a back of elegant spindles. And I wonder, 'What can Yuri do here?'"

Walter thought of his own two rocking chairs from Nathaniel Greene. Katya read *The Grapes of Wrath* to him while they rocked in those chairs.

"The floor manager pointed out, as we walked along, heaps of scrap wood, bags of sawdust. Katya, translating for Yuri and me as we walk along, tells us that the manager says that in the summer, the factory hires college students to carry out the scraps. But now the students are back in college. And Bob, the only full-time scrap man—we never did meet Bob, apparently he ended up in jail—had a habit of getting drunk. At the back end of the factory, we came to a huge bin of scraps. 'Can your friend operate a scoop?' the manager asked Boris, pointing to a small tractor with a bucket on the front for shoveling up scraps. 'Of course,' says Boris. The manager pushed a button, a big metal door rose up, and outside we see a concrete platform about five feet tall, with an empty steel bin on the ground beside it. The job was to clean all the scraps in the factory, all the sawdust, and to put them into the steel bin. A truck would take the bin away. 'What do you say?' asked the manager, looking at Yuri. Boris translated into Russian, 'Can you clean the factory?'

"Yuri said, 'Kan*yesh*na' to the man; Boris translated, 'Of *course*. I learn quickly. In one week, your factory will be clean. Then I keep factory clean. The workers work much better when factory clean.'"

"Da," said Yuri. "I work there for two weeks, and the manager he come to me and he say he *never* see the factory so clean. I don't understand all English, but I understand enough. The man is smiling while he points there and there and there in the factory, saying, 'Clean! Clean! Clean!'"

"So," continued Svetlana, "Yuri and the manager agree that Yuri will begin next Monday. Eight o'clock in the morning. Yuri and the manager shake hands. We walk to the front office, where a secretary makes a copy of Yuri's passport with American visa, and a copy of his green card. He is legal. And now he can go to work."

"My first job in Balsam Corners," said Yuri, grinning. "Once I designed complex electrical systems for nuclear submarines, so that no matter where in the world they were, they could communicate with Moscow, and now I am happy because Nathaniel Greene will pay me to work with a broom."

"We walk out of the building into the sunshine," said Svetlana, "and we say a big thank you to Boris Ivanovitch, who had found for us two jobs in less than an hour. In a little American town named Balsam Corners. Where—it was like a dream—Katya could go to school."

Walter looked at Katya, who had not only survived this epic journey, but had managed to flourish. Could any of his nine children have done as well in Saint Petersburg?

"But," said Svetlana, with weariness in her voice, "we still had to find some place to live, an apartment of two or three rooms, if such a town as Balsam Corners had apartments. Boris Ivanovitch took care of that too, for he drove us back into the little town and took us into an old house on Main Street that was now a real estate office. We spent the afternoon looking at rooms for rent, and then at houses for rent. We again said a big thank you to Boris Ivanovitch, for he would not quit until we had found this little red house, in need of some repairs, especially the water pipes. He wrote a check for a deposit and the first month's rent, so that we could live in this house. This home in America. We could move in on Saturday, and Yuri could go to work on Monday. Katya and I would visit the school on Monday morning, she to introduce us in English, and I to show that the poor child had a mother."

Svetlana looked at her daughter with abundant love, abundant pride.

Katya laughed and said, "The poor child!"

Then Svetlana reached for a serving bowl of salad and passed it to Walter. "Please, I talk too much. We must not forget our dinner."

"That is Papa's favorite salad," said Katya. "In Russia, we call it *Metropolis*. Mama makes it with potatoes, pickles, onion, green peas, and mayonnaise, and of course some kind of meat. Papa," Katya grinned, "likes his salad with hot Italian sausage from Utica."

"Da," declared Yuri, ready with his testimonial, "I am a man of thirty-nine, but the best sausage I ever eat in all my life, is from Utica. *Hot* Italian sausage."

Walter spooned a large helping of Metropolis onto his plate.

"And this one," Yuri held up a second serving bowl of salad, "is Katya's favorite. We call it *Borneo*. Tropical, from far away. Sveta makes it with rice, and crab meat, which maybe in Russia we can or can not get. And what else? Onion, corn, and mayonnaise, da?"

Walter spooned a serving of Borneo onto his plate.

"My other favorite is *Vinegret*," said Katya, holding up a third serving bowl of salad. "Mama makes it with potatoes, carrots, beet and onion, with green peas and olive oil. Oh, you have such good olive oil in Utica."

Walter spooned a portion of Vinegret onto his plate.

"And of course," said Svetlana, holding up the fourth serving bowl of salad, "what we call *Mimosa*. Boiled fish, best if fresh, with eggs, onion, carrot, and mayonnaise. Maybe also potatoes. I ask them in Utica what kind of fish. They say haddock. I ask them where this haddock comes from. They say New York City."

Walter spooned a helping of Mimosa onto his plate.

He looked at the abundance which they had set before him, which they had clearly spent hours preparing, a true Russian feast, then he looked at them, mother, father, daughter, and told them, "Thank you. From deep in my heart, thank you."

"Welcome, welcome," said Svetlana.

Then all four became quiet while they savored their Russian salads.

"So," said Walter, who was so full that he could not eat another pea, "you came to our little town in September of 2001, when New York City was just beginning to clean up the ashes."

"Yes," said Svetlana. "We came to Balsam Corners when America was in mourning. In the shops along Main Street, we see black ribbons. And for the next two years, we find ourselves in a country at war, even if the war is far away in Afghanistan, and then Iraq. While in our own country, which we had left to find a better life for Katya, our government chooses to stay out of the war."

"There's a boy from Balsam Corners over there now," said Walter. He had read about the Dyson boy in the local newspaper. Walter knew the family: the boy's father had been in Vietnam, his uncle in Korea, his grandfather on Normandy Beach.

"Da," said Yuri. "They talk about Bobby at the garage. All the mechanics know him. He was a great skier on the mountain, they say."

"Well," said Walter, "May the war end soon."

The four of them became quiet, for all four knew that wars rarely end soon.

Then Katya whispered to her father, "Papa, please, a toast to our veteran guest."

"Of course," said Yuri, the head of the family, the host, and thus the person who should propose a toast to the guest of honor. He reached for a tall, colorless, stately bottle, and unscrewed its cap. When he held it up, Walter could see that the writing on the label was in Russian letters. The Cyrillic alphabet.

"This vodka," said Yuri, "is from Saint Petersburg, imported by Boris Ivanovitch as one of many sidelines in his business." He filled each of the four small glasses, set the bottle down beside the pelmayny tureen, then raised his glass toward Walter.

"For our new friend, Walter Bower, who honors us with his visit to our home. Who honors us, because when my father and Svetlana's father were fighting in the trenches to keep the German Army from entering Leningrad, you, Walter, as Katya has told us, were flying from England and dropping bombs on Germany. We do not speak so often of that time, but neither do we ever forget. So we thank you, Walter," Katya and Svetlana now raised their glasses toward Walter, "for fighting beside us. We cannot thank anyone more deeply than we thank a veteran."

Profoundly moved, Walter raised his glass. "Then let us toast as well," he looked at Svetlana, "your father," he looked at Yuri, "and your father. I am deeply honored to be remembered among such company today."

He sipped his vodka, savored its Russian bite, while Yuri downed his entire glass. Then he took another sip. He certainly wasn't going to say a word about this to his nurse.

CHAPTER 34

All through the dinner, Walter had watched how closely the mother, father, and daughter interacted with each other. They spoke to each other as equals, and responded vibrantly, in agreement or occasionally in disagreement, to what the others had to say. Katya was no sullen teenager, silently brooding in her chair because she had been forced to join a family dinner. Yuri did not sit restlessly with an ear cocked to a football game on television in the living room.

"So in the last two years," Walter said to Svetlana, "you have advanced from dish washer to head cook at the Maple Diner."

"You must come with Katya one Saturday morning," she smiled. "I shall make *blini* for you, with wild blueberry preserves."

"I can't wait," he told her. He remembered the wild blueberry preserves that Anna had canned every summer for half a century.

Then he turned to Katya, a girl at the very edge of blossoming into a beauty like her mother, "And you, you have progressed from your sophomore year to the beginning of your senior year. Is that right?"

"Yes." She glanced with a hint of apprehension at her mother and father. "This year I must apply to universities."

He felt a pang of sadness, though he had known her only briefly. A year from now, she would be gone.

He turned to Yuri. "You spent a year and a half at Nathaniel Greene, and then the factory shut down. Last April, you, like three hundred others, were out of a job. But as I understand from Katya, you have been working at Brill's Garage."

"Da. But Walter, every evening, *every* evening, once we settle here in Balsam Corners, Katya gives her poor mother and father English lessons. I am tired from work all day, Sve*toch*ka is tired from work all day, Ka*toosh*ka is tired from school all day, but still, after dinner, we study English. So that Svetochka can do more than wash oatmeal pots. So that Yuri can do more than cough on sawdust. Sveta tries to read ladies' magazines about cooking. I try to read men's magazines about cars. When I think maybe I know something, certainly not enough but maybe something, I visit Jackson Brill at his garage on a Saturday morning in March—this is after half a year of study, study, study my English—and I tell Mr. Brill that I know Volvo. I know Saab, I know Mercedes. Mr. Brill puts me to work every Saturday with a nice boy named Raphael, just Katya's age. I teach Raphael Volvo, he teaches me Chevy. I earn as much money on one Saturday at Brill's Garage as I make in a week at Nathaniel Greene. So I work two jobs now, six days a week. Svetochka works six days a week. Katooshka studies," he smiled at his daughter, "seven days a week. So we were, until the factory closed. Then I needed another job."

Yuri paused while he helped himself to another portion of pelmayny. Walter wondered whether he should finish his vodka. His shot glass was still about half full. Telling himself to be cautious, he finished his Mimosa. Then he allowed himself another sip.

"When I first start working at the garage," continued Yuri, "in the spring of 2002, I meet a man who has an old red Volvo, in very good condition. But not excellent condition. I hear noises in the engine and I tell him he has bad rings. While I fix his rings, he watches me work— he is retired, was director of a bank—and he asks me where I am from. I say I am from Russia. He asks me—while my hands are black with grease—what sort of education I had, as if he knew an immigrant might have been an engineer, or a professor, or even a doctor, before he came to America and fixed old cars. So I tell him that I graduated from a state technical university in Leningrad, as an electrical engineer, and that I had once designed navigational systems that had guided a Soviet submarine beneath the ice cap to precisely the North Pole. He seemed pleased that I had such a background. He was a man of great curiosity, with many questions."

"Are you talking about Gerald Jacobsen?" asked Walter. "Does he still drive that old maroon Volvo? He certainly was never flashy with his money."

"Da," nodded Yuri, "I am speaking of Mr. Jacobsen. I do not know this name Gerald. Everyone in the garage, even Jackson Brill, calls him Mr. Jacobsen."

Walter knew Gerald Jacobsen, for as director of the bank, Gerald had made sure that all nine of Walter's children had a scholarship for college. His kids had worked hard in school, got top grades, and the bank—Gerald—rewarded them as he rewarded every bright kid in town who needed some help with tuition. Walter had never known Gerald personally—folks in town said that only his mother knew him personally—but he had met with the gentleman nine times in the bank director's office, and nine times, Gerald had helped to launch a youngster into the world.

Gerald Jacobsen had enabled Mary to make her way through medical school at Columbia. And he sent her a card, congratulating her, when she graduated.

"So," continued Yuri, "Mr. Jacobsen comes back to the garage every three months, for an oil change. To have winter tires put on. Once because the engine was running hot. The radiator belt was worn. And each time, we talk about Russia. He reads about Vladimir Putin, he reads about Chechnya, and he wants to know what I think. I find no one else in Balsam Corners who reads so much about Russia."

That's Gerald, thought Walter. Everyone in town knew. When Gerald loaned Bob Hendricks the money for new ovens at the bakery, he asked Bob dozens of questions about baking bread. When he helped a farmer to keep the family farm through a stretch of lean years, he wanted to know all about the cows.

"Then one day last winter—before Nathaniel Greene closed down, but everybody knows the factory has troubles—Mr. Jacobsen visits me at the garage, without his Volvo, just walks over from the bank to the garage and finds me lubing a Volksvagen and asks me if I would like to apply for a job as electrical engineer. I ask him where in little Balsam Corners can I find a job as electrical engineer. He tells me that the town has just voted to construct a wind turbine on top of the ski mountain. Bobcat Mountain, where I have never been because for a year and a half

I have been working, working, working. He tells me, 'A Danish company, DanishWind, is going to erect the wind turbine. They will check on it as part of their maintenance schedule. But they want to hire someone local with a background in electronics to monitor the turbine. To keep track of the daily readings. The DanishWind people told us that if we could find an engineer who was also handy with tools, that would be just right.'"

Yuri paused, remembering the moment when he was about to take an enormous step forward. "Mr. Jacobsen tells me, 'A lot of people will apply for that job, because when Nathaniel Greene folds, a lot of people will be out of work. But I think you are more qualified than anyone else in town. What do you think? Will you fill out an application?'

"Now I stop lubing this Volksvagen and I look at Mr. Jacobsen as if he is an angel asking me if I want to be somebody again. I of course had studied turbines at the university, and a Danish turbine could not be so different from a Soviet turbine. 'Mr. Jacobsen,' I say, 'I am grateful for maybe this job.'

"'Good,' he says. 'And your wife too. You mentioned that she has a background in engineering. Am I correct?'

"I was surprised that he had remembered. 'Yes, you are correct,' I told him. 'Svetlana and I graduated in the same class.

"'Then please,' he said, 'if you would both be kind enough to provide me with a resumé of your education and career experience.' He smiled with a joke, 'Without telling me any Soviet secrets.' Then he continued, 'I will pass your resumés on to the DanishWind people. DanishWind makes the selection, hires the candidate and provides the training.' He paused, then he asked me, 'Can a Russian engineer keep a Danish wind turbine running in an Adirondack wind?'

"I wanted to shake his hand, but of course my hand was black with grease. So I told him, 'Yes, Mr. Jacobsen, I would be very grateful to work with your Adirondack wind.'"

"You know," said Walter, "I'd like to meet Gerald Jacobsen again. I haven't seen him for years."

"Are we ready for dessert?" asked Svetlana, looking around the table at the empty dinner plates. "Katya has made an apple cake."

"Mama," said Katya, "I have a suggestion before we have dessert."

"So in February, Sveta and I write our resumés," said Yuri, not done with his narration and thus not yet ready for dessert, "with Katya's help, of course. Katya types in good English our background in engineering, and I mail the two resumés to Mr. Jacobsen at the bank. In April, Nathaniel Greene closes. In May, an American engineer from the DanishWind office in Oregon visits Balsam Corners to direct the work on the electrical infrastructure: the cables and substation on the mountain which will carry electricity from the turbine to the grid. Mr. Jacobsen arranges an interview for Svetlana and me with this man, and though my English is still," he shrugged, "an immigrant's English, we understand each other very clearly. Volts and megawatts and gear ratios. This is physics, anywhere in the world."

Yuri paused to look at his wife with teasing pride. "You were my toughest competition for this job. Equally qualified, only you were missiles while I was submarines."

"Yes," she replied with mock regret, "missiles have no turbines aboard, whereas submarines do."

"Da!" exclaimed Yuri with triumph. "So DanishWind hired me, and I spent five weeks last summer training in Portland, Oregon. In the west of America. Now I can listen to the yaw gears the same as I listen to a Volvo. I can follow electrical output on a laptop. I will supervise and maintain the turbine that will power every light bulb in Balsam Corners."

He paused, then spoke softly, with reverence, "This is a gift from God. To find this job in America, this is a gift from God."

Walter, who had survived seven bombing missions, a parachute jump from a plane with three dead engines, a month of hiding in occupied France, and a trek over the Pyrenees in winter to the safety of Spain, knew what a gift from God was. With the birth of each of his nine children, he knew what a gift from God was. He had never understood why he had been so blessed, while thousands of other men lay in graveyards in Europe, or at the bottom of the sea.

He liked this man Yuri, who so clearly brimmed with gratitude for what life had given him.

Walter raised his vodka glass, about a third full. "To the Russian engineer who will keep a Danish turbine running in the Adirondack wind."

With a grateful smile, Yuri filled his own glass—Katya and Svetlana held their hands over their own glasses, for they still had some—then the four of them toasted to the successful end of an immigrant's long saga, and to the beginning of his new career.

CHAPTER 35

"I suggest," said Katya firmly, "that we have our dessert on Bobcat Mountain. Mr. Bower, the components of the turbine are still on trucks in the Ski Center parking lot. Mama and Papa have been working with the DanishWind people all week, getting ready to put the pieces together on the peak. I suggest that we put our apple cake in a picnic basket and drive up the mountain. I think you might like to see the blades that Papa is going to spin in the wind."

"But who shall drive?" asked Svetlana. "We have been toasting."

Yuri laughed, "Where is Boris Ivanovitch?"

Walter looked at his watch: ten after three on a Sunday afternoon. "Is there any sort of taxi service in Balsam Corners nowadays?"

"I have already made arrangements," said Katya. "The nursing home is waiting to send over a van, to take Mr. Bower and his companions to the Ski Center, so that he can look at what everybody else in town has been looking at this week. Mrs. Hill, the director, quite agreed with me that Mr. Bower should have the opportunity too."

Walter looked at his thoughtful friend. He had read about the wind turbine—he had read all the arguments for and against it—in the local newspaper during the past year. He had invested in a bond to support the project. But he never thought that he would actually go up on the mountain to see the turbine itself. "Thank you, Katya."

"You are welcome." She stood up from the table and went into the living room to phone the nursing home.

* * *

Katya walked beside Walter through the living room, where the fire had burned to a bed of coals in the fireplace. They stepped out the front door and walked slowly down three concrete steps, Walter with one hand on his cane and one gripping the railing. He appreciated the way Katya walked beside him, always ready, yet she never said a word about helping him.

The van soon arrived, a dark green vehicle with TALL TIMBERS in red letters along its side. The van had a lift for wheelchairs, but Walter did not need that. He was able to walk up the steps, then to sit in the passenger seat in front, so that he could look out the windshield at his little town.

While the Cherkasov family got into the back of the van, Walter asked the driver, "Johnny, can you follow 28 to the Old Mill Inn, then take a left? I'd like to see my house on the Moose River Trail."

"Okeydoke," said Johnny.

They backed out of the driveway—Walter admired once again the little red house, tucked away in the cedars—then Johnny drove west on Fern. He turned left on Adams, right on Garmon, which became Riverside, and now Walter gazed longingly at the red and green and yellow canoes, upside down on racks, at the Moose River Canoe Livery. He and Anna and the children: the family had five canoes for the eleven of them. They had paddled on the Middle Branch, and on the Pond. How many summer nights, under how many beautiful moons, had they bobbed together side by side like five pea pods, holding each other's gunnels and eating Anna's oatmeal cookies while everyone looked up at the stars.

Johnny took a right on Route 28. Walter looked at the new shops, and the giant drug store, and the giant grocery store, along the highway. "There's your left," he said to Johnny, pointing at the street just before the Old Mill.

Johnny nodded. "Joy Tract Road." He waited for a break in the traffic—the tourist traffic was always heavier on the weekends—then he made the turn.

Walter now stared ahead and a little to the left, until he saw it: the two-story white house with green trim. With a big front porch, and the addition of a family room on the left side. He was glad that the new owners kept the original colors. That house was so pretty, with the green forest behind it.

Walter turned around in his seat as much as he could and said over his shoulder, "When we turn the corner, take a look at the house on the right. White with green trim. I raised nine kids in that house."

"Nine!" exclaimed his three Russian friends together. Svetlana said a second time, "Nine!"

"Walter," said Yuri, his deep voice filled with admiration, "I think you are a Cossack!"

Walter knew that Cossacks were strong, wild men who rode horses. "Thank you," he said over his shoulder. Then he stared at his house while Johnny turned the corner slowly. Johnny pulled to the edge of the road and stopped. Walter looked out his open passenger window.

It was almost too painful, to look at the bedroom windows upstairs and know who had slept in each room. The old wicker swing on the front porch was gone. A black pick-up truck stood in the driveway.

"Thank you, Johnny."

"You're welcome, Mr. Bower." Johnny drove east on the Moose River Trail. Walter looked left and right at the houses of his neighbors, hoping to see somebody he knew. But it was a quiet Sunday afternoon. Nobody out.

At the highway department shed, Johnny turned right onto Brown's Tract Road and began to climb the flank of the mountain. Walter had driven this road a thousand times, the car filled with kids, their skis on the rooftop rack. In a way, the kids had three parents: father, mother, and the mountain. All three taught discipline, all three taught perseverance. As much as the Balsam Corners school, it was the mountain that got his kids into college.

Johnny hooked left on Bisby Road; the van labored now as it climbed up and up the winding road through maple forest. Here on the mountain, many more leaves had turned red than down in the town. Walter let out a long breath, as if his soul could relax within the embrace of the forest.

Johnny took the left fork onto Bobcat Mountain Road. Walter inhaled the pine, inhaled the tangy beech.

Now the road opened into the Ski Center parking lot. Walter was surprised to see so many cars. Then he remembered that the chair lift ran in the autumn, so people could ride to the top of Bobcat Mountain, then gaze from the peak at the rolling carpet of color. Tourists came by the carload. "Leaf peepers," he said.

"No sir," said Johnny. "Wind turbine peepers." He pointed toward crowds of people wrapped around several trucks.

Walter stared at something big, liked pieces of a rocket ship, or a space station, loaded on the flatbeds of the biggest trucks he had ever seen.

Most of the people in the crowd were no doubt from town. He wanted to see this wind turbine, but he hoped as well to meet a few people he knew.

Johnny stopped the van near a truck that carried what looked like a long thin white feather. Walter admired the blade's astonishing length, its slenderness. He knew the propeller blades of his B-17. Here was a blade with an entirely different purpose.

Katya opened his door, then stood nearby as he stepped down from the van. He wobbled and reached out to her; immediately she took his hand. He hadn't felt it before, but he did now: he shouldn't have had so much vodka.

He heard Johnny ask, "What time shall I pick you up, Mr. Bower?"

Katya looked at her watch. "It's three-forty now." She looked at Walter. "Mr. Bower, may we have the pleasure of your company for another two hours?"

He felt fine. Not tired at all. "My pleasure. My pleasure."

"Wonderful." She turned to Johnny. "Can you pick us up at six?"

"Six'll do." Johnny climbed back into the van.

Holding Katya's arm with one hand, tapping his cane with the other, Walter walked toward the giant feather. Svetlana and Yuri walked beside him, she with a small wicker basket. Walter said to them with growing respect, "This is what you're going to spin in the sky above Balsam Corners?"

"Yes," said Svetlana proudly. "And we like it so much more than missiles and submarines."

They stood four in a row, gazing up at the feather that would not fly upon the wind, but rather would spin as the wind blew upon it.

"Walter," said Yuri, "this company, DanishWind, has installed over twelve thousand turbines in forty countries. Including five hundred in China. Other companies are installing turbines as well, so that around the world, turbines are springing up like mushrooms after rain. But two countries, Walter, two countries, are very slow to put up turbines. Your

America and my Russia still believe in coal and oil. You see, you have your oligarchs too."

Oligarchs? Walter hated to think that his country was run by such people. Yet it was certainly money that carried a candidate into the White House. The big power plants kept burning their coal. The oil boys kept poking their noses toward Alaska. And his daughter Mary, the Adirondack girl who had moved to the Big City, had made sure he understood that the administration's Clear Skies Initiative was "pure bunk." Words, empty words, while the kids today couldn't even eat the fish they caught.

"Yuri," said Walter, "I liked Truman. He was a little guy who cared about all the other little guys."

The four of them walked over to look at the turbine's housing, or "na*celle*," as Yuri called it, almost as big as a white boxcar. "Sveta and I worked inside the nacelle with the DanishWind people all day Friday," said Yuri. "We were checking that everything was in order after the long trip from Denmark."

Walter stared at the white housing that would take something as simple as the wind, and turn it into something as powerful as electricity.

This is why we fought the war, he thought. We fought the war so that others after us could build a better America, could build a better world.

"Whadya think, Walt?" he heard someone ask.

He was enormously pleased to discover Gerald Jacobsen standing beside Katya. Here was the man who quietly made so much possible for so many people. "Well, hello, Mr. Jacobsen. I hear that you've had something to do with all this."

"Oh, not so much. The mountain was already here, and the wind was already blowing." Looking past Walter, Mr. Jacobsen asked Yuri, "Are we on schedule?"

"Yes, sir. The three tower sections will be trucked up on Monday. Tomorrow. The crane will lift the base section into place on Tuesday. The nacelle will be trucked up on Wednesday. On Thursday, the crane will lift the mid section and top section of the tower into place. By Thursday afternoon, we should be able to lift the nacelle and set it atop the tower. They'll truck the blades up Friday, attach them to the hub on Saturday. On Sunday, one week from today, we thank the good Lord for bringing us this far. Then on Monday, the crane will lift the hub and three blades into place. We fly the rotor, as they say. On Tuesday, a small crane inside the nacelle lowers a cable and hook, then lifts up the electrical cable. By Tuesday afternoon, we should be connected. Then on Wednesday, two weeks to the day after the first truck arrived, we throw the switch: we start pumping three megawatts of power into the grid. And then that chair lift," Yuri pointed toward the green chairs gliding up the mountain, "will be powered no more by coal, no more by oil, no more by nuclear, but by the wind."

"That's right," said Mr. Jacobsen, satisfied with the information. "By a breeze not even strong enough to blow off your hat."

Katya quietly asked Mr. Bower, "Can you walk all the way to the chair lift?"

He looked across the grassy flats at the bottom of the ski runs to where the green chairs of the lift were gliding smoothly. He gauged the distance to be about two hundred yards. Then he looked at Katya. "My dear girl, I haven't been to the top of Bobcat Mountain for over twenty years."

Mr. Jacobsen offered, "ol' Bess is parked right nearby, Walter, if you'd like a ride to the chair lift."

"Thank you," said Walter. "But let's see if I can make it. I've been walking on the sidewalk around the nursing home all summer. Let's see if I still have any spring in my step."

So they walked, the five of them together, past the bustling ski chalet—where people sat out on the balcony eating either a late Sunday lunch or an early Sunday dinner—toward a line of people waiting to get on the chair lift. Walter held Katya's arm, though he no longer felt tipsy. Nor at all tired.

Katya and Walter stepped slowly but steadily forward in the line. Yuri and Svetlana followed behind them. Mr. Jacobsen, next in line, was already talking with a student from Utica College.

When the operator saw Walter, he pressed a button and stopped the lift. Gripping Katya's arm, Walter stepped forward until he stood on a spot of worn earth, facing up the mountain. The operator brought the chair slowly forward, then stopped it again. Walter carefully sat down, let go of Katya's arm and shifted himself so that he sat with his weight squarely on the chair. Then he laid his cane over his lap, and held it there with one hand.

The operator lowered a safety gate in front of them. "Are you ready?"

Walter had asked himself that, sixty years ago, in England, every time he climbed into the B-17.

"Ready as I'll ever be," he told the young man.

The chair lifted him and Katya into the air and carried them forward with such smooth grace that he felt as if some angelic hand had lifted them both from the earth.

They floated higher and higher among the treetops: red bushy crowns rippling in the wind. Walter listened to the cable running through the wheels of each green tower. The ride was so gentle, so quiet, so smooth, that he said to Katya, "I don't think I'll need my parachute today."

She looked at him with quiet triumph. "All you need is enough room for dessert."

"Your apple cake?"

"Yes."

"Then I guarantee, I've left enough room."

"Good!"

While they rode up the mountain, she gripped the safety bar with her two young hands; he held the green bar with one old hand, while his other hand held his cane.

Now he noticed, emerging above the upper slopes, the slender red lattice of the boom of the crane, reaching nearly straight up into the cloudy sky. More and more of the boom, and then the base of the crane, became visible as the chair approached the top of the mountain.

"Will you bring me up tomorrow?" he asked Katya. "Will you bring me up every afternoon next week?"

"Of course," she said. "If your van can give us a ride, I'll meet you every afternoon at four o'clock."

"I'd love to watch the turbine go up, step by step."

"Me too."

When the operator at the top saw Walter approaching, he slowed the chair . . . then stopped it when Walter and Katya had reached the unloading platform. The operator, a man with a beard who looked as if he'd weathered half a century of winters atop Bobcat Mountain, lifted the safety gate. "Hello, Walter."

"Hello, Roy!"

Katya eased down first. Walter gripped the crook of his cane, took hold of Katya's arm, then shifted his bottom on the chair until he eased down and stood on his two feet again. Then he looked at Katya and let out a laugh. "By golly, girl, you got me here!"

Beauty filled her face when she teased him, "Never doubt the wiles of a Russian woman."

They stepped off the platform, out of the way, then waited for Svetlana and Yuri to arrive. Katya laughed as she waved to her parents, then she whispered to Walter, "They're as happy as two lovebirds."

Svetlana and Yuri stepped quickly off the moving chair, stepped off the platform and stood beside Walter. Yuri pointed, "The town brought up a truckload of picnic tables."

Walter looked at the green picnic tables scattered around the granite dome, outside of a yellow ribbon that encircled the work area where the red crane stood. "That one's empty," he said, pointing with his cane toward an unoccupied table.

They invited Mr. Jacobsen and the college student for a piece of apple cake. But Mr. Jacobsen thanked them and said that he and Jim, a student of structural engineering, were going to take a closer look at the crane.

So Walter and the family which had adopted him made their way slowly across the glacier-polished granite to a table on the northern side of the peak. "Which way do you want to sit?" asked Katya, pointing at the table's two benches. "Looking toward the crane, or toward the Adirondacks?"

He glanced at the crane, then looked in the other direction at the rolling green-and-crimson carpet of forest. "The Adirondacks."

He sat on the bench with somebody's initials carved in it. Svetlana placed the wicker basket on the table, then took out four plates, four forks, four napkins. She lifted a plastic container out of the basket, then peeled off its lid. Walter smelled the apple cake, moaned softly and said to Katya, "I've been waiting all day for this moment."

He loved to see her smile, loved to see her happy. At least he could still do that for a youngster.

Svetlana set a plastic bottle on the table, with four glasses. "Cold water from the faucet," she explained. "The best water in all my life I have ever known."

Svetlana and Yuri sat on the bench flanking Walter, so that they too could look out at the mountains. Katya sat facing him, then she cut her cake, put a piece on each plate, and served the plates to her three guests.

Taking a first bite, he groaned with pleasure . . . and savored the sparkle in Katya's eyes.

When half the cake was gone, and forks rested on empty plates, the four of them were quiet, too peaceful for words.

Svetlana began to sing quietly in Russian. Katya blended her voice with her mother's voice. Yuri joined them, so that Walter listened to alto on his left, bass on his right, and soprano facing him. The trio sang with such sadness, such longing, and with such precision, that clearly they had sung this song many times before.

When they came to the end, and were silent, pensive, Walter waited a polite moment, then he asked Katya, "Will you translate for me?"

"I'm sorry," she apologized. "Of course."

"It is Borodin," said Svetlana. "Queen Olga's aria in the opera, *Prince Igor*. She misses her homeland."

"Yes," said Katya. "The verses are . . ." She paused, thinking, then she translated line by line,

> "Fly on the wings of wind
> To my native land,
> You, my native song.
> Fly to the place where
> We could sing you freely,
> Where we felt freedom, you and me."

Katya smiled shyly at Walter. "Forgive us for being a little home-sick."

He had been in England, in France, in Spain, in Portugal, then back in England again, before finally they sent him home. "I quite understand."

And now, seated atop a small Adirondack mountain, he felt that home had become something larger than the little town tucked into the woods below.

CHAPTER 36

Once Tony got rolling, he didn't like to stop. Once he was cruising, he liked neither the interruption of his training, nor the interruption of his thoughts.

But by the time he had reached Raquette Lake, twenty miles up the road, he needed to refill his water bottle. He stopped at the diner near the marina, said hello to Frank, busy as always at the grill, then handed the waitress his empty plastic bottle. "Thanks."

While she was filling it at the kitchen tap, Tony noticed a mayonnaise jar on the diner's counter, with a picture of a little girl taped to it. He leaned closer and read the hand-printed text below the picture: "Please help Ernestine. Our daughter has leukemia. God bless you." There was a phone number.

He looked inside the jar: a few bills, mostly coins.

The fucking bastards, he thought.

He reached into his left sock, pulled out a folded twenty-dollar bill. He asked the waitress when she came back with his water bottle if she could give him change. "Thanks."

He folded a five-dollar bill and slid it through the slot in the lid of the mayonnaise jar. He knew that most people up here in the woods couldn't afford to give more than coins and singles. But why should they have to? Why should two parents have to face the worst nightmare imaginable, when their child becomes horribly sick, and yet on top of that, they have to worry about where on earth they're going to find the money to pay the bills? One sock in the jaw was enough; they didn't need two.

He left a dollar tip on the counter, called "G'bye, Frank!", then stepped out the door and glanced up at the sky, mother-of-pearl with darker clouds scudding from the east. As he set the water bottle in its rack, he thought again, The fucking bastards. There ain't going to be any mayonnaise jars when I'm in the White House.

He mounted his bike, pedaled across the gravel parking lot, rolled onto the smooth asphalt highway, and tried to get his mind back into the biking.

Traffic on Route 28, the main two-lane highway winding through the Adirondacks, was heavy today. A lot of leaf peepers were out on a Sunday in autumn. He wore his yellow reflective vest and red helmet; he was clearly visible. He kept to the right edge of the highway, in the apron marked (usually) by a white stripe. He was wary of cracked and broken asphalt, and the occasional bottle. It was always a risk, riding on the highway.

He stopped a second time, at the gas station in Blue Mountain Lake, to put air into his rear tire. He liked to keep his tires right at 100 psi, and he could feel his rear a bit soft. At the air pump on the side of the gas station, he knelt down and fit the brass end of the air hose over the tire's nozzle. As he squeezed the lever and watched the pressure gauge, filling the tire from 83 to 100, he heard a jovial voice at the gas pump call out, "Fill 'er up!" A boy Tony's age—a boy spending his Sunday morning at a gas station to make a few bucks—said "Yes, sir" as he lifted the nozzle from the gas pump and inserted it into the gas tank of a black, Mountain-Man-Macho-Style SUV.

Tony screwed the little black cap back on the air nozzle, then he knelt at his front tire and checked its pressure. 97; he gave it a touch, 100. Good.

He coiled the air hose on its rack. Then, without looking at the SUV or the guy inside, he got rolling again.

He hated these stops. He just wanted to cruise.

He rode through the village of Long Lake without stopping, although for a moment he considered browsing through Hoss's General store, one of his favorite bookstores in the Park. But today he just wanted to cruise. He had been dreaming since the first day of school about the Newcomb Road, a long rolling stretch across one of the remotest parts of the Adirondacks.

Heading east with the wind in his face, he pumped uphill out of Long Lake to the high country, where the road, now flanking a mountainside, sometimes rose above the trees. He swept his gaze across the immense reddish-green forest rolling away to the horizon; his eyes paused on patches of orange. He liked to look ahead for a mile or two along the dip and rise in the gray mountain road reaching out to meet a gray mountain sky.

When he was cruising on the Newcomb Road, he could feel the wind under his wings.

He loved his road bike, a Trek 1200, silver and black, with twenty-seven gorgeous gears. The bike was so light, at twenty-two pounds, that he could hold it for several seconds at the end of his outstretched arm. Because he had worked full-time for three summers at the bike shop, Sunny had knocked a hundred dollars off the price. Sunny had wanted only two hundred down; the rest he would take, little by little, out of Tony's wages on Saturdays through his senior year.

For the first annual Tour d'Adirondack, Tony would graduate up to a Trek 5000, a two-thousand-dollar bike, with the same frame that Lance had ridden to Paris in 1999. Tony didn't know how he could manage the two grand, especially as he would be leaving for some university right after the race. But he was determined, win or lose, to show the world that an Adirondack rider could be a top contender. And that meant, a professional bike.

He sailed at a good clip across the bridge over Fishing Brook; he was pushing, pushing, his legs tired but not aching, his heart thumping but not pounding.

Over the sound of his tires on the asphalt, and the light running of his chain, he heard high above him, "Kee-heeeeeeeee. Kee-heeeeeeeeeeee." A broad-winged hawk, perhaps a pair, for they usually hunted together. He glanced up, but with his helmet on, he couldn't see the hawk.

So he just listened. "Kee-heeeeeeeeeee." Then a fainter, faraway, "Kee-heeeeee." Yes, there were two, hunting as a pair.

He passed one of his favorite cemeteries in the Adirondacks, tucked into a hill just outside the hamlet of Newcomb. He rolled past houses sprinkled along the highway, crossed the narrow Hudson—he was close to the headwaters—sprinted the final four miles, then braked and rolled into a park with an excellent view north toward the big burly mountains of the High Peaks.

Squeezing the brakes, he came to a halt beside his favorite picnic table, set apart from the others. He liked to have a snack at this table, while he gazed at peak after peak, each of them distinct. Leaning his bike against the southern bench, he sat on the weathered wood of the table with his feet on the northern bench. The clouds were high enough that the peaks marched clearly from east to west across the northern horizon. He felt like a king on his throne.

Once he had caught his breath, he took off his small yellow backpack, unzipped a pouch and found an apricot-oatmeal energy bar. He took a bite, then settled his gaze on Mount Marcy, the highest peak in the Adirondacks. He had climbed Marcy a few years ago in June, with his parents. The picture he had taken of them on the granite peak, holding hands and grinning like two kids at the top of the world, now stood on the mantel over the wood-burning stove.

He began to hear what Miss Applegate called his "voice." Reaching into his backpack, he found a small notebook with a pen clipped inside it. He flipped past pages of scribbled poems, until he came to a blank page about a third of the way through the book. He took the cap off the pen, then began to write:

Star Dust
The slums of the world are one slum.
From the same dust of the same exploded star,
We spun, and slowly gathered into a small ball
Orbiting around a larger hot one.
The dust beneath our feet
Is the same as the feet themselves.
This bread we break or do not break with one another:
Star dust.
This wine in fellowship or sanctity or loneliness partaken,

Once reached in expanding waves of radiant dust across
The universe,
The heavens,
The dark.
Who are we not to share?

He put the cap back on the pen, clipped the pen inside the notebook, slipped the notebook into his backpack, then stared again at the parade of jagged mountains. He would type the poem at home this evening, then give it to Miss Applegate tomorrow morning.

He ate a second energy bar, and washed it down with a drink of water from his bottle. Putting on his backpack, he took a last loving glance at the High Peaks.

Then he shoved off for the long journey home.

CHAPTER 37

Now the Big Week began.

On Monday, September 8, 2003, the three blue flatbed trucks carrying the three long white cylinders managed to make their way up the old timber road. Going one by one all the way up and all the way down, they first wound through the forest up the mountain's western flank, then climbed more steeply around the back, and then made a final turn toward the granite summit.

Folks from town began to ride the chair lift up the mountain at eight o'clock on Monday morning. The audience that gathered atop Bobcat Mountain applauded as each of the three blue trucks rumbled up the final stretch in low gear, reached the broad granite dome with its precious cargo, and came to a halt where the crane could lower its cable over the cylinder. Each triumphant truck gave three loud blasts of its diesel horn. The crowd roared with a cheer.

On Tuesday, the giant red crane set the first cylinder of the tower upright on the concrete foundation. The crane lowered the cylinder with such precision that the workers in their orange uniforms were able to line up the ring of bolts in the concrete plug with matching holes in the bottom flange of the cylinder. Then the workers turned their wrenches on the nuts that would hold the tower against winter blizzards and summer thunderstorms.

When folks rode the chair lift down the mountain later that afternoon, they had the satisfaction of having seen the first piece of the wind turbine set in place.

At dawn on Wednesday morning, a flatbed truck carrying a large yellow bulldozer made its way up the old timber road. The truck was unable, however, with its heavy load, to reach the summit. The bulldozer backed off the truck, then cleared a path for itself a short distance into the hemlock and maple. The empty flatbed truck now rumbled up the last stretch to the summit, drove on an improvised loop of gravel and beams around the work site, then headed back down the mountain. The bulldozer emerged from its parking spot, crawled capably to the summit, then waited for the job which it would do later in the day.

The long blue truck that carried the nacelle now began its climb up Bobcat Mountain. The DanishWind people had studied every bend in the road; they were certain that their long but flexible truck could make the ascent.

A crowd of well over a thousand had gathered on the summit. Most of the shops in Balsam Corners were closed. School let out at noon; the yellow school buses brought students, teachers and staff to the Ski Center parking lot. Then everybody rode the chair lift. Thus by one o'clock, every kid in town was on top of the mountain, waiting for the turbine's big white housing, atop the huge blue truck, to reach the summit.

The truck was specially designed, with three swivel points rather than just one, and thus was able to follow the old logging trail. Because of the weight of the nacelle, sixty-eight metric tonnes, the truck needed help in the final ascent to the summit. The bulldozer backed slowly down, fastened a towing cable to the front of the truck, then roared and rumbled and vented blasts of black smoke as it pulled the truck and nacelle the last two hundred yards to the summit.

When the nacelle was safely atop Bobcat Mountain, within reach of the crane, the big blue truck gave a long triumphant blast of its diesel horn, followed by four short blasts. The crowd roared with triumph: their dream was one step closer.

* * *

On Thursday morning, the crane lifted the middle cylinder of the tower into place, and then the upper cylinder. The white tube now stood eighty meters tall: two hundred and fifty feet.

On Thursday afternoon, the crane lifted the sixty-eight-tonne nacelle into the dark gray sky, swung the tapered white box with its blue stripe over the white tower, then set the nacelle atop the tower with absolute precision. The crowd of two thousand gathered on the summit had listened to the weather report that morning: they had brought rain gear and umbrellas. Nothing short of bolts of lightning was going to keep them from watching the nacelle lifted into place.

The rain held off until about five o'clock, when gusts of cold drizzle drenched the folks still riding the chair lift down the mountain.

On Friday, using a narrow-radius turning technique developed on mountain roads in Austria, the three blue trucks carrying the three white blades made their way one by one up the mountain.

Since the blades were relatively light, at 4.8 tonnes each, the trucks were able to reach the summit. As each blue truck brought its long white feather to the top of Bobcat Mountain, the crowd cheered with triumph.

Folks turned their faces into the breeze that swept across the summit from the clear blue sky to the north; soon they would put that breeze to work.

On Saturday, the crane lifted the first blade into the crystalline blue sky. With two triangulated cables running from the crane's hook to the ends of a yellow beam, then two straps from ends of the beam looped around the blade, the crane slowly hoisted the horizontal blade, then held it in place eighty meters up, so that the blade could be attached to the hub. Workers inside the hub tightened nuts on a ring of bolts.

The crane lifted and positioned the second blade; workers tightened nuts on a second ring of bolts.

The crane lifted and positioned the third blade; workers tightened nuts on a third and final ring of bolts.

When the cables were released from the third blade, the completed wind turbine stood motionless on the mountaintop. People stared up at the white box with three slender feathers, waiting up there in the sky to go to work. After the long and fierce debate, after a dozen studies, after the arduous process of government and Adirondack Park approvals, after a spring and summer of preparing the infrastructure, and after a heroic effort by the truck drivers and crane operators and the Danish-Wind engineers, the New Guy in Town was finally here.

On Sunday, the chair lift operated after church: from one in the afternoon until six. People from Albany and Syracuse rode the lift; people from Lake Placid and Saranac Lake rode the lift. Radio and television crews interviewed the people of Balsam Corners while they stood on the summit of Bobcat Mountain with the Adirondacks rolling in the background; occasionally the television cameras would point nearly straight up for a shot of the stationary blades.

On Monday, a small crane located inside the nacelle lowered a hook on a cable down the inside of the hollow tower, then lifted eighty meters of electrical cable that would connect the turbine and its transformer to a substation at the edge of the granite dome. The substation was already connected by a cable than ran through the forest down the mountain to the New York State grid. Once fully connected, the turbine was thus "commissioned": ready to operate.

During Monday and Tuesday, the DanishWind engineers conducted a two-day test cycle, during which the blades began to spin, though power did not yet enter the grid.

On Wednesday afternoon, a DanishWind engineer inside the nacelle flipped a switch. A DanishWind engineer at the substation flipped another switch. A third engineer phoned the Balsam Corners firehouse. At 2:47 in the afternoon, the firehouse blew the noon whistle. The multitude of thousands gathered on the mountain heard the whistle and roared with a mighty cheer. Their wind turbine was feeding the grid, and the grid was feeding their town.

As the people of Balsam Corners rode the chair lift down the mountain—a chair lift powered by the wind—they knew that this evening, the wind would light their homes. The wind would light their streets. The wind would heat the water in their electric teapots, the wind would heat the water for their bath.

Tomorrow morning at eight o'clock, when the first bell rang at Balsam Corners Central School, it would be the wind that powered the clanging bell.

CHAPTER 38

During the Big Week, Tony spent so much time after school on the mountaintop taking pictures, zooming his telephoto lens on both the tower as it was constructed and the spectators as they watched, that on Wednesday afternoon, a man wearing a blue DanishWind uniform walked over to the yellow tape that divided the work site from the ring of spectators and called, "Hello, young fellow. Are you shooting for the newspaper?"

Tony could hear an accent, probably Danish.

"No, I'm taking pictures for a soldier in Iraq. He's from Balsam Corners, and I thought he'd like to see what's going on."

The man stared at Tony for a moment, as if he might say something about the war. He was younger than Tony's father, and had the stub of a blond beard. Then he took off his work glove and reached his hand over the yellow ribbon. "I am Svend Nielsen, project manager. You are welcome to take all the pictures you want."

"Thank you, Mr. Nielsen. I'm Tony Delmontico, a high school senior here in Balsam Corners."

"If you would like some close-ups of the men working, I could give you a hard hat and you could come on the site."

Tony had been aching for days to get closer. "Thank you. I would very much like to get some portraits of the crew at work."

Mr. Nielsen lifted the yellow ribbon. "Come."

Passing from the world of spectator to the world of journalist, Tony knelt down and stepped under the yellow ribbon. Mr. Nielsen led him across a flat bed of gravel laid over the irregular granite to a small trailer, where he fetched a blue hard hat from a shelf and a yellow vest from a bin. Tony set his camera on a table, then put on the vest and hard hat. "Thanks. They're a perfect fit." He picked up his camera.

"You are welcome," said Mr. Nielsen, his blue eyes firm but friendly.

They stepped out the trailer door into the late afternoon sunshine. With a photographer's eye, Tony quickly scanned the work site: one white cylinder already stood upright, bolted to the concrete base; two cylinders waited on the ground, and the nacelle waited as well; a dozen men were busy at various jobs. The giant red crane towered above everything. The small white crane looked like its sidekick.

He could shoot ten rolls here.

"Ja," said Mr. Nielsen, "if you have any questions, you are welcome to ask the men."

"Thanks." Tony already had a dozen questions, especially about the schedule. He didn't want to miss the hoisting of the three blades because he was sitting in some stupid classroom. But just then Mr. Nielsen received a call in his hip speaker-phone, "Hey Svend, when's the guy comin' to grade my pad?"

Mr. Nielsen pushed the button of the microphone on his chest, "Virgil, how far is your next crawl?"

"Ten meters southwest."

"Ja. I come see you. Ten four."

Mr. Nielsen pointed across the work site at a man in the glass cabin atop the giant red crawler crane. "I shall introduce you to Virgil. To-morrow he will lift a sixty-eight tonne nacelle to a height of eighty meters, then he will position it within half a millimeter while the crew at the top of the tower line up their ring of bolts with the nacelle's ring of holes, and then torque the nuts. Virgil's touch is the best in the business."

Tony looked almost straight up at the long slender red boom of the crane, reaching into the hazy blue sky where tomorrow it would lift the last two cylinders of the tower, and then set the nacelle atop them. "What time will you lift the nacelle?"

"Nei, hard to say," said Mr. Nielsen, leading Tony across the work site. "Your weather report says rain coming tomorrow. We will do our best."

They now stood beside the chest-high tread of a crane that looked as if it could pick up Balsam Corners Central School, swing the red brick building across the sky, then set it down on the backside of a nearby mountain. Virgil came out of his cab and stood above them on a red metal walkway. He pointed down here and there at low spots in the gravel where, as Tony could see, the tremendous weight of the crane's treads had crushed the gravel down. Apparently the crane's pad had to be built back up between maneuvers.

Virgil spoke with a strong Southern accent—Tony would later learn that Virgil was from North Carolina—while Svend, inspecting the various spots that needed fixing, spoke English with his Danish accent. Tony smiled at the musical mix.

Then Mr. Nielsen said, "Virgil, this is Tony, a student from town. He'll be taking some pictures. Try not to run him over."

Virgil looked down at Tony. From the lines on his weathered face, he had operated cranes for at least three decades. "Hook yer trouser belt on meh fishhook," he said, pointing up at the crane's massive hook, dangling at the end of the cable at least two hundred feet above the mountaintop, "and I'll give ya the best view in town."

Tony laughed. He wouldn't ask Virgil yet if he could take his portrait; he'd wait until they got to know each other a little better. "Thanks. I'll make sure to wear a good belt tomorrow."

As he rode his bike home that evening—following a meat loaf dinner at the Maple Diner, and a couple of hours at the library—he stopped at Mr. Shepherd's house on Blueberry Lake, to ask if he could miss classes on Thursday and Friday. "I'd like to take pictures of the two cylinders going up, and then the nacelle. Sir, I wouldn't ask this if I didn't think it was important. It's partly for Bobby Dyson, but it's also for the town. This is history, and I'd like to try to capture it in pictures."

Tony had taken his bike helmet off and held it in his arm as he spoke with Mr. Shepherd in the glow of a porch light. Mr. Shepherd looked tired; running a school during the first weeks of September was no easy job.

"Tony," said the principal, "shoot fifty wall-hangers, and you can have an exhibit in the gym."

"You're on."

They shook hands, then the journalist hopped back on his bike and peddled up the driveway into the night.

When Tony looked out his bedroom window on Thursday morning, he saw a charcoal gray sky that boded rain. He packed his rain suit and collapsible umbrella into his backpack, along with his camera and a dozen rolls of film, so that, short of high winds and lightning on the mountaintop, he could take pictures in the rain.

He rode his bike to school, spoke with all of his teachers, and wrote down the assignments for Friday and the weekend. Then he pumped his bike up the mountain road to the chair lift, where he locked his bike to a young maple; scarlet leaves were scattered on the ground as he knelt to fasten the lock. He sat on the gliding green chair with his backpack on his lap at—he looked at his watch—five minutes to nine. He was on the peak by nine o'clock, right on time.

He picked up his hard hat and vest at the office trailer, then went to work. He photographed the men as they attached the crane's enormous hook to a red beam bolted across one end of a cylinder, then photographed the long white cylinder as the crane lifted it into the gray-black sky and set it with precision atop the tower's first cylinder, already bolted to the earth. He could hear the faint rattling growl of workers inside the two cylinders, spinning nuts on the ring of bolts that connected the circular seam.

He took pictures of the hoisting of the third cylinder, and its positioning atop the other two. The tower now looked like a huge white stovepipe, two hundred and fifty feet tall.

A truck arrived at the work site—Tony had heard it laboring up the old timber road for several minutes—with the white hub on its flatbed. The hub, looking much like a Martian flying saucer, was lifted from the truck by the smaller crane, then attached to one end of the nacelle. Tony could see the three flat circles on the steel hub, each with a ring of holes about six feet in diameter, where the three blades would be attached.

His mother had made four tuna sandwiches for him; she had also packed two apples, five stalks of celery filled with peanut butter, and a box of raisins. He had lunch with the guys—the town of Balsam Corners had provided the workers with a couple of picnic tables—and began to learn their names. Chris was a Mohawk from the Akwasasne Reserve up north on the St. Lawrence Seaway. Larry was married to an Oneida woman; they lived near the Oneida Reserve just west of Utica. Blake Patrick was a Southern gentleman from Tennessee; he shared with Tony a couple of homemade brownies which his wife had mailed to him. Tony decided that he had better bring up a bag of apples in his backpack tomorrow.

After lunch—the rain still held off, though the wind was getting gusty—the men attached the crane's hook to the top of the nacelle. The crane then hoisted the sixty-eight-tonne nacelle about seven feet. Larry, Chris, and another fellow whose name Tony hadn't yet learned gathered beneath the hovering nacelle and, reaching up with their tools, readied it for placement atop the tower.

Tony circled the work site with his camera until he found the right angle to shoot the vertical white tower, the nearly vertical red crane, and the white nacelle with the hub attached at one end as it rose into the threatening heavens. The men told him they didn't want rain to fall inside the open tower; once the nacelle was in place, it would keep the tower dry.

Two long ropes, attached to opposite ends of the slowly rising nacelle, slung down to two teams of men who stood near the outer edge of the work site. The ends of the ropes were secured by winches fastened to the backs of two pickup trucks. Three men held each rope in their gloves hands, while a fourth man worked the winch, tightening, or letting out. Thus the two crews could slowly turn the dangling nacelle to the needed position. Though the long ropes bowed from their own weight, they were otherwise taut as the men, following Svend's instructions over Larry's hip speaker-phone, shifted the nacelle by increments, then steadied it against the wind.

The crane lifted the nacelle above the height of the tubular tower. Then slowly the red boom swung the nacelle over the top of the tower. On Larry's phone, the men could hear Svend, at the top of the tower, speaking to Virgil in the crane's cab, giving him instructions. The crane shifted by increments, lowered the nacelle by increments, until the gap closed. Now Tony could hear the first faint growl of a nut spun onto a bolt. He had taken five or six pictures as the nacelle had risen into the sky, and now he took a picture of the white box with a tiny man in an orange suit standing atop it. Tony, who never cared for heights, took the picture quickly, before the wind up there blew that crazy guy into orbit.

He could hear applause from the crowd ringing the work site. The installation of the nacelle was another triumph. His parents were among the spectators, as was Mr. Jacobsen. He occasionally waved to them.

Once the nacelle was fully secured, the ground crew packed up tools and lashed down gear in readiness for the storm now sweeping a curtain of gray rain over the hills to the west. Tony put his zoom telephoto Nikon FA, an old workhorse that his uncle had given him on his fifteenth birthday, into a plastic bag, then into his backpack. He put on his rain suit, but did not bother, in the rising wind, with the umbrella. Cold wet gusts battered his back as he stood with the crew beside the tread of the crane, each man holding a blue metal cup of hot coffee while they discussed the work schedule for tomorrow. The blades would be trucked up one by one, lifted off the trucks by the small crane and laid along the edge of the work site. They must be properly lashed down. They would be hoisted up to the hub on Saturday, weather permitting.

Tony rode down the chair lift with his mother in a driving rain. He declined his parents' invitation to ride home with them in the red Jeep, with his bike in its rack on the roof. He did give them his backpack, but he wanted to ride home in the rain. In part, he didn't want to miss a day of training. But also, in a vague way, not thoroughly clear in his thoughts, he wanted to thank the rain for holding off until the turbine stood ready for its first storm.

He could tell on Friday morning, even before he got out of bed, that the air flowing through his two open bedroom windows was cold: a north wind from Canada. Peering past boughs of hemlock, he could see hints of blue in the still overcast sky. Cold clean air, Canada's finest export, would sweep away the clouds and give the crew a day of sunshine.

After a breakfast of oatmeal—his mother made a big pot of oatmeal every morning "for my two men"—he rode his bike into the wind along Blueberry Lake, bypassed school, pumped up the mountain road, and was on the chair lift by 8:45. Today, three trucks would bring three giant white feathers up the mountain. He didn't want to miss a moment.

The first truck arrived at 9:15, after a slow hour-and-a-half journey up the old timber road; the tip of the blade extended beyond the cab of the truck, and a few trees had to be cut along the way so that the tip could swing around a curve. The long blue truck growled in first gear as it emerged from a forest of hemlock and maple, drove across the flattened granite dome to the gravel work site, and halted near the crane. When it blew its diesel horn—a blast that echoed from nearby mountains—the crowd roared with triumph.

While the crew unfastened the straps over the blade, the smaller crane rolled into position. It lowered a yellow beam over the blade; the beam was supported by two short cables triangulating down from the crane's hook. Two straps hung down from near the ends of the yellow beam. The crew slung the straps beneath the blade and then attached them to the beam. Tony could see that a vertical black line at the center of the beam was positioned exactly above a small black-and-red circle on the blade: its center of gravity.

Now the crane lifted the 4.8 tonne feather from the bed of the truck, while two teams of men controlled the ropes attached to the ends of the feather. Tony could see that the men had a bit of a job, for as soon as the crane lifted the blade from the truck, the breeze sweeping the mountaintop caught the blade and swung it slightly.

Rolling slowly on its wheels across the gravel, the small crane set the blade down at the edge of the work site; each end of the blade was supported by a wooden pallet. The men quickly secured the tip of the blade with a length of rope to a block of concrete which had already been positioned. Unless a tornado hit the peak of Bobcat Mountain, the blade would stay put.

The long blue truck, designed with a turning radius of only fourteen meters, worked its way around the work site and then disappeared into the forest. It would make the journey down the mountain a bit more quickly, and then the second truck would start up.

Tony walked over to the blade and stood at its tip, where he could see along the length of the gently curving feather, proportioned like an eagle's pinion stretched to twice its normal length. The surface was shiny white. He reached up his right hand and touched the smooth tip, lay his palm flat against the tip, then began to walk, rubbing his hand along the cool smooth length of the blade. He walked for forty-four meters, a hundred and forty-three feet, until he reached the round end of the blade: a stump of quill that would attach to the hub. The blade was manufactured, as Svend had explained to him, from strips of wood laid over with a carbonfibre-epoxy blend, which was then heated in a long oven. The stub of the quill was made of steel; Tony inspected the ring of holes about six feet in diameter that would match a ring of bolts in the hub.

Then, raising his left hand and pressing it against the blade, he walked back all the way to the tip. This blade would sweep the sky for the next twenty years. Or more. He would be thirty-seven years old, perhaps a father with children, before this blade would be replaced. In twenty years, the wind turbine would generate almost three hundred million kilowatts. In twenty years, it would reduce the world's pollution by more than a quarter-million tons of CO_2. He patted his hand on the blade's very tip, as if he patted the neck of a tall white stallion, a pat of encouragement, a pat of gratitude.

The second blade arrived at 1:05, and the third at 4:10. The small crane lifted the blades from their trucks and set them on pallets parallel to the first blade, ready to be hoisted by the big crane tomorrow. The sky had cleared by noon to a breezy blue. The wind would have to settle quite a bit before the blades could be hoisted to the height of eighty meters. "They're like sails," said Larry. "We can lift the nacelle in a wind, but we like a calm day for the blades."

Thus on Saturday morning, as Tony ate his oatmeal, he looked out the window with profound satisfaction at the unrippled surface of Blueberry Lake. A blue dome of clear Canadian air now sat upon the Adirondacks. Today was the day.

At 9:05, he watched the big red crane lower the yellow beam on triangulated cables over the first blade. From the beam hung straps which the men wrapped under the blade and fastened to the beam, with the blade's center of gravity directly under the crane's hook. Tony stood with Chris, Larry and Blake as they readied the tag line attached to the blade's tip. Jerry tended the winch fastened to the end of a dirty black pickup. A second crew, clustered about a hundred and fifty feet from the first crew, handled the tag line to the blade's round stub.

When both tag lines were ready, Virgil lifted the long white feather from the earth; the men tightened their lines, holding the suspended blade steady. As Virgil slowly lifted the blade—an enormous white quill ready to scribe some epic poem across the blue sky—the men carefully let out their lines. Listening to the speaker-phone on Larry's hip, Tony could hear Virgil's instructions to the tag line crews, as well as Svend's instructions from up in the hub. Tony listened to the steady flow of instructions and cautions and occasional curses as the blade rose to the height of the hub at the end of the nacelle.

Now he could hear Svend's Danish English trading back and forth with Virgil's Southern English as Virgil brought the round stub of the blade incrementally toward the connection point on the hub. A gust—just a faint gust—brushed the blade, so that the tag line gave Chris, Larry and Blake a good tug, and Svend cursed in Danish. But with "A bump to the left, Virgil," and "Lower your wire, Virgil," Svend and his crew of four up in the hub were able to line up the first bolt. Now Tony and the ground crew could hear the faint growl of the first nut being torqued into place.

"That's it," said Blake, always generous with his explanations to Tony, whom he called "Newspaper Man." "They start with a bolt at the top, connecting the blade ring with the hub ring. Then they work down, bringing the two rings flat together."

"Give me another ton, Virgil."

Virgil eased the load by one ton, closing the clamshell slightly.

"Another ton, Virgil."

Virgil eased his cable slightly. The ground crew could hear the faint burr of nuts being torqued.

Gradually, all of the bolts passed through all of the holes and were firmly secured.

"Thank you, Virgil," said Svend. "Good job." He said "yob."

Virgil eased the cable completely, then slowly swung the crane so that the loose straps hanging from the yellow beam moved along the blade toward the hub, where a man in an orange suit and safety harness reached out through a hatch door and released the straps from the blade. The crane now slowly swung the beam with its two drooping straps away from the hub, then lowered the beam to fetch the second blade.

Once the first blade was fully secured, a turning gear inside the nacelle—a temporary piece of equipment used for the installation of the blades, powered by a generator roaring at the bottom of the tower—turned the gears in the nacelle, which in turn rotated the hub, so that the newly installed blade swung counterclockwise from its horizontal position at three o'clock up to two and then to one o'clock, then past twelve and down to eleven, where the hub was locked. Now at three o'clock was another connecting spot, ready for the next blade.

The second blade began its journey upward at 10:45; a slight breeze had risen as the morning progressed, but it was not strong enough to swing the blade unduly as the second white feather rose into the blue sky. Once again, Svend and Virgil traded brief instructions and occasional epithets as the blade was brought incrementally toward the hub and then connected. Tony could hear the hub crew torquing.

"Good yob," said Svend over the speaker-phone.

"Y'all welcome," replied Virgil.

Once the second blade was fully secured, the turning gear again rotated the hub counterclockwise, so that the newly installed blade swung up to noon and then over to eleven o'clock; the first blade was now at seven o'clock. At three o'clock, the third connecting point was ready for the third blade.

Looking up at the nearly completed wind turbine, Tony remembered the question which Mr. Jacobsen had asked, "What are the cathedrals of our age?" He knew that he was watching the construction of something more than a machine which would provide clean energy. It would uplift humanity as well, by beckoning the human spirit to awaken more fully, to rise to new heights, to reach more generously around the curve of the planet.

Then the crew had lunch. When they took off their hard hats, the warm September sun shone on their dirty faces and white foreheads. Each man sat with a happy groan on the bench of the picnic table. Tony shared his apples from Cortland County, just south of Utica; Blake shared his brownies from Tennessee.

The third blade, the final piece of the wind turbine, began its journey upward at 1:05, when the sun arching over the rolling red hills of the Adirondacks was at its zenith. When the blade was about half-way up, Larry said to Tony, "Put your hand on the tag line."

Three men now held the tag line, gripping it with gloves while they leaned their weight against it. A fourth man minded the line where it wrapped around the winch. The men holding the line sometimes pulled gently, sometimes let the line out gently, and sometimes they held steady. The man on the winch made sure that they never lost control of the line, especially by losing the line itself.

The half-inch rope rose with a big belly in it up to the "sock" on the tip of the rising blade. The canvas sock fitted over the tip, and was secured by a line to the round hub, a line which could be released from the hub. Thus the tag line was not fastened to the blade itself, but to the canvas sock. Despite its belly, the line was taut from the tip of the feather to the hands of the men.

Tony took his camera into his left hand, then placed his right hand on the tag line. Wrapping his fingers around it, he felt the line vibrate. "Is that the wind making the line vibrate?" he asked Larry. "Or is it the blade?"

"The blade," said Larry. "You can feel, it wants to go to work."

Tony knew the tugging nibble of a bass taking a worm at the end of his fishing line. Now he felt something far more vibrant and insistent: as if he held the rein to a racehorse, trembling with energy, ready to gallop. He felt the giant feather trembling in the wind, ready to catch it, ready to fly in eternal circles.

The crew let the tag line out steadily as the blade rose toward the hub. They held firmly when the blade reached the height of the hub. Now they pulled in a bit as the crane swung the horizontal blade toward three o'clock on the hub. Tony was still holding onto the tag line when he heard the first torquing from the hub. Though the quill was now being connected, the tip of the feather never stopped quivering.

Virgil lowered his load by increments, "down a ton . . . down a ton," while the crew in the hub torqued the final ring of bolts.

"Good yob, Virgil."

"Y'all welcome, Svend."

The tag line crews held firm until, about a minute later, Svend phoned them, "Ease the tag lines, ease the tag lines. Thank you, yentlemen."

With reluctance, Tony took his hand off the line. Larry, Chris and Drake eased off, while Jerry slackened the line on the winch.

Once the third blade was fully secured, the turning gear rotated the completed rotor counterclockwise, so that as each blade reached down toward six o'clock, its sock fell off.

Now the assembled wind turbine stood towering above them; its three blades, not locked, but slowly freewheeling in the breeze that caressed them, moved slowly now and then, making one rotation—with many pauses—in two or three minutes. The angle of the nacelle and thus the angle of the blades was such that as the long inner curve of each blade swept up through twelve o'clock, the smooth white length of the curve caught the light of the sun and, for three or four seconds, cupped a long radiant sheen. Tony raised his lens toward that sheen, where the sun touched the three-petaled daisy in the immense blue sky.

Tony's parents brought up three Chinese dinners, which they ate at one of the picnic tables on the spectators' side of the yellow ribbon. His parents offered to take him home in the Jeep, but Tony didn't want to leave yet. The sun would set at about a quarter after seven. The sky was still cloudless, the air extremely clear. The stars would be crystalline tonight. That's what Tony wanted to see: he wanted to look almost straight up at the slender black silhouette of the wind turbine against the stars.

He kissed his mother on her cheek, then stepped beneath the yellow ribbon and put his hard hat back on. "Thanks for dinner," he said with a wave to his parents. Then he walked across the gravel and sat alone at the picnic table on the work site, his camera in its case on the table, his backpack on the bench beside him. The orange sun became darker red and more swollen as it descended toward the maroon-black hills.

He watched the shadow of some distant Adirondack mountain as it crept up the tall cylindrical tower. The shrinking upper portion of the tower was lit an apricot-yellow. By the time the shadow reached the bottom of the nacelle, the white box and slowly freewheeling blades were pumpkin orange.

Then the sun vanished, and the turbine became pale gray against the milky blue sky.

The first star that Tony spotted was of course Vega, straight up in the crux between two dark blades, though he could not as yet see the other stars in the constellation Lyra. The second star was Arcturus, rusty red in the west, about a third of the way up the sky. Arcturus was the bright foot of a figure that slowly appeared in the darkening turquoise sky, a figure made of four stars: one the foot, one the face, and the other two the uplifted hands at ten o'clock and two o'clock. The figure's right hand (his own right hand, though it is the hand on the left as Tony looked up at him) held a bowl made of a half-dozen faint stars, some so faint that he had to stare carefully to see them all. And what was in that bowl? Perhaps it was a bowl of celestial rice, to be shared. To be shared.

The sky had fully darkened to a radiant black, and Cygnus the white swan was sailing along the exquisitely crystalline Milky Way, straight overhead and thus high above the slender black blades of the wind turbine, when Tony heard what Miss Applegate called his voice. He took his notebook out of his backpack, then wrote the day and the date at the top of the page, "Saturday evening, September 13, 2003," in the faint glow of starlight. Though he could not easily read what he had neatly written, he could see the black writing on the white paper, and thus could write line by line down the page.

On a Starry Night

Look at all that flash and tatter out there:
Nuclear sparks hurtling through a void
Laced with waves of energy.
And spinning as happy as could be
In the midst of that vast celestial desert
Is Earth, blessed with water, blessed with land,
Blessed with a gentle, steady dose of sunshine:
An oasis which the Creator chose as a cradle.

Matter which has been ordered into the form of life
Seems to be only a tiny fraction
Of all the matter in the universe.
Most matter seems to be unliving,
Unless we believe that fiery gases and chunks of frozen nitrogen
Are alive.
But only a small portion of living matter
Thinks,
Unless we believe that viruses and vegetables and ancient sequoias
Can think.

And only a small, small portion of thinking matter
Ponders its origin,
Unless we believe that apes and elephants and the singing whales
Can ponder.
That leaves
Us.
We see no clear bridge between star and starfish,
Nor between starfish and human child,
And so we ponder how we came to be.

There must have been some force that challenged
The randomness of existence,
And won.

Tony looked up at the towering black wind turbine. The blades no longer moved, for the breeze had settled at dusk.

But as the wind turbine seemed completely at home as it stood atop the mountain, so it seemed completely at home among the stars.

Part III

A SOLDIER COMES HOME

CHAPTER 39

Katya sat in her rocking chair beside Mr. Bower, the both of them gently rocking as they looked at the forest outside the window. It was late afternoon; this was when the deer came out of the woods and into the grassy yard.

While she kept a sharp watch along the edge of the trees, Katya said, "When I first came to the school in Balsam Corners, two years ago, I thought it was so strange that there was no history room in the school. No room with photographs of the veterans from the town. No photographs of other famous people from the town. Not even a photograph of the original school. The classroom where we have history is just a classroom, with maps of America, maps of the world," she shrugged, "but no pictures of the soldiers who fought to defend your homeland. Every school in Russia has such a room. Mr. Bower, if you were a veteran in Saint Petersburg, and lived in my neighborhood, your photograph would be on the wall of the history room in my school, and you would visit my school at least once a year, and I would have met you and gotten to know you. Of course!"

"Well," said Mr. Bower, "there's a few folks who still remember me. They fetch me out to watch the parade on Veterans Day, and then again on Memorial Day. The Legion is real good about remembering me."

"Do you know," she asked, continuing her comparison, "that after a wedding in Russia, the bride in her white dress and the groom in his suit, along with all of the wedding party, go to a *cemetery* to thank the people who died in our wars. Even in January, even if a half-meter of snow lies over the graves, the bride wears a winter coat over her dress while she and the two families stand before a monument honoring those who fell in the Great Patriotic War. We say thank you, thank you for what you did, so that we could have our wedding today. *Thank you.* We lay our red carnations in the snow atop the headstones of uncles and aunts, grandmothers and grandfathers." She paused, remembering the sadness, and the gratitude, and the respect that she had begun to understand as a child. "Do you see? The children in the wedding party, the veterans in the wedding party, they are all together, learning and remembering."

Mr. Bower rocked without speaking, his eyes sweeping slowly across the gray-green edge of the forest.

"Only after we have been to the cemetery," said Katya, "do we celebrate the wedding with a big dinner."

She had said enough; she could be quiet now. She knew that Mr. Bower needed periods of silence before he would talk about the war.

After several minutes, he said, "No one can understand what we went through. No one can know what we felt, what we did. Except those who were there. Those who went from being kids to being soldiers. Even Anna, who put up with my nightmares for almost fifty years, even she could never really know what it was like. So how can I expect people today to understand what it was?" He shrugged. "I don't blame anybody. I'm glad I was called upon, and I'm glad I came home. That's enough."

She looked at him; he wore a store-bought sweater, and his blue silk tie. He always wore a tie, blue, red, maroon, or sometimes dark green. "Would you like to visit our history class, to tell us about being a bombardier?"

He shrugged again. "Who would listen?"

"I would. And the others ought to know. I can talk with Mr. Larson, our history teacher. I am sure he would be glad to phone you, so that you could arrange a time."

Mr. Bower rocked in his chair. "I know Mr. Larson. Peter Larson. His father never came back from the Pacific."

Katya knew that she was asking something very difficult. "I want you to understand that of course you do not have to do this. Sometimes my father's father will talk about the war, and sometimes not. But I would like to know what you did, Mr. Bower. And I think that maybe the seniors would like to know as well."

He let out a long breath, then he looked at her; she touched her foot to the floor, rocked her chair in tandem with his.

"I never told my own children about the war," he said. "Nine kids, and I wanted them each to have a happy childhood. Without some dark shadow in it. That's why we fought, wasn't it? So that our kids could live normal lives. Happy lives, productive lives. Why the hell go back to killing and destruction?"

"So, could you tell thirty-two children in the senior class about the war? Could you tell them that war is real, and that their country is at war today? Could you give them some idea of what war is, other than the combat videos they play? I find it very disconcerting, to live in a country at war that does not know what war is."

"Our soldiers over there in Iraq know what war is."

"Yes, they know. And then they come home to the shopping malls. War and Peace are separate planets, unless the veterans have a chance to speak."

They rocked together, sharing the silence.

"All right," he said. "But I can't do the entire war in fifty minutes."

"I'll ask Mr. Larson if you can come several times. Maybe once a week."

"Once every two weeks."

"All right."

"And just your senior class. Thirty-two kids, that's fine. But I don't want to speak to some big audience in the gym."

"All right. Just the seniors. I think you'll like them."

Looking once again out the window, he watched the edge of the forest.

"Thank you," he said.

"You are welcome."

CHAPTER 40

Andy and Emily looked out the window at Emily's birdfeeder, where a red-breasted nuthatch kept the fluttering chickadees away by pointing its sharp beak at them. Finally the nuthatch chose a sunflower seed and flew to a nearby spruce.

Four chickadees quickly landed on the carpet of black seeds in the tray. They looked warily about, pecked at the large seeds, and one by one flew away.

"Whooo!" said Emily, fluttering her hands in the air like chickadee wings. She stared intently out the window, waiting for the birds to come back.

Emily sat in her wheelchair; Andy sat in a folding metal chair beside her. He was pleased that the birdfeeder was such a success. Emily's face was filled with a child's excitement. The nurse had told Andy that Emily spent hours watching the birds. On warm afternoons, she opened her window and whistled chickadee calls.

Andy opened his sketchbook, flipped through a few pages of false starts, then found the page with a rough sketch of a two-story birdhouse with Victorian gables over the holes. Showing Emily the sketch, he asked, "Emily, next spring, do you want robins or do you want swallows in your birdhouse? Robins need big holes, whereas swallows like little holes."

"I don't want chickens," she said with a firmness that precluded any further argument.

"All right, no chickens. But how about a flock of swallows? They'll swoop across the yard outside your window. My mother says they're her favorite to watch."

Emily looked at him, puzzled. "Your mother?" She clearly didn't remember his mother. But she seemed to remember him, although not always at first. Sometimes she stared at him when he arrived at four o'clock each afternoon, puzzled by his appearance. Sometimes she hardly noticed him. But usually, after a few minutes, she spoke to him as if now she remembered him again.

"Emily, would you like a Victorian birdhouse? A two-story house with a steep roof and tall gables? Or would you like a birdhouse that looks like a cottage, just one story, for one family of birds?" He began to work with his pencil, adding an ornamental chimney to his sketch of a prototype birdhouse.

"One family," she said, looking at him with eyes filled with hope. "When my brother comes home, we'll be a family again."

"That's right, Emily. Well, swallows like hotels with lots of holes, and robins like their own private house. So how about a cottage-style birdhouse with one hole big enough for robins? What color would you like your birdhouse?"

"Do you like my pink?" she asked him, smoothing the dress on her lap with her bent fingers.

"I love your pink, Emily. You are like a rose. You are like a lovely pink rose."

"Thank you, young man."

"You're welcome."

He looked at his watch. He'd been with her for half an hour. That was usually enough. She sometimes got cranky if he stayed too long.

He closed his sketchbook, then stood up from his chair. "I'll be heading home now, Emily. It was nice to see you today."

She looked up at him, worried. "Will you come again?" Even if she did not remember him at first when he came, she always asked him before he left if he would come back. It wasn't affection or friendship in her face, it was worry.

"I'll be back tomorrow, Emily. I come every day to put sunflower seeds in your birdfeeder. I have to be here so the chickadees can have their dinner."

"Yes," she said, brightening. "We have to feed the chickadees."

He liked it when she said "we." He folded the chair, leaned it against the wall, then bent down and kissed her soft cheek. "Don't worry if the squirrel comes back. We put out enough food for everybody."

She shook her fist toward the window. "I'll shoo him away!"

"That's right, you tell him to go visit somebody else's birdfeeder." He laughed, for a banquet table of twenty-five feeders now ringed the nursing home.

Emily turned her chair toward him as he walked to the door. He waved to her, while she a little sadly waved back.

Jennifer Hill was in her office, getting ready to leave for the day, when one of the seniors, the boy with an orange Mohawk haircut, knocked on her half-open door.

She had welcomed the seniors on their first day at Towering Timbers, but had not spoken with this particular boy since. The nurses had given her nothing but excellent reports about him: he had brought Emily out of her depression, and had not only put twenty-five birdfeeders outside twenty-five residents' windows, but he filled the feeders every day with sunflower seeds in some, and finch food in others.

"Hello," she called to him. She could not remember his name. "Please come in."

Today he wore a blue sweatshirt with a bald eagle soaring on it; the eagle's wings spanned the boy's chest. Across his stomach was printed in white letters, ADIRONDACK MOUNTAINS. The sweatshirt was no doubt from his parents' souvenir shop in town.

On his first day to Towering Timbers, he had worn a white sweatshirt with DRAINO BROTHERS printed in bleeding red on his chest. Clearly, Emily was doing this boy a world of good.

"What's up?" she asked him brightly as he approached her desk.

"Well," he said, holding a notebook in one hand and a pencil in the other, "I wondered if I could ask a question about Emily."

She stood up from her chair, walked out from behind her desk, reached out her hand and liked the look in the boy's eyes as he shook hands with her.

"I am Mrs. Hill, director of Towering Timbers," she told him. "And whom do I have the pleasure of meeting?"

"Andy Charboneau," he said with a likeable confidence. Then he grinned, "But Emily calls me Mr. Chickadee."

"Quite right she is, I'm sure." She gestured toward a cherry spindle chair, top of the line at Nathaniel Greene. "Please have a seat." She sat in a twin spindle chair, made of dark maple. "Now, what is your question?"

"Um, I was just wondering why Emily keeps expecting her brother to show up. I guess he went away to some war? Do you know when that was?"

Jennifer realized that she certainly wasn't going to get out of the office by five. But she also saw what she had hoped she would see when she first suggested this program to Dale Shepherd.

"Andy, Emily spent her entire life in a log cabin deep in the Adirondack forest. People in Balsam Corners hardly ever saw anyone from her family in town. The men were trappers, woodcutters and hunters, the sons and grandsons of the original lumberjacks in this corner of the woods. The women labored in the cabins, labored in the yard. They had a lot of kids, and tried to keep the kids alive. Emily's world probably did not extend more than a few miles in any direction from the cabin where she had been born."

Andy shook his head with disbelief. "You mean that sweet, white-haired lady in her pink dress once lived in a log cabin?"

"Andy, she made her own soap. She canned blueberries for the winter. She could probably shoot a red squirrel at a hundred yards and ask you before she shot, Which ear did you want her to nick?"

"C'mon," laughed Andy. "Emily?"

"Well, we don't know all that much. When we found her, she was alone in her cabin, in April, with still enough firewood, and still enough potatoes and carrots, although her preserves were entirely gone. Her husband had vanished sometime during the winter. I don't think he ran off. I think he disappeared in the forest. He maybe hurt himself somehow and then froze to death. Or perhaps he fell through the ice on a lake. And she, utterly alone out there in the forest, the last of her family, snow up to her waist, took care of herself just fine. She split logs into kindling. She kept a fire going. She kept a pot of potatoes at a simmer. She brought water up from the earth with the old kitchen pump. When the county health department, alerted by a snowmobiler who came upon a crazy old woman in the woods, followed him back to the cabin and found her alone inside, she was as healthy as could be. But she was unable to give more than the simplest answers to their questions. Or no answer at all."

"Did she ever have children?"

"Nobody knows. She never mentions any. She never mentions her husband either. The only person she ever refers to is her brother."

"Yes, she's waiting for him to come home from the war."

"We don't know his name. She never calls him by name, only as 'my brother.' He evidently signed up for military service in Utica, for there is no record of anyone from the Van Der Hooven family signing up here in Balsam Corners. No one here knew him, no one knew he had left." She shrugged. "Did he go into the Army, or Navy? Europe, or the Pacific? We don't know. Emily doesn't tell us. We only know that she's waiting for him to come home."

"But he's never coming home, is he?"

"No, he isn't." Emily's beloved brother, when he disappeared from her life, must have been just a year or two older than Andy. "So she lost her brother, she lost her husband, and she arrived here with initially some confusion. Then gradually, she found a quiet happiness. As if she had dreamed her whole life of one day going to town, and wearing a dress like in a magazine, and eating a nice meal on a nice plate, and now suddenly, here she was. The transformation from pioneer woman to civilized lady was remarkably smooth and swift. She asked us if she could wear something nice, from a store, meaning something that she herself could choose in a store. So the staff took her down to one of the big department stores in Utica, which must have looked to her the way New York City looks to us hicks, and she went shopping. She knew just what she wanted: those four long-skirted dresses, with puffy sleeves and a belt at the waist, one of them pink, one lilac, one yellow, and one pale green. She has a few sweaters too, but she doesn't put them on until snow is on the ground."

Andy thought for a moment. "Is that why she said the chickadees didn't abandon her? Because her brother never came back, her husband disappeared, and she was alone out there in the forest all winter, when the chickadees are the only birds around."

"That's right. And now she's got you."

The boy looked at her as if he understood that he had taken on a very large responsibility.

Jennifer stood up from her chair. Andy stood up as well. She shook hands with him a second time. "If you miss a day now and then, don't worry. There are a dozen people on the staff, myself included," she smiled, "who would be glad to spend twenty minutes outside, filling your beautiful birdfeeders with sunflower seeds."

"Thank you," he said, his blue eyes honest, his young smile genuine.

"You're welcome. Please stop by now and then."

"Thanks. I will."

Andy looked at his watch: 4:42. Time for a cup of coffee in the nursing home cafeteria. The coffee was free, and good. He liked to sit quietly with a cup of good coffee for a while, after he'd been with Emily, and before he entered the outside world of Balsam Corners. He liked to savor his half-hour with Emily, while he sipped the coffee and watched the staff set the tables for dinner.

But when he walked into the cafeteria, he saw the Russian girl seated at a table near the coffee machine, one hand holding a cup, one hand holding a book. She had a strange Russian name, like Cathy but something else. He had never spoken with her, though they were both seniors and had been in the same classes for two years. But of course, she hardly ever spoke to anybody. She was dark, and serious, and a little scary. Not a bad looking chick, but certainly not his type.

He almost turned around in the doorway and walked out. But he thought she might look up and see it was him. He didn't want to insult her. He just didn't especially want to talk with her either.

He kept walking across the cafeteria toward the coffee machine, set his sketchbook down on a separate table, took a white, upside-down cup from the cupboard and filled it with steaming coffee. With that cup of coffee, and a chair where he could rest a bit, he could handle the conversation.

"Hi," he said to her when she looked up from her book. "It's just me, Andy." He sat down at his table, facing her. "Whatcha reading?"

"John Steinbeck. *The Grapes of Wrath.*"

"Uh-oh. I'd better get crackin'. What page are we supposed to be up to by tomorrow?"

"Tomorrow we have the first quiz. Up to page one hundred and five."

"I'm dead. I'm dead. I'll never read a hundred and five pages tonight."

She put a marker into her book, set the book aside. "Whom do you visit here?"

"Emily. A nice lady, with a little bit of Alzheimer's. Who do you visit?"

"Walter Bower. He is a veteran of World War Two."

"Hmm." Andy wondered if Walter Bower knew Emily's brother. "Can you talk with Walter Bower? I mean, does he remember things?"

"Yes, I think he probably remembers too much."

She had that serious look, the look he noticed now and then at school, as if she was part girl, and part a much older woman.

"Well," he said, standing up from his chair, "I'd better get home and crack open Steinbeck." He finished the coffee in his cup, set the cup on a tray for used cups, picked up his sketchbook and gave her a wave. "I'll see ya."

She waved back, her dark eyes perhaps a little sad that he was leaving so soon. "Good bye, Andy," she said with her faint accent.

As he stepped out the cafeteria door, he thought that tomorrow, he'd ask Raphael what the girl's name was.

CHAPTER 41

Knowing that the weather report called for rain on Friday evening, Dorothy Ferguson made a blueberry pie. While the pie was in the oven, she stepped out on her porch, glanced at the silver-gray lake, then looked up at dark clouds sweeping across the sky from the southwest. She guessed that rain would hit in about two hours.

Returning to her kitchen, she opened a maple cabinet under the kitchen counter, took out two empty, well-cleaned mayonnaise jars, then spun their lids off. Back out on the porch, where the trees were seething in wet gusts of wind, she set the two glass jars on the railing.

When the rain hit, the jars would collect it from the very first drops.

She took the pie out of the oven, touched a fork to the golden crust, then turned off the oven. She had followed her grandmother's directions, and the pie was perfect.

At exactly 5:55 p.m.—guessing that Kate would be home and about to sit down to dinner—she dialed Kate's cell phone number.

"Kate, this is Dorothy Ferguson. I was wondering if maybe you and Raphael might like to stop by for a piece of blueberry pie. I just took it out of the oven."

"Um, hello, Mrs. Ferguson. Raphael is, um, going to pick me up at seven. We were going to drive up to the Ski Center, then take the lift to the top. But it looks like it might rain."

"It's about to pour. Why don't you bring Raphael and have some pie for dessert?"

"Um, all right. What time would you like?"

249

"About seven-thirty."

"All right. See you then, Mrs. Ferguson."

"Thank you. Kate."

Good, thought Dorothy. She hoped for the thunderstorm of the century.

She stood out on her porch in her blue rain jacket, the hood up and tied beneath her chin, as the first big battering drops pummeled her up-lifted face. She hadn't heard any thunder, had seen no flashes in the clouds. This wasn't going to be a storm, just a cold wet drenching.

Back inside, still in her rain suit and boots, she was heating cider when the phone rang. It was Kate. They were about halfway up Blueberry Lake Road and had a flat tire. Kate was holding an umbrella over Raphel while he was changing the wheel. They were both laughing and teasing because the umbrella was full of holes. Dorothy could hear, in the background, the rain battering on the metal truck.

"We'll be there in about fifteen minutes," said Kate. Dorothy heard the clang of a spanner dropped on the pavement.

"All right. Are you wet, Sweetheart? Will you need dry clothes?"

"We're drenched!" laughed Kate.

Raphael guffawed in the background, "I'm taking a bath!"

"All right. The pie is still warm, and I'm heating the cider."

After she hung up, she went upstairs to her bedroom and rummaged through several drawers for clothes that would fit them.

Rain pummeled her umbrella as she stood where the path met her driveway, watching Raphael's headlights coming up the road. He parked opposite her driveway; the lights went out, two doors opened and banged shut. Then she could hear them giggling and laughing as they came running—without an umbrella, without any rain gear, without rubber boots—down the driveway toward her. In the glow of the porch light, they splashed in their sneakers through a puddle.

"Kate and Raphael, Raphael and Kate," she called to them. Then she hurried ahead of them up the path. She opened the door and bounded in-side; they bounded inside behind her. Then they shyly, politely took off their wet shoes.

She gave them each a towel and a set of old clothes. Kate went into the bathroom first. She emerged in Dorothy's blue denim shirt and blue slacks, and a pair of dry wool socks. Now Raphael disappeared into the bathroom. Two minutes later, Raphael emerged wearing Ed's dark green Forest Ranger uniform. The shirt was a little tight in the shoulders, and the trousers a bit baggy at the waist—Kate was about in hysterics—but the red wool socks were a good fit. Dorothy gave Kate an old pair of her moccasins, and Raphael a pair of Ed's moccasins. When she looked at the two of them standing shyly together in her living room, she saw two Adirondack honeymooners, a lifetime ago.

She gave them each a mug of hot cider. They sat on stools at her kitchen counter, politely not saying anything about the cooling blueberry pie at the end of the counter.

Then, still in her rain gear, she went out on the porch—the rain was water-falling off the edge of the roof—grabbed a mayonnaise jar in each hand, then hurried back into the house. She set the nearly full jars on the kitchen counter. "Kate, here's our first sample. I'll get you a notebook. We have to write down the date, the time, the type of sample, and the pH. Anything else?"

Kate looked at her, puzzled. "But we don't have the pH tester yet. We just ordered it. It won't come until next week."

"I know. Mr. Schwartz phoned me after you spoke with him. He likes our project. He offered to bring his own tester out to Blueberry Lake, so he could show me how to use it." She opened a drawer in Ed's mother's old walnut hutch and took out what looked like a small tapered flashlight. "Mr. Schwartz let us borrow his tester. I couldn't wait to get started. I didn't want to let even one rain go by."

Kate and Raphael watched carefully as Dorothy dipped a clear bulb at the slender end of the tester into a jar of rainwater.

"Hold the tip about an inch deep in the rainwater," she told them, "stir it around a bit, then hold it steady. You'll see a digital reading in the little window." She pointed at the window; they nodded that they saw it.

Then she rinsed the tester with tap water, and handed it to Kate. "Here you go."

Reluctantly, Kate took hold of the beige plastic pH tester.

"Raphael," said Dorothy, "why don't you write down our data in a notebook?"

She handed Raphael an old battered notebook, half-filled with her field notes over the years. She hadn't made a single notation in it since Ed died.

Looking through the side of a mayonnaise jar, Kate held the little clear bulb at the tip of the pH tester an inch deep in the rainwater. She stirred the bulb around and around in small circles, then she held it steady. The digital number in the window went down from 6.1 to 5.8, to 5.5, settling at 5.2. "Five point two," said Kate, without taking her eyes off the number inside the little window.

"Five point two," repeated Raphael as he wrote it in the notebook.

"Five point two," repeated Dorothy with some satisfaction. "That is fairly acidic. That's a figure we can phone in to the radio."

Kate gave her a worried look. Then she asked, "Should I test the other jar?"

"Let Raphael test it. Rinse the tester in tap water, then put the lid on the first jar. We'll label it, and see if the pH changes after one day, two days, five days."

"All right." Kate rinsed the tester in tap water at the sink, then she gave it to Raphael, who handed her the pencil.

Raphael dipped the tip of the tester into the second jar, peered sideways into the jar to be sure he was exactly one inch deep, then he looked at the number in the window and cheered, "Five point two!"

"Good," said Dorothy. "You corroborate."

Following the first successful pH sampling, Dorothy asked Kate, "Now what are you going to tell them at the radio?"

Kate seemed to shrink into herself. "I still think that you should talk with them. Or maybe Raphael. But I'm definitely not the person for public speaking."

"Nope," said Raphael firmly. "This is your community service project, not mine."

"Kate," said Dorothy, "you ask for the station weatherman, then tell him your name and explain to him that you are a senior at Balsam High. You have tested the pH of the rain which is pouring down right now, and you have found it to be an acidic 5.2. Then you ask him if he would include that figure in his weather reports this evening and tomorrow.

That's all. Very simple. Tell him that it's a professional pH tester, if he wants to know."

Kate looked at Raphael, her eyes asking for help.

He told her, "This is your gig. You've got a great voice. The world is waiting."

Kate took in a long breath, let it out as a noisy puff. "All right. Where's the phone and what's the number?"

Dorothy led Kate to the phone on a small table beside her reading chair, picked up a pink three-by-five-inch card from the table—the card had the radio station's phone number on it—and handed the card to Kate. "WADX, Northwoods Radio, the Voice of the Adirondacks. Ask for Ben Stewart, he's the weatherman."

Kate looked as if she were about to step onto a scaffold where a guillotine waited. She dialed the numbers on the old rotary phone, then held the receiver to her ear.

"Um, hi. This is Kate Sommerfelt calling from Blueberry Lake, near Balsam Corners. I, um, we, um . . . It's raining here, and we just, um, took the pH of the rain. And we want you to know that the rain is acidic, five point two. Could you please tell people that when you do your weather report, please?"

Kate rolled her eyes: she had survived an enormous ordeal.

"Uh-huh," she said as she listened. "Uh-huh. All right. Thanks. Good bye." She set the black receiver onto its cradle. Then she looked at Dorothy as if she had been shot but was still alive.

"Well?" asked Raphael.

"He has to ask the station manager."

"Maybe you should call back and ask to speak with the station manager yourself."

"No way!"

"You should have given them your phone number. Then they could call you back. You were pretty brief."

"I did it, I did it, I did it. That's enough. All they have to say is it's raining tonight, and the rain is five point two."

Raphael let out a long sigh. "You could have told them that you're going to phone them each time it rains."

"You phone them."

"Nope. It's your gig."

At that point, Dorothy invited Kate and Raphael for a piece of warm blueberry pie. The rain, drumming on the porch, was easing off a bit. She turned the radio on, quietly, in the background. Then she sat at the table with the two lovebirds and watched them flirt and tease while they both ate two pieces of pie.

The radio did not announce the pH of the rain in its eight o'clock weather report. The weatherman gave the temperature, wind direction and velocity, and said that over an inch of rain had fallen already in some areas. But he did not announce the pH. The weather was followed by an advertisement from Flanagan's Ford.

"We'll do better next time," said Raphael. "It takes a little practice, is all."

After the kids had left—still dressed in her old clothes and Ed's old clothes—Dorothy read until nine o'clock, then she listened to the news and weather. No pH.

"All right," said Raphael to the seniors at the beginning of chemistry class on Monday morning, "listen up." Mr. Schwartz had given him and Kate a couple of minutes of class time to make their announcement. Raphael stood at the front of the room; Kate sat shrunken in her chair.

"Kate's community service project is of the scientific sort. She is testing the pH of rain, and eventually snow, to monitor how much acid rain and acid snow are falling on the Adirondacks." He paused while the seniors glanced at Kate with an approving nod. "Now last Friday evening, when it was raining cats and dogs and coyotes and panthers, Kate took a pH reading with a first class professional pH tester, provided by our own Mr. Schwartz. And that reading was five point two, which, gang, is acidic. Our sturdy Kate then phoned the results to Northwoods Radio, and asked them to include her vital piece of information with the weather report." He paused. "But no deal. They shrugged her off. They think that rain is rain, one inch, two inches, and that's it."

Tony raised his hand. "The advertisers don't like to hear bad stuff. They want to sell bass boats and gasoline and cold beer. The Adirondacks are a wilderness paradise. Everything's great."

"Well," said Raphael, "we're going to do a little lobbying. We're going to apply a little pressure. I want every senior to write, phone, or email WADX." He pointed at the address, phone number, and email address on the blackboard. "Tell them that you would very much like to know the pH of the rain falling on our beloved Adirondacks. Tell them that you have a *right* to that information. And get your Aunt Tilly to phone them too."

The seniors nodded with approval. They had grown up with acid rain, had heard their parents grumble that once there had been fish in these lakes. They had read about the rising mercury in Fourth Lake, right next door. They'd rally around Kate, with a barrage of messages to the radio station, requesting a pH reading of every precipitation to fall on the Adirondacks.

Raphael sat down at his desk, then he glanced across the classroom at Kate, who sat not quite so scrunched down in her seat. She looked at him with gratitude, and with something more.

Dorothy, for whom patience was not a virtue, yearned during the following days for another downpour. Next time, she would rehearse with Kate, so that Kate would know exactly what to say when she phoned the radio station.

Raphael had promised that he would ask the seniors to complain to the station. But they were only thirty-two kids. Maybe she should phone her friends on the wind turbine committee, the people who had fought so hard to convince the town that a turbine would benefit Balsam Corners. Certainly everybody on that committee would be willing to make a call to the radio station.

Or maybe she should phone Gerald Jacobsen first. He had been the committee's chairman. She admired how he always did his homework— "Get the facts," he'd say, "get the facts"—then he'd carefully plan his strategy. He would talk with this one, talk with that one. Yes, Gerald would know what to do.

She phoned him in the evening, explained her project with Kate, told him about the station's unwillingness to report the rain's pH, and said that Kate's boyfriend, Raphael, would ask the other seniors to complain to the station.

"Unwillingness?" said Gerald with immediate impatience. "Complain? Dorothy, did you yourself speak with the station manager, before this student phoned the weatherman? Did the chemistry teacher phone the station manager to verify that the testing would be done in a professional manner? And remember, a radio station can't just announce somebody's news just because somebody says it's news."

"Oh." Ed had always told her the same thing, 'Don't go flying off the handle.'

"You say that the seniors are going to contact the station?"

"Yes."

"Well, I hope they do so in a civilized manner."

"Yes. Well, thank you, Gerald."

"You're welcome, Dorothy. Please phone me again to let me know how you and Kate are getting along."

"I will. Good-bye."

"Good-bye, Dorothy."

Well, she thought as she hung up, that's why Gerald was the chairman and I was the flaming radical.

CHAPTER 42

On Sunday afternoon, after dropping Kate off at Mrs. Ferguson's house at one o'clock—Kate and Mrs. Ferguson would rake leaves today—Raphael drove back to the Schaeffers' house, where, as he had agreed with Mr. Schaeffer last night on the phone, he would not stack wood. He would have the full four hours to work on the Corvette. He had the new tires in the back of T. Rex; they had been delivered to Brill's last week. He'd put them on first, then dig into the engine. Points and condenser. Cap and rotor. Plug wires. Gas filter. Some tinkering with the carburetor. Certainly the brakes would need adjusting. And a half dozen other things would pop up. But maybe he could get the Chevy running well enough today that he could drive it out of the garage and across the road and down the driveway to the Schaeffers' yard, so they could wash it with the hose and a bucket of soap.

Mr. and Mrs. Schaeffer sat in two Adirondack chairs in the garage while he worked, his silent audience. They watched him crank up the jack four times as he put on the new tires. Jackson Brill had let Raphael borrow a portable air compressor. After Raphael had filled the fourth tire to pressure, then cranked down the jack to set the tire on the brown Adirondack earth, he looked at the Schaeffers. They were watching him as intently as kids at a circus. He told them, "Your wheels are ready."

"Thank you," said Mr. Schaeffer, straight from his heart.

Mrs. Schaeffer quietly applauded.

They didn't bother him any more than that. They let him work on the engine.

At ten minutes after four, with new plugs and a clean carburetor, Raphael sat behind the wheel, shifted into neutral, set the hand brake, nodded to his audience, then turned the key. As the engine roared to life, Mr. and Mrs. Schaeffer popped up from their chairs and hurried to the car, beaming smiles of gratitude. The ragtop was down; Mr. Schaeffer gripped Raphael's shoulder with a manly clasp. Mrs. Schaeffer leaned down and kissed him on top of his head.

They stood back as he shifted into first gear and slowly rolled the little red beauty out the garage door into the dappled sunshine. He called over his shoulder, "I'll meet you at your house," then he shifted into second and drove along the grassy driveway to the road. Looking in both directions, he saw Kate and Mrs. Ferguson walking down the road toward him. He gave them a wave as he drove across the road, then rolled in second gear down the sandy driveway to a spot about ten feet from the Schaeffers' gray Ford. He didn't bother with what kind of Ford it was. It was a wallflower, whereas he had just arrived in a Chevy that would prove to be, once it was washed, fire engine red.

He was putting the ragtop up as the Schaeffers came walking down their driveway with Kate and Mrs. Ferguson. He rolled up the windows. Ready for a bath.

While Mrs. Schaeffer fetched a bucket and a couple of sponges, Mr. Schaeffer uncoiled the green hose from its rack on the side of the house, then screwed on a brass nozzle. He pulled the hose into the yard and began to spray the Corvette that had once belonged to Amanda Louise, cleaning it of years of dust.

Mrs. Schaeffer had brought only two sponges from the house; she refused any help from Raphael, or Kate and Mrs. Ferguson, as she and her husband squeezed their sponges in the bucket of suds, then swept the sponges back and forth over the red hood, the fenders, the windshield, the yellowed ragtop. They each washed a white scoop along the sides. They washed the new tires.

Then Mr. Schaeffer hosed the entire Corvette, rinsing away the dirty suds. The late afternoon sun sent its beams down through the hemlocks and dappled the shiny red hood.

Mrs. Schaeffer asked Raphael, "Can we take it for a spin?"

He hated to tell her, but he had to, "Not yet. I need to test the brakes first. They'll need adjusting. And I could hear that the timing's not right. I've got to tune your fiddle a little bit more."

"But we can leave it parked right here, can't we?" she asked.

"Sure. You might want to wax her tomorrow, and maybe polish the chrome."

He was glad that Kate had walked down the road to see him as he was working on his own gig. He had told her about Amanda Louise, and why the Corvette was so important to the Schaeffers. He wanted Kate to share this moment of success.

As Raphael and Kate drove home together in T. Rex, which no one had waxed in at least a decade, but which hummed with perfect timing, she looked at him and said, "You done good."

"Thanks," he said. "I like doing it."

"Of course you like to fix up an old car. That's your great talent."

"No, I didn't mean that. I like . . . I like making people happy."

"Right," she said. "That's why I told you in the first place, you done good."

CHAPTER 43

On Sunday evening, Tony took two albums of pictures, 128 photos in all, to show Bobby Dyson's parents, so they could see what he was sending to their son in Iraq, and so he could get Bobby's address from them.

He didn't know Bobby very well, for he had been only a sophomore when Bobby was a mighty senior, racing down slopes all over the Adirondacks and winning first prize on most of them. But Tony had greatly enjoyed taking these pictures, and thought that a soldier from his hometown would find some pleasure, or encouragement, or reassurance, in a collection of hometown portraits. After the final editing of twenty-one rolls of three-by-six-inch prints, he had 71 portraits of people, most of them from Balsam Corners, 24 pictures of the construction of the wind turbine on top of Bobcat Mountain, 12 pictures of shops and the little park and the beach and the school in Balsam Corners, and 21 pictures of autumn in the Adirondacks. He had written an eleven-page letter, describing step by step the construction of the wind turbine. The other pictures did not need any explanation.

He had never met Robert and Bonny Dyson before. In the phone book, he had read: **Robert Dyson Sr., 14 Harvey Street, 369-4251.** So Bobby was really Robert Dyson Jr.

Tony had phoned them on Saturday evening; he spoke with Mrs. Dyson. She had readily agreed that he might stop at their house at eight o'clock on Sunday evening. She thought that his pictures were "a wonderful idea."

After Sunday dinner with his parents, Tony rode his bike down Blueberry Lake Road in the last faint light of dusk. He wore his reflective yellow vest, and turned on the front and rear lights. The road was dark but distinct ahead of him. He did not pedal as fast as he would during the day; by night, he might suddenly come upon a raccoon or a porcupine.

Balsam Corners was quiet as he rode through town, aside from the usual cars on Main Street, heading south out of the Adirondacks on Sunday evening. The lights were on at the movie theater, at the diner. He turned onto Crosby Boulevard; the lights were on in the library. The church next door to the library was lit too, but there was only one car in the parking lot behind it. Maybe the minister was in his office, writing his sermon for next Sunday.

He turned left on Fern, right on Harvey, then spotted the American flag at the top of a flagpole, lit by a spotlight as it fluttered gently in an evening breeze. He looked at the blue clapboard house behind the flag: here was Bobby's house, where his folks flew the flag while they waited for him to come home.

He leaned his bike against the trunk of an ancient maple in the front yard, then he stood still for a moment and listened to the quiet of autumn: no crickets, no locusts. Most of the birds were gone. Cupping his hands behind his ears, he listened to the starry sky above the roofs and treetops of town, but he heard no geese flying south by night. He heard only the flapping of the flag.

He took off his backpack, unzipped the top flap and took out the two photo albums. From this peaceful front yard, outside a peaceful home with its windows lit, in the heart of a town at peace, these two albums would travel half way around the world, to the heart of a war zone. He liked to think of these albums in Bobby's hands, and in the hands of his fellow soldiers, in whatever tent or hut they were living in. He wanted to let them know that what they were fighting for was still out here, as beautiful as ever.

He climbed the steps to the front porch and rang the doorbell. Both Mr. and Mrs. Dyson came to the door, and both seemed very glad to meet him. They invited him into their living room, where he spotted a large framed photograph of Bobby on the mantel over the fireplace; Bobby looked sharp in his Army uniform. Mrs. Dyson invited him to sit on a sofa facing the warm fire; she sat to his left, Mr. Dyson sat to his right. They were ready, right away, to see his photographs.

He had planned to show them the pictures in one album, then the other, but he saw that the best thing to do was to give them each an album, then answer their questions as they arose. Both were quickly absorbed, turning the pages slowly, smiling often, especially when they recognized someone. Now and then they showed each other an especially good portrait of somebody in town.

Tony was pleased that they liked the photograph he had taken of their home: a powder-blue clapboard house lit by the late afternoon sun on a crystal clear day. "Look," said Mr. Dyson as he showed the picture to his wife, "you can see the brass doorknob gleaming in the sun."

(For over a week. Tony had ridden his bike past the Dyson house every afternoon after school, looking for the right light on the front facade. He didn't want cloudy light, didn't want hazy light. He wanted the sharp light of a crystal clear Adirondack afternoon.)

While Mr. and Mrs. Dyson were looking at the photographs, Tony glanced around the living room. A small American flag stood atop the television. Beside it stood another picture of Bobby, taken at least two years ago, for he was wearing his green-and-white racing uniform. He was holding his skis in one hand and a trophy in the other. Tony recognized Bobby's quiet smile.

On the other side of the flag was a slightly faded color photo of Mr. Dyson as a soldier in Vietnam. He was sitting in a Jeep, wearing camouflage, looking at the camera with a confident grin.

On the living room walls were several Adirondack watercolors: a stream meandering through a bog, an old sugaring shed in snow, a loon crossing silver-black water in the moonlight. High on the wall to the left of the television was a picture of Jesus praying at night in the Garden of Gethsemene.

After the Dyson's had looked at the pictures, they invited Tony into the kitchen, where they sat around a formica table and polished off an entire pumpkin pie. Mrs. Dyson used a heavy dose of cloves in her pumpkin pie, the way Tony liked it.

He didn't know whether or not to ask about Bobby. He didn't know how much they wanted to talk about their son over there in that war in

Iraq. So the only question he asked was about Bobby's address. Bobby's mother wrote it neatly on a sheet of notebook paper:

SPC. DYSON, ROBERT

then lines of cryptic capital letters. At the bottom, A P 0, then A E 58204, but no country.

"Do I write IRAQ?" he asked.

"No," she said. "Just exactly as it is here. It'll get to him."

"All right."

He did not ask Bobby's parents about the lack of body armor when Bobby first got to Iraq; that news, stated in Bobby's first letter home, had raced around town. People were shocked, outraged; some were more patient, taking the long view.

Did Bobby have body armor now? Were his vehicles armored? What really was going on over there?

Tony did not ask these questions during his hour with Bobby's parents. He was thrilled that they liked his pictures, and was glad that he could now send them off to a soldier far from home. No need, during this quiet evening, this peaceful evening, to intrude with worry and fear.

Assuring them that he had lights on his bike and would be quite all right while he rode home at night, he swung on his backpack with the albums in it, then rolled his bike down the driveway to the dark smooth asphalt of Harvey Street.

"Good night, Tony," they called from their front porch. They stood in front of the overhead light; their faces were dark, although Mr. Dyson's grey ponytail was well lit.

"Good night," he called back to them.

He had never before put together such a collection of pictures. He had never before visited the parents of a soldier away at war.

Bobby's parents had given his pictures their blessing.

Then what he was doing must be right.

He would mail the albums tomorrow, Monday, with a quick trip across the street to the post office during lunch hour at school.

He was riding on Crosby past the Methodist Church, its windows lit, when he heard the faint but distinct music of the pipe organ. Mrs. Fisher was rehearsing. He hooked his bike into the church's driveway, rode to the back where the lone car was parked, leaned his bike against the church's brick wall, then quietly let himself in through the back door. He stepped through the room where members of the choir put on their robes, then he opened a second door and entered the interior of the church. He looked up at the pipe organ in the balcony: Mrs. Fisher with her white hair sat on the bench with her back to the pews, swiveling her shoulders, leaning forward, leaning back, as she poured out a Bach cantata.

He took off his backpack, sat in the front pew and closed his eyes. Often, other people stopped at the church to listen to Mrs. Fisher rehearse. But this evening, he was alone.

He liked the power and precision of the organ. He liked the way the organist could change the tone and color of the notes. He liked the steady deliberateness of Bach, the confidence that marched through the music.

He had been listening for about twenty minutes when Mrs. Fisher stopped playing. As she was gathering her music, he stood up and applauded from the front pew. She looked down and gave him a wave, then she continued to organize her music. After a couple of minutes, when it was clear that she would not be coming down right away, he called up to her, "Thank you, Mrs. Fisher."

"You're welcome," she called down, but pursued the conversation no further.

He put on his backpack as he walked through the choir room, stepped out the back door into the night, glanced up at the stars, fetched his bike and began the trip home.

While he was pumping up Blueberry Lake Road, sweating beneath his flannel shirt, he heard the faint but unmistakable calling of geese: from behind him on the right, then overhead among the stars, and now ahead of him on the left, passing from north to south as he headed southwest. He squeezed his brakes to stop the bike, cupped his hands behind his ears, then listened to the jubilant honking as it became increasingly faint . . . and vanished, leaving the utter silence of the forest beneath the utter silence of the stars.

By the time he rode along the shoreline of Blueberry Lake, its water dark charcoal against the absolute black of the forest along the far shore, he was hearing what Miss Applegate called his "voice." When he got home, he said a quick hello to his parents, then he fetched from his bedroom desk a small, battery-operated lamp that he had once taken on Boy Scout camping trips. Still wearing his backpack, for his notebook was in it, he stepped out the lakeside door and followed the dark path down to the dock. He took off his backpack, then sat in an Adirondack chair facing the lake. He set the lamp on a flat arm and switched it on. The glow was soft, directed downward by a metal shade. He could write in the glow, but still look up now and then at the stars.

He unzipped a side pouch and took out his small notebook, with a pen clipped to the cardboard cover. He set the backpack, with the two photo albums still inside it, on the dock beside his chair. Then he flipped through the pages of scribble in the notebook until he came to a blank page, about halfway through the book.

The voice he heard was not his own voice. It was a soldier's voice, speaking on the day that he came home alive from the war. The soldier spoke in the form of a prayer, a prayer of gratitude.

The dark lake lay flat in front of him, the black forest wrapped around him, the pinprick stars hovered over him, as he wrote in the glow of the lamp:

HOMECOMING

God, you are too far away for me to thank.
I want to grab your hand with both of mine
And squeeze it with gratitude.
I want to kneel on the green earth
And tell you with more than another daily prayer
That my heart aches with undelivered love.
I want to knock loudly on a church door,
I want to climb the steps to the organ loft
And run my fingers fervently up and down the keys.
I want to lift the roof with my thunderous joy,
Not for the pilgrim below in the pews,
But for you.
I want to look the author of the unfolding story of my life in the eye,
While I thank him for every long chapter and precious verse.
Come close, God.
I want to grip your shoulders and insist that you listen while I tell you,
Thank you for bringing me home.

When he had finished writing, he sat for a long time in the chair and stared out at the lake. The water was so still and black that he could see the Big Dipper reflected upside down.

CHAPTER 44

Once the blades of the turbine were turning, Gerald Jacobsen took the town's investment a step further. He wanted to light the ski slopes during the coming winter, as well as the cross-country ski trails. Then the town could advertise Night Skiing. Few ski areas in the Northeast had night skiing on the slopes; none had lit trails. Bobcat Mountain could increase sales of lift tickets by at least a third. The motels and restaurants would benefit, as would the shops. And everybody riding the chair lift beneath the stars could look at the wind turbine on the mountaintop, its three white blades spinning majestically in the beams of a half-dozen spotlights.

On Tuesday, September 23, the first day of autumn, Gerald held a meeting in his conference room with Yuri and Svetlana Cherkasov, and Antonio and Larisa Delmontico, two couples who had not yet met each other. He had also invited Steve Barkauskas, the manager of the Ski Center. He wanted everyone to work together, so that the mountain would be lit by Christmas.

DanishWind had hired Yuri full-time, and Svetlana part-time, as engineers qualified to keep an eye on the turbine. In actuality, the turbine monitored itself by transmitting data to Yuri's laptop, so that whether he was at home or working at the garage, he could with a glance check the wind speed, direction, blade rotation, blade pitch, and a dozen other variables. He did not need to climb up in the tower every day, unless something seemed to be wrong.

However, for the first month of the turbine's operation, he wanted to stand every morning on the mountain top, listening to the "whoosh . . . whoosh . . . whoosh" of the blades overhead, so he could hear what a normal "whoosh" should sound like. Then he climbed the ladder inside the tower up to the nacelle, where he listened to the gears, to the turbine, to the blades rotating outside, so that he knew what smoothly running gears should sound like. A good mechanic must know the sounds of a mechanism when it is running well, so that he can detect the sound of something wrong.

DanishWind required that whenever someone is working up in the nacelle, another worker must stand at the bottom of the tower—outside the cylinder, safe from falling tools or bolts or cell phones. Able to contact each other by phone, the two workers thus maintained a buddy system.

Svetlana accompanied Yuri every morning in their Volvo to the Ski Center parking lot, then she rode beside him on the chair lift to the top of the mountain. After working the dawn shift at the diner for two years, her quiet ride on the chair lift every morning—her "commute to work," as she liked to call it—was heavenly. With Yuri beside her, the two of them gliding smoothly past orange and scarlet maples at the peak of their colors, she felt completely at peace. She and Yuri agreed one morning on the way up that this was the most peaceful time that they could remember in their entire marriage.

Antonio and Larisa had never been managers before. But now they had been hired full-time by the town to manage the installation of lights on Bobcat Mountain before the coming of winter. They had met several times with the manager of the Ski Center, Steve Barkauskas; they had hiked with Steve up and down every ski slope on the mountain, sketching where the lights might best be installed. Then they had contacted a dozen electrical contractors in New York State, seeking bids on the project. Three outfits were interested; they were sending reps next week to look at Bobcat Mountain and assess the job.

Antonio and Larisa hiked as well along the cross-country ski trails that laced around the base of Bobcat Mountain. They hiked a longer trail that wrapped around the back of the mountain, a wilderness trail that skirted wetlands and a lovely pond. They planned to string lights on poles along these trails, so that folks on a wintry evening could follow necklaces of lights through the forest.

Although Antonio had spent his working years making furniture, and although Larisa had spent her working years keeping the accounts for a medium-sized company, they loved their new jobs. Their son had learned to ski on Bobcat Mountain. Nearly every child in Balsam Corners was at least an intermediate skier. The kids were healthy, they stayed out of trouble, and they developed a confidence that grew with every bold attempt to ski an even steeper slope.

Their job was to light the mountain and the forest around it. Antonio and Larisa felt they were making a genuine contribution to Balsam Corners, in small repayment for the many blessings which the town had bestowed upon them.

Steve Barkauskas loved his mountain. From the first T-bar in 1959, to the rope tow in 1962, to the chair lift in 1973, the town had developed its Ski Center. As a hometown boy, Steve had ridden up the T-bar when he was nine years old. He had gripped the rope tow when he was twelve. He rode the chair lift on its first day of operation when he was twenty-three. His father had started him on skis when he was not quite two years old; he had thus been skiing on Bobcat Mountain for half a century.

Every time he watched a kid zigzagging down one of the big slopes, he felt good. That was one less kid parked in front of a television. That was a kid building up her confidence, so that one day she could really set her sails.

And now, with the prospect of putting lights on the mountain, he could take his dream a step further. Now the kids on the basketball team, the kids in the drama club, busy with practice and rehearsals every afternoon, would have a chance to ski. He envisioned the kids coming down the slopes at night with torches, the way the Norwegians had done during the Olympics in Lillehammer. For the first time, Balsam Corners could have its Winter Carnival under the stars.

Gerald served his five guests cups of hot cocoa. Then he sat at the head of the conference table, Svetlana and Yuri to his left, Larisa and Antonio to his right, and Steve at the far end of the table, everyone now quiet and looking at him expectantly.

"Thank you for coming," he told them. "Our purpose today is to prepare for the arrival next week of three electrical contractors, who will survey the job and tender bids. They are coming on," he looked to Antonio for confirmation, "Tuesday, Wednesday, and Friday, is that right? Yes, and I would like the five of you—turbine people producing power, lighting people using power, and mountain manager—to be ready as a team to meet, and then select, the people who will put up the lights."

The discussion around the table lasted for nearly an hour. With their background in electrical engineering, Yuri and Svetlana helped the others to understand the sort of system that would be set up . . . although, as they readily admitted, they did not know how such things were done in America.

Everyone coordinated schedules for Tuesday, Wednesday, and Friday, so that all five could meet as a team with each contractor. Then they would gather again here in Gerald's conference room, on Friday evening, to evaluate the events of the week.

"Say from seven to nine?" Gerald asked. "Can everybody make it?"

No conflicts; everybody was available.

"Good." He looked at them one by one, with full confidence that they could handle the job.

"Now," he said, leaning forward in his chair, "let's take our thoughts a step further. This town has a boy over in Iraq. A boy who, by the time he was eighteen, was a living legend on skis. He had colleges offering scholarships, he had scouts from the National Ski Team watching him win every giant slalom in the Adirondacks. Bobby Dyson had a good shot at the Olympics. And he still may take advantage of those opportunities. But first, that kid wanted to serve his country. He wanted to put on the uniform, and if necessary, to fight the good fight. So instead of enrolling at the University of Colorado, he signed up for the United States Army. He didn't know when he graduated from high school in June of 2001, then went off to boot camp, that his nation would be attacked in September of 2001. He knew only that whatever was required of him, he would answer the call."

Gerald paused. The faces watching him were deeply serious now. "We all watch the news, so we have a pretty good idea of what is happening to kids like Bobby Dyson. They get shot up, they get shipped home. Some arrive on a stretcher, some in a box. Those still alive have suffered every possible sort of injury."

He paused, balancing his anger with a dream that he had. "I would like to develop on Bobcat Mountain, over the next several years, a winter sports program for the handicapped. Let's reach out to the soldiers who need a fresh start. Let's contact Walter Reed Army Medical Center down in Washington, and our own Fort Drum, just outside of the Adirondack Park. We put up the first wind turbine, now let's use that power to welcome the troops home."

Larisa raised her hand.

"Yes. Larisa."

"I'd like to be the head of that committee.

CHAPTER 45

Gerald Jacobsen had it all worked out with Svetlana. He would invite Tony to meet him one afternoon after school, not in his office, but at the diner. Katya stopped at the diner after school to see her mother, now that her mother was working the afternoon shift. Gerald and Tony would sit in a booth; Svetlana would bring Katya over to the booth to introduce her to Mr. Jacobsen. Then Katya and Tony would have a chance to say hello.

Svetlana made blini with wild bluebarry jam for Tony, blini with honey for Gerald. She served them both strong tea from a brightly painted Russian tea pot. (Folks in town kidded that the Maple Diner had become the Russian Tea Room.) Gerald knew that Tony did not usually eat a meal after school; he was usually out training on his bike. But today would be an exception. Gerald wanted to talk with the kids about college.

But first, while Gerald and Tony sat in the booth together, just the two of them, Gerald wanted to talk about the full moon in October.

"It's on a Friday night, October 10. September's full moon was clouded over. I'm hoping for better luck in October. I want to get at least five hundred people from town up on top of the mountain, with kids and picnics, by five o'clock on Friday afternoon." Gerald took a sip of tea, then dug into his third blini. "The town'll have fifty or so picnic tables ready on top, and we're installing a dozen charcoal grills. I've arranged for bags of charcoal. All folks need to bring are their picnic baskets on their laps while they ride the chair lift."

Tony poured himself another cup of tea from the brightly painted Russian tea pot, filled Gerald's cup, added a spoonful of sugar to his own cup, then drank the entire cup at a toss.

Gerald continued, "What I want you to do is organize the music."

"The music?" asked Tony with surprise.

"The town's got that old beat and battered sound system that we use in the park on the Fourth of July. Those speakers don't have any *oomf* to them. I'm working with Jim Cooper at the Music Shack to see if we can't come up with better speakers. I'd like you to talk with Ruth Fisher, the school's choir director. Ask her if the choir could give us a concert on top of Bobcat Mountain right at moonrise. The sun sets at 6:24 on October 10. We'll all be up on that peak, watching the big orange sun set over the forest to the west, and the big orange moon rising over the forest to the east. That's when I'd like the school choir to give us something appropriate."

"Shouldn't you ask someone in the choir to talk with Mrs. Fisher? I mean," Tony laughed, "I sing like a drowning turkey. I don't know the first thing about choirs."

"Tony, I've thought this through, and I want you to be my *impresario*. The man who is not a baritone, who is not a high-leaping dancer, but the man who gets things organized."

"An impresario."

"Yes. Like Diaghalev, who took the Russian *corps de ballet* to Paris, where they were a smashing success."

Training on a bike was a solitary pursuit. Gerald wanted some balance in the boy's community service.

"All right," said Tony. "I'll talk with Mrs. Fisher tomorrow. Then she and the choir can figure out their repertoire."

"Fine. A concert of about forty-five minutes."

"I'll tell Mrs. Fisher, forty-five minutes."

Both Gerald and Tony now focused in silence on their blini.

Tony saw Katya come into the diner with an armload of books. She smiled at her mother, pouring coffee behind the counter. They said something in Russian as Katya set her books on the counter and sat on a stool.

Tony didn't know Katya well enough to call hello. They had gone through two years of classes together, but they never had lunch together in the cafeteria, or phoned each other to confer about an assignment.

Katya's mother came out from behind the counter and walked with Katya toward the booth where Tony sat with Mr. Jacobsen. Katya glanced at him with that wary look in her dark eyes that was there every day at school. He hardly knew who she was, rarely heard her speak, had no idea if she did well or poorly on exams.

He said, "Hi, Katya."

She said, "Hi, Tony," then she turned her attention to Mr. Jacobsen, to whom her mother was introducing her.

"Katya, this is Mr. Jacobsen, the man your father and I talk about so much. This is the man who can see twenty years into the future."

As Katya shook hands with Mr. Jacobsen, he gestured toward Tony's side of the booth. "Won't you join us?"

Tony shifted over on the bench.

Glad to meet the man who had given her parents their first real job in America, Katya sat down in the booth across from Mr. Jacobsen. He was a handsome gentleman with blue eyes full of humor, yet eyes which saw everything. Her father called Mr. Jacobsen "the mayor," even though Mr. Jacobsen was not the officially elected mayor. Papa, like every Russian man, knew where the power was.

At her mother's insistence, Katya agreed to have two blackberry blinis with a cup of tea. She knew that if she ate so much now, she would not be hungry for dinner. But clearly Mama wanted her to join Mr. Jacobsen, to spend some time with him.

She glanced again at Tony, gave him a cordial smile. He rode a bike. He read an occasional poem out loud in English class. His parents were putting up lights on the ski hill.

Then she turned to Mr. Jacobsen and told him, "My parents take turns every morning climbing up to the nacelle. Papa says the gears are of an extremely high quality. Mama says the electronics are as good as anything they had in Leningrad. I want to thank you, Mr. Jacobsen, for your help to our family."

"You are very welcome, Katya. You are very welcome."

"But," she wondered, "how did you know to bring a wind turbine to Balsam Corners? There are so few in America, so many in Europe. In Russia, we have almost none. So I wonder, how did you know to bring a wind turbine to Balsam Corners?"

Mr. Jacobsen set down his fork, leaned forward and stared at her with eyes that now had an edge of anger in them. "Because I hate war."

Katya noticed a reaction from Tony beside her. He looked up from his blini and gave Mr. Jacobsen his full attention.

"You see," said Mr. Jacobsen, looking at the two of them, "that wind turbine is a college. A college that teaches democracy. A global college, that teaches global democracy."

With a nod, Katya's mother went back to work at the counter.

Mr. Jacobsen drank his tea, looking at Katya, looking at Tony, over the top of his tea cup.

Then he said, "No one ever started a war over a wind turbine." He shrugged, as if it were obvious: "The wind and the sun knock on all doors equally. For the first time in human history, the peoples of the world are able to work together, globally, as we learn to harness the wind, to harness the sun. Why not do the job together? Why not share what we learn? Why not link up universities in every nation around the world?" He thumped his fist lightly on the table, jolting slightly the cups of tea. "Why not enable Africa to design, produce, and sell the best solar panels in the world? Why do we let a few fat boys pump the oil, when the sun and the wind would give *all of us* a share of the power?"

Katya understood what he meant by a global college. Universities in Russia would benefit enormously if they were linked to other universities around the world. Together, they could tackle a challenge as big as the space program.

"But why do you say," she asked, "a college of democracy?" She almost added, but held her tongue, 'I see so little democracy in America.'

"Because," he swept his hand, presenting the evidence, "the wind belongs to all of us, not to nations, not to stockholders. The wind and the sun would teach us to share, not to hoard. They would teach us to learn from each other, rather than to stifle ingenuity. Don't you see, they would bring us together, as equal partners in mastering the challenges of clean energy. One, we clean up this poor filthy planet, and two, we become a hell of a lot more civilized as we do it."

Anger flashed in his eyes; he spoke as if he were about to spit. "We quarrel over oil, and claim to fight our wars for democracy. But what is more democratic than the wind turning turbines for all, equally? Providing electricity for all, equally. And thus providing jobs and classrooms for all, equally."

She remembered the phrase which she had learned in Russia in eighth grade, when her class was studying the history of America: 'All men are created equal.' She had wondered then if all the people were really equal in America. And now here was Mr. Jacobsen, talking about students around the world as being equal. He was a dreamer, and yet she couldn't deny it: he had enabled this little town to put a wind turbine on top of its mountain.

"I think," he said, the anger gone from his eyes, replaced by a look of determination, "that if our Benjamin Franklin and your Peter the Great were to come back and join us today, they would be in neither Philadelphia nor Saint Petersburg, but in Denmark. They would be observing experiments with electricity, observing experiments that will change the very nature of the world."

Mr. Jacobsen concluded, his blue eyes locked first on Tony's eyes, then on hers, "No one ever fought a war over a wind turbine."

He shuffled sideways along his bench, then stood up. "I'll tally up with the waitress. You two finish your tea."

He walked over to the counter, spoke quietly with Katya's mother as he paid the bill. He gave a quick wave to Katya and Tony in the booth, then walked out the door.

Katya asked Tony, "Do you know Mr. Jacobsen very well?"

"He's my community service person."

"Oh. What are you doing with him?"

"I'm learning to think more along the lines of Ben Franklin from Philadelphia, than the boys in Washington."

"Yes," she nodded with understanding. It wasn't her place, as a guest in his country, to offer her opinion of the American government. Nevertheless she said, "You Americans are so quick to accuse our Putin of being undemocratic. But your crew are certainly not a beacon of integrity."

He let out a long sigh, as if he could speak for an hour on the subject, or just shake his head and say nothing at all.

Then his brown eyes brightened as he told her, "Your mother makes magnificent Russian pancakes. I never had a blini before, rolled up with blueberry jam in the middle."

"We picked the blueberries last August."

"You did?"

"We wanted to pick mushrooms too, but you don't have mushrooms here the way we do in Russia."

"Do you have maple syrup in Russia?"

"No."

He grinned. "Well, there!"

After they had said good-bye to her mother, and stood together on the sidewalk outside the diner, he surprised her by asking, "May I walk you home?"

"Actually, I was going to the library."

"Then, may I walk you to the library?"

She nodded her assent.

He held the handlebars and rolled his bike between the two of them as they walked along Main Street to the corner, then turned left and followed the sidewalk along Crosby.

"What are you working on at the library?" he asked.

"I am reading about World War Two, as you call it." How much should she tell him? A bit more. "We learned in Russia about the Great Patriotic War, when Germany attacked us, and we fought back. Now I'm learning about the western view of the war: what was happening in England, while my people were under siege in Leningrad."

"Good," he said with genuine interest. "And why do you want to learn about England during the war?"

"My community service person is a veteran of World War Two. He flew in a bomber from England over France and Germany in 1943. He will be speaking in our history class next week. So I am reading about Flying Fortresses. Mr. Bower was the bombardier; I found a picture in a book of his position in the plane. When the bomber was approaching the target, the pilot let the bombardier take over, so that Mr. Bower himself flew the B-17 until he released the bombs precisely over the target. I want to understand this as well as I can, so that when he speaks to our class, I can ask the right questions."

They reached the library quickly; it was only a short ways up the street.

They paused at the sidewalk leading to the library's door. He was clearly not coming in, but would ride his bike.

Yet he paused for a moment, then he asked, "Would you do me a favor?"

"Maybe," she said.

"Some time, would you tell me about the siege of Leningrad during the Great Patriotic War?"

She could see in his eyes that his interest was genuine.

"First," she said, "you must do some reading. You cannot do it the American way, by watching television. You might start with a book by an American author, Harrison Salisbury. *The 900 Days.*" She nodded toward the building behind her. "It's probably in the library."

"All right," he said, and began rolling his bike up the sidewalk toward the yellow brick building.

He found the book, a thick one: *The 900 Days: The Siege of Leningrad.* He checked it out at the desk, then he walked over to the table where, with papers spread around her, she was reading a book.

"Thanks," he said, holding up the thick book of Russian history in his hands.

"You are welcome," she said, holding up her book with a picture of a Flying Fortress on the cover.

He put the heavy book into his backpack, swung the backpack onto his shoulders, then gave her a little wave, "See ya."

As he walked out the library door, she wondered if he knew how to waltz.

CHAPTER 46

Raphael had just come out of Miss Applegate's classroom on the second floor, and was walking beside the railing overlooking the central staircase, when he heard Kate's voice at the bottom of the stairs, singing "Summertime, when the livin' is easy . . ." Her voice, rich and vibrant, resonated beautifully in the stairwell. Then he heard Katya, who was just starting down from the upper landing, as she sang the second verse, *alto* to Kate's *soprano*, "The fish are jumpin', and the cotton is tall." Katya sang with a different tone, one that blended beautifully, as if a clarinet were playing with a flute.

Kate continued to sing as she came up the stairs, and Katya continued to sing as she went down the stairs. Both of their voices resonated richly in the stairwell; the girls, emboldened, sang with stronger voices.

They passed each other on the middle landing as they sang together, "Your Daddy's rich, and your Mama's good lookin' . . ." Then they continued on their way, Kate to the second floor, Katya to the first, singing "Hush little baby, don't you cry."

Raphael applauded them over the railing, then he told Kate when she reached the upper landing, "That was beautiful!"

She gave him a confident smile. "The school choir is practicing 'Summertime.'"

"And you two are the lead duet. You sounded great."

"No, we're not a duet. We're just . . . in the choir."

CHAPTER 47

At 8:15 on Monday morning, September 29, 2003, Walter Bower rocked in his chair in a state of nervous anticipation. In fifteen minutes, the Towering Timbers van would pick him up at the front door, then drive him to the school, where Katya would meet him. An elevator would take them to the second floor, then they would walk to the classroom of Peter Larson, Katya's history teacher. Walter had fifty minutes, during second period, to begin his talk about World War Two. Peter, who had been a classmate of his daughter Mary, had phoned him a week ago, welcoming him as a guest speaker. Peter had reassured Walter that of course one fifty-minute period would not be enough to cover a subject as important as a veteran's experiences in World War Two. They'd see how far Walter got today in his address to the students, then Walter could continue with another visit in a week or two.

Walter wasn't nervous about speaking. He didn't know the seniors, but he probably knew most of their families. And after raising nine of his own, he certainly had no qualms about being in a room full of kids.

What made him anxious was the fact that for the first time in his life—with the exception of his talks with Anna—he was going to tell people what he had done in the war. Even if he didn't get any further today than the first bombing mission over Hannover, Germany, he was going to have to tell them about losing the gunner. Tech sergeant Ethridge Lamm, a nineteen-year-old lamb from Oklahoma, killed on his very first mission. Nineteen, just two years older than the kids he'd be talking to today.

285

He had never told his own children about the war. Now, at the age of eighty-two, with his nine children scattered across the country, he was going to tell the children of Balsam Comers. And a girl from Russia. Maybe they would find it interesting. Maybe they would be bored to death.

Ethridge Lamm. The rest of the crew had teased him during flight training in California about his name. "Ethridge?" they called to each other, their voices ping-ponging back and forth across the table at dinner while the poor boy blushed. "*Ethridge?* What sort of name is that?"

It was Lamm they should have paid attention to. The first to go: the sacrificial lamb.

Walter looked at his watch. He straightened the cuff of his brown tweed coat, ran his fingers down his maroon silk tie.

He heard the footsteps of his nurse coming down the corridor to fetch him.

Could he really do this?

When he arrived in the van, Katya was waiting for him. Standing beside her at the curb was Dale Shepherd, the school principal, who had been in Billy's class. The warmth of their greeting as Walter climbed slowly out of the van, then stood with them on the sidewalk in the sunshine, left no doubt in Walter's mind that his visit today was an Event. He was received as an honored guest.

Holding a model airplane in one hand—his tiny plastic Flying Fortress—and his cane in the other hand, he entered the school which had sent his nine children into the world. He enjoyed the curious faces of children peering at him as he walked along a corridor, Katya on one side, Dale on the other. Walter knew the school well, for he'd had a child in every classroom in the building.

As they rode the elevator to the second floor, Dale asked Walter, "Would you mind if I attended your lecture today?"

Walter was honored. "Do you really want to hear an old soldier's story?"

Busy as he must have been, the principal told him, "I wouldn't miss it for the world."

Dale and Katya escorted Walter along the second floor corridor to the history room, where Walter met Peter Larson, whom he had known when Peter showed up at the front door forty years ago to escort Mary to the prom. Peter now met Walter at the classroom doorway, greeted him with both cordiality and respect, then invited him into the room.

Peter had hung a map of Europe at the front of the room. The map was at just the right height: Walter would be able to point his finger at various spots in southern England, as well as in France and Germany. He set the model airplane on the teacher's desk.

Peter gestured toward an oaken chair behind the large oaken desk. "Mr. Bower, do you want to sit here behind the desk?"

"No," said Walter, "I want to stand. I may want to walk around a bit."

"All right. Here's the pointer, if you want to use it." Peter laid a wooden pointer across the desk.

"Thank you," said Walter. No, he would use his finger to point out places. This was not a lecture about geography. This was a lecture about war.

The seniors arrived noisily at the classroom door, talking and laughing with each other as they came in from the corridor. When they discovered that they had a guest, they quieted and took their seats. Katya sat in the front row, to the left of the teacher's desk, smiling at Walter with encouragement.

The thirty-two seniors filled five rows of desks. Two extra chairs had been brought in; they stood empty at the back, waiting for Dale and Peter. Principal and teacher now stood with Walter at the front of the classroom, ready to introduce him.

When the bell rang, the room became almost silent, though someone was whispering in the back. Peter Larson gestured toward Walter, who stood in front of the map, as he addressed the students, "Seniors, we have a very special guest today. This is Mr. Walter Bower, a native of Balsam Corners, who is here today to talk about his experiences during World War Two."

Walter nodded shyly toward the thirty-two expectant and very young faces.

"Mr. Bower, the senior class has been studying the American Revolution during the month of September. But to prepare for your visit, we spent last Thursday and Friday getting at least a glimpse of what World War Two was all about, especially in the European Theater. So the students are familiar with Nazi Germany, the German invasion of

Europe and Russia, and the fact that England remained an unconquered island. I think you can take it from there."

"Well," said Walter. "I shall try."

Dale Shepherd now clapped his hands lightly, as a signal to the students, while he said, "Welcome, Mr. Bowers."

The students joined his applause of welcome; Walter nodded with gratitude.

Then Dale and Peter walked to the back of the room and sat in the two chairs.

Katya looked at him with her dark eyes; she was clearly proud of him. The moment had come.

He walked around the teacher's desk and stood in front of it with his cane. "Anna and I were married in October of 1940. There was a war on in Europe, but the war had not yet touched America. We had been married only a little over three months when I was drafted into the Army, in January of 1941. I wasn't the first man from Balsam Corners to be drafted, but I was the first married man. And that was hard."

His beautiful Anna. All he had wanted in all the world was just to live with his beautiful Anna.

"I served one and a half years in the 9th Infantry Division at Fort Bragg, North Carolina. I had only one month to go of military duty, and then I would be discharged and I could go home to Balsam Corners, and to my Anna. But the Japanese bombed Pearl Harbor in December of 1941. So there was no discharge. We were at war now, with both Japan and Germany, and like all the other soldiers, I was in for the duration."

He felt a wave of ancient sadness wash over him. So many dreams for so many people were about to be dashed, devastated, destroyed.

"I didn't want to go to war in the infantry. I wanted to be something more than a foot soldier. A buddy of mine had heard about the Army Air Force. I thought I'd try it. I applied for flight training, and I was accepted. I reported to Bombardier School in San Angelo, Texas, from which I graduated in January of 1943. I will mention here that I did manage to spend some time with my wife when she came to visit me in Texas for a week in December of 1942."

Yes, we had been married for over two years, and finally had a week together, in Texas while I was learning to drop bombs. But Anna never complained a peep.

"After Texas, it was Gunnery School in Florida. A B-17 bomber had eleven fifty-caliber machine guns on it." He picked up the model of a B-17 and showed the students where the plane bristled with guns. "They fired from the nose, the sides, the top, the bottom, and the tail. That's why the B-17 was called a Flying Fortress. We were well armed to shoot down any German fighters that attacked us."

He pointed to the front bottom of the bomber's glass nose. "Here was my position, behind a big curving window, so I could look down and forward toward the target. One pane of glass, here," he pointed at a specific window, "was flat, not rounded like the other panes. That flatness eliminated any distortion in my view as I navigated with absolute precision toward our target."

He set the model plane on the desk, then glanced at the students. Was he boring them? They seemed to be listening. Nobody had walked out yet.

"From Florida, they sent me to Salt Lake City, where I was given my Combat Crew assignment. A B-17 had a crew of ten: the pilot, co-pilot, navigator, and bombardier, all of them officers, plus the flight engineer, and five gunners. One gunner doubled as the radio operator. Our crew was assembled in Salt Lake City, then we shipped to Blythe, California for the first phase of actual B-17 training. The second phase was in Walla Walla, Washington. But before we even got to Washington, we had to make an emergency landing in Redmond, Oregon. We had an engine on fire. One of the propellers flew off as we were landing. Fortunately it did not slice through the plane."

He glanced at Katya. She nodded: he was doing fine.

"The third phase of flight training was in Oregon. Then we flew to Grand Island, Nebraska, where a new B-17, fresh from the Boeing factory in Seattle, was waiting for us. We flew it in Nebraska for two weeks to calibrate the instruments. Then we flew to Bangor, Maine. Then to St. Johns, Newfoundland, where the weather was dismal for six days. Finally the sky cleared and we flew the big one: across the Atlantic Ocean to Prestwick, Scotland. We arrived on July 3, 1943. The folks back home would have hotdogs and fireworks tomorrow, whereas we would soon be watching German fireworks, something altogether different."

He walked back around the desk to the map. "After two weeks of more flight training, we were assigned to an airbase in Alconbury."

Though little Alconbury was not on the map, he pointed to the region of southern England that he had called home. "We were assigned to the Eighth Air Force, 92nd Bomb Group, 407th Squadron. I had been in the service from January of 1941 to July of 1943, two and a half years, and now, in England, preparing to fly over the continent to bomb the enemy, I was finally at war."

He paused for a moment, unsure whether to add a personal detail. He finally decided there was no harm in it. "I will add that my wife Anna had informed me that she was now pregnant with our first child. To be a soldier at war is difficult, but to be a father-to-be at war was, sometimes, almost unbearable. I was twenty-six at the time, with no guarantee that I would ever see twenty-seven."

He paused, grateful once again, grateful as he had been a thousand times, that he had survived.

Then he continued, "The British had been bombing German cities at night. The British bombers were a bit safer from German fighters in the darkness of night. But at the same time, it was harder for the pilots and bombardiers to pinpoint the target. The Americans had a different idea: we would fly by day, so that we could do precision bombing on specific factories, and airfields, and the submarine pens along the coast. Daylight bombing was far riskier, but potentially far more effective. The Brits and the Yanks pounded the Germans by night and by day, taking the war deeper and deeper into Germany."

He took a drink of water from a glass on the desk. So far it was all background. Now the real stuff would begin.

"Any questions?" he asked.

Not a question. The students were watching him intently; even the boy with an orange Mohawk was listening.

"All right, then." He thumped the rubber tip of his cane on the floor. "Our first mission, on July 26, 1943, was to Hannover, Germany." He pointed at Hannover in north-central Germany. "Here is Hannover." Then he pointed further east, "And here is Berlin, much further from England. Berlin was, of course, the ultimate goal. One day the B-17's would reach Berlin. Whether our crew of ten would still be alive, we had no way of knowing. But if the Allies were to win the war, then the Air Force was going to have to destroy key factories, and the Nazi headquarters, in Berlin."

He pointed at southern England, then moved his finger slowly east, from green to blue, from land to water. "As you can see, our formation of about two hundred bombers had to fly northeast across the North Sea, at a safe distance from the German coastline, before we turned southeast, toward the German coast. Flying over the North Sea meant no place to land if you had an engine on fire. No place to land if you had a dying pilot. And certainly, no one wanted to parachute into that cold water."

He walked around the big desk and again stood in front of it, then he thumped the rubber tip of his cane. "Once we had crossed the German coastline, German fighters came up to tear us apart. They were generally of two kinds, Messerschmitts and Focke-Wulfs. The Messerschmitts had an engine-mounted 20mm cannon that could shoot a wing right off a bomber. The Focke-Wulfs carried four machine guns and two cannons. They would fly almost straight toward us, coming from," he held his arm out toward the middle of the classroom, "twelve o'clock," he swung his arm, "one o'clock, two o'clock. Low, or high. When one of our crew spotted a German fighter, he would alert the gunners through the intercom, "Twelve o'clock high. Two o'clock high." Then our gunners would try to hit those tiny racing planes while they shot their cannons at our nose and wings and tail."

He pointed a finger straight up. "To protect ourselves, we flew at a very high altitude, 25,000 feet, about five miles up. We wore arctic coats and gloves against the frigid cold. We had to breathe oxygen through masks. The German fighters had a harder time getting at us while we were up so high. However, the Germans on the ground fired flak at us. The flak was set to explode at exactly our altitude and thus to blast us with hot shrapnel."

He looked out the classroom window at the blue sky with scattered white clouds. "We had to have good visibility, which meant that we needed good weather over England and good weather over the target in Germany. We didn't have the fancy technology back then that they have today. Our navigator read a few basic instruments, and compared the land below with his map. He had to bring us close to the target, and then I would take over. You see, on the final leg, the bombardier was given control of the plane. I had to navigate and pilot us to the point of precision bombing, and then I had to release the bombs. Ten five-hundred-pound demolition bombs. That was my job in this war. I would call through the intercom, 'Bombs away!' alerting the crew that our load had been dropped, although they could feel it from the tremor of the plane."

He looked at the seniors, one by one; after his seven years in a nursing home, they looked so young. "But I'm getting ahead of myself. We are on our first bombing mission. We're ten scared kids in a large airplane filled with explosives. We are flying in a complex box formation, with three 21-plane groups, 63 bombers in all. When we crossed the German coast on our way toward Hannover, all hell broke loose. We saw other bombers in our formation explode into flames with their entire crew aboard. They dropped in a long arc toward the earth, trailing a tail of black smoke. We saw bombers lose a wing, a tail, then go spiraling down. For a second or two, we watched to see if any parachutes opened in the sky, at least two or three out of ten. I saw . . ."

He had to stop. He looked at Katya, whose dark Russian eyes understood war. "I saw one man jump out of a B-17 that was in flames. He opened his chute too soon. He should have waited until he was clear of the plane. The chute opened, then caught fire, just a bit of it, but enough that it couldn't catch the air. That poor fellow fell from five miles up, probably completely alert to his situation. Maybe, maybe, he blacked out for lack of oxygen. But then he would probably have awakened again before he hit the earth."

He pointed at various boys in the class. "That man was probably a kid only two or three years older than you."

The boys stared at him, their faces deeply serious.

"We were now crossing Germany on a southeast heading, on our way toward Hannover. Suddenly our tail gunner reported that a wounded B-17 was trying to fit into our formation. You see, a plane in formation was protected by the others, for all the planes had batteries of machine guns. But a bomber out of formation was an immediate target for the German fighters. They would pounce on it, rip it apart.

"Our tail gunner reported that the wounded bomber's windshield was sunbeamed, badly cracked by enemy fire. The co-pilot seemed to be fighting with the pilot for control of the plane. So our own pilot, Lieutenant Ralph Bruce, lifted our plane up above the formation, enabling the crippled plane to take our place."

He thumped his cane. "But then *Bam*! we were hit. A Messerschmitt from eleven o'clock poured machine gun fire into our top ball turret."

He picked up the model airplane and showed the students the glass bubble on the top of the plane. "Our gunner was hit and badly wounded. Our copilot gave the gunner a bit of first aid, stuffing wads of bandages into punctures and gashes to slow the bleeding. Then he went back to his station. The gunner, Ethridge Lamm, kept calling over his intercom for help. We could all hear him, until the copilot turned off Ethridge's microphone. We had to get to Hannover, we had to fight off swarms of fighters, we had to dodge flak, we had to dodge pieces of airplanes falling through the sky, until we had bombed the target. So there wasn't much we could do about the wounded gunner."

He tapped his cane, lightly. "I can still hear, sixty years later, the desperate, weakening voice of that dying boy. A boy who had worried in Utah, who had worried in California, who had worried in Washington and Oregon, who had worried in Nebraska—right next to his home state of Iowa—and then who worried all the way across the Atlantic. The war for Sergeant Ethridge Lamm was never a jaunt, never an adventure, never a way of seeing the world. It was just a huge, pointless interruption, when he should have been home helping his old parents to take tare of the farm. Other guys wrote letters from training camp to one girl, to a half dozen girls. But Ethridge wrote only to his 'poor old mother and father,' as he called them. There was a drought, there was too much rain, the chickens were sick. That was Ethridge's world, until the war made him a top ball turret gunner, bleeding to death, freezing to death, while we flew our load of bombs toward Hannover."

Walter looked out the window again, at scarlet maples on the hillside beyond the edge of town. Sometimes it was good just to stare at a bit of peace for a while.

Turning to the seniors, his silent, patient audience, he continued, "It was customary on those missions that even if you had an engine on fire, even if half your tail was shot off, even if five or six of your crew were dead, the pilot, navigator and bombardier would still try to reach the target."

He tapped his cane. "We did. Peering down through my Norden bombsight, I pinpointed an aircraft factory at the northern edge of Hannover, then I pushed the button. We could feel the plane lift as the weight of the bombs was released. The tail gunner reported a perfect hit. After two and a half years of training, I had done it just right. But now we had to get home.

"The entire formation of bombers dropped its load of bombs, then the entire formation swept in a broad turn and headed back toward the sea. Swarms of fighters were still ripping through us. Clouds of flak sent shrapnel tearing through wings, through a fuselage. Through the tubes of an oxygen system. Through the wires of an intercom system. Through cables to the flaps. A plane was so vulnerable in so many places. If one bit of flak hit a gas tank, a bomber became a ball of flames five miles up.

"When finally we reached the coastline and flew out over the North Sea, the flak ended and the fighters flew back to their bases to refuel. We could breathe again, and take stock of our wounds. I crawled back from my position in the nose, then climbed up to the top ball turret, where I saw that Ethridge was still alive, still conscious, but clearly dying. I gave him several shots of morphine, then stuffed new bandages into his wounds. Some of his wounds had stopped bleeding because they were frozen.

"Then I held Ethridge in my arms, a twenty-six-year-old man holding a nineteen-year-old kid, and I prayed into his ear the Our Father. I prayed all the way through the Rosary, the Hail Mary, the Glory Be, all by heart, over and over, and I didn't even know if the kid was Catholic. That was the one time I didn't hold Rosary beads while I prayed; I held Ethridge Lamm instead."

He paused; let the students hold, for a few moments, a dying boy in their hearts.

"We had one engine shot out. But at least it wasn't on fire. The mission had been a long one, and all of our fuel warning lights were on. We were so low on fuel that the rest of the crew was preparing to ditch in the North Sea. I was still up in the ball turret with Ethridge. But we managed to reach a Royal Air Force base at Foulsham. As we hit the runway, Sergeant Ethridge Lamm died in my arms. The jolt let him know that we were back in England, safe, and he let go."

Walter walked with his cane along the aisle through the center of the classroom. He stopped in front of the boy with the orange Mohawk and said to him, "That gunner was two years older than you are today. All he wanted to do in all the world was to grow corn. Grow corn, and take care of his old mother and father."

He walked to the end of the aisle and said to a girl with long brown hair, "He had a fiancée. Her name was Sue. She was a town girl, wanting to move out on the farm with him. She was going to keep an eye on the cows while he kept his eye on the corn." Walter paused, deep sadness competing with even deeper anger. "When we went through Ethridge's personal effects, we found eleven letters from Sue. Ethridge had kept his love life completely secret. He didn't want the guys kidding him about Sue."

The poor girl, he thought, sad at her loss, angry at the absurd waste of war.

He glanced at Dale, at Peter, listening as intently as the kids. Then he walked back up the aisle and stood once again in front of the big desk.

"Now all of this took place during the last week of July, in 1943. During that same week, roughly four hundred B-17's flew missions against Nazi targets, each bomber with a crew of ten on board. Nearly one plane in four was shot down. Over nine hundred men were dead, wounded, or missing. Daylight precision bombing was so horribly expensive, in terms of planes, in terms of men, that some members of Congress back in Washington questioned whether the bombing should continue.

"The crews had to fly twenty-five missions before they could be rotated home to the States. However, most crews didn't get beyond four or five runs. Those were the odds, day after day after day. You hoped for low drizzly clouds, you hoped for the worst dreary weather England could dream up, because on those days, the planes couldn't take off, much less gather into formation. And you dreaded sunshine, because then you had to go up into that blue sky on another suicide mission."

He glanced at the clock on the classroom wall: he had five minutes left. "That was mission one, out of seven missions. We lost Ethridge, but we hit our target, and we made it home." He tapped his cane. "I think I'll stop there, because maybe you have some questions."

The students stared at him, silent, almost motionless. Dale Shepherd said with an encouraging tone from the back of the room, "Any questions for Mr. Bower?"

Silence prevailed. Then Katya raised her hand.

Walter nodded toward her with a smile of gratitude. "Yes, Katya."

"I learned at the library that most of the B-17's had a name. Did your plane have a name?"

"Yes, on the side of her nose, we painted 'Bruce's Boys,' to honor our pilot, Lieutenant Ralph Bruce. Some of the other crews painted women on their planes, such as 'Miss Minookie,' and 'Memphis Belle,' and . . ." He almost said, 'The Careful Virgin.' "But we weren't that kind of crew."

Katya smiled, "Thank you."

"You are welcome. Any other questions?"

A boy on the opposite side of the room raised his hand.

Walter nodded to him, "Yes?"

"Hello. My name is Tony. I was wondering, whether, with your perspective from the Second World War, you would have an opinion on our present war in Iraq."

Well, thought Walter, this kid's a heavy hitter.

He hadn't expected such a question.

"Tony, my purpose today is to talk about my own experiences during World War Two. I am well aware that discussions about today's war in Iraq can quickly become angry and divisive. So I'm not sure that this is the place and time for me to get into all that. Perhaps, Tony, you might visit me at Towering Timbers, room 126. Then an old soldier will let you know what he thinks about the present mess."

"Thank you, sir."

"You're welcome."

He glanced again at the clock, and in that moment heard the bell ring.

With a smile of triumph, Katya began to applaud. The other seniors followed her example. Walter first nodded, then gave the class a slight bow.

As the applause quieted, Peter Larson asked, "Shall we invite Mr. Bower to come back and continue his story?"

Walter heard, "Yes. Yes. How about tomorrow?" from throughout the classroom. He was immensely pleased.

Then the seniors did something which he had never anticipated. The boy named Tony walked up the aisle and shook Walters hand. The others followed his example, so that all thirty-two seniors, Katya the last, made their way forward to shake his hand. Their faces somber, they said, "Thank you." Some said, "Thank you, sir."

Dale and Peter both shook his hand. Dale said quietly, after all the seniors but Katya had left the room, "I have never seen our students line up like that to shake a speaker's hand. Walter, you have our deepest gratitude."

Walter hadn't expected this. He had merely hoped that most of the students would be interested in what he had to say.

"When can you come back?" asked Peter. "In two weeks, on Monday morning, October 13?"

"Sounds good to me," said Walter.

With his model plane in one hand, his cane in the other, he walked out of the classroom, feeling that somehow a great burden had been lifted from his soul.

CHAPTER 48

Dorothy Ferguson had not always been an impatient person. She had lost her patience as her anger grew, until, living now with a deep seething rage, her patience had vanished.

She had worked for forty-one years as a pediatrics nurse, caring for newborn infants. Two or three times a week, whenever there was a difficult delivery, she assisted the obstetrician in the delivery room. Her job had been to bring children into the world, then to keep them in the world. She had focused for years on the health of the children, and only as she and Ed had watched their lake die did she begin to focus on the health of the world.

Ed had spent his career with the New York State Department of Fisheries. He knew when a lake was healthy, or when it was dying. He saw the budget cuts, he saw information stifled, he saw a federal government prancing on a leash held by coal and oil. The sulfur in coal became sulfuric acid in the clouds, and then the rain fell. The nitrogen in gasoline became nitric acid in the clouds, and then the snow fell. She and Ed watched the government pass out loophole after loophole: the "grandfather" clause to the coal-burning power plants, and the "small truck" clause to the automobile industry. The coal and oil kept burning, as did the accountant's midnight oil, as he penned an unrelenting record of profits.

And then one day in January, eight months ago, she and Ed were out skiing along an old timber road through the forest. They stopped at the "picnic bench" that Ed had built years before: the smooth trunk of a beech, laid across two stumps at the edge of the trail. The bench was about waist-high in the summer, but just the right height in the winter, with three feet of snow. They could back their skis under the beech log, then sit on it and have a most wonderful picnic.

They had eaten their sandwiches, and were peeling their oranges, when Ed stood up in his red jacket, then sat back down and collapsed sideways into the snow. Calling his name again and again, she struggled awkwardly on her skis until she lay in the snow beside him, his head in her hands. She knew from his absolute stillness—her ear at his mouth: not a breath, not a breath—that he was gone.

Leaving her utterly alone. She and Ed had brought five beautiful children into the world, but they had all migrated west, three as far as California. Ed had been busy enough with his fish, and she with her newborns, that their empty nest never threatened their deep happiness with each other. But when he was suddenly gone, and the only local person to phone, after she had raced on skis back to the house, was a public official—the ambulance, the police—she wondered how she was going to survive.

The town responded with a warmth that surprised her. Old friends and distant friends phoned her. Whereas she had thought that perhaps a dozen people might come to Ed's funeral, over a hundred stood in a light snowfall in the Balsam Corners Cemetery, honoring a man who had spent his life taking care of their Adirondack lakes.

He not only left her alone, but bequeathed to her his share of the battle. For decades, he had gathered the information, whether biological, chemical, economic, or political, while she had put it all together time and again in a cogent letter to a congressman, or governor, or senator, or quite often, to the President in the White House.

Now she had to do it all alone.

She knew that in a human embryo only four weeks old, nestled deep inside a mother's uterus, a tiny primordial heart was already beating.

Through her stethoscope, she often heard the racing heart of a newborn child, while that child took his first breaths.

She had listened to a thousand hearts, ten thousand hearts, most of them well, some of them struggling.

And now she was supposed to watch the mercury level go up in her lake, threatening any child or pregnant woman who might eat a fish?

She was supposed to hear silence in the stead of a yodeling loon, after mercury had done its work?

She was supposed to watch the last kingfisher and the last heron disappear, because there was nothing left in the lake to eat?

She had begun, a couple of months after Ed died, to hear the voice of a child, a child not yet born. It was an angry voice, filled with bitterness at the people living in the world today.

Finally she wrote down what that voice was trying to say. She sat in a green Adirondack chair on the dock, on a gorgeous day in July—a day when she and Ed would no doubt have been out in the canoe—and let that child, a girl, have her say. With her notebook on the broad arm of the chair, and her pen scribbling line after line, she wrote:

BREAKING THE LAW

Let me tell you about the law, pal.
You think it's legal to pump that gas, "Fill 'er up!"
I am one of the "unborn millions"
Whom General Washington wrote about at the end of the Revolution.
He was thinking about tomorrow's Americans,
And as he set no limit on America,
So he set no limit on tomorrow.
"We the People" did not refer only to those folks living at the time.
When Jefferson wrote, "All men are created equal," he assumed
That the creating would continue.

I am your unborn great granddaughter, coming in 2048.
If you want to sprinkle arsenic on your corn flakes, pal,
Go right ahead.
But stop poisoning my rainbow.
I may or may not ever know you,
But I will certainly have to breathe the air that you bequeath me.

You claim that you are doing nothing illegal,
That you're entirely within your rights, by county law, state law,
Federal law, the Constitution,
And what's more, the Ten Commandments.

What about the laws of nature?
What did you ever do to make the sun to rise,
The rain to fall, the wind to blow,
And the geese to come back every spring?
What part did you ever have in the making of an oak from an acorn?
So suddenly you think that you can make up your own rules?
Rules based on economics, convenience, who won the election, and
Your belief that Technology, like your mother, will clean up the mess.
It's the laws of biology, pal, the laws of chemistry,
And the laws of physics, divine, complex, and wise,
That spend nine months building a perfect child.
No Gross National Product, no pork barrel Congress,
No computer upgrade with fancy files and fonts
Ever yet spun an earth 93 million miles from a sun
And bid life to begin.

The petty, ephemeral laws that allow you
To continue burning gasoline,
To continue burning coal,
To continue hiding your plutonium (Pluto, the god of death),
While you ignore the sun, while you ignore the wind,
(Because it's hard to register shares of sunshine
On the New York Stock Exchange,
Because it's hard to buy futures of wind,)
Are laws in direct contradiction to natural law, the law of life.

You're breaking the law, pal.
If you are dead and gone in 2048,
(Buried with your rigid fingers still gripping the steering wheel
Which the undertaker thoughtfully laid upon your chest,)
We shall build a wind turbine right on top of your grave.
We shall turn the state of Texas into one huge solar panel.
And we shall keep the empty factories in Detroit,
The same as we keep the camp at Auschwitz.
Lest we forget what you legal thieves have done to us.

Dorothy decided that the child who was speaking was a little girl named Helen. Dorothy typed Helen's words in more legible form than the scribble on the pad, then she mailed the poem as a sort of letter to the President in the White House.

Dorothy had mailed Helen's letter last July.

Now it was the beginning of October. Helen was still waiting for an answer.

CHAPTER 49

The impresario worked with great efficiency. Tony spoke with Mrs. Fisher, the school choir director; he spoke with Mr. Shepherd, the principal; he spoke with Mrs. Hill, the director of the nursing home; and he placed an announcement in the local newspaper, the *Adirondack Express*, inviting the town to gather on the peak of Bobcat Mountain on the afternoon of Friday, October 10, with picnics. He called the event, "Full Moon Festival: an Early Thanksgiving." The sun would set at 5:24, and the moon would rise at about the same time. That's when the choir would begin to sing.

He met with Mr. Cooper, who owned the Music Shack on Main Street, in Mr. Jacobsen's office. The three of them discussed a new sound system for the town: a ring of powerful speakers that would encircle the wind turbine tower, and thus broadcast the concert to a ring of picnickers at picnic tables and on blankets around the rim of the mountain. The choir would assemble and sing on the side of the mountain toward the rising moon.

At four o'clock on Friday afternoon. Tony stood with his camera about fifty feet in front of the chair lift loading platform. He focused his zoom lens on couple after couple as they were lifted into the air. His growing collection of pictures for Bobby Dyson would continue through the autumn and winter, the spring and summer, for as long as it took until Bobby came home.

Most of the leaves were down now; the maples lining the ski slopes were nearly bare. Only the beeches still clung to their fluttering yellow leaves. The pale blue sky was clear, promising a bright full moon tonight. The late afternoon sun turned a deepening copper-red as it swung toward the woods to the west. People on the chair lift wore coats and hats: they were expecting a chilly evening.

Tony took a portrait of Katya and Walter Bower as they launched into the sky on the chair lift, each with a smile of delight.

He took a picture of Kate and Raphael; they had spotted him while they were standing in line, so for their picture, Kate kissed Raphael on the cheek, while he gave the camera a thumbs-up.

He took a gorgeous portrait of Katya's mother and father, their peaceful faces tinged with red as they stared at the sun.

He took a picture of his own mother and father, with the old wicker picnic basket on his father's lap. The Cherkasovs and the Delmonticos were picnicking together tonight, a mountaintop dinner that would be a bit of a celebration. The poles for the lights on the mountain would be installed next week, and the lights themselves would be mounted in early November. If all went well, the lights would be turned on right around Thanksgiving. Bobcat Mountain would almost certainly have lights by the beginning of the ski season. A lot of work still had to be done, but at least the project was started. Reason enough for a bit of celebration.

When his parents spotted him pointing his zoom telephoto lens at them, his father waved and his mother blew him a kiss . . . CLICK. Perfect.

He took a picture of Mr. Jacobsen riding in the chair beside Dorothy Ferguson. Mr. Jacobsen was explaining something, pointing toward the top of the mountain, Mrs. Ferguson was looking up. Neither one noticed that he took their picture.

Now he spotted Robert and Bonny Dyson in the line, ready to ride the chair lift. He waited for them to step forward, sit on the chair, then glide up into the air, each with a look of quiet determination. CLICK. Bobby's father wore a canvas hunting coat over a red-and-black Adirondack shirt; Bobby's mother wore a black wool jacket over a red turtleneck. They looked as if Bobby's father had spent the day grouse hunting, while his mother had spent the day picking apples. Perfect.

Then Tony took a picture which he hoped would be a wall hanger. The chair lift stopped. Andy wheeled Emily in her wheelchair onto the loading platform. Then Emily, with Andy's help, stood up in her rose-pink dress, pivoted on two shuffling feet (somebody wheeled her chair out of the way), and sat on the chair lift. Andy sat beside her, pulled down the safety bar, showed Emily how to grip the bar, then nodded to the operator. The chair began to move, lifting Andy and Emily into the air. Emily cried "Whooooo!" with a child's excitement, while Andy grinned like a proud father. CLICK.

One of the town trucks would carry Emily's wheelchair up the old logging road. A wooden walkway had been built from the upper loading platform to a nearby picnic table. Andy and Tony had worked together with the town to make sure that everything was ready for Emily's arrival on the peak of Bobcat Mountain.

The moonrise concert was a grand success. As a huge apricot moon rose in the darkening sky, the choir sang "Swing Low, Sweet Chariot" with well-practiced harmonies. The people of Balsam Corners, some at picnic tables, some standing, some stretched out on a blanket, heard the voices with crystalline clarity through the new speaker system. High above them, the steadily turning blades of the wind turbine made a soft "whoosh . . . whoosh . . . whoosh." As the moon rose and brightened during the concert, the three white blades shone with moonlit clarity against the night.

The choir sang "Summertime," a song by George Gershwin which featured, as they were now billed, "Catherine and Katherine," the Balsam Corners international duet. For the first time ever, the audience, who for years had listened to Kate's clear but timid voice in church, now heard the confident voice of an angel. Her soprano seemed to reach up to the first twinkling stars. Katya's voice complemented Kate's with a rich and vibrant harmony. The two of them seemed to have been singing together for years.

Then Katya sang a solo, "Somewhere, there's a place for us," from *West Side Story* by Leonard Bernstein. The people of Balsam Corners heard the Russian girl sing what had always been for them a very American song, and they welcomed her into their hearts.

Now Kate sang a solo, "Somewhere, My Love," by the French composer Maurice Jarre, from the movie *Doctor Zhivago*. The longing in Kate's voice echoed the longing that had been in Katya's voice.

Mrs. Fisher conducted the entire choir as it sang, in English, "Queen Olga's Aria" by Aleksander Borodin. Then, while the choir hummed in quiet harmony in the background, Katya sang in Russian about her native land.

The choir's powerful rendition of "Amazing Grace" was so moving that several hundred voices on the mountaintop joined in.

Now in the quiet of the chilly night, while the turbine whispered "whoosh . . . whoosh . . . whoosh" to the stars, the choir began to sing once more, with soft clear voices, "Swing low, sweet chariot, coming for to carry me home . . ." The chariot would sweep down from the starlit heaven, would fetch a peaceful believer, would carry her home.

When the choir had finished, the peacefulness of the evening was so deep that people hesitated to applaud. But then they did, with a hearty roar that lasted almost a full minute. The Balsam Corners Mountaintop Concert Hall had been magnificently inaugurated.

Following the concert and a bountiful picnic dinner, Tony and Katya walked in a slow circle around the dome of Bobcat Mountain, saying hello to people as folks gazed out at the rolling black mountains beneath the stars. Tony, as impresario, wanted to savor the evening with his "guests."

He and Katya sat for a while on a park bench with Bobby Dyson's parents. All four faced north, and thus were able to look down at the lights of their little town. They looked straight out at the Big Dipper, low to the horizon and nearly as level as if a pot sat on a stove. They looked up at the North Star, faint in the moonlit sky.

After a long silence, Robert Dyson leaned forward and looked past his wife as he said to both Tony and Katya, "If I could go back forty years, to when we were building up our firepower in Vietnam, this is what I would give to those good people. All they wanted was the same thing that people here want: a night of peace. That's all that anybody wants, in every country around the world. Just to look up at the stars on a night of peace."

He wrapped his arm around his wife's shoulders. "That's an old soldier talking. An old soldier who wants all the young soldiers to come home."

Above them, the wind turbine whispered, "Whoosh . . . whoosh . . . whoosh."

CHAPTER 50

On Monday morning, October 13, Walter once again visited Katya's history class. He stood with his cane in front of the big desk, wearing his suit and a blue silk tie. Katya sat in the front row to his left. Dale and Peter sat in the back. The seniors were in their seats, absolutely quiet, staring at him with their full attention, when the bell rang.

Today, Walter's plane was going to drop out of the sky. Somehow, he had to convey the reality of that war to these kids.

"We left off two weeks ago at the end of mission one. As I said then, we flew six more missions, for a total of seven. If you finished twenty-five missions, you could go home. Back to the United States. But almost nobody reached twenty-five."

He paused, then he counted them off.

"Our second mission was to Kassel, in the Ruhr Valley, one of Germany's largest industrial areas. By hitting factories, we were crippling the Nazis. Kassel was protected by extensive batteries of flak guns. Flak was an airborne grenade, fired up at us by artillery, set to explode at whatever altitude the planes were flying. The exploding flak sent hot shreds of shrapnel ripping through our wings, through our fuselage, through our men. The sky was filled with jagged metal trying to tear the guts out of your plane.

"We were hit by flak several times, but those B-17's were designed to fly even if half the tail was blown away. Our fuselage looked as if buckshot had blasted through us, but we kept flying. Toward the target. We kept flying until I as bombardier took over piloting the plane, and navigated us to our precision bombing position, and pushed the button, and spoke into the intercom, 'Bombs away.' Until you hit the target, you did not waver, no matter how badly you were hurt. As long as your plane could fly, even if it was limping out of formation, you focused primarily on your target."

He pointed out the classroom window at the gray drizzly day. "That's the weather we hated, and loved. Hated, because we couldn't fly in bad weather. And loved, because we couldn't fly in bad weather. We were soldiers in a war, but at the same time, we wanted to live."

Walter looked at Tony, seated near the back of the room to the right, where he could glance, as he often did, out the window. Tony had come to visit him at the nursing home, last Saturday evening. He and Katya were on a date, except they were pretending that they were just visiting Walter. But he saw it from the moment she walked into his room and introduced Tony to him. Her eyes sparkled.

He continued, "Our third mission was to Le Bourget, the airfield near Paris where Lindberg had landed. Le Bourget was now a Luftwaffe airfield. We were to strike the German Air Force, in one of the first blows that ultimately would clear the skies over France of German aircraft. During the landing at Normandy in June of 1944, almost a year later, British and American aircraft had nearly absolute supremacy in the skies over northern France.

"Again we were hit on the way in, but again our patched and repatched plane survived. We dropped our bombs and made the big turn and flew back to the blessed soil of England."

England, a country he had come to love almost as much as he loved America.

"My fourth mission was with another crew, for they needed a bombardier. That was the famous Schweinfurt Raid. The *first* Schweinfurt Raid. Our target was a ball bearing factory. You see, every engine, every wheel, in the German military machine depended at some point on ball bearings. We were going to hit them in the you know what." He tapped his cane.

"Our own fighters, P-47's, the Thunderbolts, escorted us as far as the German border. But then they had to turn back toward England or they would run out of fuel. So the formation of bombers was on its lonesome just at the very point when we really needed those fighters. Because the

Germans hit us immediately with their own fighters. They came at you one at a time, two at a time, four at a time, screaming down at you from the sky in front of you and firing their cannons at your 'office,' where your pilot sat. Your own guns, firing back, shook the body of your plane. At three, four, five miles up, if you lost your glove, your hand froze. If flak cut through your oxygen, you would black out.

"I can tell you that we made it to Schweinfurt, and that I flew the Bonny Belle from my position in the nose, staring down through the flat piece of glass at a large German city. The plane no longer dodged fighters or flak, for I paid no attention to them. I had to fly now single-mindedly toward that ball bearing factory. I can tell you that this bombardier was extremely precise in his precision bombing, and that when I let go, those bombs went nowhere but right through the roof of that ball bearing factory. The tail gunner told me over the intercom that I'd put a bomb right down the chimney."

He still felt a soldier's pride in what he had done. The marksman had hit the mark.

"We were making our turn when the flak hit us, or we hit the flak. A piece of it grazed my face." He touched a finger to his cheek, but the scar was lost in wrinkles now. "It missed my eye by an inch, but knocked me flat on my back and covered my face with blood. I could vaguely hear the navigator telling the crew, 'They killed the bombardier.'

"But the bombardier was still alive when our B-17 touched down in England. We weren't at our own airbase. We were at another American base, making an emergency landing for fuel. They carried me out of the plane, washed me up a bit, took me to a clinic and gave me seven stitches. Then they loaded me back on our plane for the flight home. I was told not to fly for a week, or the wound might become frostbit."

He glanced at Katya. During the summer of 1943, her people were fighting too. Even though she herself had not been there, she understood. She too had refrained from telling her war stories, primarily stories that she had heard from others, though he could see in her eyes that she understood a great deal of what war was about.

"I will add that on that first Schweinfurt Raid, we lost sixty bombers out of our formation. We lost six hundred highly trained men, on one day."

He paused, to let the seniors think about those six hundred men.

Then he continued, "Because of my injury, I didn't fly with my crew on their fifth mission. But that was just as well, because their mission was aborted. While they were flying in formation east over London on the way out, a supercharger on one of the engines blew up. A supercharger, you see, was a part of the engine that increased the volume air charge, thus increasing the power of the pistons. Flying on three engines, the pilot had to drop out of formation and turn back."

He tapped his cane lightly, just a touch of the rubber tip to the linoleum floor. "I joined my crew for our sixth mission, to a German air base in Amiens, France. I was able to glimpse the cathedral from my window. We were again hit by flak, but again were able to make the trip home."

Now it would begin. All that had been preamble. Now was the stuff that only Anna knew about.

"Our seventh mission, our final mission, was to Rommilly Sur Seine, an air base near Paris. We were on our way in, still northeast of Paris. The visibility was poor, with a deck of low clouds. This was on the third of September, 1943.

"We had a new group leader, who turned the formation to the right too sharply. At least, too sharply for us, because we were flying in a position called Tail End Charlie, down in Purple Heart Corner. You know when you're ice skating and you all hold hands and play crack-the-whip? Well, we were the last plane on the whip, and we couldn't keep up.

"As soon as we were thrown out of formation, the German fighters hit us. Twelve FW 190's, Focke-Wulfs, hit us from three directions in one pass. Four came at us from twelve o'clock high, four from eleven o'clock, and four from one o'clock. They were extremely skilled at it, focusing all of their firepower on us while they kept out of each other's way. Within a few seconds, they hit the top ball turret, the bottom ball turret, and three of our four engines. Lieutenant Ralph Bruce, our pilot, dropped our wheels. Sometimes, if you dropped your wheels, the fighters would give you time to bail out.

"The top ball turret gunner was wounded. We gave him half a minute of first aid, clipped his parachute hook and tossed him out. His chute opened, then we began to jump ourselves."

He paused, then thumped his cane harder. "Now here is what I want you to understand. We had one engine, the outer engine on the right wing. Our pilot kept circling to the left, while trying to maintain altitude, in order to keep the left wing up. That gave his crew time to bail out. We still had our bombs aboard, and more than half of our fuel. With three burning engines, we could explode into a fireball at any moment.

"Mac bailed out through the nose hatch, then the navigator jumped, then Cassidy, the flight engineer. The four gunners jumped from further aft. That left Lieutenant Bruce and I still in the plane, he at the controls and me standing over the open nose hatch. The plane was shaking like a freight train sledding down a mountain on rocks. The wind was screaming through a dozen holes. The engines looked like bonfires in a hurricane. But I didn't want to jump, because I didn't want to leave Lieutenant Bruce alone. Six times, he had brought the crew safely back to England. But of course, he couldn't bail out until all of his crew was safely out. So I jumped.

"Only when everyone else was out, nine out of nine, did Lieutenant Ralph Bruce set the plane on automatic pilot, destroy the secret documents that he was carrying, and put on his own parachute. Back at the controls, he could see a French village ahead. He aimed the Flying Fortress toward some fields outside the village, then finally he jumped out through the nose hatch.

"We had bailed out at 23,000 feet, more than four miles up. A man should never open his parachute immediately, for he is moving at the same speed as the plane, too fast to deploy a chute. The sudden jerk can snap his spine. He has to fall for a while, actually slowing down, and only then does he pull the ripcord. I myself fell for about three miles before I opened my chute. While I was falling, I was able to watch our B-17 drop to the earth and explode with all the ordnance on board. Had our plane hit that village, it would surely have killed half the people living there."

He glanced at the clock, saw that he had a little less then ten minutes. "Any questions?"

The students stared at him in silence, until the kid with the orange Mohawk said, "Hey, wait a minute, you have to finish your story."

"No," said Walter, "I think we'll stop right there for today. Maybe you will be kind enough to invite me to visit you again."

With a grin of delight, Katya gave him a thumbs-up.

CHAPTER 51

Kate was beginning to be a bit brave. She had sung a solo in the Bobcat Mountain Concert; she had stood alone at the microphone, with the people of her little town gathered in front of her, and with the stars wrapped over her, and she had sung "Somewhere My Love." The song was from the movie *Doctor Zhivago*, a movie about Katya's country. Kate had rented a video of the movie, and had listened to the song weave all through the story. She did not understand the history in the movie, and she knew that the movie stars were not like real Russians. Nevertheless, she opened her eyes upon Russia. She discovered something deeply beautiful, and deeply sad. And that's what Kate put into her song when she sang that night on Bobcat Mountain for the people of her town, and for Katya.

Well, if she could sing a song on a mountaintop, she could certainly make a phone call to a radio station. But first, she had to be better organized. A whole lot better organized. She had to speak with the station manager, explaining the project to him. She would suggest that he speak with her chemistry teacher, Mr. Schwartz, to confirm that the pH testing was done with a professional instrument. If the station manager still resisted, Kate would ask Mrs. Ferguson to phone him. If he still resisted, then she would ask the senior class to inform the radio station that they wanted pH readings with their weather report, or they were going to change channels.

To her surprise, when she phoned the radio station—on the Monday evening after the concert—the station manager liked the idea of reporting the rain's acidity. He liked the idea that a senior high school student, here in the Adirondacks, was doing the testing. He invited her to phone him during every rain storm, every snowfall. If he was out, she should leave the pH reading in a recorded message.

Then he asked her, "May we use your voice over the phone? We could patch you in live, then we could repeat you with subsequent weather reports on tape."

"Yes," she said, "you may use my voice over the phone."

"Good. Well then, Kate, let's wait for the next crack and dazzle thunderstorm."

"Yes. Thank you."

"You're welcome, Kate."

She hung up the phone, having just spoken as smoothly as could be with a radio station manager. The pH part was going to be easy.

Later that night, she was awakened by the first drops of rain on the leaves in the trees outside her bedroom window. She was ready. The pH testing kit had arrived from Cole-Parmer in Illinois; the tester and two buffers were on her dresser. She got up, put on her bathrobe, then carried the kit down to the kitchen, where she turned on the dim light over the stove. Then she glanced out the kitchen window at the quart mayonnaise jar which she had put on the porch railing before she went to bed. It was now filling with the very first rain to fall. Perhaps the rain at the front of a storm had a different pH than the rain in the main part of the storm. She would test both, just to see.

First she had to calibrate the tester. She dipped the clear bead at the narrow end of the tester into small beakers containing two buffers, one at pH 4.01, and one at pH 7.00. She rinsed the clear bead with tap water between calibrations, and rinsed it again before the actual testing.

Now she went to the closet by the front door and found both an umbrella and her rubber boots. She slipped her bare feet into the boots; if her feet got cold out in the October rain, she'd put on a pair of wool socks.

Feeling like Christopher Robin with her boots and umbrella, she stepped out the kitchen door to the back deck. But before she fetched the jar—which already contained almost an inch of rainwater—she just stood in the night rain and listened to it pound on her umbrella, and patter on the wooden deck. She could hear a deep gurgle above her: the rain pouring down a gutter.

She stood out in the rain until her feet got cold, then she stood a while longer. Finally, remembering her mission, she picked up the jar with its inch and a half of rainwater and returned to the kitchen. Clomping in her boots, she set the jar in the dim glow of the stove lamp, then folded the dripping umbrella and laid it in the sink.

When she dipped the clear bulb of the tester into the rainwater, she almost cheered. The digital number in the little window went down and down, to 4.9. That was more acidic than last time, which had been 5.2. Who would have guessed that a lovely autumn rained contained a touch of acid in every drop?

She knew that if she phoned the radio station now—at 2:45 in the middle of the night by the kitchen clock—nobody would be there. She would get the answering machine. Perfect.

She did not use her cell phone, for it would make her voice sound tinny. Using the wall phone in the kitchen—an old rotary-dial telephone that always worked, even when the power went out and all the "modern" phones were useless—she dialed the station's number. She listened to the message, waited for the beep, and then she said, "Hello, listeners of WADX. This is Kate Summerfelt, a senior at Balsam Corners High School, letting you know that the rain falling on our Adirondacks tonight, at 2:45 a.m. on Tuesday morning, October 14, has a pH of 4.9. That is 4.9, which means that tonight we are getting a bath of acid. Acid in your forest, acid on your farms. Stay tuned for further reports. This is your correspondent, Kate Sommerfelt. Good bye."

She hung up, her heart thumping.

Tomorrow morning, during breakfast, she'd turn on the radio for the seven o'clock news and weather. She hoped that her mother and father would both be at the breakfast table. And she hoped that the station manager wouldn't let her down.

At 7:01, while she ate her Cheerios, she listened to the beginning of the news. Her father was reading the sports page. Her mother was flossing her teeth in a nearby bathroom.

At 7:05, the weather report began. Kate continued to chew her Cheerios. Then at the end of today's weather, and tomorrow's weather, and the five-day forecast, the station manager's voice came on: "And now, a public service announcement from Balsam Corners." And then she heard herself, smooth, confident, speaking very clearly. She even had a bit of a lilt in her voice. Her message seemed very brief, but she had stated the figure twice: 4.9. And she had even said, "Tonight we are getting a bath of acid." Good girl!

Her father was staring at her. Her mother came out of the bathroom and stared at her. "Was that you?" she asked.

"Yup," said Kate. "Your correspondent, calling in with every thunderstorm."

After she had finished her Cheerios, and before she walked to school, she phoned Mrs. Ferguson with the good news.

CHAPTER 52

On Tuesday, November 11, Balsam Corners Central School honored Veterans Day. We had never really done so before; we had certainly never devoted an entire day, with all normal classes cancelled, to Veterans Day. But in October, Katya Cherkasova came to my office and said, "Mr. Shepherd, may I tell you what we do on Veterans Day in our schools in Russia?"

So I let her take charge. She organized the entire day: she talked with teachers, she talked with students, she talked with Veterans organizations. Then on November 11, 2003, our school opened its doors to twenty-two veterans, men and women both, some from town, some from as far north as Blue Mountain Lake, and as far south as Utica. Each Veteran spoke during the day in various classrooms, to middle schoolers, to high schoolers.

Katya asked the senior class to host the Veterans on Veterans Day. The seniors then broke into committees: the invitation committee, the transportation committee, the reading and drama committee, and the lunch committee, which renamed itself the Banquet Committee. The Banquet Committee worked under the direction of Katya's mother, a professional cook, as they prepared, in the school kitchen on the morning of Veterans Day, a roast beef banquet. The banquet would be served at 3:30, at the end of the regular school day, to the twenty-two Veterans and thirty-two seniors, in the cafeteria, which would become their private dining hall.

During the day, Walter Bower spoke about World War Two, not so much in terms of his own personal experience—he saved his story for his visits with the seniors—but rather as a general chronicle of events, beginning with America's reluctance to go to war.

Robert Dyson Sr. spoke about the war in Vietnam, focusing less upon himself than on the mistakes America had made, both military mistakes and political mistakes, over the course of the twenty-year war.

Philip Schaeffer spoke about the war in Korea. "The conflict in Korea has been called 'the Forgotten War,'" he said. "I imagine that most soldiers will tell you that every war quickly becomes the forgotten war."

A sergeant came from Fort Drum, the Army base just west of the Adirondack Park, to talk about his experience in Iraq. The students understood, from their homeroom teachers that morning, that they were welcome to ask questions, but they were not, under any circumstances, to get into a debate or argument with our Veteran guests.

Tony and Robert Dyson Sr. set up a display in one corner of the auditorium of printed digital pictures sent by Bobby from Iraq. There were only twelve pictures, but they showed Bobby's Humvee on a street in Baghdad, some of the soldiers he worked with, their Iraqi translator, and—eight of the twelve pictures—Iraqi kids. Kids clustered in a street, kids in a schoolyard, kids with a broad brown river behind them. Clearly, Bobby liked the kids.

As principal of this school for eighteen years, and assistant principal for another ten, I can say that I have never experienced such an extraordinary day at Balsam Corners Central School. The kids were on their absolute best behavior, for they knew that what they were learning that day was important. Our guests seemed to appreciate the earnestness of the students, even if their understanding of history may have been a little weak.

We had our regular lunch period, Veterans and students together in the cafeteria, despite the coming banquet. Then after lunch, the middle and upper schools gathered in the auditorium, with our Veteran guests seated in the two front rows, for a concert of patriotic songs and patriotic readings. The seniors read from Walt Whitman, Abraham Lincoln, Stephen Crane, Ernest Hemingway; they sang "Over There" and "Tie a Yellow Ribbon Around that Old Oak Tree." No one told them what to read, no one told them what to sing. The seniors organized it themselves.

The banquet was conducted with a tone of dignity. The seniors and Veterans sat, as much as possible, in alternate chairs, so that the two groups were well mixed. (The junior class served as waiters, hurrying back and forth between the tables and the school kitchen; their turn would come next year.) The seniors, each dressed in his or her Sunday best, rose to the occasion magnificently. Tony stood up and clinked his glass, then gave a toast to "our honored guests." Walter stood up and gave a toast to "the Class of 2004, from whom we expect great things."

Everyone was in complete agreement the following day that Veterans Day at Balsam Corners Central School should become an annual event. Each class would look forward to its turn as host.

As principal, I sent a handwritten note to Katya Cherkasova, thanking her. Not once did she try to introduce Russian history, Russian wars, into our American Veterans Day. She simply wanted the Veterans to be honored.

CHAPTER 53

"Now where were we?" asked Walter, standing in front of the big desk with thirty-two seniors facing him. He pretended not to remember where he had left off in his story, over a month ago.

"You fell for three miles before you opened your parachute," said the kid with the orange Mohawk. His arching tuft of hair was a little less orange, as if the dye were fading. It was also a little less well-defined, a little less arrogant, for the rest of his hair was growing in. The kid might even one day look normal.

"That's right," said Walter. "What's your name, son?"

"Andy."

"You work with Emily at the nursing home, right?"

"I sure do. She's a corker."

"Good work, son."

"Thank you, sir."

Walter glanced at Katya, always in the same seat, front row left. "My parachute opened, and I floated now over France, where German snipers might be waiting to shoot me as I drifted down. We could guide our chutes to some degree by pulling on the shrouds, so I headed toward a brown field flanked on two sides by a fairly large woods. I didn't know a word of French. Even less German. Then my boots hit the ground, I rolled and lay low to the earth, alive."

He paused. He was getting better at the pauses. They were part of the story.

"I listened, my ears straining in every direction. I heard no voices. Heard no heavy trucks, or shooting . . . though I could hear, up in the sky, the distant flak. I took off my parachute harness, gathered the chute and shrouds into a tight bundle, then I dashed with the chute under my arm from the field of corn stubble to the woods.

"Once I was in that woods, about twenty feet in, I stood in absolute silence with my back against an oak tree, for about five minutes. I heard a breeze rustling the yellow leaves of September. I heard a crow. My first French crow, which did sound a little different from our American crow, and yet I could tell, even without seeing it, that the bird which cawed while sailing above the treetops was a crow.

"I heard a dog bark, about half a mile away. And I may have heard a rooster. But I think I was straining too hard and just thought that I heard a rooster."

He paused. A good long pause.

"And then I heard, from the direction of the village, a bell, tolling four times: four o'clock in the afternoon, on the most peaceful September afternoon you could imagine. Except that I had just dropped out of the sky, and I was in the middle of a war, and what was I supposed to do next?"

He looked slowly around the classroom, his eyes moving from face to face. "Any suggestions?"

They stared at him in silence, shy, uncertain.

He continued, "Well, the good people of the village of Trilbardeau knew what to do. The *French* people of Trilbardeau. They had watched me float down into one of their fields. They knew I would hide in the woods. I wasn't there any longer than ten minutes before a boy about sixteen years old came walking through the trees, looking for me. I whistled to him. He immediately froze and stared in my direction. I was kneeling behind a bush; I stood up, stepped into view and said, 'Hello.'

"'Eengleesh?' he asked.

"'American,' I told him.

"He smiled. 'Americain!' He waved his hand, indicating that I should follow him. He led me around the back of the woods, along a hedgerow, through a farm yard, then into the village through a back gate that donkeys used. We hurried along a street, went around a corner, then a door opened and I was waved inside by a man glancing warily up and down the lane. I hurried into the house, heard the door close behind me, then followed my host, with the boy right behind me, up a flight of stairs, along a short hallway with closed doors off both sides, then up a narrower flight of stairs, and found myself in a warm stuffy attic. The boy now stood in front of me and put his finger over his lips." Walter put his finger over his lips, indicating to the seniors: Keep quiet.

Walter looked out the long classroom window at the bare trees on the hillside beyond town: November trees. Bare and bleak beneath a gray November sky.

"The good people of Trilbardeau brought me food, brought me French clothing, brought me French identification papers. They kept me hidden for over a week, then one of them transported me, by train, to the Underground in Paris. The French Underground provided me with more papers, and another train ticket, toward the Spanish border. There I would be met by a Dutch escort, who would take a group of us through the Pyrenees Mountains on foot, past German border guards, into the sanctuary of Spain."

He tapped his cane lightly.

"I would not be standing here before you today, had it not been for the courage and the generosity and the big-heartedness of the French people of Trilbardeau. I would never have seen the faces of my nine children, not even the one child who had been born on the day, August 17, 1943, that we bombed Schweinfurt. Without the kindness of those brave people, who could have been lined up against a wall and shot for even giving me a slice of bread, I would never have been able to return home to see my wife and firstborn son."

He tapped his cane harder now.

"So don't tell me about Liberty Fries in the stead of French fries. Don't tell me that the French are no longer our friends. Don't tell me to turn my back on them with an arrogant shrug. Because they risked dozens of lives to help get one American soldier home."

He was too damn angry now to say anything more. He stared out the window at the bare trees while he cooled down.

Finally he turned to the seniors and continued, "We hiked through the Pyrenees Mountains in France to the Pyrenees Mountains in Spain. We walked for thirty-five hours without stopping, up and down steep rocky slopes, through snow, then sleet, and then freezing rain, led by two Basque guides who knew the mountain trails. Our Dutch escort, who had gathered together a dozen fellows like myself, said only that his name was Martin, and nothing more."

Martin, a man of enormous endurance. A man of immense courage.

"Now I was not dressed for the mountains, nor did I have the proper boots. I had been hiding for over a month in an attic in Paris, with French identity papers, French city clothes, and French city shoes. I rode the train west from Paris to the Pyrenees, met Martin at the station, then began this hike into enormous jagged mountains during the worst kind of weather. I hadn't had any exercise for a month, my legs were weak, and my whole body was soon nearly frozen.

"When I became so exhausted that I could not walk any further, Martin wrapped one of my arms over his shoulders, wrapped his strong arm beneath my shoulders, and kept me stumbling forward. He would give me lumps of sugar, then he would say to me, 'Walter, you are an American. I am Dutch. We are all fighting for freedom. You can't give up now.' Then he would tell me some joke, about the chicken soup we were going to eat in Spain. That Dutch fellow kept me going."

Walter looked at Katya, the girl who kept him going. She was watching him with her dark, serious eyes.

"The Germans were patrolling the trails, patrolling the roads, and of course patrolling the border itself. But our Basque guides knew trails that the Germans had not yet discovered. One Basque kept telling us in English, 'In few more hours, in few more hours.' In a few more hours, we would be in Spain."

"And then, sometime in the middle of an endless day, as we staggered forward in a freezing drizzle, we reached a Spanish border marker beside the trail. Martin and I knelt and rubbed our hands over it, feeling it, taking into our exhausted minds the hardness and realness of that weathered wooden post.

"We followed a goat trail, with fresh goat droppings on it. I slipped at one point on loose rocks and nearly fell down a cliff to a certain death hundreds of feet below. I managed to grab hold of a small but ancient pine, which, thank you God, stayed rooted to the earth. Martin, who had been helping a French officer to walk, reached down and squeezed my arm in his strong grip, then he dragged me back up to the trail. He kept saying, 'Come on, Walter. If the goats can make it, you can make it.'

"We came to a mountain stream that we had to cross. It was flowing very fast, carrying chunks of ice. We skirted along it, found a spot where the stream became shallow enough that we might at least get a grip with our feet, then waded in. We braced ourselves against the strong current, struggling step by step with freezing water up to our knees. If a man lost his footing, he would simply be swept away. But none of us did. Martin walked downstream from me, but I made it without his having to try to grab me.

"Then we walked. We had been walking for what seemed to be a week, but we could not stop walking now or our legs would freeze. We walked on numb stumps. We walked on feet that ached as they thawed. We walked on knees that seemed ready to drop us in a heap. We walked through the fading light of late afternoon. We walked into the growing darkness of evening. If we stopped walking, we would sleep for a month, so we did not stop.

"Then the light of a window appeared ahead of us in the snowy dark. We came to a farm, a Basque farm. The family that met us was related somehow to one of our guides: the bearded farmer was perhaps his brother. They fed us goat soup. I had to make myself eat with a spoon, and not pick up the bowl and gulp it all at once. They gave us the most wonderful warm bread, bread that I dipped into a second bowl of soup. Then they gave us each a glass of anisette. We toasted our gratitude to our two Basque guides and to the Basque family, 'Gracias, gracias!' And I am quite sure that each man in our ragged group said a prayer to his God above, be he Dutch or French or American, 'Thank you, Lord, that I am alive, and safe.'

"The following morning, we walked a few miles to the small city of Pamplona, where Martin helped us to turn ourselves in at a Spanish police station. In the company of a half-dozen Americans, most of whom were trying to get back to England, and with Martin as our unerring escort, I traveled by train to Le Cumberi, then to Madrid, where we boarded a train bound for Lisboa, Portugal.

"I shall never forget the beauty of that train ride across Portugal to the coast. Whenever the train stopped in a village, we could buy fresh Portuguese oranges, just picked from the trees. Those sweet juicy oranges, eaten while we stood on a railroad platform beneath a blue sky with the sun warm on our faces, meant peace for me. Peace, even if temporary. I had to get back to England, had to get back to my base and join another crew. But on that day in Portugal, hopping back on the train each time the whistle blew, I was deeply, deeply at peace."

He let out a long breath. He had told his story, had almost reached the end. He had gotten it out. He looked at Katya, his heart filled with gratitude.

"In Lisboa, the capital of Portugal, we boarded a British ship, a corvette named *Sayonara*, which took us south along the Portuguese coast to the British naval base in Gibraltar." He walked around the big desk and pointed to Gibraltar on the map. "In Gibraltar, it was almost impossible to sleep, because they were setting off depth charges in the harbor day and night, to keep German frogmen from attaching magnetic mines to the hulls of British ships. *Boom! Boom!* All night, the never-ending, watery *Boom!* I was back in the war again.

"I was flown by the Royal Air Force back to England, then I went straight by train to my base. Mac and Cassidy showed up about two weeks after me. They too had been smuggled out by the French Underground. But they, the lucky dogs, were shipped out on a boat back to the States, whereas I was sent to the Royal Air Force base at Highgate, where I lectured at the Escape and Evasion School for military intelligence officers. The Brits wanted to know how I had managed it in France.

"Back again at my own air base, I was told that I could be home by January, 1944—A-1 priority, which meant by plane rather than by boat—if I would go on a lecture tour to the bomber training bases in America. I of course agreed, flew from England to New York, rode the train north to Utica, and on January 14th, 1944, my wife's birthday, I met my family at the Utica station. Anna was holding our son, who was five months old, on the crowded platform. When I stepped off the train and hugged both my wife and my son in my arms, I felt the greatest happiness and the greatest peace that I have ever known in my life. That day was a hundred times bigger than our wedding day. A thousand times bigger. I still say a prayer every night, thanking the good Lord for that miracle: the day I came home."

He paused for a moment to think quietly, Thank you, Lord. Thank you.

"I did my lecture tour, told the young bombardiers what I thought they needed to know, then I settled for the remainder of the war at a base in Laredo, Texas, teaching Escape and Evasion, and playing golf. Until we dropped the first salvo of the nuclear age on Hiroshima, and then Nagasaki. Those two bombs brought the war to an end, and I went home for good. I've been right here in Balsam Corners ever since. Put nine kids through this school. And today I have the pleasure, and the honor, of addressing a group of hard-working seniors. Who will one day build a better America. Who will one day build a better world."

Now he paused. He had brought them into the story.

"Let me give you some figures." He picked up a piece of chalk, then wrote on the blackboard: 12,731 B-17's. "Twelve thousand, seven hundred and thirty-one B-17's were built in the United States, then flown to war zones around the world. By the end of the war, over five thousand had been shot down." He wrote 5000 above the other figure, then drew a line between them, making them a fraction. "Each Flying Fortress carried a crew of ten. Sometimes they all bailed out. Sometimes only one or two got out. Sometimes they burned alive in their plane as it plunged to earth. By the end of the war, around the world, seventy-six thousand American airmen were killed or missing." He wrote the figure: 76,000 men.

"Ethridge Lamm was one of those airmen. I never found out what happened to his parents, or the farm, or Sue. It may seem strange, but I never stopped wondering how she is, his fiancée, Sue."

He glanced at the clock. Five minutes left. Just right.

He walked around the big desk, scanned the fresh young faces, then he said, "I shall finish by telling you that for the rest of my life, I have had nightmares almost every night. I am up in that B-17. We have just been hit by those twelve German fighters, three engines are dead, the plane is shuddering as the pilot tries to fly it, and I know that we have to get out before the plane either crashes or explodes."

He paused.

"I have my chute on, the nose hatch is open at my feet, but I don't want to jump. Because I don't want to leave the pilot alone in that shot-up cripple. Lieutenant Ralph Bruce brought us home to England six times. I didn't want to leave him alone."

He could feel the plane shaking, heard the wind shrieking, and felt again the raw fear that a soldier learns to live with.

"That's when I wake up. Sweating, shaking, unable to talk for a minute or two. And then, once I realize where I am—in my own bed, at home, in Balsam Corners."

He looked at the now familiar faces around the room. "So I would like to thank you, the Senior Class of 2004," he looked at Katya, "to thank you with deep gratitude, because you have enabled me finally to let the demons out."

All right, enough of the personal stuff.

"You, all thirty-two of you, now live in a nation at war. In June, seven months from now, you will graduate from this fine little school, and you will go off to your colleges and universities. To your jobs. Or to one of the branches of the Armed Forces. Keep in mind that war is real, that from one moment to the next it can entirely engulf you. Tread carefully, step wisely."

He tapped his cane. "Thank you very much."

Once again, the seniors lined up to shake Walter's hand and to thank him. As Katya, the last in line, shook his hand, she kissed his cheek. A Russian thank you.

CHAPTER 54

The installation of lights on the slopes and trails of Bobcat Mountain, a joint venture which combined the local knowledge of the Delmontico family with the electrical knowledge of the Cherkasov family, proceeded on schedule. Aldridge Electric, a contractor based in Utica, had done a professional job, on time. By the end of the third week of November, only a few small details remained.

On Friday evening, November 21, Antonio, Larisa, Yuri, and Svetlana met with Gerald Jacobsen in his conference room, upstairs at the bank. The five of them decided that the switch should be flipped, and the mountain lit, on the following Thursday evening, November 27, after everyone had finished eating Thanksgiving dinner.

The Delmontico family invited the Cherkasov family to have Thanksgiving dinner with them at their home on Blueberry Lake. Walter Bower was of course invited, as were Walter's daughter Mary and her husband Arthur, who had driven up from Long Island.

Larisa and Mary showed Svetlana how to cook a turkey, a real American turkey for a real American dinner. They showed her how to make dressing, and how to bake a pumpkin pie.

Antonio, Yuri, Walter and Arthur bundled up and went for a walk along the road that followed the shore of Blueberry Lake. Walter walked a quarter of a mile before he decided he had better turn around. While they were walking back, the men heard two flocks of geese going over. One flock, a big rippling V, passed directly overhead, traveling due south.

Tony and Katya disappeared in the canoe. Ice had not yet formed on the lake. Leaving the dock, they paddled south, toward the wilderness end of the lake. They returned at 2:45—both wore their watches—in time for dinner at 3:00.

Gerald had Thanksgiving dinner at Dorothy's camp on Blueberry Lake. They were joined by her neighbors, Philip and Margaret. Gerald brought two bottles of French Bordeaux. Philip and Margaret, on their second glass, told the tale of their trip through the Adirondacks in their little red Corvette. For a week in early October, they had driven a big loop around the Adirondacks when the leaves were at their peak. They hiked on trails they had hiked years ago. Some nights they camped, and some nights they stayed at an old inn. They rented a canoe and paddled on a lake which, in October, they had entirely to themselves. They took pictures of each other, standing at the edge of the lake, and standing beside the Corvette's red fender.

"It was our second honeymoon," said Philip.

"It was like our courting days," said Margaret. "We were as happy as two larks in our little red Corvette."

Dorothy held a platter toward Gerald. "More turkey?"

Emily had Thanksgiving dinner with Andy and his mother and father in their home on Riverside Drive. Andy walked that morning to the nursing home, then rode in the special van, able to accommodate wheelchairs, that brought Emily to his house. She was delighted to go somewhere new, and though she may or may not have recognized his parents, she liked their company, liked the bustle in the house as they worked together in the kitchen and prepared the table for a big dinner.

She wore her lilac dress with white lace at the cuffs and collar. Andy gave her a white gardenia for Thanksgiving; he helped her to pin the fragrant flower to her lilac lapel.

"Thank you, young man."

"You're welcome, Emily."

She wheeled her chair across the living room to a window that looked out on the Moose River. Most of the leaves had fallen from the trees, so she could see the shimmering gray water.

Andy moved a dining room chair so that he could sit beside Emily. He opened his sketch pad on his lap. He had been studying gothic cathedrals in an art history book, so that he could design a gothic birdhouse for Emily.

"Your birdhouse will have four gothic turrets, one at each corner," he told her, showing her a sketch, "with a gothic spire rising from the middle of the roof. If you want, we can make it not a birdhouse, but a bird hotel, with four holes and compartments, or eight holes and compartments. We could build a two-story, eight-hole hotel, gothic style. That's the sort of accommodation that swallows like."

She studied his drawing. "Maybe chickadees will move in."

"Chickadees don't like bird houses. Our bird book says that chickadees like cavities in rotted stumps, or an old woodpecker hole."

"Rotted stumps?"

"Well, each to his own. Listen, if we build a single-dwelling house, we might attract robins. Would you like a pair of robins outside your window?"

She thought for a moment. "I'd rather have flamingoes."

"I know you would. But the flamingoes don't come in the spring and summer. They come in the winter, when the snow is deep."

"Are you sure?"

"I promise, that as soon as the snow is at least a foot deep, in January maybe, a big flock of pink flamingoes is going to arrive right outside your window."

"Well then," she said, staring at him as if they shared a great secret. "We'll just have to wait."

"Yup. We'll just have to wait."

Kate and her parents had Thanksgiving dinner with Raphael and his parents, and his brother Ezekiel, at Raphael's home in the hamlet of Thendara, on the southern side of the Moose River. Kate's parents and Raphael's parents had gone through high school together, so they spent much of the afternoon, while working in the kitchen and watching a TV football game, reminiscing about old times.

Raphael's brother Ezekiel was in his bedroom, emailing friends. One of the friends he emailed—he was sending greetings on Thanksgiving—was Bobby in Baghdad. Ezekiel got a reply at 1:47 in the afternoon,

Balsam Corners time, 9:47 in the evening, Baghdad time. Bobby had just come back from a night patrol.

Kate and Raphael spent over an hour in Raphael's bedroom, the door wide open, working together at his desk with a half-dozen library books and his computer. On this day of thanksgiving for America's plenitude, the two of them wrote a short essay—Raphael at the keyboard, Kate standing behind him with her hands on his shoulders—an essay that described how acid rain was causing the Adirondack forest to starve.

The nitric acid and sulfuric acid in rainwater leached the calcium out of the thin Adirondack soil, then washed it away into the streams and lakes. Trees need calcium just the same as people need calcium; take away our calcium and our bones collapse. Slowly, year after year, the Adirondack earth was incrementally depleted of calcium. The trees were starving. They lost their resistance against the cold of winter, against the invasion of insects and disease. Now, with the slowly increasing global temperatures, in both summer and winter, insects and bacteria and molds which had never before lived in the Adirondacks would be able to move north. The already weakened forest might easily succumb to a blight. And how, one could ask, does one replant a dead forest, in soil depleted of nutrients?

Raphael and Kate worked on their public service message until Kate could read it smoothly in just under sixty seconds. The next time it rained a 4.9 downpour, she and Raphael were ready.

The chair lift began running at three in the afternoon on Thanksgiving Day. By five o'clock, a crowd of folks from town had gathered on the top of Bobcat Mountain, while another crowd had gathered at the bottom of the ski slopes. A few people climbed up, or down, the brown grassy slopes. Those at the top would be close to the wind turbine when the spotlights came on, shining up at the white tower and nacelle and spinning wings against the night sky. Those at the bottom would be able to see necklaces of lights festooned down the slopes. A few folks hiked along the cross-country trails that laced around the base of the mountain, for the trails too would be lit.

People wore their woolies, warm hats and heavy coats, winter gloves and winter boots, for the lights would not be turned on until six o'clock, when the evening was good and dark.

Almost everyone wore a watch. This was far more exciting than New Year's Eve. When the lights came on, illuminating the slopes and trails of Bobcat Mountain, Balsam Corners would be able to offer Night Skiing to the world. Every skier would contribute to the town's coffers, and every skier would ride the chair lift toward the wind turbine that was lighting him and lifting him.

At one minute before six p.m., everyone at the top and bottom of the ski slopes seemed to hold his breath. Yuri, in the Ski Center office, looked at his watch, glanced out the office door at Svetlana, Antonio, and Larisa standing in the dark on the lawn outside, then looked again at his watch . . . and threw the switches.

Necklaces of light appeared one by one across the dark face of the mountain, while a cheer went up from the crowd at the bottom as if they were watching fireworks on the Fourth of July.

Then Yuri threw another switch, to the spotlights on the mountaintop, aimed almost straight up. Folks at the top stared up at the unbelievably tall turbine: the white cylindrical tower rose up to the November stars; the nacelle looked like a house that lived among the stars; and the three white blades, facing into the prevailing west wind, spun majestically in the night, as if they were sweeping star dust out of the sky and dispensing it gently to the earth with each "Whoosh . . . whoosh . . . whoosh."

Both on top and below, everyone applauded, for here was the first real sign of their investment. The rest had been figures on paper, but here were lights shining down from well-spaced poles. The lights shone now on brown grass, but soon there would be snow; folks imagined how pretty the white slopes would look beneath the lights.

The chair lift ran until ten o'clock that night. Folks at the bottom wanted to ride up so they could stare nearly straight up at the enormous white blades that were harvesting, harvesting. Folks at the top wanted to ride down so they could admire the necklaces draping down the face of the mountain, and the big pools of light on the lawn at the bottom.

Nobody said so, but folks were quietly proud. Their little town had done something. Something for themselves, something for the forest, something for the lakes, something for the world.

Their wind turbine, and the clean lights which it powered, were their way of saying Thank you, to the forest, to the lakes, to the world.

CHAPTER 55

And then the war came home.

The phone rang in the Dyson home at 9:32 on Friday morning, November 28, 2003. Bobby's father, a logger, had the day off. He was sitting with a cup of coffee at the breakfast table, wearing a blue bathrobe over his pajamas, when the phone rang. He picked it up while he read on the sports page about the Syracuse Orangemen. "Hello?"

An Army officer, calling from an office in Washington, introduced himself, then asked, "To whom am I speaking?"

"Robert Dyson Senior."

"The father of Specialist Robert Dyson Junior?"

"Yes."

Now the officer was telling him that Robert Dyson Junior had been injured the night before while on patrol, and was now being evacuated to a hospital in Germany.

Robert dropped the newspaper on the table and stood up. "How bad is he hurt?"

"I do not have access to the full medical report, but our information indicates that he suffered chest wounds during an attack on his convoy."

"Was he wearing body armor?" Robert sent the question like a shot down the phone line to Washington.

"My information indicates nothing about personal or vehicular armor. I know only that he was brought back to base, given immediate medical treatment, then airlifted out on a transport to Germany. I will notify you with any further information as we receive it."

Bonny was standing beside him now, in her pink bathrobe, clutching his arm.

Robert asked the officer, "Is there a phone number in Germany where I might reach my son?"

"We'll have to wait until we know in which facility he's quartered. I will notify you with any further information as we receive it."

"May I have your name again, and your phone number, please?" Robert wrote down the officer's name and number on a pad beside the phone.

"Thank you, Lieutenant Meyers."

"Keep your chin up," said Lieutenant Meyers.

Robert set the phone in its cradle, then he wrapped his arms around Bonny and said, "Our Bobby is still alive."

Because the town would want to know, Robert phoned the radio station in Canton, asked for the station manager, then told him that Robert Dyson Jr. of Balsam Corners, while serving proudly in Iraq, had been injured during a night convoy, and had been evacuated to a hospital in Germany. He said nothing about body armor; he would find out the truth from Bobby himself.

He asked, "Can you add that to your news report? He's a local boy, and a lot of people in the area would like to know."

"Mr. Dyson, we'll run it at the next half-hour break, and then right on through the day."

"Thank you so much."

"You're welcome. I'm deeply sorry, Mr. Dyson, for what you and your family are going through. Your family will be in my prayers."

"Thank you."

Robert hung up, stared at his half-cup of coffee, and wondered how much two airplane tickets to Germany would cost.

Some people in Balsam Corners learned about Bobby from the announcements on the radio; others learned about him when a friend or a neighbor phoned them. In the grocery store, at the garage, in the pharmacy, people asked each other, "Did you hear about Bobby Dyson?"

People had known, of course, that Bobby could get hurt. He was a soldier in Iraq. But much more in their minds, he was the ski champion. He had come down his first bunny slope on Bobcat Mountain when he was three. By the time he was ten, he was training with the high school ski team. And by the time he reached high school, he was bringing trophies back from Whiteface Mountain in the High Peaks. He wore a dark green racing suit, Adirondack green, with number 1 on it.

So when the news flashed around town that Bobby was in a military hospital in Germany with chest wounds from a night attack on his convoy, some people had trouble putting the two Bobby's together: their Bobby coming down through the flags of the giant slalom as if his skis were rockets, and the other Bobby, who had joined the Army to serve his country, the same as his dad had served in Vietnam, the same as his uncle had served in Korea, the same as his grandfather had served in Europe during World War Two. So of course Bobby had wanted to serve too. But he was supposed to come home and coach the ski team.

During that long weekend, a black Friday, a black Saturday, and a black Sunday, Robert and Bonny received no more news, and thus the town received no more news. Friends came to visit them, often with a potato salad or a still-warm ham. The collection in the town's two churches on Sunday was for plane tickets to Germany.

Then on Monday morning, Robert learned from Lieutenant Meyers that Bobby was on his way to Walter Reed Army Medical Center, in northwest Washington. He was stable. "You are certainly welcome to visit him," said Lieutenant Meyers.

On Monday afternoon, Robert and Bonny began the long drive south to Washington. They would use the money collected in church for their hotel and meals.

While they were gone, the town held its breath.

CHAPTER 56

The snowfall was light in November. Blueberry Lake remained open water, silver-gray beneath a gray sky, all through November. Then cold Canadian air swept down from the north and cleared away the clouds. The southern end of Blueberry Lake froze on the night of December 2. The northern end froze the following night. No one could walk on the ice yet, but winter had set in.

Both frigid nights had been quiet, without any wind. The layer of ice that formed was consequently very smooth.

During the next week and a half, the December sky was clear powder blue during the day, and filled with bright stars during the night. Nighttime temperatures had dropped to zero by Thursday, to ten below by Saturday, although the sunny days were a little warmer. The full moon on Monday evening, December 8, shown down on dark forests and dark fields, with little snow on them yet, and on the most perfect smooth ice that a skater could wish for.

But was the ice thick enough? Dale Shepherd ventured out on the ice a short distance from his dock, shuffling his feet in the moonlight, while Cindy stood on the dock with a long bamboo pole which he had told her would not be necessary. He drilled down through the ice with an old hand-crank awl, then he knelt and measured with a ruler and flashlight: "Five and a half inches. Best to wait until it's at least six."

On Thursday evening, December 11, Dale measured the ice again: "Seven and one-quarter inches! I say we invite the gang to go skating on Saturday."

"Wonderful," said Cindy. "We haven't been out on the blades for years."

Everyone who lives in the Adirondacks knows that perfect conditions for ice skating do not come every winter, nor do they last long. Usually, the first ice to form on a lake is quickly covered by snow. And if perfect ice does form, snow will surely come within two weeks. Thus Mr. Shepherd made an announcement over the school public address system on Friday morning, inviting every student, every teacher, and every member of the staff to go skating on Blueberry Lake tomorrow, Saturday, all day and into the evening. Pancakes and hot cocoa would be provided at one of the docks.

The Adirondacks thus offered a balm to the stricken town. The deep forest, blue sky and frozen lake offered a day or two of normalcy, so that people could put on their figure skates, their hockey skates, their racing skates. Robert and Bonny had not returned home yet, and certainly Bobby had not returned home; but Bonny, who did all the telephoning to friends in Balsam Corners, always reported that Bobby was stable. For two weeks now, Bobby had been stable. The people of Balsam Corners allowed themselves a day or two of ice-skating under a brilliant blue December sky, on a long, narrow Adirondack lake with camps along one shore, and state forest, "forever wild," along the opposite shore. The southern pocket had no camps along either side, and thus approached as close to pure wilderness as the Adirondack Park would get. Folks allowed themselves a day or two away from the phone, away from the war.

People from town parked their cars on the brown grass around the little chapel at the north end of the lake. The chapel's windows were covered with boards. The bell in the white tower was silent. As folks carried their skates to the edge of the lake, they swept their eyes across as beautiful a sheet of ice as they had ever seen, wrapped by dark green forest. The winter sun, low over the southern end of the lake, cast a yellow sheen across the silver-blue ice.

Folks stepped out on the ice, gingerly at first, then with more confidence. They sat down on one of a dozen green park benches which the town had provided, took off their boots and put on their freshly sharpened skates. They pulled the laces tight, tied good firm bows. Then they stood up warily on the somewhat wobbly blades, pushed off on a first cautious glide, and hoped they wouldn't break an arm today.

* * *

On Saturday morning, Kate and Raphael were told by their respective bosses at the beauty shop and garage to "Get lost!" The town looked with fresh eyes upon its children, for one was injured now. Shopkeepers refused to keep the kids working inside on such a beautiful day. Thus Kate and Raphael did not have to wait until five in the afternoon before they could rattle and rumble in Raphael's old truck up to Blueberry Lake; they were on their way at five minutes past nine.

Both had skated before, though neither was very good. They were able to glide along together at a slow but steady pace. They especially enjoyed exploring, now in December, the parts of the lake which they had explored by canoe in September.

"Do you know what?" asked Kate as they glided between two brown bogs. The stunted tamaracks that grew on the bogs were bare skeletons now, without their needles.

"What?" asked Raphael, looking ahead at a beaver house built by the edge of a bog. As he and Kate skated past the dome of sticks, he noticed a white doily of frost capping the top of the dome: the frozen breath of beavers sleeping inside.

"This is our nineteenth date."

Raphael looked with a grin at Kate. They were both wearing sunglasses as they skated toward the morning sun. "I count only sixteen," he teased.

"That's because you're not paying attention."

As they skated deeper into the southern pocket of Blueberry Lake, wilderness wrapped its arms around them. They wore small backpacks; they had brought lunches. Today, they could be two happy kids, in love, in the sanctuary of a beautiful world.

At Dale's invitation, Yuri and Tony skated with him to Dorothy's dock, the last dock on the western shore, for pancakes and hot cocoa. Philip and Margaret had set up their gas camping grill on the dock; they were producing pancakes from their black griddles as fast as they could. Dorothy poured hot maple syrup over the pancakes, served on a thick paper plate with a plastic fork and knife. The skaters reached up as Dorothy, three feet higher on the dock, reached down. The skaters then set their plates on the end of the dock—a little below waist-high as they stood in their skates—and carefully cut the rapidly cooling pancakes with their fork and knife. The first pieces of pancake were very hot, and exquisite. The last pieces were getting a little cold, for the temperature had risen from ten below last night to only three below by ten o'clock in the morning.

Gerald Jacobsen was part of the work crew on Dorothy's dock: he was heating two pots of cocoa on his own gas grill, and set a cup of steaming hot cocoa on the dock beside each plate of pancakes.

Dale, Yuri and Tony each had three pancakes and a cup of hot cocoa.

Gerald told Dale, "That'll be $29.95 per serving, plus a four-way tip."

"Add it to my account," bantered Dale ask he handed Dorothy the proper amount, "Three times five is fifteen," which would benefit the school library.

With their stomachs pleasantly full, the threesome now skated out toward the middle of Blueberry Lake.

"What do you say we take a tour all the way around the lake?" asked Dale. "We'll follow the entire shoreline, and end up back at Dorothy's dock."

"Da," said Yuri, always game, always agreeable.

"Let's go," said Tony, restless because he had been off his bike for three weeks. There were patches of ice on the roads now, from a freezing rain in November. He would be very glad for some exercise on skates.

Mr. Shepherd opened his stride, immediately gaining speed toward the far shore. Tony and Mr. Cherkasov wore hockey skates, but Mr. Shepherd wore long racing skates. Tony wondered if his principal had ever competed. When Mr. Shepherd slowed down enough for the other two to catch up, Tony asked him, "Hey, Mr. Shepherd, did you ever race on those skates?"

Mr. Shepherd laughed, "I taught Hans Brinker all he knows."

Tony understood, as they were skating across the long, narrow lake, that Mr. Shepherd wanted the three of them together for some reason. The reason seemed to have to do more with skating than with talking. Mr. Cherkasov had clearly learned to skate well in Russia. Mr. Shepherd had clearly trained to race on skates. Tony had never fallen in love with skating the way he had fallen in love with the bike. But he was good enough, and strong enough, that he could keep up with Mr. Cherkasov, while the two of them tried to keep up with Mr. Shepherd.

Now they headed north along the eastern shore, weaving among other skaters out on the lake. They heard a burst of laughter when somebody thumped on his bottom on the ice. At the lake's broad northern end, they skated a gradual turn to the west, sailing past the point of land where the chapel stood. In the sharp wintry sunlight, the little chapel was bright white against the fringe of dark green hemlocks behind it.

Then instead of skating south along the western shore—the ice beyond the docks was crowded with skaters—the three men skated to the middle of the northern end of the lake and then headed south. The other skaters in the middle of the lake were scattered enough that Mr. Shepherd could open up into an untiring sprint of increasing speed, with a mile and a half of ice ahead of him before he reached the imaginary finish line of Mrs. Ferguson's dock.

Tony and Mr. Cherkasov increased their pace, pushing with each stride, swinging their shoulders with the rhythm, wary of people ahead and correcting course when necessary. But as Mr. Shepherd drew steadily further and further ahead of them, they knew they would never catch up.

Feeling great, for finally he was cruising again, Tony called to Mr. Cherkasov, skating twenty feet to his right, "Ka-ra-SHOW!" That meant *good* in Russian. He had learned the word from Katya.

Mr. Cherkasov beamed a smile at him. "Ka-ra-SHOW!"

A ring-shaped crowd of spectators on skates formed around the ice where Svetlana was skating. The ring expanded until it was about two hundred feet in diameter. The Russian woman who made blini with blueberries at the Red Maple Diner, and who had begun a second job as assistant electrical engineer on the wind turbine, had never told a soul at the diner that she could figure skate. Now here she was, skating like an angel. One of the stars from the Russian Olympics seemed to have found her way to Blueberry Lake.

Svetlana had trained after school every winter from the third grade to the eleventh grade. She won many competitions around Leningrad, and even two in Moscow. But she had never let the skating take away time from her studies, so when she entered the university, she hung up her skates.

Today, however, without a coach and strict discipline and growing exhaustion and aching ankles, but with a golden sun shining down from a deep blue sky upon a sheet of perfect ice, she felt her wings.

She warmed up at first, then tried a jump—a single spin—and came down firmly. As the other skaters noticed her and began to give her room, she jumped a one-and-a-half and came down sailing backwards. A quick hop, and she sailed forward again, now on one skate, her body horizontal, her arms extended, as if she were a swan.

She skated into an increasingly tight circle, then into a stationary spin. She finished with a flourish, coming to a sudden halt with her arms raised and her face lifted toward the sun. One moment, and then she sailed off on her next run. She could hear applause from the crowd that was now expanding to give her a full-sized rink.

The opening theme of Tchaikovsky's "Swan Lake", with its deep, threatening tones, flowed clearly from bar to bar in her mind. That had been the music for her winning routine during her last year in high school. She knew the moves by heart, and though she would not attempt a double jump today—she did all the singles, and replaced the doubles with singles, landing each one—she flowed through the entire routine as if she had been practicing it just last week.

When, at the conclusion, she knelt one knee to the ice, held out her arms and bowed her head as a dying swan, someone shouted from the crowd, "Ten! Ten! A perfect ten!"

When the yellow December sun disappeared behind the black spires of balsam, people could feel the temperature drop. By 4:30, the first stars were appearing in the turquoise sky. Only the hardiest, and the most in love, were still out on their skates.

Though their feet were nearly frozen, Kate and Raphael skated beside each other in big easy circles near the pale white chapel. Kate wanted to skate under the Milky Way, which she had done once as a little girl. Tonight was the night: clear, with no moon. If they could keep going for another hour, their nineteenth date would be absolutely perfect.

Antonio and Larisa skated with Yuri and Svetlana in the broad belly of the lake. Those who could savor a cold and silent Russian night in December joined those who could savor a cold and silent Adirondack night.

As the entire sky became a silvered black, they skated on ice so smooth and black that it reflected the stars. The Big Dipper, or "Great Bear" as Svetlana called it, prowled just above the trees at the northern end of the lake. The four brightest stars in the Bear were reflected upside down on the black ice.

The North Star shone high overhead, and shone on the ice as well if one looked almost straight down.

Pegasus and his upside down twin galloped across the southwestern corner of the lake.

As the foursome skated with a universe above and a universe below, they rarely spoke. They did not discuss the kilowattage of strings of lights on the mountain, for now they glided, and pirouetted, and skated a backwards hourglass, under the lights of heaven.

Kate and Raphael skated to a stop in front of the starlit chapel. They looked up, almost straight up, at the luminous white stripe of the Milky Way, as crystal clear as Kate had ever seen it. She had her wish, and on this night of perfection, she leaned against her man—cautiously, on their skates—wrapped her arms around him, felt his strong arms wrap around her, and then they kissed. She had no more doubts, no more hesitations. She kissed him not as a girl but as a woman, a woman who had made her decision: yes. Yes without clouds or clutter. Yes, with a surge of exuberance. Yes, with a deep bedrock of love.

This is the man with whom she would be, forever.

Tony and Katya skated along the channel leading into the far southern end of the lake. They skated past the black dome of sleeping beavers. They skated past black spires of balsam that pointed like bushy arrows into the blaze of stars.

He was from America, she was from Russia. He wanted to bring some benevolence and common sense to the White House, whereas she wanted to go home to help her own country. And yet . . . And yet . . .

They could talk for hours together. The conversation never actually stopped, but paused, then immediately continued when they were together again. For each had thought about what the other had said, and now had a question or two.

Most of their "dates" were at the library. With Mr. Larson's encouragement, they worked together on a twelve-page essay about the causes of the American Revolution.

They followed that endeavor with an extra-credit sixteen-page essay about the causes of the Russian Revolution. Katya called Tony her Minuteman; Tony called Katya his Comrade.

Tony quickly understood that Katya had no idea where she might go to college in this foreign country. He also understood that she should attend one of the top universities. She was extremely bright, and deserved four years with the best teachers.

He wasn't sure how he was going to manage it, but he hoped that they might both spend those four years together at Georgetown.

Most of the time they were companions, friends, but once in a while, she flirted with him. It seemed to be a matter of her increasing courage: the more she trusted him, the more she—occasionally—flirted. Then those dark Russian eyes teased him, while at the same time they admired him, and he began to begin to wonder if he might sometime tell her that he was beginning to love her.

Katya began to feel less and less that she was a Russian girl lost in America. First she had found Walter Bower. Then her parents had begun to work with Tony's parents. Then, after two years in classes together, the handsome boy who seemed so quiet and capable in everything he did, and whose girlfriend seemed to be his bicycle, began talking to her. He seemed apologetic at first, as if he should have said hello much sooner; but she had been very deep in her own silence.

Now as they skated along the gradually narrowing channel of ice, with black forest along both shores, and black forest cupping around the end of the lake ahead of them, she wondered, their skates cutting stride after stride in almost perfect tandem, whether two people so different from each other could really understand each other. For in order to marry someone, the understanding had to be comprehensive and deep.

He had astonished her by reading all six hundred pages of *The Siege of Leningrad* in less than a month. As he read, and asked her questions, she could feel that his respect for Russia, and for her parents, and for her, gradually deepened. Half way through the book, he had told her, "Now I understand why Russians go from the wedding ceremony to a cemetery, before they go to the banquet. They go to the cemetery to say 'Thank you.' Of course they do."

Then he said more softly, "Of course you do."

Maybe, one day in Saint Petersburg, they would go together to the cemetery to visit Maxim.

They stopped before they reached the end of the lake, for a stream trickled into the southern tip and the ice would be thin. They both understood that they had waited for a special time, a special place, for their first kiss. Not at the bike rack, before school and after school. Not behind the stacks of books in the Balsam Corners Library. Not even while holding hands as he walked her home from the library. They wanted a place apart, distant from the world's uncertainties, where, without words, and with only a brief moment's hesitation, a glance that asked, *Are you ready?* they could face each other on skates, hold each others cheeks with mittens, with gloves, and gently, gently kiss. They affirmed to each other a tenderness, and a devotion.

He pressed harder, and she responded. Thus they gave each other a promise, that one day, when the time was right . . .

A frozen tree cracked in the frigid night. An owl hooted in the black forest; across the lake, another owl hooted back.

As Katya and Tony skated along the channel toward home, a shooting star blazed like a white spark across the sky, and blazed as well across the black ice.

CHAPTER 57

On Monday evening, December 15, Robert Dyson Sr. phoned Tom O'Donnell, a fellow Vietnam Vet in Balsam Corners, to tell him that Bobby was weakening. The chest and abdomen wounds had been extensive: the stomach had been torn open and the lining around the heart cavity had been severed by shrapnel; one kidney had been so damaged that they had taken it out; the other kidney couldn't keep up with the infections that kept flaring up here and there inside Bobby.

"He wasn't wearing any body armor on his chest," Robert said to his fellow soldier from Nam. "Bobby told me they never issued him any. Promises, promises, the old crap. Now what do I do, Tom? I'm down here in Washington, and if my kid dies, I may go ballistic."

"Listen, Rob," said the man who understood war and death as much as any living man could, "you're got to keep a grip. What would Bobby want? Dignity, Rob. He wouldn't want any crazy dramatics in Washington. Bring your son home, Rob, and let the town wrap its arms around the three of you."

"All right, Tommy. But this is the ultimate, ultimate shit."

"I know. They never quit, do they? But Rob, bring your boy home."

"Thank you, Tom."

"You're welcome, Brother."

Robert Dyson hung up the pay phone in a ward of Walter Reed Army Medical Center. His friend Tom O'Donnell hung up the phone in his home on Adams Street.

The final vigil had begun.

* * *

On Wednesday morning, December 17, Bonny Dyson phoned her minister at the Methodist Church. Bobby had died at dawn. She and Rob had both been with him in his room, a room he shared with two dozen other mangled soldiers. Rob was keeping under control. They would be home on Friday, or Saturday, she wasn't sure.

"You just let us know how Bobby is coming home," said Reverend Knowles, "and the town will be there to meet him."

"Thank you. Thank you."

The students at Balsam Corners Central School, in the middle of their end-of-semester exams, listened to Mr. Shepherd's announcement on the public address system on Wednesday morning, telling them that Bobby Dyson had died. All end-of-semester exams were canceled. The exams would be given sometime in January.

The shopkeepers up and down Main Street talked with each other, then took down their Christmas decorations and put up black bunting instead. The highway department brought the cherry picker back out and unstrung the arches of Christmas lights over Main Street. The two churches took down their Advent decorations, then draped a black shroud over the arms of the cross on the altar.

A contingent of well over fifty friends, neighbors, veterans, and town officials had gathered at Hancock Airport near Syracuse when the military plane arrived with Bobby's coffin. Rob and Bonny were on the plane; Tom had arranged for an agency in Washington to drive their car north to Balsam Corners. The coffin was carried off the plane and loaded into a hearse from a funeral home in Utica that had a branch in Balsam Corners. A procession of twenty cars—five of them in front of the black hearse, the other fifteen following—all with their lights on and a piece of black ribbon tied to the radio antenna, departed from the airport, drove south on Interstate 81 to the Thruway, followed the Thruway east to Utica, headed north on Route 12 to Alder Creek, then turned northeast on Route 28 and entered the Adirondack Park. The procession arrived in Balsam Corners at 4:10 in the afternoon on Saturday, December 20, five days before Christmas.

The procession drove slowly along Main Street, which the police had closed to regular traffic. People gathered along the sidewalks watched the long black hearse drive slowly by. The flag in front of the fire station was at half-staff. The procession turned onto Crosby Boulevard, drove past the library, past the Methodist Church where the funeral would be held, then turned left onto Fern Street. The hearse pulled into the driveway of an old white house that had been refurbished into a funeral home. Three of the cars, including Tom O'Donnel's car with Rob and Bonny riding in the back seat, stopped beside the curb. Philip and Margaret Schaeffer, Bobby's uncle and aunt, parked behind them. The other cars drove home.

Rob and Bonny walked across the brown grass, then they entered the funeral home where they had been with Bonny's grandmother less than a year ago.

The coffin was brought inside. An American flag was laid lengthwise over it.

Rob and Bonny spoke with Reverend Knowles, and with the director of the funeral home. They decided that the funeral would be held on Monday, December 22. Then the families of Balsam Corners, in whatever way they were able, could have their Christmas.

CHAPTER 58

The snow finally arrived that night.

The first real dump of snow, a foot and a half in twenty-four hours, after weeks of flurries and melts and freezing rains, began to fall just after one o'clock in the morning on Sunday, December 21. It was as if the snow had waited. Had waited for the skier to come home, before it covered the mountain with white. Had waited for the boy from the Adirondacks to come home, before it heaped fluffy white billows of snow along drooping pine boughs. Had waited for the kid from Balsam Corners to come home, before it blanketed the town with what, in a normal December, folks would have called "perfect Christmas snow."

People welcomed the snow. They didn't mind plowing their driveways so they could get to church on Sunday morning. The snow was like a balm, a blessing, as if winter in the Adirondacks had laid her hands over their town, bringing a hush, a beauty, the reassurance of nature's peace. Although grief had laid a black shroud upon the town, the sky laid down a shroud of white.

Bobby lay in an open coffin in the Methodist Church on Sunday, from one in the afternoon until five. He was not dressed in his Army uniform. During the final night of anguish beside Bobby's bed in Walter Reed Hospital, Rob and Bonny had both agreed, as they stared at the sagging face of their unconscious son, that he would be buried in his green racing suit, with number 1 on his chest. He would not be buried in a military uniform. They wanted to remember him as he had lived, not as he had died.

Bobby would have an American funeral, but not a military funeral. There would be no stiff soldiers, no taps.

They did not ask their son whether he would prefer a military funeral or a Balsam Corners funeral. They talked with him, when he was conscious, about how proud the town was of him, as a skier, as a soldier. His eyes lit up when they called him a skier. He shook his head slightly when they called him a soldier. So when he closed his eyes, and they could see they were losing him, they decided that he would be dressed in Adirondack green.

If anyone in town objected to the lack of a military funeral, no one said so. As the procession of mourners moved slowly all Sunday afternoon past the open coffin, people stood and stared at the hero they had known on the mountain, the boy who had put Balsam Corners on the map, the kid who took it all quietly in stride, and who then went off to serve his country.

The folks from town offered a handshake, offered a hug, to Bobby's parents, standing near the coffin. Robert wore a dark suit, not his dress uniform; Bonny wore a black dress, with a black hat and black veil. She did not wear black gloves, for she wanted to reach out and hold the hands of friends who had come to comfort her.

CHAPTER 59

At about three o'clock in the morning on Monday, the snowplow drivers noticed that stars were beginning to appear. The clouds were clearing. The big dump was over: they could move now from the plowed highways to the smaller roads.

When folks peered out their bedroom windows and front doors on Monday morning, they saw a pale silver-blue sky. A little after seven-thirty, the sun cast its first yellow-pink light on the drifts. Bobby would have a beautiful day, for no day was more beautiful in the Adirondacks than the day of blue sky and sunshine that followed a blizzard.

When people began to enter the Methodist Church at noon for the one o'clock service, they were bathed in the dignity and reassurance of Bach, resounding from the pipe organ in the loft above them. The coffin, at the foot of the altar, was closed, covered lengthwise with an American flag. Hundreds of bouquets stood across the entire front of the church. People nodded their greetings but said little as they settled into the pews.

Robert and Bonny Dyson entered the church just before one o'clock. They walked down the long aisle where once they had walked in the opposite direction as man and wife, then they sat in the front pew.

Reverend Knowles conducted the first portion of the service as befits a Methodist funeral. Then he called upon Walter Bower, "a Veteran of World War Two in the European Theater," to address the mourners.

Walter stood up from the front pew, where he had been sitting between Katya and Tony. He walked with his cane up the three steps to the altar, so that he could look out at the packed church from a slight elevation. Robert Dyson Sr. had asked him to speak, as a Veteran.

"Mine was a very different war," he began. "There was no doubt in our minds as to who our enemy was. We knew what we were fighting for. And we had been reluctant to fight . . . until we were attacked at Pearl Harbor. So the entire nation knew exactly why we were at war."

He paused.

"The situation today in Iraq is quite different. But though the causes and conduct of a war may be marred, the sacrifice made by the soldiers is offered in the name of something much higher than politics. No matter what war they are fighting in, their belief in building a better world is genuine."

He looked up at the balcony, packed with people. The silver pipes of the organ rose up the wall behind them.

"We shall bury our Bobby today in the Balsam Corners Cemetery. But we shall also bury Bobby in one small corner of Arlington Cemetery. For Arlington is the resting ground for soldiers who believe that all men are created equal. All men, all women, all children, around the world. Because when the Founding Fathers raised their torch, they hoped that it would light not just their America, but the entire world."

He turned and looked up at Jesus, kneeling at prayer among skulls on Gethsemane, in the stained glass window above the altar.

"Let us remember that the man in whose church we are assembled today did not conquer with a sword. He did not use a superpower arsenal. Few are the converts who are convinced by force of arms."

He scanned his audience, the largest audience he had ever spoken too, for now he had come to what he really wanted to tell them.

"When we visit our little cemetery later today, and lay our beloved hero to rest, let us borrow a bit of Bobby's energy. The energy that enabled him to come zigzagging and zooming down the mountain." Walter smiled at the memory, then tapped his cane as if to say, *Bravo!* "Let us use that exuberant energy to reach out to the world, as Bobby would have reached. The kid had so much good in him. Let us ourselves try to dispense as much of that good as we can."

Walter stepped carefully down the stairs, then walked to his place in the pew between Katya and Tony. When he sat down, Katya grabbed his hand and Tony wrapped an arm around his shoulders.

Ruth Fisher, at the organ keyboard, now let Bach speak to the matter of death. She summoned his faith, she summoned his confidence, rendering both with pipes that rumbled majestic cadences of chords. Those chords had marched with no lessening of their fervency for two and a half centuries. They reached down now to every pew, to every nook and corner in the church, and though the music could not banish the grief that gripped the hearts of people who had come to say farewell, the chords and cadences could shake that grief, could challenge it, let it know that human life is not without divine purpose. Ruth Fisher knew how to lift the roof of the church with her Bach, that the light of heaven might shine in.

Reverend Knowles now introduced the second speaker, Bonny Dyson. She stood up from the front pew and walked in her black dress up the three altar steps, then she turned slowly and faced the people who had watched over her when she was a little girl, people who had cheered her on the volleyball team, people who had wished her well when she was married, people who had congratulated her on the birth of her first (and only) child. People who had cheered her fearless son down the mountain.

She had already cried so much, she had no tears left and did not worry that she would break down and be unable to speak. She had lived through the horror of two weeks in Walter Reed Hospital. She could speak today, with words of crystalline truth.

"My friends, most of the pictures that Bobby sent home from Iraq were of children. With his camera, he took pictures of children who live in the middle of a war. Many of you saw these photographs in the exhibit at school on Veterans Day."

She looked at Robert, watching her from the front pew. No love should have to be forged by the fire of what they had been through; but strong as their love had been, it had been forged even stronger.

"When Rob and I spent two weeks visiting Bobby in Walter Reed Army Medical Center in Washington, we saw children of another sort. Yes, you can of course say that those broken soldiers are young men and women. But to their parents, those beautiful young people, nineteen, twenty, twenty-one years old, are still children.

"Every American should visit Walter Reed Army Medical Center. Every American television should take us on a tour, for two hours every evening during prime time, night after night after night, until the war has ended. Because until you see and fully comprehend what has happened to those children, you cannot claim to be able to cast an educated vote."

She paused. Never before had she spoken so openly to so many people.

"I am one mother who is tired of war. I'll bet I could find another such mother in Iraq. Though I sometimes feel now that I would gladly lie in the earth beside my son, I will not rest while other children are dying. I cannot say now what sort of service calls me," she looked down at Robert, "calls Robert and me together, but it shall not be service under any nation's flag. Bobby wrote in an email that he wanted to return to Iraq one day to help the kids. Maybe one day, in Iraq, or some other such struggling country, under the blue flag of the United Nations, Robert and I can do that job for him."

She looked down at the coffin, covered by an American flag, surrounded by flowers, and then she looked at the multitude of faces beyond it. "Thank you for coming today. Bobby would have been deeply honored."

She walked down the steps and sat beside her husband. He gripped her hand.

Now Katya and Kate assembled with the rest of the school choir near the coffin. Every student was dressed in black. With Mrs. Fisher directing, they sang "Swing low, sweet chariot, coming for to carry me home." People remembered when the choir had sung that song on top of Bobcat Mountain, while the orange moon rose. The kids of Balsam Corners were singing for one of their own.

Reverend Knowles stood up and looked at Robert, who nodded: yes, he would speak. Reverend Knowles introduced Robert Dyson Sr., "a Veteran of the War in Vietnam." Rob squeezed Bonny's hand, then he stood and climbed the steps. He looked out at the folks who had kept him alive during those first years back from Nam. He looked out at the folks who were keeping him alive right now.

"When Bobby won the Whiteface Challenge in January, 2002 with a record time, a journalist from an Albany paper asked him, 'How does it feel to have conquered the mountain?'"

Robert had been standing nearby, proudly watching his son as the boy responded to the press.

"Bobby shook his head and replied, 'I never conquer a mountain. The mountain teaches me, and I learn from it, so that we can work together.'"

Robert clenched his hands, for they shook with anger.

"Bigger mountains waited for him. Bigger lessons. Bigger work. There's no telling what he might have done, if he could have had another sixty years."

He locked eyes with Tom O'Donnell, sitting in the second pew. He kept a grip, though he could have shrieked, he could have roared.

That was all he could say by way of an elegy for Bobby.

The rest of the message, on Bobby's behalf, was going to clarify a bit of history.

"It is a little-known, under-reported, and much neglected fact . . . that during the 1980's, our government supported Saddam Hussein in a big way. He was our guy against the Iranians, who, in 1979, had held our embassy people hostage. Though we now thump our chests and proclaim Saddam to be a monster, we were very glad for an entire decade to buy oil from him.

"Further, we provided Iraq with over 500 million dollars in financial credit, so that Saddam could buy American grain to feed his people, especially his army, which was then at war with Iran. Much of the 500 million dollars went to American farmers, who were glad for it. Even after the world knew that Saddam was killing the Kurdish people in northern Iraq with poison gas, we decided to provide him with *another* 500 million dollars worth of food. In our eyes, he could do no wrong."

Robert shook his head. "You won't hear much about this ten-year alliance on the evening news these days. You won't hear that we provided Saddam with export-import credits, enabling him to purchase American goods . . . including chemicals. You won't hear that in November of 1984, America restored diplomatic relations with Iraq, although we knew about the torture and executions in Saddam's prisons."

Robert studied the faces that stared at him, wondering if anyone was going to stand up and walk out of the church.

"As Franklin Roosevelt once said about a Central American dictator, 'He's a son of a bitch, but he's our son of a bitch.' There you have American diplomacy in a nutshell. Only when Saddam threatened our oil by attacking Kuwait, did we see him in a different light."

He looked again at Tom O'Donnell, sitting with his wife Ernestine. Tom gave him a nod of encouragement.

If he was going to talk about Iraq, he was going to have to keep his rage under lock and key. He had kept a grip in Washington; he would do so here today.

"I will not belabor my Republican friends with my thoughts about the present administration. But I will tell you what I heard from Bobby himself: that again and again he was ordered to accompany a convoy through the streets of Baghdad, and along the highways of Iraq, every one of them a war zone, even though he was never supplied with the proper body armor. Further, he was not the only soldier lacking the ceramic plates that protect the chest area. And thus I would ask," he steadied himself, "why did Halliburton have a handle on the oil, but not on the body armor?"

No one stood up. No one walked out. They were being polite.

He called out, nearly shouted, so that his voice might reach more than a congregation, more than a community . . . so that his voice might reach an entire nation, "America, we have given you our *best*."

He looked down at the coffin, covered by the flag that had asked so much of his family. Slowly, his pride began to outgrow his grief. "Thank you, soldier. Thank you for believing in the best in America." Then the soldier from Vietnam saluted the soldier from Iraq.

He looked at Bonny, his bedrock. She held him with her loving eyes.

Then he looked once again at the people who had come to honor his son. "Thank you, my friends, for coming today. Never shall Bonny and I forget how this town has held us in its heart."

He walked down the steps and sat beside his wife, who took his cheeks in her hands and kissed him on the lips with a love that would endure forever.

Reverend Knowles concluded the funeral service with a prayer asking for strength. He then invited the mourners to the burial in Balsam

Corners Cemetery, at three o'clock. The roads to the cemetery had been plowed, and the sidewalks within the cemetery had been snow-blown.

The church bells began to toll, slowly, majestically. They tolled for the next half-hour, while the pews slowly emptied. People heard the bells chiming as they walked forward and stood one more time near the coffin. People heard the bells ringing while they walked down the long aisle, then waited in line, speaking quietly with each other now as they shuffled forward.

When they stepped out the church door into the cold wintry sunshine, folks heard the bells proclaiming a steadfast faith.

Looking up, they saw the deep pure blue of God's eternal heaven.

CHAPTER 60

Gerald Jacobsen stood apart from the mourners gathered around the coffin beside the open grave. He could see, off to the left, the sharp contrast of fresh brown earth heaped on white snow. The uppermost layer of earth had no doubt been frozen, but the town's backhoe had managed to cut through.

Looking beyond the ring of several hundred mourners, he could see, above the treetops and a jumble of white hills, the snow-clad peak of Bobcat Mountain. He had never noticed before that you could see the mountain from the cemetery so well. With binoculars, you could probably see the chair lift.

On top of the mountain, facing the low yellow sun that would set in less than an hour, stood the wind turbine. Even with his old eyes, he could see the three blades spinning with majestic steadiness.

If Bobby looked down now upon his little town, he would see that folks hadn't just sat where they were at. They had talked it out, made their decision, then offered each other a breath of fresh air.

That, and more.

No soldier ever went to war over a wind turbine.

About the author

With a doctorate in literature from Stanford University in 1974, John Slade has taught at both the high school and college levels in the United States, the Caribbean, Norway and Russia. His research in the field of wind turbines has taken him to a manufacturing plant in Denmark where the giant blades are built, and to the top of a newly constructed wind turbine in his native New York.

Dr. Slade firmly believes that the coming global generation, now students at their desks, can take up the hammer and beat the blades of our myriad swords into the blades of wind turbines. We can forge an unprecedented harmony with each other, and with our one precious Earth, by investing in an international Renaissance.